REPUBLIC *of* WOMEN

Merrill Findlay was born in Condobolin in central western New South Wales and spent most of her childhood
on her family's farm near the village of Bogan Gate. She
returns to the farm regularly to refresh her spirit but has
lived in many places since she left boarding school, and
has done many different things — often to the complete
despair and bewilderment of her family and friends! She
currently lives and works in the inner Melbourne suburb
of St Kilda, from where she founded the small environmental organisation, Imagine The Future Inc. Merrill has
been involved in a broad range of progressive social
movements in Australia and overseas throughout her
adult life and sees this on-going commitment as integral
to her praxis as a writer. For more information visit her
web site www.merrillfindlay.com.

REPUBLIC *of* WOMEN *Merrill Findlay*

UNIVERSITY OF QUEENSLAND PRESS

First published 1999 by University of Queensland Press
Box 42, St Lucia, Queensland 4067 Australia

Typeset by University of Queensland Press
Printed in Australia by McPherson's Printing Group

Distributed in the USA and Canada by
International Specialized Book Services, Inc.,
5804 N.E. Hassalo Street, Portland, Oregon 97213–3640

This project has been assisted by
the Commonwealth Government through
the Australia Council, its arts funding
and advisory body.

Cataloguing in Publication Data
National Library of Australia

Findlay, Merrill.
   Republic of women.

   I. Title.

   A 823.3

ISBN 0 7022 3078 2

For all the people — friends, family, and strangers —
who supported me so generously and in so many ways during
the writing and publication of this book. Thank you.
And for my father who died before it was finished.

First Chaos came and then broad-bosomed Earth
The everlasting seat of all that is,
And Love.

Hesiod

THE phone rings, someone pushes the security buzzer and Daphne Downstairs pops in the back door. At the very same moment, Marie hits her thumb with the hammer. Damn, she says and sits on a fruit crate. The phone's still ringing, the buzzer's still buzzing and now her thumb is throbbing. She sucks it then leans out the window. Look, I don't believe in god and I'm really busy, she tells the two Jehovah's Witnesses at the security door below.

But there's going to be a big change in the world and you can be saved, the one clutching the black book says. If you obey Jesus.

I'm sorry, but I'll just have to save myself, she says.

The phone's stopped ringing: I'll be in town Thursday, and was wondering … her caller is telling the answering machine. It's the man she fell for at that conference last week. She scrambles across the loose timber and pulls back the white dust sheet protecting the chaos of her desk but he hangs up just as she reaches for the receiver. She stares at the answering machine. Her thumb is still throbbing and Daphne Downstairs is still at the back door: I won't keep you a moment dear, but just have a look at what they've done to my pelargonium. It's the junkies again, Daphne says. They're worse than the possums.

Marie joins her on the staircase and together the two women lean over the railing in silence, shoulders touching to stare at the pelargonium which, just half an hour ago, had almost filled Daphne's tiny garden under the broken staircase. Now the bush is bent and vandalised. I've just got to get away from here, Daphne says. It's getting worse. I never thought I'd be spending my retirement in a place like this.

Look, it's OK Daphne. We'll fix the pelargonium. The stem's not broken right through, and if we splint it ... have you got an old stocking? And what's wrong with this place anyway? Marie says. I love it. It's got life. It's got diversity. It's got passion. You can be anyone you want to here.

Yes dear, but I'm seventy-three. I've had my passion. Marie giggles. They splint the wounded pelargonium, gossip, admire the alyssum, the impatiens, the native creeper that's beginning to wrap itself around the horizontal wooden beams supporting the stairway. Pull a few weeds, bemoan the aphids.

I'll have to make up some more garlic spray, Daphne says. She says it every time they chat about the garden.

Upstairs, Ursula The Rose is accompanying a young soprano. Follie! Follie! Delirio vano è questo! the student is singing. Povera donna, sola, abbandonata in questo popoloso deserto che appellano Parigi. Poor woman, abandoned and alone in this crowded desert called Paris ...

Verdi. *La Traviata*. The sanitised story of Violetta Valéry, a French sex worker who dies of TB. Her aching notes tumble down the stairs from Ursula's flat on the second floor: What can I hope for? What should I do? Enjoy all the good things in life and drown my sorrows in a whirlpool of delight?

Marie perches on a step, leans her head against the railing and unconsciously caresses a petal of the wounded pelargonium. Sempre libera degg'io, the student sings. I must always be free to enjoy myself, to never refuse a good time. I dedicate my life to pleasure and will live it to the full, always seeking new delights and ever more exciting thrills.

The voice changes as the old music teacher sings Alfredo, Violetta's lover. Her notes fall like dry petals, wrinkled and frail:

Amor è palpito dell'universo intero, she sings. Love is the pulse of the whole universe. Mysterious and noble, both crucifix and joy of the heart.

The music ends. Marie climbs the stairs to her own flat but Verdi's tune lingers. She steps over the loose timber on her bedroom floor and listens to the message on her answering machine — then dials his number. Yes, I'll be home Thursday. Great. I'll look forward to it.

It was once a shearing shed, this timber stacked on her bedroom floor. Before that, a sparse forest of Murray pines growing on the flood plains of this island's major river system — the track of the rainbow serpent, the old people said. They're all but gone now, the trees. Cleared, burned, cut for fence posts, or for shearing sheds and houses. The old people too, they've all but gone — back into the earth from where they're being re-born to reclaim their mother land, whole forests of young saplings. And the sheep? They're still there. You can smell them in these logs. Lanolin mixed with the faint dry scent of shit. I must've been mad, Marie told the truckie who delivered them. Then she touched the old timber: merino smooth, lambswool soft ... no, these logs will make a lovely bed, she said. Despite their history.

She rotates on her studio chair and looks again at her room: four Murray pines are growing vertically from the floor. On top of them a sleeping platform of wooden slats. On the slats a wool-filled futon, unbleached cotton sheets and a feather doona covered in the antique lace that once hung as curtains in her grandmother's sitting room near Ballarat. Beside the futon, a glass vase of flowering eucalypts and a nest of books. She spins back to her desk, picks up a pencil, sketches a quick plan, stares at it, erases a few lines, redraws them — then gazes out the window to Fitzroy Street.

It would of course be easier to find another flat but she likes it here, the village life of the street. And the rent is cheap, which is an important consideration for an aspiring young architect in the last decade of the twentieth century.

DENIS is sunbaking on the back landing, waiting, he says, for Heinrich, Marie's Prussian neighbour. This week Denis is a blond. His face is waxed and he is wearing kohl around his eyes. He has stripped to a tiny yellow g-string and risks serious sunburn. When Marie appears, he reaches for his shirt and apologises for his near-nakedness. It's OK, Marie says. At least you're not shooting up. Yesterday I came out here and there was this girl sitting on the step filling her syringe. If she'd shot up while I was looking I'd have fainted.

Heinrich told me he'd kill me if he ever found me doing that, Denis says. So I'm trying to go straight. I mean, really straight.

Really straight means not doing drugs and not working O'Donnell Park. That's where Heinrich found him, or Denis found Heinrich. A conventional pickup. Heinrich's in his car at the kerb, Denis asks him for the time, Heinrich plays the game, they discuss money — and come back to the flat where Heinrich dresses Denis in an old military jacket, plays with his genitals, exposes his own cock, then demands head. And gets it. Well, that's how Denis describes it anyway.

I've bought him a present, Denis says as he takes a small package from his shirt pocket. Five sepia-toned postcards of naked Sicilian boys with enormous circumcised cocks.

I got them at that second-hand market in Greville Street, he says. Stole them. They match the big photo on his bedroom wall. *Paternal Chastisement* I think it's called. This naked guy with a droopy moustache is whipping a boy's bare bum with a sapling. Heinrich says it's by some famous German called Wilhelm von something. He's into whips, Heinrich. Riding crops, mainly.

He doesn't whip you, does he? Marie says.

Not really. Not hard. He just likes being kinky sometimes.

They sit in silence looking at the old postcards. Photographer Wilhelm's boys are draped around ancient columns and urns, waterfalls and craggy cliffs. In their hair are flowers and olive leaves, and at their lips the flutes of Pan. Their young bodies are polished with milk and oil. Their muscles glow.

How come they have such big cocks? Marie says. Did they pull themselves or something before the photos were taken? She pauses. But then how'd they keep 'em up long enough for the exposures? Like, those postcards are from old glass plates and you had to stand still for, well, at least a couple of minutes.

Denis doesn't know about exposing glass plates, but he does know about male genitals.

Their cocks aren't erect, he says. They're just big. That's what Italians and Greeks are famous for.

Jesus, Marie says.

Haven't you ever fucked a Greek or Italian?

No — well, not yet.

She stares at the sepia postcards. The photographer's name is Wilhelm von Gloeden. Marie has seen his work before. He exposed these images in Taormina when it was a village clinging to Sicily's eastern cliffs. Only shards, an amphitheatre and a temple to a goddess remain from its more glorious Greek past but these arte-facts were enough, it seems, for Wilhelm to re-imagine the sons of Taormina's peasant folk as young Jasons and Odysseuses. But in these boys' gene pool swim the sperm of every imperialist, every myth-maker who ever sailed the Mediterranean. Because this is-land, this virgin whore, has lain, legs open, for every conqueror who has ever wanted her. For every man with every battle axe, every sword, every gun. And in every generation these boys ... but this evening their images will pass again between lovers. Heinrich will come home from work, pour two glasses of beer, switch on the TV and sit with Denis on the vinyl couch. Denis will pull the postcards from his pocket and pass them to Heinrich — who'll unwrap them, examine each of them slowly and unconsciously stroke Denis's hand. They'll kiss, grow hard, then Heinrich will search through his collection of uniforms for a jacket someone told him Mussolini's favourite aide once wore. He'll dress Denis up, play with his genitals, caress his naked arse, and whip him. (But softly.) Then he'll sit again on the vinyl lounge and spread his legs. Denis will kneel before him, unzip his fly, lick his cock, nuzzle his balls, tease him, then swallow his penis whole. With his lips, his tongue, he'll suck his lover limp, then curl up like a child in Heinrich's arms to watch 'Neighbours'. Later they'll order charcoal chicken and chips from the Lebanese take-away across the road and go to bed — where, below Wilhelm von Gloeden's *Paternal Chastisement*, they'll cling to one another as though their very lives depend on this intimacy. Then Heinrich will roll over and go to sleep.

In the flat next door, Marie will dream her own Adonis. A Sicilian lover with glowing olive skin and a big, yet sensitive, cock.

TUESDAY, tute day and seventeen undergraduates await. Soon she'll be asking them whether calling those new clock-towers and granite-faced columns on St Kilda Road 'postmodern' actually means anything. And if so, what. It's mid-morning, raining, and the tram is late.

There's this guy at the stop, Marie's seen him before. Blond, dressed by Country Road. Hip hairstyle, briefcase. Earrings. (In one ear only.) And a mobile phone. He gets on the number sixteen in front of Marie and takes the last vacant seat. She hangs on from the ceiling strap behind him.

By the time they've crossed the Yarra the tram is crowded and he has already answered three calls. Then a lover phones. You always pick the worst times to ring, he says. He listens then calls her a Fucking Whore. And sex with you is really boring, he says. Marie catches the eye of the woman sitting in the opposite seat, an office worker with shoulder pads and red shoes. They raise eyebrows and grimace together. What a jerk, the office worker says.

Mobile Phone gets off at Collins Street and Marie takes his seat. The girl behind her shakes her short-back-and-sides. Aren't men bastards, she says, like she's been there herself.

If a man told me that ... the office worker says.

They'll all tell you that eventually, says a pensioner with a fresh perm and rinse.

SHE picks up a chisel, places the blade on a length of Murray pine and lifts the mallet. Her maternal grandfather bought these tools at a bush clearing sale. You can feel the history in these things, he told her. They don't make mallets like this any more.

The sounds of the street. The trams, the passers-by under her window, the sparrows. Shadows on the wall. The wood-on-wood rhythm of her mallet striking the chisel. Wood chips gathering on the floor. Memories. You can feel the history in these things, he says. They don't make mallets like this any more. Her first clumsy mortice and tenon join. I was still a child, she says. Her grandfather's hand on hers as she holds the chisel, those first cautious hits, those first slivers shed as the blade follows the soft grain of the Douglas fir, the years of growing, the young girl, the tree. See those bands in the wood? he says. They tell the story of that tree, the good seasons and the bad, a new ring every year, a new page. Maybe four hundred years this tree grew before someone cut it, floated it down the river to Vancouver maybe, and loaded it on to a ship. We all sailed here on ships, except those who didn't, she says, those who were already here. Blood on this chisel and this mallet, blood on my inheritance. How many blacks did they shoot and rape and poison, my relatives? But they died fighting too. Under the southern cross on those golden fields of Ballarat. Your great-great-grandmother helped sew the flag, grandfather says. It was silk, she worked all night by candle-light hemming the stars, tucking the edges, the points, and then the double row of fine running stitch. A flag as big as a double bed sheet, she says, as she watches it unfurl over the stockade and hears the Republic of Victoria proclaimed. The boys say it's their game, no place for a woman here but I too dream dreams, great-great grandmother says. And I stitched the stars on to the Southern Cross. I heard the first shots, saw the bayonets. My flag torn down, blood on my sheet, my cross, my stars dragged through the mud and the Republic stillborn. She boils the water, tears up her cotton petticoats for bandages, and rushes to the Eureka stockade. Where is he? Billy, Billy, oh my god …

The wood-on-wood rhythm of the mallet, sounds of the street below, sparrows. Shadows on the wall. All because he didn't want to pay a licence fee each month, grandfather says. Thirty shillings, but it wasn't the money. The traps'd come and demand your licence, grandfather says, so you'd have to climb all the way up again, just for them to spit in your face, or chain you to a tree if your licence was out of date. The government wanted the Diggers' money but didn't want them to have a say in making the laws they had to obey. Because only squatters could vote, you see. Only men of property.

The wood-on-wood rhythm, shadows on the wall. Those seams of gold in Ballarat, those sweating shafts and only picks, shovels and windlasses to mine those shining dreams of freedom. You claim that we Diggers take away other men's property by digging upon the common, Gerrard Winstanley says. Yet you live on theft. Will you not be wise, O ye rulers?

The wood-on-wood rhythm, wood chips falling to the floor, and those hidden dreams like buried gold in Ballarat. But a dawn of reason is rising on the world, Tom Paine says. A new order of things will follow naturally the new order of thoughts. This res publica, this libertas. For a nation to be free it is sufficient that she wills it, says Lafayette.

The wood-on-wood rhythm, the din of dreams. We hold these truths to be self-evident, that all men are created equal, that they are endowed by their creator with certain unalienable rights, that among these are life, liberty and the pursuit of happiness, says Tom Jefferson. And the right to fight oppression, declare the new citizens of the French Republic. Ah, how every place has its Bastille and every Bastille its despot, Tom Paine says. But how can the bird that is born for joy sit in a cage and sing? says William Blake.

Men from every nation with every dream of liberty, every dream of getting rich. Because why else are they digging here for new-world gold in Ballarat, these refugees, these adventurers, these Chartists, these liberal democrats, these socialists, these communists, these anarchists, these convicts, these dreamers who've escaped from every prison, every potato famine, every dark satanic mill, every nationalist movement, every barricade, every insurrection against every ancien régime? For here we'll build a great and independent nation, a refuge for the oppressed of every European land, a New World free of all the evils of the old.

But where are your licences? the traps are saying.

We've burnt them, the Diggers are saying. Because taxation without representation is tyranny and we've come here to be free men.

A young officer raises his sword.

Aux armes citoyens, a Digger says.

And so they fall in line, two abreast behind the Southern Cross, to march up Bakers Hill shouting their now-familiar slogans. No licences without representation. Victoria for the Victorians. All power rests in the people.

They build their stockade, swear their oaths, arm themselves with guns and sharpened pikes — then go off and get pissed at the nearest pub. By dawn, only 150 hangovers are left to fight for freedom. Took the troopers just fifteen minutes to clean 'em up, grandfather says. And so another ancien régime was saved.

Ah, how the past weighs like a nightmare on the brains of the living, Karl Marx says. But I too dream dreams, great-great-grandmother says. And I stitched the stars on to the Southern Cross. Heard the first shots, saw the bayonets, the blood on the sheet. My stars dragged through the mud ...

UPSTAIRS the piano again. Ursula and her student. La Traviata, the fallen woman. Sempre libera, Violetta sings. I must always be free. Lyrics by Francesco Piave, music by Giuseppe Verdi, a nationalist composer with an acronymic name. V.E.R.D.I. Vittorio Emanuele — Re d'Italia. Vittorio Emanuele, King of Italy. Viva Verdi, they're screaming at his operas. Viva Verdi, they're spray-painting on Italia's walls. Because in Europe another nation state's being born — with guns and bayonets. Guns and bayonets at Verdi's birth too. An army marching through his village. Soldiers. His mother Luigia snatches Giuseppe from his crib, flees with him to the chapel. Another woman panics, freezes, a man in uniform grabs her, forces her against the organ loft and thrusts. His cock, his bayonet. Blood. Luigia hides in the belfry, holds her baby to her breast, clings to him and prays. They live. Years later papa Verdi buys Giuseppe an old spinet. The village priest teaches him to play. Sempre Libera.

The mallet striking the handle of the chisel, wood-on-wood, the steel blade slivering through the Murray pine. The smell of lanolin, of sheep. Shadows on the wall. And her cello leaning there, soft curves under a cotton dust cover that's like a shroud on this melancholy afternoon. She lifts the sheet, carries the instrument, the bow, the resin to the fruit box she's been sawing timber on, sits, brushes the wildest wisps of her red hair from her face, spreads her legs and places the cello, yes, between her thighs. She bends over it, hugs it, lays her head against its neck. Plucks a string, bows, and listens as the sound changes the silence of her room. The notes fall together imperfectly but with infinite yearning. Not Verdi but Elgar, the first movement of his Cello Concerto. She played it in a school concert more than a decade ago. In Ballarat.

The deep, dark harmonics of the strings, the shadows and, from the wall, Guilhermina Suggia smiling as she smiled from Marie's grandmother's wall, a beautiful Mediterranean woman with dark, dark hair and skin painted in fresh goat's milk. She's wearing a long velvet gown the colour of cinnabar and cut low across her breasts. Europe's greatest cellist, grandmother said, by one of Europe's greatest painters, Augustus Johns. Marie grew up believing all cellists were exotic dark-haired ladies with skin the colour of goat's milk and breasts that were full and soft. This is what I want to be, she told her grandmother then, a cellist like Guilhermina Suggia making the sound of cinnabar velvet.

She inhales, exhales deeply as she bows. This moment, these notes, this room vibrating now with music, with memories, with the wood shavings of a new-world tree. This bed she is building. This life.

UPSTAIRS the faded voice of the old teacher singing up her past. He was German, the man she married all those years ago, another refugee who had made St Kilda home. All he owned when they first met was his violin and a number tattooed on his wrist. Me or opera, he told her then. Because opera means Europe and in Europe there's no place for me. She made the easier choice — she loved him, and that's what women did in those days. He didn't mind her singing or teaching but only in her spare time. So she'd cook his meals, wash and wipe his dishes, hang the tea towel on the rail to dry, remove her apron, then quietly leave the kitchen to sit at her piano and sing her dreams. Only lonely widowed wine dreams now, cheap claret, cream sherry dreams. This evening they stain the air with sadness. Tutto e follia nel mondo cio che non e piacer, she's singing. Everything in the universe is madness except for pleasure. So let's fill this evening with delight because love is but a flower that quickly blooms and fades. E un fior che nasce e muore. A flower that blooms and fades.

La Traviata, the fallen woman is seeping through the floorboards into Marie's flat below, note by trembling note, like tears. Vio tardaste! You're late! What happened? the tenors are singing. We were playing cards at Flora's and no one noticed the time, the basses respond in molto vivace. Ursula sweeps forward in her finest imaginary silk and lace to greet them: Flora and you, my friends, the whole night remains. Let's make it glow … She signals her invisible servant to pour the champagne. I depend on these amusements, they're the drug I need to help me forget the way I feel, she sings. For pleasure's the only thing worth living for.

A door opens out of nowhere and Gaston, Vicomte de Létori-ères, strides into her apartment with a stranger he introduces as Alfredo Germont. I'm sure I'll like him as much as I like you, Ursula sings to Gaston as the stranger kisses her hand. My darling guests, be seated: relax at my banquet and open your hearts, she sings as she lifts her glass of cream sherry. Her baby grand becomes a rosewood table set with the finest cutlery and china as she sips. Long white candles in golden candelabras, a bowl of fresh white camellias, wine sparkling in long crystal flutes. Champagne is the secret potion that cures all our ills, her guests are singing. Alfredo stands to propose a toast: Libiamo ne'lieti calici che la bellezza infiora, he sings. Raise your chalices and drink with me in this lovely place, and, as each hour passes, we'll drink deeper of delight. Drink and taste this sweet arousal which love alone excites. He lifts his own glass to his hostess. Ursula smiles from her keyboard. Tra voi dividere il tempo mio gioconodo, she sings. I'll share my gaiety with you because everything else is madness — except for pleasure. Tutto e follia nel mondo cio che e piacer. She leans across her supper-table keyboard to Alfredo: La vita é nel tripudio, she confides to him in an inebriated trill of intimacy. Life is in the thrills.

But only when you have no true love, he responds.

Don't talk to me of something I know nothing about, she sings — then pauses, rises from her piano stool, and glides towards an elaborate drawing room that's opening in a blank wall of her tiny flat. She stumbles, takes another step forward, falters again and clutches the mantelpiece above her little gas heater. Her imaginary guests rush towards her. Che avete? they sing. What's wrong? What's the matter? Nothing, nothing at all, Ursula hums. Just a little trembling. It'll pass. Please go on and enjoy yourselves. I'll be with you in a moment.

Her guests move through the marble archway into the drawing room, all of them except Alfredo. Ursula leans on her mantelpiece and gazes into the mirror. I look so pale, she sings, then notices Alfredo's reflection. Voi qui!

Are you all right? he sings. You'll kill yourself living like this. You must take care of yourself.

E lo potrei? How can I?

He reaches his hand through the mirror. If you were mine, he sings to Verdi's melody, I'd protect you and take care of you so tenderly.

You'd take care of me? I don't know anyone who'd do that.

Only because you have no one who loves you.

No one?

Only me.

Are you telling me the truth?

I'm not deceiving you.

How long have you loved me?

For a year now. From the first time I saw you I knew love was our destiny.

If this is true, then leave me, she sings. I can only offer you friendship. I can't love anyone and I couldn't bear such a noble love from you. I'm a very candid and simple person so forget me and find someone else to love.

I'll leave.

Is that how it is? She removes a camellia from the invisible corsage nestling in the invisible lace at her breast. Then take one of my flowers.

But why?

Because you could bring it back to me.

When?

When it has wilted.

O ciel! Tomorrow?

Tomorrow.

He takes the flower and exits. Io son felice! he sings. I am so happy.

His words are carved into my heart, Ursula hums to herself as she gazes again into the mirror. Alfredo's reflection gazes back at her. A dark-haired man with serious blue eyes, a violin under his arm and a tattoo etched into his being. Follie! Follie! Delirio vano é questi! she sings. Such vain madness. Povera donna, sola, abbandonata in questo popoloso deserto che appellano Parigi. This poor woman, abandoned and alone ...

VERDI'S music lingers till morning in Marie's flat below. That damn melody, she says as she hums another bar. Follie! Follie! Delirio vano è questo! She's clasping her first cup of coffee for the day and is still in her favourite spotted flannelette pyjamas. Outside, the elm trees have grown more golden since the last time she looked and each breeze brings another flutter of falling leaves. Soon there'll be drifts along the paths and lanes followed by all those long bare-branch days which always seem so much colder and wetter than they were the year before. But even bare-branch days will pass, or so we're told, she says. The elms will blossom and seed again and on every breeze clouds of gossamer-winged seeds will swirl down Fitzroy Street instead of golden leaves.

A number sixteen tram is rattling up St George's hill with a load of suits and shoulder pads. Glad that's not me today, she says. But look, there's Lilith across the street. I'd recognise that limp anywhere. She must've been up to the post office to collect yesterday's mail. That old woman, she gets the most interesting mail I've ever seen, not just bills and things like the rest of us do. Maybe it's another letter from Sokrates in Alexandria, or from one of those students she's supporting in Eritrea. She showed me photographs of this underground school she'd financed during the war, the whole next generation hidden in desert valleys so they'd be invisible to the Ethiopian Migs flying overhead. Schools, hospitals, factories, whole de facto government departments literally built underground so they wouldn't be bombed to blood and rubble. Or that's what Lilith said. That old iconoclast, she drives you nuts sometimes but she walks her talk like nobody else I know, though to see her limping down the street like that, you'd never guess.

Lillian — or Lilith, as Marie calls her, after Eve's Sumerian predecessor, who refused to lie down for the biblical Adam — is reading as she walks, she and her Abelard, the effusive neutered labrador she named for a medieval scholastic who was once the most famous philosopher in all of France. He was castrated after he fucked one of his students, a gifted scholar twenty years his junior whose name was Heloise. She became pregnant, had the baby and reluctantly agreed to marry him — but she never wanted to be a wife. Heloise's guardian sent his heavies in anyway, who knows why? A quick slice between the philosopher's thighs … and after that, Heloise became a bride of Christ. The easiest choice available for a woman who wanted to be free, Lilith said. Eventually Heloise became a great abbess, and a great scholar too. Like Lilith.

Across the road at the USA Cafe, Angelo and Jana are serving the morning breakfast trade. Back-packers mainly with pancakes and maple syrup, or lonely men with runny eggs and bacon on thick Vienna toast. Must be school holidays, Marie says, because the kids are there. She watches as Lillian stops to chat with Jana, hands Abelard's leash to one of the boys then goes into the Vietnamese bakery. Maybe I'll go over and have a croissant and coffee on the pavement with her, Marie says, but nah, don't feel much like talking yet. Lilith's probably reminiscing about how Dan's croissants remind her of Paris, though I don't suppose she's telling him how she entertained the North Vietnamese during the peace negotiations there, because Dan and his family come from the South. Dan's mob in the eighties, Elle's in the fifties and sixties, mine a hundred years before that and all of us boat people. Lilith's too — but there must be something different about being a Jew because, like, she says it makes you feel guilty for having survived. She was born the year the Nazis won the Bavarian elections, so I guess that explains what she means, and she joked once that the only person who knew what was going on that year was Werner Heisenberg because he was talking about Uncertainty while everyone else reckoned they knew the truth.

Marie sips her morning coffee again. But nothing much has changed in the forty or so years between her birth and mine, she says, even though Lilith claims it has — just because a couple of men went to the moon around the time I was born and looked over their shoulders to see this little blue island in space. But I dunno.

Doesn't seem to have made much difference to what we've done to the planet since, or to one another.

THE letter Lillian is reading is from Sokrates, her now-and-then lover of more than thirty years. He is writing from Alexandria, that ancient Greek city on Egypt's Mediterranean coast. Lillian stops at the USA Cafe to chat with Jana and puts the letter in her basket. One of Jana and Angelo's little boys takes Abelard's leash while she goes into Dan's bakery to buy a loaf of unsliced multi-grain, a carton of calcium-enriched milk and some croissants. She glances across the road to Marie's flat and for a moment considers pushing the security buzzer to invite her to coffee and croissants, but no, Lillian says, it's probably too early for those young ones yet. She chats with Dan, asks him how his wife and new baby are, collects Abelard from the cafe and moves on along the street. She pauses at the pawn shop and waves to the Afghani man behind the counter. He grins and points to the large silver samovar she has been admiring for weeks, but she shakes her head. Where would I put it? she says, then notices Millie listing towards her in a man's checked woollen dressing gown over a see-through floral op-shop dress that's much too short for the bright pink nylon slip she's wearing underneath. Lillian checks for the pack of cigarettes she carries with her every time she ventures into Fitzroy Street, even though she despises the tobacco industry, and waits. Millie stops dead in front of her as usual, and, in a very bad imitation of smoking, moves two fingers to and fro in front of her lips. Millie does this to almost everyone she passes in the street, sometimes to the same person five or six times a day. Most people ignore her, or worse still, swear at her, but Lillian reaches into her basket for her Millie-pack and a box of matches, puts a single cigarette carefully between the street woman's lips, lights it, then hands her another cigarette as a spare. In return, Millie gives her gummiest, most beatific smile and hobbles on.

Still don't know if I'm doing the right thing, Lillian says to herself, but what else does the poor old thing have to look forward to each day? And there but for … She was about to say but for the grace of God, but stopped herself just in time. Those archaic phrases, they just slip out from between your lips almost without you even noticing, she says. She's so preoccupied with the hidden power of language that she almost bumps into Helga, the office manager at Leo's Spaghetti Bar. They've been acquainted since the 1960s when Helga was a young waitress who hardly spoke a word of English, and Lillian was one of her most conspicuous regulars who'd sit alone for hours over an espresso reading the latest European journals. Because Leo's was one of the few places in the whole country where you could get a decent coffee, she says, or even a bowl of pasta. Australia was a wasteland then, especially for intelligent women. That's why I went to Paris, to find the kind of conversations I could only dream of here. But you can never leave your past behind which is why I always return.

Abelard is pulling at his leash. He wants to visit the nearest lamp post, and Lillian has little choice but to follow him and wait while he sniffs around and pisses. Even without their balls, these males have to mark their territory! she says, then remembers the letter she still hasn't finished reading. She takes it out of her basket, unfolds it and reads while Abelard completes his business with the lamp post.

THE possums have been at the potted geraniums again, and at the struggling herbs. This is not the back balcony of Marie's imagination. Inside her head there are tomatoes and rhubarb and spinach in big pots, and grape vines co-existing with the herbs and geraniums. Between what is and what could be, are the possums. But at least they're better than the junkies, Daphne says.

There's a family of them living in the roof cavity: a gutsy and inquisitive female, a male with extraordinarily large biceps, and an indescribably cute babe that has outgrown the pouch. Each night they sniff the air, scramble down the plane tree onto Ursula's second-storey porch, sniff again, shit, nibble at anything green, scurry down the railings to the first-floor landing, sniff and shit some more, then either attack Marie's pot plants or nip the buds from Daphne's native creeper wherever it dares peep out from under the stairs. Marie calls the possum family an ecological disaster. Ursula calls them her last link with the wild, and at night she feeds them stale bread.

You're only encouraging them, Marie says. They're not domesticated animals, you know. But some evenings, especially when the baby looks at her with those big brown eyes, even Marie returns to her kitchen for a crust and holds her breath while the little one creeps towards her outstretched hand.

It's not just the pot plants on the balconies they're eating, though. They're also killing the plane tree that gives its shade in summer then drops its leaves to give the winter sun. The old population-growth story: once big daddy wasn't big daddy but a cute little cuddly that was probably born and nurtured in the roof of the park rotunda or in someone else's ceiling cavity. Little mother emerged from the loft of an old St Kilda shed perhaps and they met, mated, claimed new territory and colonised it. A plentiful supply of food at first, and each year, another cute little mouth to nibble the plane tree and pot plants until all the leaves are gone, and then the emerging shoots …

They've got to go, Marie says to Denis through Heinrich's open kitchen window. Denis is washing the dishes again. Will you give me a hand to shift them some time?

You're not going to kill them, are you? Denis says.

I couldn't do that. Anyway they're a protected species. We'll have to stick 'em in a couple of bags and find a gum tree for them or something.

The only mature eucalypt left in St Kilda is the corroboree tree in the park on the corner of Fitzroy Street and Marine Parade. An ancient ghost that burst from its gum nut when Australia was still an Aboriginal island and only Arab, Chinese, Indonesian, Dutch and Portuguese traders knew. Most of those visitors chose not to stay. That this tree survived the next invasion is a miracle.

THURSDAY. The guy who rang from Sydney visits. For coffee.

Do you like the Romantics? she says as she slips Rimsky-Korsakov's *Scheherazade* into the CD player. She fills a saucepan with water, ignites the gas and grinds some coffee beans. The smell of Ethiopia where the first beans grew, of slave ships crossing the Atlantic, of plantations, of monoculture. She opens the cupboard and reaches for the tiny floral cups, pot, cream jug and sugar bowl of her grandmother's coffee set. It was a wedding present, her grandmother had said, from Joan and Ted McMillan, but you probably don't remember them. You probably weren't even born when they left Ballarat.

By the time the coffee is ready, Sinbad's ship is sailing up the mother of all estuaries towards Basra and Baghdad, and Scheherazade, that plaintive violin voice in Rimsky-Korsakov's symphonic suite, is composing her next story for Shahriyar, her sultan spouse. Sydney is listening from the couch. He comments about the music, the exotic smell. Marie sits opposite and lays the tray on the low table between them.

Do you take sugar? she says.

He nods.

And milk?

MARIE, Maria, Mary. She gives us words: we conceive our descent from her, our past, our future. We the first historians, the first myth-makers; we the first prophets, and seers.

She gives us flame; we rub two sticks together, to keep warm, to keep safe, to cook. We the first fire-makers, the first chefs. She gives us wood, stone, bone; we chip, rub, rasp, grind, sharpen, flatten, polish with a slow, eternal rhythm. Clubs, dibble sticks, awls, querns, brushes, palettes, blades, fish hooks, spear points, arrow heads, spinning wheels, looms, cradles: we the first tool-makers, the first artisans. We incise secret meanings, paint sacred songs: we the first artists. She gives us clay; we mould, shape, incinerate. Bowls, basins, bricks, urns. We the first potters, the first manufacturers.

She gives us wild grasses, wild fruit; we harvest them, select the best, scatter the seeds and channel the water to help them grow: we, the first farmers, the first hydrologists; the first botanists, the first genetic engineers. We grind the grain, add water, fire: we, the first millers, the first bakers. Process the leaves: we the first herbalists, pharmacists, the first paper-makers. Ferment the grain, the grape: we the first brewers, first wine makers, the first biochemists.

She gives us wild beasts: ewes, rams, does, bucks, cows, bulls, sows, boars, mares, stallions, bitches, dogs. We crossbreed, shepherd, domesticate: we the first pastoralists. We shear them, refine their fleece: the first spinners, the first weavers. We flay them, make sandals, boots, jackets, cloaks: the first leather-workers, tanners, furriers. Stretch their skin: the first drummers. String their sinews: the first musicians. Separate their milk, curds from the whey: we the first cheese-makers, the first bacteriologists.

She gives us good seasons, surplus, so we barter with strangers: we the first traders. We measure our boundaries, our harvest, we count our sheep, our goats and determine the exchange rate: we the first mathematicians, the first statisticians, economists, accountants, managers.

We plan, design and construct houses, temples, roads: we the first architects, the first civil engineers, the first builders of cities.

But sometimes the load is too heavy, the distance too far or too high for women to lift, carry, push, or haul. So we innovate, invent, create. Of our actions, our knowledge, we make records, marks on wet clay: we the first scribes, the first teachers. And afterwards we write our praise, our love for her, for our children, for one another, for our men: we the first poets, the first novelists. We who make the past, the present, we who give the future birth. We the daughters of her.

Do you take sugar? she says. And milk?

He nods.

She meets his gaze, undoes the pearl buttons on her cardigan, soft black like night and embroidered with flowers, slips the strap from her shoulder and exposes her breast. The nipple darkens, grows erect. Droplets of milk condense like dew. She leans forward, picks up a tiny cup, lets the milk drip into the coffee and passes it to him. Again for her own. They sip in silence.

Would you like another?

Just the milk, he says.

No, don't fuck me. Let me sip you too, inhale you, let me let you slip, all warm and damp, between my legs; let me let you curl up in my womb, listen to my heartbeat, to my blood swirl around my body. Let me let you be born again, a new man. Kiss me, caress me, my belly, my breasts. Let me nourish you. I am mother, lover, intimate. Maria, Mary, Marie.

But all they have is coffee. And a shy kiss at the door.

FOR weeks the future of the possum family, their rights as an indigenous specie versus the rights of introduced species, is debated up and down the old wooden staircase at the back of the block of flats. Eventually a consensus is reached: yes, the possums really must go, but no one is to get hurt, especially not the possums. And not the non-indigenous humans, either.

The game plan is as follows: Ursula upstairs is to lure the possums from the eaves with her crusts and let them nibble just enough to whet their appetites. Daphne will tempt them further down the tree and onto the railing with pieces of apple, where Marie, Heinrich and Denis will bag them as quickly as possible, in the only bags that are available — the ones St Kilda Council distributes to the local human inhabitants for recycling their glass, paper, and aluminium cans. Marie is to take the mother, Heinrich the father, and Denis wants the babe because she (or he) is so cute, Denis says. Ursula will meanwhile open the gate through which Heinrich, Denis and Marie will leave to relocate the possum family in the corroboree tree.

The first part of the plan (Ursula's crusts and Daphne's apples) works well enough, but basically possums don't like being bagged. While no one expected them to passively cooperate, the violence of their protest seems excessive. Indeed the male possum, he with the big biceps, hisses and claws himself right out of Heinrich's bag and back up the plane tree. Heinrich is mortified. Marie suggests he make a cup of tea for Daphne and Ursula while she and Denis take mother and son (Denis says he checked) up the road.

Jeannie the bag lady is already asleep under the front stairwell as they leave the apartment block. Old Jim, the guardian of Fitzroy Street, is still on his usual street bench with Josephine, his adoring border collie, and his bottle of beer which is eternally camouflaged as a brown paper bag. It's the possums, Marie says in answer to his raised eyebrow. We're taking them to the corroboree tree.

Mary and the boys are still down there, he says. Better ask them first.

Mary White (who's big and black) is the regent of Fitzroy Street. She's in residence only seasonally or when the mood takes her, but when she is, everyone knows. Because this is her country, right, and she's not gunna take no fucken shit from no one, see. Her clan of koori cousins and other refugees simply follow in her wake. Tonight she has led them to the corroboree tree, a warm camp fire of scavenged fence pickets and a cask that they bought from the bottle shop after Mary and her volunteers did the length of the restaurant strip biting the bourgeoisie.

The camp site is hidden in the reconstituted bush that was planted after a Council resolution to attract indigenous wildlife back to St Kilda. The wildlife the councillors had in mind were birds, the ones that sing sweetly, look pretty and eat the insects in their European gardens. Mary White's only recorded comment at the time was that the bush should be reconstituted from the bay right back to the 'Nongs, those mountains at the edge of Melbourne's sprawl. You'd have plenty of native wildlife then, she said.

Mary and her clan have now reclaimed this sanctuary, not for indigenous wildlife but for indigenous people. A fine plume of smoke, a country strum of an old guitar and the Aboriginal flag painted illegally on the old toilet block proclaim their sovereignty. Entry to this black nation is open to anyone who dares, to anyone who is ready to sit on the ground and share the post-colonial ritual of the cask.

Hey cuz, come and 'ave a sip, a very mellow yet regal Mary shouts when she recognises Marie.

Nah, not tonight thanks all the same, Marie says. But is it OK if we let these possums go here? We thought this'd be the best place for them.

They bin spearin' ya sheep, missus? a black voice says from near the camp fire but Marie hears only ex-Mission laughter as she wades through the reintroduced native grasses to the corroboree tree — under which she and Denis lay their still hissing, still heaving recycling bags. Marie unties hers carefully and mother marsupial disappears instantly. Denis wants to say a slow and cuddly farewell to his and reaches into the sack. Fuck, he screams as he quickly withdraws his arm. Scratches and flowing blood. The baby hisses and disappears up the tree. Marie digs into her pocket for a handkerchief and reaches to wipe Denis's wound.

Don't touch me, don't touch me, he says.

Hey, what's wrong? I just wanna help.

No. Don't come near me. I'm positive.

He leans against the gum tree, closes his eyes and lets his poisoned blood drip onto the ground. Marie leans against the tree trunk too, stares at the moon for at least thirty seconds then reaches across to him. Here, take my hanky, she says, and let's go home. I'll clean you up and give you some antiseptic cream. It's OK. I won't get it.

She picks up the two now-empty bags. Denis follows her along the track back into whitefella territory. European elms, asphalt, tram lines …

WHEN did you find out? Marie says.

A couple of years ago. I had a job at this, like you'd call it a brothel, and we all had to have this test. I think I got it from drugs, though.

Does Heinrich know?

Yeah. He doesn't think he has it but he won't go to the clinic to find out.

They cross Park Street to the dull throb of the drums and bass guitars from the nightclubs, the electric metal-on-metal of the number sixteen tram, and the scream of an ambulance siren.

Another junkie dead, Denis says. Marie opens the security door to her block of flats. Denis follows her up the front stairs and turns to knock on Heinrich's door.

No, come to my place first, she says.

She runs warm water into the bathroom basin, cautiously wipes the scratches with cotton wool and squeezes a tube of ointment. It's your war wound, she says as she wraps a gauze bandage around his arm. What will happen to Heinrich if I die? Denis says.

✦ ✦

BUT HER REAL NAME is Marguerite Gautier, the intellectual property of Alexandre Dumas, the only son of Catherine Labay, a single working mother, and her lover Alexandre Dumas, who's now known as Dumas père, the one who wrote *Les Trois Mousquetaires* and *Le Comte de Monte Cristo*. Marguerite Gautier is the son's invention. He calls this fictional character La Dame aux Camélias and claims he had a real-life affair with someone very much like her, in Paris in 1844. Verdi based his opera on her. La Traviata.

It is my considered view, young Dumas says in the opening of his book about Marguerite, that no one can invent fictional characters without first having made a lengthy study of people. Since I am not yet of an age to invent, I must make do with telling a tale. I therefore invite the reader to believe that this story is true. All the characters who appear in it, with the exception of the heroine, are still living, he says.

11 Boulevard de la Madeleine
Paris
January 1847

I know I'm dying. This cough, this blood I'm choking on, this pain, I know it's incurable, that it's punishment for the way I have lived my life. But before I go, I want to tell my story. This darkness of my soul, this loneliness, this desperate longing to see him once more.

I laughed at Armand when we first met. A mutual acquaintance had brought him up to my box at the Opéra-Comique. My laughter must have offended him because he returned to his seat in the stalls. He was such a serious young man. Weeks later, my neighbour Prudence Duvernoy and that young Gaston brought him around to my place for supper. I drank too much champagne that night, out of boredom I suppose, and so my coughing started again. I rushed, stumbled from the dining room to my boudoir so no one would see the blood and collapsed exhausted onto my sofa. Armand followed me. He was shocked by what he saw. You're killing yourself by living this way, he said. I glanced at myself in the mirror. I seemed so pale, so dishevelled. He took my hands and kissed them. Just look after yourself, he said.

It's too late for that, I told him. Looking after yourself is only for society ladies with families and friends, and husbands to pay the bills. Women like me can't afford such luxury. Our job is to feed men's vanity. When we can no longer do that, we're abandoned.

I'd take care of you if you let me, he said.

I laughed at him again. He was still holding my hands, kissing them, drawing me closer. Then he told me he loved me, that he had loved me ever since he'd seen me outside Michel Susse's gallery more than a year ago. I tried to make light of it. I told him he was being far too serious but that if he could accept me the way I was, perhaps I could love him too. But I had to be free to lead my own life the way I wanted to, I said. I'd always dreamed of that, you see. Of finding a young man who could love me without thinking of me as his property and who'd let me give myself freely to him, no questions asked. He agreed with my conditions and he tried to kiss me. I pulled away. We'll see, I said.

When?

Later.

Why not now?

I removed a single red camellia from my corsage and passed it to him. Sometimes it's better to wait, I said. I'm sure he understood, because everyone knows that for four or five days each month, I wore my camellias red. We'll see what happens when they're white, I said. Perhaps tomorrow night.

The next morning my creditors were at my door again, including my florist! In those days my annual expenditure was around one hundred thousand francs, which meant I needed at least four or five very rich lovers to pay my bills. And I mean very rich. Even a man with an annual income of five hundred thousand francs, a huge fortune, would only have been able to cover a fraction of my costs on top of all his own expenses — his servants, carriages and horses, hunting estates, entertaining, gambling, travelling, and a racing stable perhaps. And more often than not, a wife and children as well. With all that he'd only be able to spare me forty or fifty thousand a year, which to most people is still a great deal of money, I know. Most working men and their families have to survive on two thousand francs a year if they're lucky and women only earn half as much — if they earn anything at all. Most of them do what I do but never get paid, the poor things.

On this occasion, it was the old Duke who kept my creditors happy. He's worth tens of millions and has been my greatest asset — though even from him, I couldn't ask for more than seventy thousand a year. I met him at the sanatorium in Bagnères. He told me I looked very much like his daughter, who'd died of consumption there, and he promised to give me anything I wanted if he could visit me. I explained what sort of a woman I was, that I needed my freedom, and he accepted that.

After I had paid all my bills, all I wanted to do was go straight to bed alone — because having to worry about money is so stressful, don't you think? But then Armand arrived to remind me of my promise. Nanine, my maid, showed him into my boudoir and we'd just settled down in front of the fire when the doorbell rang again. It was Count de N. He'd picked the very worst time to call and didn't I let him know! I snapped at poor Nanine too. I'm so tired of men knocking on my door for the same thing! I screamed. Paying me for it and thinking that's enough. If girls only knew what this trade was like they'd sooner be chamber-maids! And what's more, this dress is too tight, I said as I stormed into my dressing room. Get me my robe. And bring me some punch.

You'll kill yourself, madame, poor Nanine said.

Good! I told her. And bring me something to eat as well.

Nanine returned with a cold chicken, a bottle of Bordeaux which she said was better for me than punch, a bowl of strawberries, plates, cutlery and two long-stemmed glasses. I slipped into bed and beckoned Armand to sit beside me. When he was close enough, I popped a strawberry into his mouth and handed him a glass of wine. He gulped it down and began to relax. I did too. We sat together in bed like naughty children feeding one another chicken breast and strawberries and when there was no food left, nor any wine, I put the tray on the bedside table. As I moved, my robe slipped open. I could feel Armand's eyes clinging to me. I lay down, took his hand and put it on one of my breasts. He touched me as though I were the Virgin Mary, then he bent to kiss my nipple. I held his head there, caressed him like a mother and let him suck me. But he was so inexperienced, so inept in the art of desire, my poor darling, that he lost control and nearly smothered me in his frenzy. I pushed him off just in time. If all you want to do is jump on top and poke it in and out a few times, I told him, you might as well relieve yourself in the privacy of your own room. So then I introduced him to the art of love. He was a very good student.

Unfortunately I had to ask him to leave around 5.00 a.m.

because my old patron often visited me early in the mornings — and he liked me to be all fresh and pure and virginal. He used to send me scented soap and perfume and have exquisite night dresses made for me to his own design. White silk, long and almost transparent, with fine, hand-made lace at the collar and cuffs and little mother-of-pearl buttons right down to my navel.

The Duke was already near his eighties by then and most of the time, all he wanted to do was pretend. Nanine would often set up a small table for two by the window so we could have petit déjeuner and read the papers together. Sometimes I'd slowly unbutton my night dress all the way down and let it fall from my shoulders as I passed him his coffee. He'd take my hand as if I were a little girl and lead me to the sofa then, and sit me on his lap. I'd rest my head on his shoulder, nuzzle him, call him Your Excellency and tell him I was his to do with as he liked. He'd smile and caress my breasts with his gnarled old hands and I'd sigh and act as though he was the only one who'd ever touched me that way, then he'd slip his hand beneath my night dress, over my tummy, my arse, between my legs and sometimes he'd cup my mound in his hand, let his fingers slip between my lips. I'd press my body into his hand again and again, let my thighs fall open, bite his shoulder, contract the muscles of my cunt and my arse and say oh Your Excellency, I'm coming, I'm coming. And sometimes I wouldn't have to pretend.

Afterwards I'd curl up in his lap and sometimes even fall asleep if I'd had a busy night. Other mornings he wasn't so gentle. He never wanted to go to bed with me, though, and I never saw his old body fully naked. He was my most undemanding patron, and my most generous. But after that first time with Armand all I could think about was seeing him again. I'd just lie in other men's arms daydreaming about how I could buy more time to be with my true love, somewhere away from Paris where we could be alone. A country house overlooking the Seine, perhaps, with trees and flowers.

One night when we were lying together in front of the fire I told him about my idea. All it needs is for you to love me as much as I love you, and to share in my profits! I said. He wanted to know what I meant by that but I knew I could never tell him. What does it matter? I said. In a month's time we'll be in some lovely little village strolling hand in hand along the river bank and drinking milk fresh from the cows just as I did when I was a child. He hesitated even then, so I hugged and kissed him and caressed his cock. Please let me have this simple happiness, I begged. While I still have time. He just fell into my arms then. I'd let you have anything you wanted, he whispered.

I set the next night aside for financing my summer with Armand, but I knew by then that I could never tell him the truth. So I sent him a note telling him I was ill, that my doctor had advised me to stay in bed.

The next morning I received a note from him. I trust that yesterday's indisposition has not proved too troublesome, he wrote. I called at eleven last evening to ask after you and was told you had not yet returned. Monsieur de G. was altogether more fortunate, for he arrived a few moments later and was still with you at four o'clock this morning.

Oh, the silly boy, I said to Prudence at the time. People compose letters like this in their heads but they never actually send them. Why does he have to be so jealous? Does he think he owns me or something?

A few days later I received another letter, full of repentance, and begging me to let him visit me again. By then I was curious to see where he lived, so I decided to go to his place instead. His manservant let us in and I waited on the sofa in his drawing room. You should have seen his face when he saw me! He fell to his knees, took my hands in his and smothered himself in my lap. I lifted his head and kissed him on the lips. This is the third time I've had to forgive you in as many days, I said.

But why did you deceive me?

Look Armand, I said, if I were a Duchess with two hundred thousand francs a year and you were my lover, you might have the right to ask me that question. But I'm not a wealthy duchess. I'm Mademoiselle Marguerite Gautier and I have debts of forty thousand francs and I want to spend my summer in the country with you and I don't want you to have to pay, because I'd never contaminate our love like that. He kissed me again and accompanied me back to my place for supper. He stayed until dawn.

We saw a lot of one another after that and he really took care of me as he said he would. He gave up his gambling, drinking and smoking, and watched over me to make sure I ate the proper foods and rested, until soon my coughing was gone. One day we went for a drive — though I didn't tell him why. We lunched in Bougival, about an hour and a half from Paris by carriage. You can see the Marly aqueduct from the restaurant there, and the Ile de Croissy. And all those new factories in the background with Paris almost hidden under a low black cloud. In the afternoon, we rowed across to the island to stroll through the glades. That's when I saw it. The prettiest stone house I'd ever seen, with climbing roses right up to the first-floor balconies. Why don't you get the Duke to rent it for you? Prudence whispered to me — which is exactly what I'd been planning all along.

I took the Duke to see the house the next day, and of course he agreed. I think he was delighted to get me out of Paris and away from the spying eyes of his family. While he was paying for lunch, I booked a hotel suite for Armand and a week later we moved, Armand to the hotel and me to my country house, but you can imagine where Armand spent most of his time. Soon my servants were calling him Sir.

It was perfect, those first weeks. Everything I'd hoped for. But then the Duke found out. There was quite a scene, really. He demanded that Armand leave immediately and never return. I needed the Duke's money, but by then I also needed Armand. So I made my choice — even though I had no idea how we'd get by without the Duke paying the bills.

We didn't set foot in Paris for two whole months after that. We spent our time doing silly romantic things, like chasing butterflies in the garden or picking flowers or just lying in the grass watching the clouds pass by. Sometimes we'd stay in bed all day, discovering new things about ourselves, like the hardly-touching trace of my finger across his lips; him sighing and closing his eyes, kissing, nibbling my hand; me caressing his stubbled cheeks, the softness of his neck; him turning towards me, opening his eyes and smiling at me; me leaning into him, kissing him softly on the lips, entwining him with my legs, feeling his cock tight against my belly, moving my hips in that slow ancient lovers' dance. Just gazing into one another's eyes, seeing, feeling like we were a single being. And then Nanine knocking on the door to bring us breakfast or lunch or dinner on a tray. And we'd gaze at one another again and caress and kiss and I'd slip his cock inside and rock my hips to continue the dance to whatever rhythm we felt was right. A waltz perhaps, or an allemande. A gavotte, a minuet, a pavane. A wild passionate Gypsy dance or a pas de deux so slow we'd hardly move.

I'd never felt like this with any of my lovers before and only knew it was possible because I'd read about it in books. But books always had a final page — and that was my greatest fear. That I'd turn the page and find he'd grown tired of me. I'd tell him this sometimes, how afraid I was. He'd hold me and swear he'd always love me, that he'd never leave me. Then we'd kiss again and watch the moon rise, or listen to the wind in the trees, or just hold hands in silence. And another day would pass.

But still there were things I couldn't talk to him about. Like the letters from Prudence about how my creditors were threatening to repossess my things because the old Duke was refusing to pay my bills. That's when I decided to pawn my jewels, to sell my horses and my barouche so I could buy more time with Armand. I took him for a picnic on the island so Prudence could collect my things without him noticing. I had to lie to him about what had happened to my things. When he noticed that the coach was missing, for example, I told him I'd sent it away for repairs. But that night he went through my drawers to see what else was gone, and the next day took the train to Paris. He said it was to check his mail but he went straight to Prudence's place. I know because I asked Nanine to follow him. When he got home, he shouted at me. Why didn't you ask me for the money? he said. Because I don't want money to come between us, I told him. And anyway, why can't you love me just as well without my diamonds and pearls, and my fine horses and carriage?

I'd changed in those few months with Armand. All those things that had once meant so much to me were no longer important. All I wanted was to be everything Armand wanted me to be. I'd even been thinking of liquidating all my assets, paying off all my debts and investing what remained so Armand and I could live together indefinitely on my income. We'd be poor, but at least we'd have each other. And I even daydreamed that he might ask me to marry him, and that one day I might have his baby. But then I received a letter from his father, Monsieur Duval. He wrote that he wanted to see me. Alone.

MARIE'S back door is open. Heinrich and Denis are on the landing. Marie can hear them talking … so they made them out of fir and oak and beech trees from the forests of Macedonia or from around the Black Sea, Heinrich says. Or southern Italy. Trees eight or ten metres thick at the base. Hundreds, thousands of years old. Their ships were very shallow-draughted and no good in the open sea, so they'd just cruise along the coasts or island-hop and go ashore each night to sleep.

He's sitting on a fold-up chair at a fold-up picnic table as he speaks, squinting like a Cyclops through a single robotic eye that's a black jeweller's lens. He dips a brush only a few hairs thick into a miniature pot of liquid bronze and applies it to the prow of the shrunken Athenian trireme that's wedged between the eroded limestone ridges of his thumb and forefinger.

By the fifth century BCE Athens had to import all her timber, he says, and most of her grain too. That's why she became a colonial power — to secure the resources she needed to sustain her own people. The alternative was mass famine, complete economic collapse and social disorder. Hey, get out of my light! he says as Denis's shadow moves across the tiny ship.

Well, why couldn't they just plant more trees to replace the ones they cut down, not have so many babies and be nice to their neighbours, Denis says and rests an arm on Heinrich's shoulders. Why did they have to go to war?

You're so naive, Heinrich says.

Denis grimaces like his heart has been pierced by a javelin. He lifts his arm from Heinrich's shoulder and moves away. Heinrich looks up and catches Denis's hand: but that's one of the things I like about you, he says. Your innocence.

Denis turns again to his lover, drapes his arms around him from behind, runs his fingers through the hair on his bare chest and kisses his neck. Soft lips on bare, soft skin. S'pose you still want me out of the way this afternoon though, he says.

Heinrich dips his brush into the liquid bronze to gild another Athenian prow. You'd only be bored, he says.

Do they know about me? About us?

We never talk about that kind of stuff, Heinrich says.

Denis leans back against the balcony railing and exhales a sigh of blind acceptance. I'll piss off before they come then, he says.

Heinrich nods and checks his fleet against the drawings in his reference book, ship by tiny ship. The markings match exactly. Next he checks his field commanders in their plumed helmets and red cloaks of office: Nicias, Lamachus, Demosthenes, Cleon ... He lifts the tiny lead figures individually and dabs a touch of bronze onto each of their shields to represent the gilded form of Athena, their patron deity. His last general, Alcibiades, is wrapped not in a red cloak like the other Athenian leaders, but in royal and ostentatious purple. On this general's shield is his own patron deity, masculine Eros armed with a runic bolt of lighting. In the game of life that was the real war Heinrich is preparing for, this tiny tin warrior determined the destiny of the entire Athenian empire. Or so Thucydides says.

The Athenians of lesser rank are waiting patiently in their corslets, helmets and greaves in Heinrich's second bedroom, the war room as he calls it. This room is decorated with prints of famous battles and portraits of his favourite military leaders — Pericles, Hannibal, Caesar, Napoleon, Radetzky, Bismarck, Nelson and MacArthur. And on the shelves along the walls, generation upon generation of tiny hand-painted soldiers are waiting to be blood sacrificed.

MARIE climbs the wooden stairs of the restored stable loft at the back of the Esplanade Hotel and knocks on Elle's door; inside, small feet on timber floorboards, the dragging of a chair, excited breathing. Marie puts her face close to the security lens and sticks out her tongue. A child giggles. More chair sounds. Marie hides against the wall. The door opens as if by magic. Marie waits. Sophie waits. Then simultaneous Boos! Marie catches the little girl in her arms, lifts her and holds her tight. Got you, she says. More giggles. Let me see your tooth!

Sophie opens her mouth and wobbles a tiny incisor. Is there really a tooth fairy? she says.

Leave your tooth in a glass when it falls out, and if it disappears, then you'll know, Marie says.

Will I see her if I stay awake all night?

Marie brushes the child's long dark hair from her face. What'd you do if you did see her?

I don't know, the little girl says and giggles again.

A shout from the back of the apartment. That you, Marie?

Yeah, Elley. Just passing. Thought you might like a game of pool while there's no one in the pub.

I could do with a break from these guys, Elle says. She's in the corridor now and advancing on the small living room. Garibaldi's about to invade Sicily, she says. You should read this stuff.

It's probably in Italian, Marie says as she flops into the lap of an elderly armchair.

There are translations for you monolinguals, you know, Elle says. But what I'm on now is in English. Found it down at that second-hand book shop in Barkly Street, by some sycophant from Cambridge called Trevelyan. The ultimate male romance. Hero lands on this unknown island with a thousand dreamers all dressed in red shirts, or some of them are, to free the natives from tyranny and unite Italia — da Trapani al Isonzo, dal Taranto a Nizza. But the boys in Turin have given Nice away. To Napoleon III, and Savoy too. Part of that deal with France to get the Austrians out of the rest of Italia.

She settles herself astride a frayed armrest of her faded Edwardian sofa. I'm getting really pissed off with this Trevelyan, though, she says. He reckons the Sicilian peasants were so naive they thought they were fighting for some princess called La Talia. But my forebears knew more about fighting tyranny than anyone. They'd been doing it for millennia, like Sicilian Vespers and all that. And they were the first to the barricades in 1848 while the rest of Europe was still sitting around in their cafes talking about it. She picks up an elastic band from the coffee table, runs her fingers through Sophie's hair, gently pulls it back into a ponytail and slips the elastic over. You wanna see if Lilith's home, Soph? she says.

You could ask her about the tooth fairy, Marie says. Lilith's the one who'd know.

And maybe I can dust the dolls, Sophie says.

The child gathers her shoes and runs down the back stairs of the converted stables. Elle watches from the kitchen window as she crosses the bluestone lane, reaches through a familiar hole to unlatch Lillian's ageing wooden gate and, with exaggerated effort, drags it across the path — to be greeted by a very excited Abelard.

IT'S two o'clock in the afternoon and five European field commanders are pouring their first libation in Heinrich's war room. A man in jungle greens lifts his can: to Zeus, he says. This man's nom de guerre is John. He has no personal history — because these men don't talk about that kind of stuff, or so Heinrich says. Today Anonymous John is playing Sparta and the Peloponnesian League including Corinth. Anonymous Carlos is the Persian Empire, Anonymous Pete is both Macedonia and Thebes, and Anonymous Alexie is umpire, chief scorer and banker. Each of these commanders, including Heinrich, has spent the last fortnight preparing both men and machines for battle. And themselves, for even in a war game, victory is more than a casino.

Alexie the banker lifts his stubby: to Sparta and Athens he says. May the best side win.

We already know who won! Heinrich says. Anonymous Pete of Macedonia grins and reaches across the map for his first foreign intervention.

LILLIAN appears at the fly-screen door, bends for a kiss then waves her OK-I'll-look-after-Sophie signal back across the cobbles to Elle at the stable window.

Who needs a tooth fairy with Lilith across the lane? Elle says. Do I want any money?

Nah. I've got enough for a game and a couple of drinks for both of us, Marie says.

Elle grabs a floppy velvet hat and fake leopard-skin jacket from the back of the sofa, checks the back door, closes the front, and follows Marie down the stairs. They've known one another since childhood, these two women. At first it was just a smile across the pumpkin and potatoes once week when Marie's mum stopped to do her fruit and veg at Elle's parents' shop. But it was music that gave them this friendship. All those Saturday mornings spent climbing the grand marble staircase of the Ballarat Art Gallery (Marie with cello, Elle with her accordion) to play under the baton of Sister Beatrice, the provincial saint who rejected no child who wanted to learn music. Nineteenth-century music that is. The sort Ballarat's founding fathers listened to before they had themselves hung in heavy gold frames on the art gallery walls. And each Christmas for most of their high-school years, the two girls played carols outside the fruit and veg. Cello and accordion.

They shared such innocent dreams in those days — like Elle's father must have dreamed before he left Sicily for the Fiat factory in Turin. Or Turin for his uncle's market garden on the outskirts of Melbourne. Or the market garden for the shop in Ballarat. And Elle's mother? She never dreams, or that's what Elle says. And if she does, it'd still be in dialect, because Elle's mother has never felt comfortable with English, nor even with formal Italian. To Elle, she just works too hard too long in the shop, goes to church too often, and prays too much. To Mary, holy mother of god. Especially when Elle got pregnant, like Mary and Heloise, and wouldn't marry the guy. Wouldn't even name him.

Such a scandal in the fruit and veg. For months a procession of migrant women throwing their arms around Elle's mother as if her daughter were dead. But she was only in St Kilda, another refugee giving birth in a stable. Between breast feeds and sleepless nights, she studied and played music to supplement her single-parent benefit. Keyboards in rock bands, and lead vocals, which is why she's so good at pool. All those hours waiting between brackets in pubs while Lillian and Marie took care of little Sophie. She still does music and still studies. A women's band called Lip Service and this thesis on sovereignty.

So how's it going, anyway, your Garibaldi and his boys? Marie says.

Fascinating, Elle says. Amazing connections. Like did you know he visited Australia? He was captain of this ship and came ashore on some island in Bass Strait for water. One of Nellie Melba's singing teachers even fought with him in Rome. And like, remember your grandfather telling us about Eureka when we were kids? How your great-great-grandmother or someone sewed the stars on to the Southern Cross? Well, it seems like there were some of Garibaldi's boys there too, some of the ones who escaped after the fall of the Roman Republic. But what a pissweak little rebellion Eureka was compared with what was happening in other parts of the world!

LILLIAN appears at the fly-screen door, bends for a kiss then waves her OK-I'll-look-after-Sophie signal back across the cobbles. Both dog and child rush into the kitchen. Have they sprouted yet? Sophie says as she scrapes a chair from under the jarrah kitchen table and kneels to reach a terracotta shard in a saucer of water. On the shard is a scatter of barley seeds, the garden from which Adonis was born, a harvest deity and the most perfect, most beautiful son of the virgin goddess queen. Each year he was born anew to be sacrificed, bled and buried, and on the third day he rose again from the dead to ascend into heaven through his mother's most secret, most sacred gate. But Sophie doesn't know this yet. She's still dragging the terracotta shard of barley seeds across the table. Within each tiny grain the whole universe of barleyhood is sprouting. But they'll die if they have no dirt, Sophie says.

Lillian's sitting on the edge of the table rolling up the sleeves of her most bedraggled cardigan. They're meant to wither and die, Soph, she says. It's a symbolic garden like our grandmothers used to make thousands of years ago along the Tigris and Euphrates rivers, and along the Nile and all around the Mediterranean. Each one of those little seeds represents Adonis — or Damuzi or Tammuz or Attis or Dionysus or Jesus or whatever he's called in whatever place — being born again from his mother's womb. If we planted them in a real garden, they'd grow up tall and flower and by summer you'd have a whole crop of barley seeds like this. Then you'd harvest them with your sickle and hide the seed in pits or big terracotta pots so you'd have enough to eat for the rest of the year and enough for next year's crop. That's if there were no droughts or plagues of insects or rodents, and no wars, because then you'd starve. But if your crop ripened, by summer you'd be able to harvest it — and then you'd plough the stalks back into the earth. That's how nature works, Soph, in cycles. Later you'd go to your temple and reap your harvest deity in the same way, or your priestess would, and they'd let his blood flow to symbolically fertilise the earth. He'd die like these barley sprouts will, but the goddess, his mother, would lie with him again to bring him back to life.

So when these sprouts wither and die, we'll take them down to the beach and throw them into the sea like our ancestors did. Because they believed that the ocean was the goddess's menstrual blood, that it would take you back to her womb to be born again. Like spring.

Does that mean they killed him? Sophie says.

It was a long time ago, Soph, and you'll have to wait a few years before you can understand. But, Lillian silently reminds herself, we sacrificed real boys then. Because males are more expendable than females, biologically speaking at least. The priestesses would cut off his genitals with a ritual sickle shaped like a crescent moon and the people would tear him apart and eat him so they could be part of his resurrection too. Later we sacrificed young rams or goats or bulls instead, and now in some religions it's just bread and wine. Because these days we sacrifice our young men differently.

Sophie is dragging the grains of barley around the Garden of Adonis with the end of a pencil she's picked up from the kitchen table. Abelard is wagging his tail and thumping it against the table leg. With each thump, another earthquake in the sprouting crop, another tidal wave across the saucer sea.

What's he look like? Sophie says.

Adonis? The most beautiful boy you've ever seen.

Like Barbie's boyfriend Ken?

Well, I'm not sure he was ever white or spoke with an American accent! Lillian says. I don't think I've got one here to show you, but you know some of his mothers.

She moves into the living room. Sophie and Abelard follow. Ten thousand years or more of female deities are standing, squatting, sitting, reclining along the shelves on either side of Lillian's marble fireplace. These are Sophie's favourite dolls.

Lillian reaches for a small clay figure. This one is Nana, she says. Remember her? One of the boy god's earliest mums. Lillian holds the deity and caresses her pregnant belly, her fecund hips, her ballooning buttocks. The goddess is cupping her breasts in the palms of her hands: here, drink of me, she's saying. She who gave birth to the Tigris and Euphrates rivers and to the first human beings, who in turn gave birth to her. They created her in their own image from river mud mixed with their own menstrual blood. Nana of Iraq. Inanna. Queen of the Persian Gulf. The Sacred Harlot, the Holy Womb. A literate deity this, who taught her people how to write but only in Sumerian which was a matricentric language with no word for father, only a plural sign for the men who give your mother pleasure, who fulfil her most divine desire. Because once upon a time, that was men's role, to give the goddess pleasure, and we women took it on her behalf as often as possible. And Nana is insatiable. Each year, she gives birth to a son who is called the Christos, the saviour, the good shepherd. The only begotten one. And each year, she sacrifices him and washes her genitals in his blood to fructify the earth. But then she despairs at what she's done. She weeps and wails and cries Damu, Damuzi my son, my lover, my darling, where are you? Come back, for the rivers they won't flood without you, the crops they will not grow. No flowers for honey, no fruit for wine. Without you, my breasts, my womb are empty. Damuzi my son, my people will perish without you.

For three days she searches the other side, and for three days the moon doesn't shine. The temple howls, ululates. The city mourns. And Nana, she's running, screaming, falling through her city's darkest, most inner alleys, bleeding, sobbing, choking as she searches for her son her brother her lover who is the other part of her. Her clothes are torn, her jewels are lost, her seven veils are ripped off one by one as she plunges through the maze of her most deepest despair. Damu, Damuzi my Christos, where are you? I want you, I need you in my arms, at my breast, I need you deep inside. Come unto me and let me give you life.

Every year she does this, and every year she finds her lover brother son, lies with him and lo, he rises from the dead and ascends into heaven through her pearly gate. My precious sweet resting on my heart, she says, my brother, he did it fifty times one by one, tongue-making. And again her belly, her breasts are full; here, drink of me, she says. While far away in the Hindu Kush the winter snows are melting. In Anatolia the rains come. And so the rivers flood. The crops grow, the birds sing, the flowers bloom. And it is spring.

But even the milk of a goddess can't guarantee eternity, Lillian says to herself. For where is Sumer now? Those lush green fields, those irrigation canals? Those temples that were once centres of women's wealth and power? Those mud-brick houses, those bazaars, those narrow alleys of Uruk and Ur? Because as Leonard Woolley once said, if Ur was an empire's capital, if Sumer was once a vast granary, why has the population dwindled to nothing, the very soil lost its virtue? And why, I might add, was Sumer bombed in America's last war?

Ah! Nana, you taught your people how to farm and irrigate, how to build cities, how to read and write, which was nice, Lillian says. But you forgot to teach us how to live in peace. With ourselves, with one another, with you, with the earth …

MARTHA is feeding St Kilda's cats under the paperbarks in the parking lot behind the Fitzroy Street motel again. Black cats and dark gray, with one or two marked in white. Milk in take-away containers, and tinned cat food from her pension cheque. Because they'd starve without me, she says. Between Martha's formal feeds, the cats stalk St Kilda's streets and lanes with all the other scavengers. Denis too. He's stalking the lanes en route to lunch at the Mission of the Sacred Heart because Heinrich's playing his war games again. Old Harold passes. He's already eaten. You can tell by the damp gravy on his shirt and the two loaves of day-old bread he's collected from the table by the Mission door.

What's on? Denis says.

Stew, Old Harold says without changing his gait.

Denis keeps walking too. Up a narrow lane between two high paling fences and into the park behind a nineteenth-century mansion that's now a seedy rooming house. Old Jacko's catching the morning sun in the rotunda there, him and the brown bottle that kept him warm last night. He ignores Denis, or pretends he does — because it's hard to ignore Denis when he's wearing his checked flannel shirt tied at the waist, the new lumberjack boots he spent his last pension cheque on, and his favourite, most frayed jeans that are cut off just below the crutch to expose the whites of his cheeks.

Denis turns into the back yard of the Sacred Heart and the smell of rotting rubbish bins. The queue's inside the Mission hall, a familiar shuffle as the plates are filled. Stew and boiled veg and a how-are-we-today-dear from the cook's volunteer. Nothing ever changes here, except for some of the faces, Denis says to a couple of friends behind him, Ralph the Rat and Monica.

Yeah, well Sharon's gone since I seen you here last week, Ralph says. Strangled on the weekend by some jerk at the Gatwick. And you remember Trudy? Throat cut in the parking lot a few days before. And River and Sunshine ... he sticks her fork into the vein of his right arm. Reckon they got it from that cunt Lionel. The social worker found them. And Johnny. Shot by the pigs. Like Colleen. Five times in the chest while he was hacking himself with a bread knife. He was schizo too. He pushes his plate away. God this place stinks, he says. You want some jelly for seconds? Or a piece of cake?

I WAS VERY NERVOUS about meeting Armand's father but excited too. I felt sure that when he saw how much Armand and I loved each other, he'd accept me and maybe even welcome me into his family. But no. He was rude, arrogant, even abusive, like many men of his class. He told me he had come to save his son from me, because, by expecting Armand to foot the bill for my extravagant lifestyle, I was destroying any chance he might have of living a respectable life! You can imagine how shocked I was by that. When he told me that Armand had signed over to me a small income of around 750 francs a year he'd inherited from his mother's estate, I exploded. I explained that I knew nothing about the inheritance and would never accept Armand's money. And as for the bills, it was me who was making all the financial sacrifices. I even showed him the pawn tickets for my jewels and told him how I'd sold my horses and carriage. I said I'd be happy to sell everything if it meant I could stay with Armand.

So then he tried another approach. He apologised for his rudeness and took my hands. Madame, he said, I don't deny your great beauty and your generous heart but you must understand that mistresses are one thing and the family quite another. I'm begging you now to make a sacrifice far greater than any you have ever made before.

I pulled my hands away and stumbled to the window. The leaves of the trees were turning gold and red. Some had already fallen. Monsieur Duval kept talking. There comes a time, he said, when a young man has duties beyond passion. If my son wants to be respected, he must find a secure job appropriate to his station in life. You may not understand this, but if you were to sacrifice all your worldly goods to live with him, you would damage him, and me, far more than you could ever know. Other people would see only one thing: that Armand Duval allowed a kept woman, a whore, to sell everything she owned for his sake. He would lose any respect people might have had for him as my son, and soon he'd be blaming you for his failure in life. How would you cope then when your youth and beauty are gone and my son's future is destroyed?

I was still staring out the window. He was still talking. If you love Armand, he said, prove it to him in the only way you can. By sacrificing your love for his future.

I couldn't believe I was hearing these words. I turned to face him: Sir, you are in my house, and now I'm asking you to leave!

He didn't move, didn't shift his eyes from mine. I have no choice then, he said, but to tell you the real reason I've made this trip. He moved closer. Armand is not my only child. I also have a daughter who is young and beautiful and as pure as an angel. She is also in love and the man she is in love with has asked her to marry him. As his wife, she'll become part of a very respectable family. I have to tell you, madame, that this family has found out about Armand's affair with you. His father has advised me that unless Armand severs his liaison with you, arrangements for his son to marry my daughter will be cancelled.

I could feel the blood draining from my face, and my story plummeting towards its final page.

So this, madame, is why I have come to see you, Monsieur Duval said. My children's future is in your hands.

I leant my head against the window. He begged me then. In the name of your love for Armand and your repentance, he said, give me my daughter's happiness. And my son back to me. Please, Marguerite.

I was sobbing now. How naive I had been to think that Armand and I could live happily ever after. I stared out the window at the garden. Autumn and then winter. I was weeping, sobbing.

Do you believe I love your son? I whispered.

Yes, he said.

That money has nothing to do with it?

Yes.

Do you know how important your son's love is to me, that it's the only thing that gives meaning to my life?

I do.

Well, Monsieur Duval, I will give him back to you. For his sake. For his future. And your daughter's.

I was clinging to the back of a chair as I spoke those words. He came towards me and kissed me on the forehead. You are a noble-hearted young woman, he said. God will recognise what you have done.

I was numb now. A machine. I went to my desk, took a sheet of my best scented paper from the drawer and wrote a note to Prudence. Please make arrangements for me to have supper with Count de N on Tuesday, I said. I'm returning to Paris and to my former life. I sealed the envelope and passed it to Armand's father. He embraced me. I felt his tears of gratitude on my head like a baptism. And then he left.

I was still crying when Armand returned. I clung to him, wept, sobbed in his arms. He begged me to tell him what was wrong but I couldn't. I just prayed to God to give me strength to fulfil my promise to his father.

The next morning Armand went to Paris again. A few hours later I too caught the train. I went straight to Prudence's place and left a letter there: By the time you read this, Armand, I wrote, I shall be another man's lover. Consequently all is finished between us. Go back to your father, my dear. Go and see your sister who knows nothing of all our miseries. With her, you will very quickly forget what you have suffered in the hands of this fallen woman named Marguerite Gautier who, for an instant, you truly loved and who stands in your debt for the only happy moments in her life, which, she hopes, will not last much longer.

The next morning I woke in Count de N's bed. After that I never missed a party, an orgy, a ball. All I wanted to do was drown myself in champagne. Without Armand, all I had was loneliness and despair.

He was hurting too. I know, because one day when I was walking in the Champs-Elysées with Olympe, I saw him. He was in a cab and looked at me with such utter contempt that I grabbed Olympe's arm to steady myself and sobbed all the way home. I saw him again at Olympe's ball. I was there with Count de N and Armand arrived alone. He flirted with Olympe, danced with her, gambled and drank all night. By the next morning he was her lover. How could you do this to me? I shouted at her when I met her in the street a few days later. And then I fainted. The next morning I received an abusive letter from Armand telling me to respect Olympe because she was the woman he loved. I knew he was lying but his words still hurt me. I stayed in bed for days after that until finally Prudence went to see him to beg him to stop torturing me. That's when he invited me to meet him at his place. To talk.

By then I was feverish and very thin and weak. I wore black because I felt I was in mourning. I covered my face with black lace. He opened the door to me himself. Here I am, Armand, I said. You wanted to see me, so I'm here at your request. Then I burst into tears. You've hurt me so much these past weeks, I sobbed. Surely there are much nobler things to do with your time than torture someone as frail as me.

Are you happy? he asked.

Do I look happy? I said.

It was your choice.

No, Armand. I had to leave. There are many things you don't know.

Well, tell me.

I can't. It wouldn't help and it might make you hate those who are closest to you.

What do you mean?

I can't tell you.

Then you're lying, he said.

I shook my head and walked to the door. He stepped in front of me. No, don't go, he said. In spite of everything you've done, I still love you.

I just collapsed into his arms then. I'm yours, I told him. Do with me what you will. But by now I could hardly breathe, and I was coughing again. He sat me by the fire and went outside to dismiss my coachman. I removed my hat, my veil, my black velvet cloak, loosened my bodice and huddled towards the flames. I was so cold. He returned and knelt beside me. He took my hands and kissed them, and held me so I could feel all his pain too. Then he undressed me and carried me to his bed.

Let's leave Paris, he whispered in the morning. Let's go away.

I panicked. It's impossible, I said. We can never be together. Please understand. And then I dressed myself and left.

He came to see me the next night. Nanine answered the door and told him I was not alone, that Count de N was with me. So he scribbled a note: You left so quickly this morning that I forgot to pay you, he said. The enclosed is your rate for last night.

It was a 500 franc note. The final insult. I slipped the money into a fresh envelope, addressed it back to him and escaped to England. But as you can see, I've returned to Paris now to die. All my friends, all my old lovers have abandoned me except for the old Duke, who took pity on me, and my loyal Count de N. And Julie, my new maid. And, of course, Prudence. But she only cares because she thinks she might get something out of me when I'm gone. I've not heard from Armand, although I write to him every day. A friend of his father's came to see me once and gave me five thousand francs on Monsieur Duval's behalf. Maybe it was a salve to his conscience.

I've got to rest now. Writing this is exhausting me, and these final pages are blotched with tears. But is this how my story had to end? What if I'd refused to listen to Armand's father? Would Armand be here with me now? Please God, just let me see him once before I go. So he knows I died loving him.

5 February

Oh, come to me, Armand, for I suffer torments! God, I am about to die! Yesterday I was so low that I felt I wanted to be somewhere other than here for the evening, which promised to be as long as the one before. The Duke had been in the morning. I have the feeling that the sight of this old man, whom death has overlooked, brings my own death that much nearer.

Although I was burning with fever, I was dressed and taken to the Vaudeville. Julie had rouged my cheeks, for otherwise I should have looked like a corpse. I took my place in the box where we had our first rendezvous and kept my eyes fixed on the seat in the stalls where you sat that day: it was occupied by some boorish man who laughed loudly at all the stupid things the actors said. I was brought home half dead and spat blood all night. Today I cannot speak and can hardly move my arms. God! God! I am going to die! I was expecting it but I cannot reconcile myself to the thought that my greatest sufferings are still to come, and if ...

THREE slim fingers stretch from the Balkan hand of Chalcidice across Heinrich's war table into the Aegean Sea. The westernmost finger, the Isthmus of Pallen, is guarded by a small walled town called Potidaea, a colony founded years ago by Sparta's ally Corinth but now paying tribute to Sparta's enemy, Athens, that tyrant city-state to the south. To the east of Potidaea is the Hellespont, which is named for Helle, a Boeotian moon princess who fell into the sea (or was she pushed?) when she tried to escape her father and her brothers aboard a flying ram, the one with the golden fleece that Jason and his Argonauts sailed through her pont to find. Her pont being the passage to the Black Sea, to the timber and the grain from Crimea and the Ukraine that Athens so badly needs. And west of Potidaea is Anonymous Pete's Macedonia.

Pete throws the dice into the pond of the Mediterranean and quietly watches the ripples become a revolt against the United States of Athens. Heinrich responds with his citizen hoplites, takes civilian hostages, ravages the Potidaean countryside, erects his siege engines against the town walls and threatens to starve his ally back into submission. A pall of smoke spreads across the map like a shroud. Another toss of the dice and Heinrich and his hoplites win a pitched battle on a blackened Potidaean plain. Heinrich moves in his triremes to blockade the Chalcidice coast. Potidaea's mother city, Corinth, forces Sparta to intervene. Sparta's other ally, Thebes, besieges Athens' ally, Plataea. The United States of Athens bans all allied trade with Sparta's ally, Megara. Sparta makes demands on Athens — which everyone knows Athens can't meet. Or won't. And slowly another trade war breaks into blood, as everyone knew it would.

ELLE pushes the back door of the Espy open: inside stale tobacco and a hard blues bass from the beer-stained baby grand. Zoe the resident muso's already practising, as she does every morning before the action starts. Behind her another punter is scoring his next pinball million playing the Terminator on a machine called Judgement Day. A round of automatic gun fire, a thrust from the left, another from the right and a tiny silver ball is propelled at significantly less than the speed of light through a tunnel marked Cyberdine Artificial Intelligence Laboratory, around a bend and into the Skynet Command Centre. Good shot, good shot, the machine screams, and discharges another volley of meaningless flashing lights.

You wanna rack 'em while I get the drinks? Marie says as she and Elle skirt the bins of last night's empties. Gwen the licensee is already at the bar. Marie puts two fingers to her mouth and whistles like the TV ad for cider. Gwen grins and bangs two cider stubbies and two glasses onto the bar. Elle remains at the back of the pub. The green baize table waits for her like an altar in a halo of malted light. At one end, a wooden triangle hints forgotten meanings. I'm the Pharaonic glyph for woman, it says, the Tantric yoni yantra, the letter Delta in archaic Greek. She releases the balls, one black, one white and fourteen coloureds, gathers them into a nest and arranges them into their secret geometry, the sign to women's most holy place, the source of all life. My blood, my body, here drink in remembrance …

Marie puts the stubbies on a laminex bench, pours and passes a glass to Elle. Here's to your Garibaldi and his boys, she says.

Elle sips and reaches for her cue. Doesn't all this make you feel horny? she says as she chalks the tip. She blows the loose chalk-dust off, raises one dark Sicilian eyebrow, slips the grip between her legs and moves up and down, up and down. Their laughter mingles with the volleys from the Day of Judgement machine.

Looks like that guy'd better watch out, Marie says as she nods towards the Terminator. He doesn't hear. She removes the rack and signals Elley to break.

THEY'RE nestled together on the sofa, Lillian, Sophie and Abelard. Abelard's head is resting on Sophie's lap, Sophie's head is on Lillian's breast, and Lillian's arm is encircling them. The afternoon sun is creeping under the bull-nose of the verandah roof, over the window-sill, along the polished timber floor, across the rich Persian hues of the silk carpet and towards the cedar coffee table to illuminate the bowl of Sasanqua camellias Lillian picked from her garden early this morning. My Tao blossoms, she calls them because of their Yunnanese origin, and within her small camellia grove she has planted a statue of Hsi Wang Mu, China's Great Mother, Lady-Queen of the West. This morning the lady-queen was covered with pale pink petals and dew.

Lillian idly caresses Sophie's arm: what will this child's life be, this darling surrogate granddaughter? What choices will be available when her time comes? They'd be adults now, my own babies, perhaps even with children of their own, but what would my life have been if I'd given birth to them? It's never easy to have an abortion, especially in France, those sad, sad, secret visits to the illicit clinics, and yet I knew I couldn't have children if I was to do all the other things I wanted to do with my life. Writing, teaching, travelling … And I was so frightened of losing my autonomy, even with Sokrates, who meant more to me than all the rest. Dear, dear Sokrates, my Adonis, my Shiva, it's just on a year since we last met. I had some work to finish off in Paris and he was in Athens so we decided to meet half way. I wonder when I'll see him again. And that apartment in Alexandria overlooking the Mediterranean, that big, antique bed … He never knew how close I came to staying with him and it would've been so comfortable, so safe because he takes his manhood so seriously in such an Old World way. Man as provider, as he who takes care. But for some reason I had a New World vision of what it is to be a woman that was incompatible with the Old. I didn't want to be taken care of. I wanted to do it all myself and, as far as possible, on my own terms. Perhaps because I'd watched my own mother, who was so gifted in so many ways, shrinking into frustration and mediocrity in a conventional marriage. She never found the courage to escape, even after my brother and I were old enough to flee our father. And her. She died a bitter old lady and I never wanted that to happen to me. But I guess I never thought I could have it all either. Few of us who escaped in those days ever did. For little Sophie, for Elley even, the choices will be easier, I hope, although there are still plenty of futures that'd keep us in chains. Like that stopover in Jedda when I wasn't allowed to leave the airport because I was an unescorted female, and the Taliban in Afghanistan telling my friend Adiba to cover herself from head to toe and never to leave the house. So now she's forced to practise her medicine underground and every day risks being stoned. And all those Hasidic women pushing their prams up my street in Montreal, always with a row of kids in tow and another on the way, and not just Jewish fundamentalists either but Christians too. How could I forget the nationalism, the conservatism of that city dedicated to one of my little deities. Cathedrals, basilicas, churches, chapels to her everywhere, including that great dome in Boulevard René Lévesque just across the loop from McGill, what's it called? That's right, the Basilica of Mary Queen of the World, how could I forget!

There's a wriggle on the sofa. Sophie has been dancing Nana up and down Abelard's back and now she's bored. Tell me another story please, she says.

You know the stories better than I do Soph, Lillian says. I've heard you talking with those deities woman-to-woman like they're your oldest friends. Why don't you tell me one instead?

Because I like yours better, Sophie says. They're different from mine.

Just one more and then I've got to get back to my cyberloom. Which one do you want?

The little girl untangles herself from Abelard, sits on the edge of the sofa and carefully studies the divinities on the shelves. A clay woman stares back at her with a calm abstracted face and eyes that are just slits. She's pulling her knees up to her shoulders to expose her swollen vulva, this deity, who's about to give birth to the universe, to the first human beings. She who was born in the image of her creators, and lived for who knows how long in her people's imaginations before she was abandoned — like all these Mothers. Abandoned and then rediscovered beside some prehistoric hearth with the charcoal flesh of a once live tree still ticking radiation. Those who found her measured the difference between our lives and hers in units of decay time: eight thousand plus or minus — but what does this figure tell? Lillian says. About her or about us?

Next to this mother, another preliterate deity is squatting in the same eternal labour. Full breasts, ballooning belly, bulbous thighs, and between them a child's head. She was chipped from soft stone, this woman and her birthing, when great forests of cedar, oaks, beeches and pines covered her mountains, and fields of barley and wheat grew wild in her valleys. She taught her people how to farm and live in villages, how to grind axes and edge their wooden sickles with fine flakes of volcanic stone, which she thought were appropriate technologies then, a revolution even. How could she foresee the consequences?

Even Artemis of the wilderness, that virgin hunter with her big strong hips and thighs and tiny waist, queen of the leopards, lionesses, elephants and pygmy hippopotamuses who once shared her south-west Asian domain, how could she know? She's resting on a leopard now, on Lillian's highest shelf, holding the leopard's cub in her arms. Beside her stands that dancing deity from Crete who once ruled the Aegean, who howled with the wolves in the island's forests, and roared with the island's bears. She's wearing a long full skirt with a very tight bodice that's open to her waist to expose her breasts, and in her hands she's holding her sacred totems, a serpent and a double-sided axe.

But Sophie points to an Egyptian deity, Nut the Vault of Heaven who's reaching over Geb, her twin. In her belly, Nut is carrying all creation and a daughter whose name is Aset. That's the one I want, the little girl says.

INSIDE the besieged walls of Potidaea it's winter and starvation. People are burning anything they can to keep warm, and eating one another to survive. Outside the walls of the polis, the besieging army of Athenians is also suffering. One in every three soldiers is dying from the plague brought from Athens. Everyone wants the siege to end but the Potidaeans do most of all. They negotiate terms. Heinrich offers them complete capitulation in exchange for their lives. Every surviving Potidaean is to abandon the town, men, women and children, with nothing but the clothes they're wearing and a few coins in their pockets. But where are they to go? To anyBalkanwhere that isn't Potidaea, Heinrich says. Because Potidaea is to be ethnically cleansed and repopulated with Athenians. The Potidaeans are now refugees dragging themselves over the horizon and out of history's view.

LILLIAN takes Nut the Vault of Heaven from the shelf and passes her to Sophie. But let's talk about the little baby in her belly, Lillian says. I am what is, what will be and what has been, Nut's daughter's Egyptian stelae say. The beginning and the end. No man uncovered my nakedness and the fruit of my birthing was the sun. This is the deity who teaches the people of the Nile delta how to grind grain, bake bread, and spin and weave the flax that grows in the delta's fertile soil; how to rule with law and how to write, how to sing and how to play the flute. Her name is Aset and she too has a twin who shared her mother's womb. His name is Ousir. And now he shares his sister's bed.

After her twins are born Nut the Sky bears another child, another brother for Aset. His name is Set, a violent red-haired deity who slashes his way out of his mother's belly, or so Plutarch says. He plots his conquests early, this upstart god, and camouflages them with sweet words and fine wine. One day he invites his brother Ousir to lunch and shows him a wooden box he claims he made just for him. What a lovely thing, Ousir says.

Why don't you hop inside to see if it fits? says wicked Set.

Ousir lies inside as Set suggests — then crash and darkness. Set nails the lid shut like a coffin, throws the box into the Nile and watches it float out to sea. That night, there's a storm over the Mediterranean and the box is washed up on a lonely beach near a timber town called Gubla, also known as Byblos in ancient Greek. But now its name is Jubayl, a village north of Beirut.

Another wave crashes onto the beach and the box is tossed against a tall tree, a cedar of Lebanon, Lillian says. Or is it a sycamore fig, or an apple, or a tamarisk? The books aren't very clear about which specie it is but it must be a very magic tree, because it grows instantly around the coffin and its dead god. The king of Phoenicia hears about this magic tree so sends his slaves to cut it down. When their axes bite into its flesh, it exudes a perfume like heaven, mellow as myrrh. Aset smells it even from Egypt and instantly rushes towards Lebanon. The waters of the Red Sea part for her, yes Soph, like they did for Moses. And yes, maybe she did ride a camel there. When she reaches Lebanon, she meets Astarte or Asherah, the goddess the people of Gubla worship. Solomon built a temple for her in Jerusalem but that's another story. Because right now Asherah is stealing the magic tree from the king of Phoenicia for her sister Aset, who takes it back to Egypt — yes Soph, on her camel — and hides it among the papyrus reeds in the wetlands of the Nile delta.

But on that very day, her wicked brother Set is fishing in the wetlands with his long spear and he finds the tree, cuts it open, and who does he see inside? Yes, his brother Ousir, embalmed in brine. Set swears and curses, and slashes Ousir's body into fourteen pieces with his sword. Plutarch and his translators are very specific about the number.

Aset is watching all this from behind a clump of papyrus reeds and remains hidden until Set and his entourage leave. That night the moon and the evening star lay a path of light across the marsh for her so she can find the scattered pieces of her crucified brother lover son. A head, an arm, a leg, a torso … She puts them in her basket and carries them to the shore, where she gives them what the books call the kiss of life. And lo, Ousir rises again from the dead. He stretches and feels himself all over — but one piece is missing, Soph, and without it Ousir says he's not a god. Yes, that's right. Plutarch's translators say a crab swallowed it but I don't think that's true.

Anyway, Ousir is really upset about not having a penis. He shouts at Aset and tells her that he's not going to reappear on earth without it, that he'll rule the dead in the underworld instead. That's OK with Aset, because by now she's pregnant again and a new dynasty is rising in her belly. No, Soph, I don't know how she did it without Ousir. Lots of virgin deities have babies that way. Asherah, Aphrodite, Mary. No, I don't know if your mother was a virgin when she had you. They don't happen much these days, virgin births. Yes, I know. It's called in vitro fertilisation but I don't think it's quite the same thing. And maybe the wicked brother Set was the father. Or maybe she did it parthenogenetically like algae do. Or by cloning. Or maybe it was magic. Who knows?

This new baby is born on an island in the delta of the Nile like his mother Aset was. The people on that island worship a falcon called Hor. Aset likes that name so she calls her baby Hor too, or Horus. That's Hor in his mother's lap on the second shelf, reaching for her breast. Or is it Osiris? Or Serapis? Because by now, Aset's real name is Isis, goddess from whom all becoming's born, oldest of the old. Giver of life, giver of death, maker of kings, saviour of the human race.

Her new lover brother son is now called the Redeemer King, but he's still sacrificed and she still weeps for him. Each year she floods the Nile with her tears. Thou givest life unto the flocks and herds, her people sing to her. All the land drinks thee when thou descendest, when thou comest the whole land rejoices. Thou art the bringer of food, though art the mighty one of meat and drink, thou art the creator of all good things. Thou fillest the storehouses, thou heapest high with corn the granaries, and thou hast care for the poor and needy.

But then a new godking comes along, Soph, a Latin peasant called Justinian. He says it's wrong to worship Isis and her son and her lover because he worships Mary and her son and her lover. One empire, one law, one church, he says. Look, there's Mary on the third shelf, one of our last little goddesses. But how about some Milo and a biscuit? Because I want to get back to my loom. Yes, of course you can dust the deities. I'll get the step-ladder so you can reach them but you'd better send Abelard out first. You know how dangerous his tail can be when he gets excited.

ELLE steps forward, bends her front leg, straightens her back leg, grips her cue firmly with her right hand, rests an elbow on the side of the altar, spreads her left hand on the green baize, slides the cue into the groove between her thumb and first finger and leans forward. Then squints to line up her shot. A few vector calculations around angles of impact, a brief rehearsal, and then — convergence. The tip of her cue hits the white ball just below centre, it speeds forward in reverse-spin and collides with the sign of the goddess's cunt. Fourteen coloured balls plus a single black dance the length, the breadth of the altar. Fourteen colours divided by two equals seven per player. Seven balls, seven deadly sins, seven pillars of wisdom, seven days of the week, seven planetary spheres, seven heavens of Islam, seven terraces of the ziggurats, seven heavenly midwives, seven mothers who make decrees, seven Hathors of Egypt, seven branches of the menorah, seven petals of the lotus, seven gates of Inanna's descent, seven judges of the Great Below, seven valleys your soul must cross, and those seven sisters, the Pleiades: Maia, Taygete, Electra, Alcyone, Celaeno, Asterope and Merope. Of which two now fall into the pockets of the underworld — ready to rise again as another game.

They relax, Elle and Marie, sip their ciders, joke, slip into autopilot as they move around the table, and flip back into old conversations: so Garibaldi agrees to invade Sicily, Elle says, but only if the Sicilians rise up against the ancien régime first. By themselves, like they're serious about wanting to be free. Poor bastards, they've rebelled against every Mediterranean power in history and here's this eccentric fifty-year-old revolutionary from Nice telling them to try again.

Everyone wants the Neapolitans out of course, even many of the feudals. Or maybe they just want a bet each way like that prince in Lampedusa's *The Leopard*. She pauses. A difficult shot off the cushion. Another coloured ball ricochets into a pocket to descend into the underworld.

There's this baron who'd throw parties in his palace, see, and between waltzes or whatever they did in Palermo then, the blokes'd disappear upstairs to make cartridges and bombs, Elle says. In their evening dress.

What about the women, then? Marie says. She's just potted her fourth ball. I mean, wouldn't you be up there making bombs or something too? Or printing pamphlets. You could hide anything under those ball gowns they wore in those days.

Who knows what the women did? Elle says. When you read the history books, it's like they never even existed. She pauses while

Marie lines up her next shot. It was probably the sex workers who were the most useful, though, she says, because they'd get to know what the enemy's doing. The baron and his mates in their fancy clothes probably got a thrill out of manufacturing ammunition and stuff, but seems like they didn't want to do anything really useful like cleaning up their own corruption or strengthening civil society. They left the dangerous stuff to the peasants and workers and tradespeople. My mob. People with nothing much to lose, like this plumber called Francesco Riso. That's who the baron was smuggling the explosives to, plus a bit of cash to buy arms. A little wooden cannon and some old blunderbusses and muskets from the mountains, the only place the Neapolitan military didn't search house-to-house. He hid them in his wagon under his tools and stashed them in a building attached to this monastery just across the alley from where he lived. When the day for the revolution came, Francesco and his mates burst out of the monastery firing their blunderbusses, shouting Viva l'Italia, Viva Vittorio Emanuele, straight into the arms of the Neapolitan militia.

Good shot, good shot, the machine called Judgement Day screams across the pub, as it discharges another volley of flashing lights.

So the survivors drag their dead and wounded back into the monastery, ring the tocsin, hurl a few of the nobles' bombs — which didn't explode — bolt the monastery door again and wait for the military to roll their cannon in to blow it open. When the Neapolitans eventually get inside, they shoot or arrest all the rebels, tie up all the monks and gut the church, Elle says. Apparently it was all over by 8.00 am, at least for Francesco and his mates. And then the retribution.

LILLIAN returns to her study, sits herself before her loom and stares at the blank screen. You'd think after all these years I'd have overcome this fear, she says, but it happens every time I begin a new chapter and there seems to be nothing I can do but trust that this time too, something will emerge from the random access of my mind to fill the void. She leans back in her chair and clasps her hands behind her head. Like those times we'd meet in Alexandria, she says aloud and for no apparent reason keys in the city's name. And then another word — Sokrates. And then another — Hypatia, the name of Alexandria's last great pagan philosopher, who was murdered by Christian fundamentalists because she challenged their patriarch. They dragged her from her chariot, stripped her and scraped her flesh from her bones with flints and oyster shells, or so the story goes. Lillian moves her fingers across the keyboard and a whole sentence grows upon her screen: I have walked in the steps of Hypatia, she writes, then stares at her screen with relief. At last I have a starting point, she says, and now the panic's gone.

But those days in Alexandria ... She deletes the city's name and does the same with the name of her lover. No one need ever know how I arrived at that opening sentence, she says, but like every good line, the path to it was carnal. She reaches across her desk for his last letter, unfolds it and reads it again. I remember once we were lying in one another's arms, Sokrates says, and you wondered aloud what the world would be like if Plato had never immortalised my name, if those papyrus scrolls he'd written on had disintegrated and settled as dust between the cracks of his Academy floor. But no, history has preserved his ideas like viruses to contaminate our minds for millennia, and look at the results, you said. And then you reached across and stroked my cock as if you were forgiving me for the sins of my fathers, and we made love again. Do your remember? You were much younger then, Lily, and much more passionate in your views, and though I was never able to tell you at the time, I loved you very much. And I still do.

Lillian smiles to herself. No, I can't remember the conversation, nor that particular night, she says, but I'm sure those events occurred if Sokrates says they did, because he has a much better memory than me. And yes, I was much younger then, and I suppose, quite attractive in an unconventional sort of way but I never did anything with it. I certainly wasn't this wrinkly old crone I seem to have become — although despite what the mirror tells me when I bother to look, I really don't feel any different inside, except perhaps a little wiser, a little more patient — and certainly more contented with my life. But what would my world have been like if I'd never met him, if I'd never even heard his name — let alone the name of his more famous predecessor?

She's daydreaming again, staring out her window without seeing a thing. Next door her neighbour is practising his clarinet, and for no apparent reason, she remembers a grand marble staircase in Alex with ornate wrought-iron balustrades. Ah, that's when it was, she says, the night Sokrates and I had our argument about Plato. The sound of a flute behind those closed double doors as I climbed the stairs to Mahmud Helme's apartment in the old Greek quarter, six flights of white marble because the lifts never work in Alexandria. We talked in his library, Mahmud and me, surrounded by books in Arabic, Turkish, English and French, and objets d'art from all over the world. African masks, Chinese porcelain, antique silver, Alexandrian glass, Pharaonic amphorae, and a little golden-winged moth he'd found on his balcony the night before ... They're my soul, he said when he saw me admiring them. Yes, that's right, he'd just completed a paper on the evolution of Arabic calligraphy and was preparing the illustrations for it, sketches of Paleolithic hands and stick figures from the walls of a cave in Libya. His own paintings, his most recent ones, were stacked against the bookshelves, gentle watercolours in a style he called symbolic realism, visual allegories that were inspired by his wanderings in the mountains of Anatolia each year after Ramadan. Opalescent blue and purple peaks between vast empty spaces, a small Sufi figure in the foreground, and in the distance a darker, more luminous spot that was his mystical destination. So different, these images, from the abstract canvases he was painting when I first met him. Abstract art is about representing what comes before rational thought and so it comes naturally to me — because Muslim culture is very abstract too, he told me then. But these new paintings ... I know you understand them, I can feel it, he said as he slipped a tape into an archaic machine. The haunting sounds of Sufi flutes and drums spilled into the darkening room. But what about those who say music and dancing and painting are against the word of Allah? I asked. Oh, ignore them, they're just ignorant people, he said. Music is life, it's balance, it's mathematics, and therefore it glorifies God. He got excited then. But do you know what's gone wrong with the world? he demanded. Greek philosophers! he said. That's what. Because Greek philosophers preached materialism. And what is the end result of materialism? Science! he said as he lifted his old body from his chair and limped to the window to throw open the shutters. Look at that! The trees are gone because they've all died from pollution, there's a hole in the ozone layer, and the atmosphere is warming ... He shook his head. Science is the destruction of the world! But in the East, we're not quite so materialistic because we give half our day to something greater than ourselves. If there's no mosque or other quiet place to pray, we take our prayer mats into the streets ...

As I was leaving, his wife gave me a finely worked scarf from her native Anatolia. I covered my head with it and walked down the marble stairs and out into the narrow treeless streets. And that was the night Sokrates and I had our argument, yes, about Plato and his rationalism. We often disagreed but the alchemy that kept us seeing one another never changed, so I suppose what he says in his letter is true. That I reached across and stroked his cock ...

BUT HER REAL NAME is Alphonsine Plessis, born to Marie Deshayes and her partner Marin Plessis in Saint-Germain-de-Clairfuille in Normandy in 1824. The year Louis XVIII died.

Alphonsine's mother was the daughter of Anne du Mesnil d'Argentelle, the last of a once great feudal line that failed to adapt to the changes the Revolution wrought. The girl's father, Marin, was the son of a village girl and a local priest. The context of their intercourse was never recorded.

Marin was illiterate, drank too much, rarely knew what it was to have a full belly, and was much too poor and ignorant to enjoy any of the Rights of Man and of Citizens that his elders said they'd fought the Revolution for. So he wandered from village to village mending people's pots and pans and kettles. He and Marie Deshayes also picked up a few weeks' work each year at sowing or harvest time, back-breaking hours from dawn to dusk for a few francs a day. It was never enough to feed and clothe a family though. And anyway Marin had wanted a son, not this howling brat of a girl with nothing but a hole between her legs. It's all your fault, you cunt, he shouted at Marie Deshayes as he bashed her again. You knew I wanted a boy. She fell to the floor of the hovel they called a home and he kicked her in the belly, the womb in which she grew Alphonsine and her other surviving child, two-year-old Delphine.

And so it came to pass that Alphonsine's mother packed the dress she wore to mass in a bag and left Saint-Germain-de-Clairfuille to support herself any way she could. Eventually she found a job as a companion to an English woman. And then she died, Marie Deshayes — of cholera, typhoid, dysentery, tuberculosis, pneumonia or sheer exhaustion. To Alphonsine's mother it doesn't matter which cause of death you choose.

Alphonsine was six years old at the time. Her father sent her to her mother's cousin's house where, like a little Cinderella, she cleaned and served and carried water from the well. Soon she too was labouring in other people's fields to earn a few extra family francs a day. At twelve, she did what every twelve-year-old village girl does, or dreams of doing: she disposed of her virginity in a hay stack with a fellow farm hand. She made the mistake, however, of confessing her adventure to the local priest who told her mother's cousin, who sent her back to her father, who apprenticed her to a local laundry. Sixteen hours a day bent over tubs until your back breaks, arms up to your elbows in hot, caustic water, your knuckles skinned bare from scrubbing other people's dirt. Filling, carrying, lifting heavy buckets of wet clothes, hanging them out to dry. And those heavy irons, heating them on the fire, and testing them to see if your spit bounces off the hot metal surface. A bowl of gruel at supper time and then collapsing onto the pile of straw that is your bed for a few hours' exhausted sleep and getting up before dawn to work another sixteen hours. And the boss expecting you to give him sex as well.

One evening her father visited the laundry and took her for a walk along a dark and narrow lane to a big house. He knocked and an old man opened the door as if he was expecting them. He looked at Alphonsine, her slim young body, her pubescent breasts, her pretty face, her big brown country-girl eyes, gave Marin some money and led the child inside. Wash her, do her hair, find her something clean and loose to wear, he told the housekeeper. Then bring her in to me.

Alphonsine escaped five days later and found her way back to the laundry. You didn't show up so we gave your job to someone else, the supervisor said. So she went to the village hotel and got a job as a maid. Bed and board plus all the rest and sixty francs a month. Then her father visited her again. This time, he took her to Gacé, an industrial town on the river Touques, where he apprenticed her to an umbrella manufacturer — although some books say he sold her to a Romany clan. Two months later she found herself in Paris, the big city where rural people go when there's no future left at home.

In Paris she boarded with a distant relative who ran a grocery shop, or so some books say. She worked six days a week in the shop and the seventh at the local dance hall, where she flirted and picked up men for a few extra francs. Or that's what those books say. Others say she found a job in another laundry washing, ironing rich men's shirts and sheets. After working at the laundry, she did piecework for a milliner, stitching flowers onto fancy women's hats.

A few weeks later, thirteen of the monastery rebels are executed down near the Palermo docks, Elle says. Francesco himself was wounded in that first rush and is dying in the prison hospital. This Neapolitan officer visits him and promises to spare his father's life if Francesco will name his accomplices. So what can the poor bloke do? He names the names, including the baron. But then the hospital chaplain tells him his father's already dead, that he's been shot with the other rebels down near the docks. I mean, how would you feel?

You sort of feel you've heard it all before, Marie says. Or seen it. John Wayne playing Francesco Riso in every TV western. But you know the good guys'll win in the end ...

Yeah, well, this isn't Hollywood, Elle says. Francesco knew his time was up but — like, you know that male thing — he wanted to avenge his father's death before he died and reclaim his family's honour. So he asks this priest to grant him a final wish. A pistol and a single bullet. Some medical student smuggles the gun into the ward, but next time the Neapolitan officer visits, Francesco's too weak to shoot. Guess he dies with the gun under his blanket still.

What about the baron?

Arrested on Francesco's evidence, Elle says. And the other nobles too. Everyone protested, of course. Thousands of people in the main street of Palermo shouting Viva l'Italia, Viva l'Italia. Demonstrations every day and arrests until the prisons are overflowing like in Dili. Or Tiananmen. But when Sicily is finally liberated, it's the baron who's carried through the streets a hero — he and the other nobles who've been smart enough to support the winning side. No one even remembered Francesco Riso or his mates.

But where's Garibaldi while all this is going on?

In Genoa, or rather at Quarto on the eastern Riviera. He's in contact with Sicily though, through these blokes from the forty-eight revolt who are hiding out in the Insera Mountains near Monreale where the Normans built that fabulous cathedral. They've got this secret printing press up there. Fratelli vincuemo. Brothers we shall conquer, the leaflets said. Signed — Il Comitato. The committee.

Fuck! Marie says. She leans against the pool table and sips her cider. Like this is really powerful stuff you're telling me and I really want to get into it but like, there's no place for us, Elle, with all that Fratelli vincuemo! I mean, it's just a boys' game. How do you cope with having to write about this crap?

I hadn't really thought about it like that, Elle says. She rests her cue against the wall and sits in a torn vinyl chair. Maybe that's why I've been feeling a bit down these last few weeks, like I'm just an apostrophe in someone else's story. She watches as Marie lines up her next shot. Guess it's like Lilith always tells us, that equality, freedom, human rights, democracy, all that stuff, they're never shared by those in power. They have to be snatched. And I guess I'm still snatching for my little bit of sovereignty.

SOPHIE'S trying to send Abelard outside so she can dust the deities. Out! she says in her sternest six-year-old voice. Lillian smiles. The back door squeaks open. Out! Sophie says a second time. You know what Lilith says about dusting the dolls while you're around!

Lillian chuckles to herself as she watches from the rear window of her study. Abelard has bounded into the garden and is sitting on the path with one of his silliest Labrador grins, waiting to retrieve sticks, stones, his frisbee, the world, anything if Sophie will only throw it for him. The security door bangs shut. Abelard gazes back through the gauze with that most heart-wrenching expression of a Labrador who's just been tricked by the person he thought was his best, his most trusted friend.

Sophie returns to the living room and drags the step-ladder to the shelves so she can remove the deities one by one and place them in the pool of light on the Persian carpet. Lillian follows the child's movements through the open door of her adjoining study. That should keep her occupied for a while, she says as she lifts her fingers to her keyboard. The words seem to flow easier now. Must be that letter from Sokrates, she says. Damn him, I still need his emotional support, but I wonder what's happened that he tells me he loves me after thirty years of intimacy? Good years too, in general — perhaps because we've never actually lived together full-time. Ah, those northern winters we'd spend together in Alexandria.

She shifts her gaze from her screen to the world outside. Port Phillip Bay emerges as an unfocused strip of blue beyond the Babylon palms and the memorial park. I'd spend the first few nights alone at the Cecil in a room overlooking the Mediterranean while we negotiated our terms, and only when that ritual was complete would I agree to move into his apartment. I'd hire a horse and carriage in front of the hotel even though Sokrates' place was only a block further down the Corniche and I'd tip the driver extra to carry my luggage up the stairs because those damn lifts in Alex … It seems silly now, but Alexandria is such a seductive, passionate, perfumed place — like those lilies I used to buy from the woman in the flannelette nightie and ragged scarf who'd steal them every morning at dawn from yesterday's graves. By mid-morning she'd have found me sitting in a street cafe where she'd sell me her freshest, most fragrant blooms. Tuberoses, I think they were. I'd give her an Egyptian pound, a fortune in her eyes, and the dignity of her gratitude nearly broke my heart. Sokrates never understood. Lillian smiles at herself. Funny what you remember, especially about Alex, where the past is so rich in celebrities: Roxanne and her Alexander in his crystal sarcophagus, Helen of Troy and her Paris, Cleopatra and her Romans, and my Hypatia at her Serapeum. And yet it's a poor woman and her dying lilies ...

Her reveries are interrupted by Sophie's chatter in the next room. The little girl is sitting on the Persian rug surrounded by the deities and dressing and undressing them in an old singlet duster and miscellaneous antique lace doilies she has borrowed from around the living room. Who are we, where have we come from, where are we going to? Sophie asks them, but in her own childish way. The deities answer in their native languages but Sophie's not impressed. Well, why did you let those bully boys take over? she says.

And what are you going to do about it, Soph? Lillian says from behind her loom.

But I'm only a little girl, Sophie says as she reaches for the goddess Nana and cradles her to her chest.

The sun spills deeper over the window sill, the sparrows flutter in the eaves, the tram rattles by, and passing pedestrians throw shadows on the walls. Sophie wraps Nana in the holey singlet duster and puts her to bed on the couch, then lays the other deities beside her. All except one. A madonna and baby girl.

THE YEAR IS 1838 and Alphonsine Plessis is fourteen years old. Algeria has almost been conquered. The first real French railway track has just been laid between Paris and Saint-Germain. The first steam ships have crossed the Atlantic. The price of colonial sugar has collapsed on the emerging global market. And Louis Daguerre has coated a copper plate with silver iodide and exposed it to light. One of his first photographs is taken from the left bank of the River Seine looking towards the Palais des Tuileries and the apartments of the citizen king, Louis-Philippe of Orleans, who once called himself a Jacobin and watched the Bastille fall, but changed his mind when he was offered the old king's throne by the businessmen and bankers who won the last revolution. The one that left another six thousand workers and students dead at the barricades. July 1830.

But what's all this to a young girl from a village in Normandy who's weaving her way through the beggars in the streets, who's jumping the gutters flowing with excrement to reach the other side of Paris where the women who wear the hats she makes meet the men whose shirts she irons? She stares in awe at these beautiful people and strains to catch the crumbs of cafe culture that are falling from their lips, half-heard conversations about books and ideas and the sex lives of famous men. Hugo, Dumas père, Gautier, Balzac, Delacroix.

She goes to the nearby theatre district and watches the carriages arrive. Women in gorgeous gowns escorted by men with neatly trimmed beards. And music. The notes of a piano tinkling onto the pavement like stars. Why can't I play music and dance and read and write and wear beautiful clothes and have supper in cafes and drive around Paris in my own carriage? she says as she crosses the Pont-Neuf. She stops at a fried-potato stand and stares so longingly that a man with a cane and a diamond ring buys her a cornet of pommes frites. She snatches the treat like a hungry cat and disappears into a side street. Holy Mary, mother of god, she says, why can't I have nice food and books and music and beautiful things in my life too? I'd do anything if I could.

A year later she is living in her own apartment on rue de l'Arcade. The rent is being paid by Monsieur Nollet, a restaurateur she met at the Galerie Montpensier. He also has a key to the flat. By the next year she has moved to a more fashionable address, twenty-eight rue du Mont-Thabor. Her patron is a young and wealthy nobleman called Agenor. Some books say he really loved her. But by now her real name is Marie Duplessis. Marie for the Virgin and for her own mother, Duplessis because she wants to buy the Plessis estate at Nonant, she says, and at sixteen she now believes she can. She's also learning to read and write, to play the piano and to dance, all at Agenor's expense, or his father's. Eventually the father intervenes, as everyone else knew he would, and Agenor disappears from the story of her life. Years later, he becomes a famous politician.

Duplessis' next recorded lover is a vicomte attached to the Ministry of the Interior. She accompanies him to Versailles where she gives birth to a son. The vicomte sends the baby to a wet-nurse in the country and tells Marie he died from pneumonia. But one day a young man about the right age will visit her sister Delphine in Normandy. He was the spitting image of her, Delphine will say. He had a job in Tours, I think he told me. In the civil service.

The vicomte moves on but Marie Duplessis' business grows. Soon her clients include all the most fashionable young men in Europe. She rises late, reads the daily newspapers over breakfast, practises her piano, dresses in the most elegant clothes, drives around Paris in her own landau, is seen at the most expensive restaurants and cafes, dances like a princess at every ball, and gambles as if she's been doing it all her life. She never misses a first night at the theatre and the régisseurs provide her with a stage box at the theatre company's expense. To the old ouvreuse at the Opera, she's already La Dame aux Camélias and her apartment is filled with flowers.

But that cough. The fevers, the night sweats. The blood in her sputum. Her doctors say it's consumption, that there's nothing they can do. Her priests say it's god's will, punishment for her sins. The poets — that it's her destiny to die so young and beautiful. To them, she's a Romantic tragedy. Marie herself is not so sure. If I believed in all that, she says, I'd still be ironing rich men's shirts. So she fights this disease too — by immersing herself in the waters at Spa in Belgium's fashionable Hautes Fagnes, where she meets Baron de Stackelberg, a wealthy Polish diplomat who is old enough to be her grandpère. He tells her about his daughter, who died of the same disease, about how lonely he's been without her. You remind me of her so much, he says. I'll give you anything if you'll keep yourself pure and chaste like her.

Marie allows the baron to rent her a new apartment in the boulevard de la Madeleine across the road from la Magdalene's church, where she goes twice a week to hear mass and pray. Forgive me, Mother, for I have sinned, she says. The Magdalene smiles, not in Latin like the priests do but in peasant French, because for thirty years, this Mary lived in a grotto near Marseilles, or so some stories say. She sailed there in her crescent moon to tell the world what happened in that cave in Palestine. It must be true because someone found her bones at Vézelay, and at vintage time local wine makers light candles for her.

Marie Duplessis lights a candle too: I am the first and the last, I am the honoured one and the scorned one, I am the whore and the holy one, the Magdalene says. It was me who supported that boy and his disciples, so why do they forsake me now?

Marie is weeping as she kneels. Will they forsake me too? she says. Because I don't want to be forsaken. I want someone to hold me close at night, someone to love me. My bed feels so empty now.

It's so lonely, Mother, being so chaste and pure like the baron's daughter was — even if it does mean I'll go to Paradise. She wipes her eyes with the back of her hand like a little peasant girl, lights another candle, crosses herself, and stands to curtsy to the Magdalene, to the Magdalene's lover, to his mother. She then leaves the church to meet the baron for a shopping spree. Because shopping makes you feel so much better than prayers, don't you think? she says, as he hands her into his coach. But it must be Louis XV because it's so spiritual, so romantic, don't you think? And don't you just love all those fluffy little cherubs, all those shepherdesses and naked goddesses? Like *Psyche Crowning Eros* by that painter Jean-Baptiste Greuze or the *Triumph of Venus* by François Boucher. And all that gilded bronze. She orders an ormolu sofa upholstered in Beauvais tapestries and a marquetry dressing table for her boudoir. Plus a savonnerie carpet for her drawing room, with medallions of spring flowers and acanthus leaves like you see carved into those ancient Greek columns. Oh, and a gold mantel clock which the man in the antique shop says belonged to la Marquise de Pompadour — who's real name was Jeanne-Antoinette Poisson, the daughter of a butcher. She attended a masked ball once dressed as Diana, the pagan huntress, a silver-blonde goddess with sans ombre skin. Louis XV said she was the most beautiful woman he'd ever seen, but Jeanne-Antoinette told him that mais non, she wouldn't sleep with him unless ... So the king made her chief mistress of the royal bed chamber. Soon she was his most trusted adviser and one of the most powerful politicians in all of France.

She died, la Pompadour, in 1764 and was succeeded by Madame du Barry whose real name was Jeanne Bécu, whose mother once ran a pub. The king died too. Of smallpox. And Jeanne Bécu? She was guillotined in the Terror that was yet to come. Mais encore un moment, monsieur le Boureau, encore un petit instant ... she said as her fellow citizens led her from the cart. Monsieur le Boureau, forgive me, but you're making a terrible mistake. I'm the illegitimate daughter of a common publican. I'm one of you.

Aм I in your story? Sophie says. She's standing at Lillian's study door with the terracotta madonna and child in her hand.

You've been a part of my story all your life, my little goddess.

The child silently places the madonna beside the keyboard. Lillian saves her text and stretches in her chair. Who've you got there? she says.

I forget.

Looks to me like Demeter and her little Persephone.

Did Demeter sacrifice her baby too? Sophie says.

Not exactly, Soph. This is a different story.

The child drags a low cane chair across to Lillian's desk, kneels in it, rests her elbows beside the computer, and waits.

OK, Soph, but I'm warning you, there's no happy ending to this one either, Lillian says. Or so far there's not.

Sophie smiles and nestles into the chair. Lillian gazes past her screen to the world outside: the Lady-Queen of the West, Hsi Wang Mu, in her camellia grove; the white picket fence; the Babylon palms and shorn green lawn of the memorial park; the plaque marking the site of the first white man's hut; the ziggurat to the local boys who died killing Boers; the white marble statue of the man with a gun commemorating another war; the Seaspray Women's Health Club known locally as the post-sultanic harem; the Novotel monstrosity where the Streets of Paris dance hall and the skating rink used to be; Mr Moon grimacing at the entrance to Luna Park; Captain Cook staring out to sea from his granite pedestal ... yes, the past's all present and accounted for. Lillian swivels her chair and puts her feet up beside Sophie. So let's start at the beginning ...

Anonymous John of Sparta lights another Gitane. He inhales and exhales across the Mediterranean, then rests his cigarette in a gunmetal ashtray. A plume of smoke rises, twists, swirls, divides into random wisps and slowly dissipates towards the ceiling of Heinrich's second bedroom. The rules of this game state that the player representing Sparta must leave his three strongest units at home to control the majority indigenous population. That'll keep the bastards down, Anonymous John says as he complies with the regulations. He marches the rest of his men north towards the Isthmus of Corinth where he pauses, sacrifices to the deities, sings a hymn with his troops, and formally addresses them: Remember always that what we are fighting for is freedom, he says. To liberate Hellas from the tyrant yoke of Athens. The hopes of all Greeks are marching with us.

His army moves on through Boeotia, crosses the border with Attica near Mount Cithaeron, burns all the still-ripening grain, chops down all the fruit trees and vines, and besieges the small fortress town of Oenoe. He moves a ravage marker to the spot and waits for an intercept from Athens. But no intercept comes — because Heinrich has moved his entire rural population inside the city walls and has ferried all the livestock to the island of Euboea just as his hero Pericles did in 431 BCE.

Only the richest Athenian landowners can afford houses within the city walls. The common folk find shelter anywhere they can — in the homes of relatives or friends, in the temples or shrines, or in tents and humpies that are hastily erected along the walled road to the port. Some, the very poorest, are even living in the Pelasgian, that most ancient and holy enclosure below the citadel — despite the Pythian oracle's forewarning that a great disaster will befall Athens if people inhabit this place.

No one wants to live this way, but Heinrich has spoken and the demos has voted, that small slave-owning male elite whose voices drown out all others' in this now festering demokratia.

Outside the city walls, a veil of smoke covers the earth like mourning. But let's not weep for property, Heinrich says. On land the Peloponnesians are much stronger than us, therefore we'd be foolish to let them provoke us into a battle we might not win. Our strength is in our navy and our empire. So let's put our faith in men — for men create property. Property does not create men.

IN the beginning, Chaos, nothingness, an empty page, Lillian says. And from Chaos came Gaia the deep-breasted, the universal mother who gave birth to the night sky Uranus and lay with him. Soon her family included six Titan daughters and six Titian sons, three Cyclops she probably adopted from a previous age, and three pet monsters who were as big as mountains, Soph. Each monster had fifty heads with long black tongues dripping from their monster mouths, and a hundred arms waving from their monster shoulders.

Sophie's eyes widen.

For many years Gaia and her family lived in peace and harmony, Lillian says, or so the story goes. Then conquerors invaded her territory, men who rode in war chariots and fought with swords of iron. They believed a male deity created the universe and invited Gaia's youngest son Kronos to audition for the part. But look, mate, you'd have to cut off your father's genitals, sleep with your mother and marry your sister, the new script-writers said, because that's what skygods do. That's fine by me, young Kronos told them, as he packed his bags for Mount Olympus. And I'll take my sister Rhea to play my wife.

Rhea felt she had little option but to accept the new role and it caused her untold pain. He gets drunk and forces me to do the most awful things, she sobbed next time she visited her mother. I know, darling, Gaia said as she gently pulled a chair out from under the kitchen table for her daughter. Rhea buried her head in her hands. Mum, I just can't take it any more, she said. But the worse part is, he swallows my babies when they're born. And I'm pregnant again … What am I going to do?

Gaia filled the kettle and put it on the stove. There's a place I know in Crete, she said, a secret grotto. I'll take you there to have this baby and you can let him grow up with the island nymphs. Give Kronos a rock wrapped up in a baby's shawl and if you do it when he's drunk, he won't even notice the baby's not there.

Sophie giggles and wriggles in her chair. Lillian tickles the child's toes. So Rhea had her baby in the grotto in Crete and left him on the island with the forest nymphs as her mother had suggested. But there was something funny about this little boy. Perhaps it was in his genes. Because little Zeus — for that's what Rhea called him — he wanted to be a skygod too, and it wasn't long before he was chatting up Metis, the goddess of Wisdom, and promising her the world if she'd help him steal his father's throne. Because no skygods can do anything by themselves.

Well, that silly goddess believed him and agreed to whatever he asked — so soon she became pregnant too. When she told Zeus, he laughed at her so hard he swallowed her up, both Metis and her unborn baby girl. But believe it or not, Soph, Metis's little girl survived to one day burst fully grown from her father Zeus's head, dressed in battle armour! He named her Athena, the patron deity of war.

Zeus tried Demeter next, the goddess you're holding in your hand. She called what he did attempted rape and told him that sex was still creation and should only be performed for mutual pleasure. He laughed at her too and told her she was being old-fashioned — but that he'd get her anyway. That night while she was sleeping he mutated into a bull and gored her — which is how her daughter

Persephone was conceived, the little baby Demeter's holding to her breast.

⇥ ⇤

Marie duplessis rests la Marquise de Pompadour's clock on her mantelpiece to measure out her hours. Long and lonely Magdalene hours filled with beautiful, lonely things. She stares into her Louis XV mirror and brushes a strand of long brown hair from her face. I look so pale, so thin and dishevelled, she says and coughs again. I want to live some more before I die. I want to laugh and love and be loved too but no one wants me when I'm chaste. Even the baron hardly visits me now.

She calls Clothilde, her maid. Am I still beautiful? she says.

Of course, madame, people say you're the most beautiful woman in all of Paris.

In that case, Marie says, I'm going to the theatre. Please advise the kitchen staff that we'll be having a crowd for supper.

She seats herself at her Louis XV desk, takes a page of scented monogram, dips her nib in ink and writes. A sheet of fancy paper for each of the wealthy young lions of the Jockey Club who once knew her so very well, and another for the régisseur at the Théâtre des Variétés requesting her old stage box for tonight's performance.

The show is really very boring, but everyone is there. Even Franz Liszt, that Hungarian pianist who sleeps his way around the bedrooms of Europe, and a handsome young army officer, Comte Edouard de Pérrigaux, the son of the banker of the king of France and the lover of Alice Ozy, that other young woman who mines the wealthy young males of Paris. Oh, and that aspiring young writer of romances someone brought up to her box. He said his name was Alexandre Dumas. Marie knows the father quite well but not the mother, who's a seamstress and raised the boy alone. But please, do all come for supper, she says.

Later that evening, Liszt suggests he give her some private piano lessons. It would be an honour, monsieur, she says, to be taught by such a gifted man as you.

She was the most absolute incarnation of woman who ever existed, he'll soon be saying, the first woman I was ever in love with.

Marie falls in love with Franz Liszt too. So does every other woman in Europe. But it's Comte Edouard de Périgaux, the king's banker's son, who stays with her when everyone else is gone. I often see you riding in the Bois-de-Boulogne, monsieur, Marie tells him. Your mount seems to delight in carrying such an accomplished cavalier. Well, what man can resist such a line! He uncorks the champagne, even pours it himself, and asks her to accompany him to the races the next day.

A week later he takes her driving in the countryside. They lunch in Bougival, about an hour and a half from Paris by carriage. You can see the Marly aqueduct from the restaurant there, and the Ile de Croissy. And all those new factories in the background with Paris almost hidden under a low black cloud. In the afternoon they row across to the island and stroll through the glades. That's when they see it. The prettiest stone house with climbing roses right up to the first-floor balconies. Why don't I buy it for you? Edouard says.

They spend the summer there and that's where he asks her to marry him. They're walking together by the river. Oh Edouard, I love you so much, Marie says, and kisses him. But if I married you, I'd be nothing but your chattel, your slave. I'd have to ask you for permission for everything I do and you know I could never be a nice submissive little wife like that. I wouldn't even be allowed to manage my own business affairs! So if you don't mind, I'd rather you remained my lover, my friend, my closest companion. Because, my darling, I do so need to be free.

They marry anyway, who knows why, but in England so the marriage is not recognised in France. The papers are signed at the

Kensington Registry Office, 21 February 1846. And so the village girl from Normandy becomes la Comtesse Marie, successful businesswoman, spouse of a nobleman, and daughter-in-law to the banker of the king of France. Holy Mother, lover of God, she says when she visits la Magdelene again, thank you. I've nearly tasted it all.

SOPHIE'S impatient. But what about Demeter and her baby girl? she says.

Well, Soph, when Demeter found out she was pregnant, she returned to her mother's clan to wait for Persephone to grow inside her belly, and while she waited, she did what any ancient goddess does. She ground the grain to make the family's bread, dried the figs and grapes and fava beans for food for the winter months, fetched water from the village well, and at night she'd spin and weave and sing the phases of the moon. One moon song and Persephone was like a little tadpole floating in her mother's cave; three moons and she was swimming with fully formed arms and legs; five moons and she was a mermaid covered in soft lanugo hair; seven moons and she could hear you, see you as shades of light and dark; nine moons and she was kicking against her mother's ribs; and ten moons she was ready to begin her descent. She dropped her little head into Demeter's pelvic cavity, tucked in her little chin, folded her little arms across her chest, and waited for the waters to gush from her mother's spring.

When Demeter knew her child was ready to be born, she gathered her own mother and sisters around her, squatted against a wall and pushed and pushed again as the muscles of her abdomen spontaneously contracted. And very slowly little Persephone emerged from between her mother's legs into her grandmother's waiting hands — her dark baby crown, her forehead, her eyes, her squashed up little nose, her ears, her mouth, her neck, her shoulders. Lillian forms a wrinkled vulva with her own hands and drags it down Sophie's anatomy as she speaks. The child giggles with delight at being born again in this caress. Soon one of Demeter's sisters is clearing the blood and mucous from Persephone's eyes and mouth, and then the sacred blade ...

Sophie inhales nervously and grimaces at this word.

It's OK, Soph. The blade's only to cut the umbilical cord that nourished Persephone while she was in her mother's womb. We all have umbilical cords when we're born. That's where we get our belly buttons from. Lillian tickles Sophie's tummy and the child laughs again. And soon little Persephone is snuggling into her mother's arms and sucking contentedly at her breast. So that's what your little terracotta goddess is saying: Here, drink of me ...

What happens to the baby then? Sophie says.

She grows up into a beautiful young woman just like you will, my little deity. But now I've got to get back to my loom.

MARIE is at the Seaspray, the women-only health club on the hill overlooking Port Phillip Bay. For those who can afford the membership fee, it's a hallowed place where women get fit and strong for no one but themselves. And some are getting very fit and very strong, even Marie. She's on a treadmill now walking at 6.8 US miles an hour (because these machines were made in California) up a fifteen per cent elevation, and little beads of sweat are forming on her brow. She lifts the hem of her T-shirt, wipes her face and walks on.

Kate Ceberano is doing her latest album over the sound system. Change! Gotta bring more meaning to our lives, Kate is singing. Yeah, yeah, we gotta change. Gotta get more meaning in our lives. Marie hums along as she strides up her fifteen per cent to nowhere. Her heart is thumping and endorphins are surging through her body. On either side of her, women are walking, running, climbing, cycling towards the bay on their own machines without ever getting any closer. Some are reading as they exercise, like the woman with the long painted nails who's into *Cleo* magazine, an article about how to get the most out of your orgasms. On the next treadmill an overweight woman is reading *Vogue*. Does she really think she'll ever look like that? Marie says as she strides up her incline. And would she even want to?

Between the gym and the bay is the memorial park with its ziggurat to all the St Kilda boys who died in South Africa fighting Boers for Queen Victoria. A cluster of grey-haired women in loose trousers is spreading across the lawn. One of them has a limp. Lilith and her Tai'chi Ch'uan, Marie says to herself as she watches. Lillian plants her two feet firmly on the earth and gazes across the bay to the blue-brown haze that is the horizon. She is about to grasp the tail of the bird to begin the first set of movements in her mystical martial art. Softness and firmness, positive and negative, lightness and darkness, action and non-action, substantiality and insubstantiality, retreat and advance, passivity and aggression, yin and yang. In slow motion she grasps the tail with one hand, repeats the movement from the opposite side, turns and steps forward into the sequence translated as ward-off-slantingly-upward. She completes the movement, pulls her body back, presses forward, and with her arms outstretched, pushes an imaginary attacker with her open hands — to slowly become a stork cooling her wings.

Marie wipes her brow again and walks on. The machine is counting her every step, her every calorie, her every second on the treadmill. Yeah, yeah, we gotta change, gotta get more meaning to our lives, she's humming with Kate. So what am I doing on this treadmill then? she says and closes her eyes. That last walk up that last mountain last month at Wilsons Promontory and down the other side. The narrow track through the tree-fern glades, the wooden bridge across the creek, the boardwalk through the melaleuca swamp and just when you think you need to rest, the most perfect picture-postcard bay like the beginning of creation. A pair of black swans, a mob of pelicans, a carpet of tiny blue crabs scampering across the sand, and you stare in wonder because there can never have been a more perfect, a more pristine place. But then you look closer and there's a rotting pylon and you remember that this place is called Sealers Cove, that this perfect beach, these perfect islands at the entrance to this perfect bay, were once covered with the lumbering basalt boulder shapes of heaving, breathing seals. And that now the seals are gone. And I am walking up a treadmill …

In the park below, the pattern is changing again. The stork is clenching her fists to attack an imaginary foe. She strikes, deflects a counter-attack, steps forward, parries, punches, then steps back to repulse the monkey. Because when Tai'chi was invented in China there were monkeys to repulse. Soon the invisible monkey becomes an invisible tiger to be carried up an invisible Taoist hill.

Marie is hypnotised by the transformations taking place on the lawn below her. Storks becoming monkeys becoming tigers becoming monkeys again. It's so graceful and so — mystical, she says, then glances self-consciously at herself in the mirror at the far end of the gym. A slim-enough young woman with wild red hair, black tights, faded purple T-shirt, green socks, old white runners, and a faint sense that what she's doing must look ridiculous from Lillian's point of view. She can feel a little river of sweat flowing down the small of her back, and her armpits have turned into springs. Fresh streams are running down her triceps to her bent elbows. A drop of sweat falls onto the treadmill. All this expenditure of energy and yet I'm getting nowhere, she says to herself.

On the lawn downstairs, the monkeys and tigers are evolving into white snakes, horses, and seven stars. Softness/firmness, positive/negative, lightness/darkness, action/in-action, substantiality/insubstantiality, retreat/advance, passivity/aggression, yin/yang, a dance that will end only when Lillian shoots the tiger with her arrows and chops her imaginary opponent with her closed fist. Because that's what you do in Tai'chi Ch'uan.

Marie pushes the stop button. The machine beeps at her and flashes a list of digits — how long, how far, how many calories she has walked, but nothing about the view of the bay from the window, or that walk up and down the mountain to Sealers Cove, or Kate Ceberano's song, or the eternal dance of yin and yang being performed in the park below. But what could a dumb machine know about such things? Marie says and strides into the change room.

The woman who was reading *Cleo* is reclining in the spa. Marie smiles at her and says she'd like to have one too but has to hurry because she wants to meet a friend downstairs. She strips and wraps a towel around her waist. Her body is moist and pungent. She opens a shower cubicle, throws the towel over the top of the door, turns the taps, tests the temperature and steps in. The water is hot and hard against her flesh. She closes her eyes, lifts her face to the spray, sighs then reaches for the soap to lather the soft sweaty hair of her armpits. Her chest, between her breasts, under them, her belly, her pubes, between her legs. She lets the shower wash the sweat and soap away then reaches for the shampoo. The lather runs down her back and over her gluteals, the muscles of her arse. She turns the water off, wipes herself, wraps her wet hair in the towel and leaves the shower cubicle smelling sweet and feminine again, like an ad in *Cleo* or *Vogue*.

━►━   ━►━

AFTER THE MARRIAGE CEREMONY Edouard returns to his family estates, to his hunting lodge, or to the army to kill Algerians, the books don't say which. Marie Duplessis returns to her apartment with her cough, her fever, the blood in her phlegm. I can't bear this life, she tells Franz Liszt at her next music lesson. I won't be able to cling to it much longer. Take me away with you, take me away wherever you want, she says. I won't be in your way. I sleep all day and in the evening you'll let me go to the theatre. At night you can do with me what you like!

Liszt says he'll take her to Constantinople with him, but he never does. She goes to Spa again instead and then to Baden, her last attempt to cure her cough. She returns to Paris exhausted and with all her hankies stained in blood. Clothilde helps her up the stairs, undresses her and puts her to bed. Her husband and the old Baron de Stackelberg return to hold her hand. And her creditors and priests. And her doctors, who prescribe infusions of poppy seed. So she's resting now in fields of poppy flowers, red like in Normandy. Above her a rococo choir of cherubs is humming the Liebesträume Liszt wrote for her and Boucher's doves are spreading poppy peace and love. In the corner, her favourite Sèvres statuette is dancing for her, a virile bacchante, and by her side, the Magdalene — naked now like Venus, except for a halo of moonlight.

She stirs, la Divine Marie. I want to say goodbye, she says. One last night in my box at the Palais-Royal. Clothilde helps her dress. A long white gown, a veil of gossamer lace, a velvet cloak lined with white fur, and a corsage of white camellias. Two lackeys in golden livery carry her up the marble stairs to her box, from where she claims the audience's fullest, most whispering attention. And then she leaves. A pale but still beautiful young woman, four white horses, and a green landau.

Across the street, a young country girl is shivering by a lamp post. Why can't I dress in beautiful gowns like her and go to the theatre and drive around Paris in my own carriage, she says. I'd do anything if I could …

SHE dies on 3 February 1847 at the age of twenty-three, Marie Duplessis. She is killed not by destiny, as the poets might have wished, but by an invisible, unknown something called *Mycobacterium tuberculosis*. Clothilde wraps her thin body in the lace shawl she wore to the Théâtre that night and fills her coffin with flowers. At her own request, she is buried at dawn in Cimetière Montmartre. Only Edouard, Clothilde and the old baron are there to mourn. And la Magdalene.

LILLIAN is chatting with her fellow Tai'chi practitioners on the lawn when Marie emerges from the Seaspray to claim a park bench under a palm tree and wait. In front of her are the Ottoman domes of the now-abandoned St Kilda sea baths and the matching cupola of the clock tower memorial to Carlo Catani, who, the bronze plaque below his bust states, was a distinguished public servant in the years 1876 to 1917. Coincidentally, these were the same years in which the Ottoman empire was collapsing into bloodshed and Australia was achieving her nationhood at Kallipolis, a town that was once an Amazonian stronghold ruled by Artemis Kalliste. Kalli as in Greek for beautiful, derived from Kali Ma, the deity who invented the Sanskrit language and inscribed the letters of its alphabet on the skulls of her rosary. I am the beginning and the end, this goddess says. Alpha and Omega. The Ottomans occupied her polis in 1354 but these days it's a Turkish town called Gallipoli — which is Australian for the place where a nation was born. In a corner of the park a white marble soldier holds his gun above his head in silent surrender to these convergences, lest we forget.

Lillian approaches. Marie smiles. I was watching you while I was working out, she says. I didn't know you could move so gracefully.

I don't know about graceful! Lillian says. But it feels wonderful. Like what Lao-Tze called practising eternity.

Makes my work-out seem really silly then, doesn't it! Marie says.

There was this new Kate Ceberano number on the stereo though and I can't get it out of my brain! Yeah, yeah, we gotta change. Gotta get more meaning in our lives, she sings. Maybe Lao-Tze was trying to tell me something!

Maybe, Lillian says and laughs. But I think we're about to be interrupted ...

Two familiar figures are striding across the park towards them. Elle and little Sophie. We're going to the beach, Sophie shouts as soon as she's within range. Can I take Abelard?

Dogs aren't allowed up this end, Lillian says.

But he won't hurt anyone, Sophie says.

All right, then. He's in the back yard. You go and liberate him while I get his lead.

The three women follow Sophie across the memorial park. So this Sokrates ...? Elle says. I mean, is it serious, Lilith? Like, you're not thinking about going back to Alexandria or anything are you? I couldn't stand that.

Lillian laughs. You want me to tell you about my love life, do you! she says. I'm flattered that you think an old thing like me still has one! But no, I'm not thinking of leaving St Kilda, or not permanently. This is my home. Sokrates and I have been friends and lovers for a long time now, which, I suppose, makes our relationship fairly serious! And somehow it works despite the distance, although he seems to be getting more sentimental about it these days ...

Why are you living on opposite sides of the planet then? Marie says. She's holding the picket gate open while Lillian collects Abelard's lead and frisbee from a cane chair on the verandah. Abelard is wagging his tail, his whole body in anticipation of a run with Sophie. He almost drags the little girl out the gate.

Well, I don't really know, Lillian says. We're in fairly regular contact though. Letters and phone calls and e-mails when he can get his computer working. He's not very technical you know! But I guess he belongs to a different world from me. His family grew cotton in King Farouk's day and managed to hang onto some of their property after the revolution, including the old apartment block overlooking the Mediterranean, so his family has a long history in Egypt. He's passionate about Alexandria and I'm passionate about Australia, I guess. I'm bonded to this place. So I suppose that's why we live where we do.

But don't you miss him sometimes? Marie says. I mean, the sex and intimacy and stuff?

He's not the only man I've slept with over the last thirty years, Lillian says. I've always retained the right to sleep with anyone I choose and I expect him to do the same. And I have plenty of other companions. You three for instance. But yes, sexual intimacy is an utter delight and I still really enjoy it. And sometimes I even miss it. Does that shock you?

No, Elle says. Marie remains silent.

I guess that's what my collection of goddesses is about, Lillian says. Women's erotic potency. It's the basis of all religions — but don't get me started on that …

Sophie is waiting to cross the street because she knows she'll be reprimanded if she attempts it alone. A number sixteen rattles by. Elle takes her daughter's hand and reminds her about checking for cars. Sophie rolls her eyes in six-year-old exasperation then leads her mother, Marie and Lillian across the now-empty Esplanade. Abelard rushes ahead of them to the beach. Sophie chases him. The women follow and nearly collide with a bare-chested, sweaty, and very hairy jogger. It's Heinrich, Marie's Prussian neighbour. He apologises profusely for the near collision then calls out to another semi-naked male further up the bike path. It's Denis on his roller-blades.

You look like an ancient warrior in that get-up, Lillian says as he glides back towards them in his scarlet helmet, corslet and matching padded greaves. Denis grins, flamboyantly kisses each of them, then glides off after Sophie and Abelard. Hey, Soph! he shouts as he scoops the child up in his arms and swings her around. Abelard barks and wags his tail. Heinrich excuses himself. Can't talk, he says. Gotta keep my pulse-rate up, and my war-game mates will be arriving again soon. He turns and continues his run. The three women gaze at his retreating torso in admiration.

What a pity he's gay, Lillian says.

I'm sure Denis doesn't think so, says Marie.

Alfredo is performing his most passionate arioso. Act II, Scene I. Lunge da lei per me non v'ha diletto! he's singing. I take no delight in life when she is far away. Alfredo Kraus remastered for Ursula to add to her CD collection, although it wasn't the Czech baritone she was interested in at the time, but rather the New York-born coloratura of Greek descent who's known simply as La Divina — Maria Callas, recorded live in 1958. Unfortunately not the 1955 Visconti production at La Scala, Ursula says, just the Teatro National de Sao Carlo in Lisboa. But still …

Alfredo has been out hunting and is now alone with his gun in the living room of Violetta's country house. There's a mirror above the mantelpiece. He glances at his own reflection and smoothes his hair. Volaron gia tre lune dacché la mia Violetta, he sings. Three months have gone by since Violetta gave up her life of ease, luxury, and honours in which she enslaved everyone with her beauty, to be with me in this quiet country house. She has left her old life behind to be happy here with me. Near her, I feel like a man reborn and am invigorated by the passion of love. In the joy of being with her I've forgotten the past. Scordo ne'gaudi suoi tutto il passato.

The key changes. The strings surge. Guilhermina Suggia smiles from her portrait on Marie's wall. Ah, that languid legato of my

Portuguese cellos, she's saying. Ah so, io vivo quasi in cielo, io vivo quasi in ciel. I live as if in heaven.

ANOTHER summer, another season of war inside Heinrich's second bedroom. Once more the Peloponnesian army invades Attica and camps near Eleusis, Demeter's sacred site. They burn the crops and houses, destroy the olive groves and vines and march on to Acharnae, just seven miles from Athens, where they burn the crops and houses, destroy the olive groves and vines and move on. Hey, pass me some more ravage markers, Anonymous John of Sparta says. This game's just starting to get interesting!

I need some help with the bed, Marie says over the phone. A pause. Fab. See ya when you get here.

She returns the phone to its cradle, her attention to the dead trees. Two trunks are leaning against one bedroom wall, two against another, and across the fruit-box bench are four ex-shearing-shed beams. She picks up the drill and presses the trigger. A dull electric scream, another hole in another beam. Another hole and another. The bit burns through the timber, warm forest smell, fragrant wood dust and a sudden change in pitch as the other side is reached. Then quiet. Marie returns the tool to her fruit-box bench and sits to ponder her next challenge: how to get the beams from the improvised bench to the top of the tree trunks that are now leaning against the walls. She stands, lifts one end of a beam to rest on a midway ladder rung, lifts, heaves the other end, strains and drops it neatly into its waiting mortices at the top of the recycled tree, returns to the ladder end and lifts until that too drops into its waiting mortice. She picks up the drill again, climbs onto a fruit crate, wobbles and nearly falls, steps down, rests the drill on the crate, drags the ladder into place, lifts the drill, climbs the ladder. Another electric scream as the bit bites into the timber. Then peace. She descends, returns the drill to the fruit box, opens a packet of brass screws, unloads them into her shirt pocket, grabs her screwdriver, ascends the ladder, slips a screw, long, golden, shining, into the first hole, rests her left knee on a ladder rung, fits the tip of her tool into the groove of the screw, grasps the wooden handle, leans her weight into the tree — and twists and slowly turns the screwdriver. The thread of the screw eats into the pine ring by ring, season by season, year by year. Extra pressure for the final turns and now only a shining brass circle on the surface of the beam.

Another screw, another twist, another turn, the slow rhythm of manual labour. Sparrow songs, shadows on the walls. And sex. Because you can't screw screws into tree trunks without certain thoughts rising from the wood. The rhythm of manual labour, slow turns from the wrist, firm twists. She caresses the smooth handle of her tool with her thumb. When will he be in Melbourne again? She descends the ladder and moves it to the other trunk. Another screw, another hole, slow turns, firm twists but not like this, she says, not a metal screw into an empty hole. She strokes the handle again and puts it to her lips. It becomes a rosebud, like that painting on Lillian's wall, delicate and pink. Sparrow songs, shadows on the wall. Her tongue is caressing the petals now, the sprouting bud, the soft, soft inner core. She's kissing it, warm silken flesh against her lips. The rosebud is responding in her imagination, aroused and erect and filled with life. What would the world be like if men thought this, that between their legs, rosebuds grew? she says. Not a drill to penetrate, a rod or staff to conquer with — but something gentle yet strong. Does he believe in rosebuds too? She hums Violetta's aria, the one that seeps through her floorboards every other night from Ursula's flat upstairs. Ah, fors'è lui che l'anima ... is he the one I dream about? È strano! È strano! In core scolpiti ho quegli accenti! His words are burned into my heart.

ANOTHER northern summer, another season of war in this eternal game. The Athenian navy cruises the Peloponnesian coast, burns the coastal crops and houses, destroys the olive groves and vines, slaughters the villagers and the livestock, then sails on to the next inlet, the next village or town … Hey, pass me some more ravage markers, says Heinrich of Athens.

AND another screw in another hole, another twist, another turn. Yes, a rosebud, Marie is thinking, like that painting on Lilith's wall. An adolescent boy hovering in a pale blue sky and, from his loins, a long-stemmed rose. He's holding it, placing it on a table as if for a feast. Of sensuality, of life. Above him, his guide, his angel, his muse, that other person through whom we discover, through whom we express. Our sex.

I met him, Lillian had said, the artist who painted this picture. His name is Apollinario Cruz. Another refugee. He told me that when he was a boy, an elder took him down to the river, a special place near his village in the Philippines. The old man was carrying a blade and a wooden tool shaped like a swan. We stretched our penises, us village boys, slipped our foreskins over the swan's head one by one, Apollinario had told her. He picked up a wooden stick from his studio bench and wrapped a paint rag around it to represent the penis head. A quick razor slash with his fingernail to demonstrate, but it didn't hurt, he told her. Just a slit to show I belong to something more, and it's still there, my foreskin. Like a rose petal. That's what the painting's about. Rosebuds. About becoming a man.

━┿═ ═┿━

BUT HER REAL NAME is Giuseppina, the daughter of Rosa Cornalba and the composer Feliciano Strepponi. She was born in Lodi in September 1815, the year Napoleon's dreams were massacred at

Waterloo. Her father died while she was still studying voice at the Milan conservatorium. Soon her mother was selling the family furniture to survive, and sending the youngest child to an orphanage. Her late father's friends organised a benefit concert to pay her student fees, but it wasn't enough. The Conservatory let her complete her course for free — that girl has such talent, her teachers said, she'll go a long, long way. And yes, soon she's singing five, sometimes six nights a week to support her widowed mother and her siblings. A young woman, beautiful, talented, intelligent but with that most fatal of female flaws: she's looking for a father to love her and finds only men who don't.

Her first mistake is conceived, she says, with her manager. She christens the child Camillo and gives him her own family name, Strepponi. Within two months she's back on stage and back on her back looking for love. By the time she makes her debut at La Scala, she's five months gone and showing. Then Florence and the Teatro Alfieri. Her second child is born six hours after the last curtain call, just thirteen months after baby Camillo's birth. She christens this one Giuseppa Faustina Strepponi and nurses her for three screaming, sleepless, lonely, winter weeks, then leaves her in the turnstile at Ospedale degli Innocenti. Because what else could I do? she says. I just couldn't cope alone and the theatres were holding me to my contracts. To them I'm just another pretty voice.

She drags herself back into her singing and back into the arms of another unplanned pregnancy. This child is stillborn. She abandons the tiny body in the parish of Santa Maria della Passione in Milan and goes back to her career again and back into another mistake with another man who doesn't love her any more than the last. She christens this next child Adelina Rosa Strepponi and leaves her with a poor couple in Trieste. Well, what else could I do? she says. Adelina dies a year later of dysentery.

THE security buzzer. Marie descends the ladder, rests her screwdriver on a fruit box, and steps over the piles of timber to reach the intercom. It's Elle. What on earth is that! she says as she enters the bedroom and sees what will become Marie's bed. Looks like you're making a bomb shelter!

It's meant to be back to natural forms, Marie says. Strength, simplicity, integrity of design. All that. It's like a grotto, see, four sides and the bed on top. These two sides near the walls will be lined with shelves so I can fit all my books in. This third side near the door'll have shelves up to waist height so I can use it like a dressing table or a sideboard. The shelves'll just slip into those grooves I've dug in the trunks. They're what'll hold it all together. On paper at least!

I'm impressed, Elle says.

Yeah, but I really want to get it up today — the uprights joined at least so I can start putting the slats on for the futon. I'm sick of sleeping on the sofa because this room's such a mess!

Elle repeats that worn phrase about making your bed and lying in it.

You sound just like my mother, Marie says. Both women laugh.

When's that guy from Sydney likely to be here again? Elle asks.

That's got nothing to do with it, Marie snaps. And anyway you're being a bit premature even thinking about that, she says, I mean we've only had a cup of coffee together so far. And maybe we'll only ever be platonic.

Come on, Elle says.

Well, yeah, it'd be nice to give the bed a work-out but I've got to get the bloody thing finished first! All the mortices are done, see, and I thought I'd have another cross-beam in by the time you arrived but I got sidetracked. I was daydreaming about that painting at Lilith's, you know, the boy with the rosebud?

IN Heinrich's second bedroom, Athenian business is war-booming. Merchant ships are docking with cargo from all the known world: timber, grain, charcoal, pitch, resin, iron ore, copper, gold, wax, ochre, salt, pickled fish, cheeses, cured meats, honey, livestock, perfumes, exotic furnishings, fine silks. And slaves. A new shipment of war captives arrives from south-west Asia consisting of young females to work the state brothels and young males for the silver mines, those ever-hungry, ever-lethal drachma pits that resource this demokratia. For silver drachmas are almost all that grows on Attica's degraded ridges now. Silver drachmas, marble columns and clay pots. Olive oil and wine. And the empire pays the deficit, as Heinrich said it would, in the currency of subjugation.

So how long am I going to be holding this log up? Elle asks. Marie's on the ladder screwing brass screws through another wooden beam. I won't be a sec, she says. Just a few more turns then I'll come down and do a bit of temporary bracing. She's leaning into the screwdriver as she speaks and another golden screw is eating into the flesh of another dead tree. You haven't told me how the gig at the Espy went the other night ...

Well, we got paid so economically it was a hit, Elle says. Don't know how it was musically but we did that new one, you know, about going down and licking clit. Very heavy punk. Got the whole pub chanting the chorus over and over again! Nearly lifted the roof off! But I kept wondering whether the words'd translate into anything good when the audience got home! Like if any of those women'd actually demand a good lick!

Marie's descending the ladder. Have you ever had a guy who's really into that, though? she says. Like I've never done any quantitative research on the subject but I suspect most men are still really into women sucking their dicks but hate the thought of the other way around. Jesus, I've even had guys who've tried to push my head down to try to make me suck 'em! I mean, they're so inarticulate they can't even discuss what they like or don't like. All they know is force. And it's so risky anyway because you gotta trust 'em not to come in your mouth. With AIDS and STDs and stuff. Like, it's very tacky politics what happens in people's beds.

Yeah, well that's what the song's about, Elle says, but quite frankly, I'd rather 'em use their fingers most of the time anyway, wouldn't you? Like I feel I lose the guy when he sticks his head down there. Or when we both stick our heads between one another's legs. I'd really rather just gaze into his eyes and kiss and nibble and whisper and nuzzle and caress and massage and move in rhythm together from above the waist. Or mostly above the waist! But I reckon most men'd still think sex is all about sticking it in and ejaculating. I mean it's nice to feel it go inside you sometimes when you're all slippery and smooth and wet, and you can squeeze your pelvic muscles and hug it tight for a while, but after that it just becomes a bore. And if you're not ready, it fucking hurts.

✦ ✦

I'VE ALWAYS BEEN CHEATED and deceived, Giuseppina Strepponi says, and for every bad thing I've always had to pay an enormous price. Let's hope it'll all be over soon … And then Giuseppe Verdi. He's bleeding too. Both his own babies have died as well as their young mother Margherita. What's more, his second opera is a flop. He locks himself in a room and swears he'll never write another note of music. But Nebuchadnezzar intervenes, the king of Babylon who's also known as Nabucco, the one who enslaved the Hebrews. The notes fall frantically, sobbingly from his nib. Oh my patria, so lovely and lost! Nabucco's captives sing. Oh, such dear memories but so torn with despair. Giuseppina accepts the role of Abigaille, the militant princess/slave who steals Nabucco's crown. Oh my country, so lovely and lost, she sings. Oh my country, myself.

The first-night audience applauds till their hands burn. It's we who are enslaved, our nation that's being denied. Viva l'Italia! Viva Verdi!

They understand! Verdi tells Strepponi as they take their seventh curtain call. They understand! Not even the Austrian censors can stop us now!

By the end of Act III, Nabucco's crown is restored, the Hebrews are liberated, Verdi is a revolutionary hero, Abigaille is dead, and Giuseppina Strepponi's voice is ruined. She has lived too hard, her doctors say, and now she's paying the price. She must never sing again.

What do you mean never sing again? Giuseppina says. I'm only twenty-six and I have a family to support. My voice is all I've got.

But don't you get like a bitch on heat sometimes and just feel like a really good hard fuck? Marie says. She's examining an off-cut as she speaks, picks up the saw, rests the off-cut on a fruit crate, holds it down with her left knee, and saws a quick forty-five degree angle into one end.

For sure, Elle says. And the most obscene things go through my mind! Like I was sitting on the tram the other evening, it was crowded and there were these quite cute suits standing up in the aisle next to me. Have you ever thought about that? That when you're sitting down in a tram, you're just at the right height to pull their zippers down, and quietly tongue it and play with their balls. I mean you could have a whole row of Collins Streets bulging down the aisle of the number ninety-six. And fuck 'em one by one.

Marie giggles. I can see it! I can see it! she says as she picks up the hammer and a couple of nails. A dozen suits clenching their briefcases not knowing where to look!

They both laugh. Marie is resting one end of the off-cut against the trunk that Elle is holding, and the other end at an angle against the wooden floor. A couple of strong confident stokes of the hammer against a nail and the trunk is temporarily but securely braced. Anyway, I didn't do it! Elle says. I mean even thinking about it is probably sexual harassment! So I just went home and gave myself a good wank and then I felt fine. It was just a bit of sexual tension and like, you can relieve yourself of that any time any place! And fucking's not about fucking anyway, I reckon. Or am I just being mushy? Like you don't want to just fuck that guy from Sydney, do you, for fucking's sake? Like a bitch on heat?

Marie's about to slide a shearing-shed floorboard shelf into two of the grooves she has already gouged across the now-erect tree trunks. I hardly even know him! she says. But no, I don't want to just fuck him. It's about tenderness and intimacy and sensuality. And just being together. Basically all I want is to feel loved.

The shelf fits. She stands back to inspect it, then picks up a hammer and a couple more nails to secure the recycled floorboard to the trunks. Sex is not unimportant though, Elle, she says. I mean I do think about it an awful lot! She's holding a nail at an angle on the shelf as she speaks. She hits it once and then again. But look, what I reckon's most important is — can he cook? Is he good in the kitchen?

Elle lets go of her now secure trunk and laughs. And does he put the toilet seat down! she says. Jeez, you haven't even slept with him and you're already asking him to move in!

Bullshit, Marie says with a grin and slips another floorboard shelf between two waiting grooves. Another floorboard and another. She wipes the wood dust off the recycled boards with an old tea towel. This is really gunna work, she says with pride. Elle licks a finger and rubs it along one of the shelves. The pattern of the tree's growing bursts through her saliva slick. Look at that grain, she says. It'll really glow when you wax it.

Yeah, Marie says and rests an elbow on Elle's shoulder. But do you reckon we can get this last log up before you've got to collect Soph from Lilith's place?

She disengages herself from Elle as she speaks and bends to drag the fourth tree trunk across the bedroom floor to where they can hoist it into position. Some very inelegant heaving, pushing and pulling, and slowly the last horizontal log becomes vertical. Elle holds it in place while Marie moves the ladder. Some more heaving, pulling, pushing and another wooden beam slips into its waiting mortices. The ladder, the electric drill, the screwdriver, a pocket full of brass screws, another scream of the drill. So all I'll have to do after this is fit the shelves in, put in a few supports so they won't sag, and build the steps, Marie says. Oh, and put the slats in for the bed. Easy, eh! She picks up the screwdriver again. Another twist, another turn and another golden circle on the surface of the beam.

AND another foreign ship from another foreign port in Heinrich's second bedroom, this time Egyptian wheat for overcrowded Athens in exchange for military assistance against Persia. The sailors are sweating and feverish. They drop their oars and surge towards the taverns and the brothels like the Nile in flood. But my head, my throat, one sailor says. He takes a wineskin from his belt and squirts alcohol over his burning face as he wanders through the putrid lanes of the Piraeus towards his regular brothel, his regular slave girl. He finds her marketing herself naked as Athenian law demands. She rushes towards him when she sees him. My daddyo, my favourite, she says, come inside, come inside of me and worship in my shrine. She reaches between his legs and drags him towards her cubicle. He tosses the overseer a coin but by now he's not feeling much like a screw. His head is throbbing, his throat is dry and his blood is scalding in his veins. He stumbles and collapses at the slave girl's feet. She rolls him over, fumbles for his purse, hides it beneath her mat and drags him back into the courtyard by the legs. Daddyo, daddyo, my pretty boy, my favourite, she says to the next man. Come inside of me and let me show you paradise ...

The sailor coughs, struggles to his knees and pulls himself to his feet. By now his head is throbbing even more, his breath is foul and his tongue and mouth are raw and bloody. That fucking whore, he says. He stumbles towards the fountain, strips and immerses his head and shoulders in the water to cool the fever. Ulcers are erupting from his back and chest, red and oozing. He lifts his head from the water and collapses against a statue of Hermes.

The slave girl is also coughing and burning and retching bile, as are all the slave girls who served the sailors from the Egyptian ship. All their later clients are coughing, burning, retching too. Pustules are bursting from their skin and soon they're suffering violent belly cramps, diarrhea, dehydration, and internal ulceration. All the sailors from the ship; all the slave girls from the brothel and all the brothel clients; all those who've drunk from the same wells; all those who have nursed them — slaves, wives, lovers, children, friends, neighbours; the doctors who bled them, prescribed them herbs; the barbers who shaved them; the priestesses, the priests who accepted their sacrifices; the worshippers who shared their prayers in this war-stressed polis. Even the dogs and vultures. Soon bodies are lying on top of one another in the streets, and the temples are full of rotting human flesh. The virtuous are dying like the wicked — the young, the old, the weak, the strong, the poor, the rich — until no one's left who cares enough to offer prayers and hymns and sacrifice, to light the funeral pyres, to collect the bones and bury them outside the city walls as tradition says they must. And without these rites, we mortals are doubly doomed: for if our bones are not returned to the earth, how can we be reborn? the slave girl asks. Oh

Mother, why hast thou forsaken us? Are we just pawns in someone else's game?

WOW, Marie says. I never thought we'd do so much today. They're sitting astride the fruit crates in Marie's bedroom admiring their afternoon's labour. The recycled Murray pines are standing erect on the bedroom floor with four ex-shearing-shed beams slung between them, plus the shelves made from the boards of the shearing-shed floor. All the sweat and blood and lanolin that's passed across those boards, Marie says. All those dark satanic mills where the sheep's wool sailed to, says Elle.

Late afternoon shadow time on the walls and sparrows. The window-muffled rumble of a number sixteen tram. And Ursula Upstairs singing with her student. Oh god, it's Act II again, Marie says. Più non esiste — or amo Alfredo, the student is singing. History does not exist — I love Alfredo now and God has wiped away my past with my contrition.

This is where the hankies come out, Marie says. Remember when we took Denis to see the Zeffirelli version! I don't think I've ever cried so much in a movie as when Violetta got done, and Denis was even worse! Jeez, I hope that girl gets the part she's practising for, so we won't have to listen to this sentimental drivel any more. Act II always gets me down.

You'd still have Ursula and her piano, Elle says. And her Verdi collection with every soprano who ever did La Trav!

Yeah, Marie says. And I'd miss old Ursula if anything happened to her. Verdi too. I mean he did write some really cool music. It's just this opera. And Violetta …

So who's getting all sentimental now? Elle says. She pauses. Anyway, no one ever listens to the words in opera!

Just as well! Marie says as she gets up to wipe the fresh dust from her floorboard shelves. What about that cup of coffee we were talking about? You wanna try the new place, the Victory, up the road in the old St Kilda railway station?

Shit no, not the Victory, Elle says. You seen who goes there? It's all brand names with mobile phones, double incomes and 2.3 designer kids a pair!

Let's make it the George, then. Though I don't see the difference. I mean, their wine of the week is seven dollars a glass!

IN Attica the barley is ripening, so Anonymous John and his Peloponnesian League invade again. Across the Aegean on the island of Lesbos, Mytilene's oligarchs are planning revolution.

Ah, the isles of Greece, the isles of Greece! Where burning Sappho loved and sang, Anonymous Carlos of Persia says. His fellow players stare at him. He continues in his strongly migrant voice: Where grew the arts of war and peace, Where Delos rose, and Phoebus sprung! Eternal summer gilds them yet ... He lifts his beer into the embarrassed silence of the war room. Byron, he says. The only English poet I know. A philhellenic. He died of malaria in 1824 at Mesolongion supporting the Greeks in their war of liberation. They mourned him as a national hero.

Really! Heinrich says as Byron's poem drowns in the map of the Mediterranean. Anonymous Carlos slides apologetically back into his corner, leans against the wall and gulps his beer like a real man should. Ah, but the isles of Greece ... For one liberating moment he'd forgotten the rules of antipodean masculinity. Now only the dice rolling across the map, the metal-on-metal rumble of the trams in Fitzroy Street, and the Doppler purr of internal combustion engines. Because Australian men don't talk about that kind of stuff, like poetry and freedom and who you are and what you feel. It's the rules of the game.

THE George, once a palatial pub named for England's pagan saint, is now a posh cafe and gallery with a big door of glass and gilded metal embossed with the saint's pagan name. Marie holds it open for Elle, then follows her to a table by the window. Outside, Grey Street — the battle front between St Kilda's poor and St Kilda's rich: the sex workers, rooming-house tenants and homeless people who claim the street their own, versus the nouveau developers who claim the nineteenth-century real estate. Inside the George, the battle's already won — but in the very best quality-of-life taste!

Marie drags a bentwood chair across the fashionably polished concrete floor. We did OK today, she says. Couldn't have done any of it without you. Ta.

It was fun, Elle says. But I want to see it finished and fully tested! She grins.

Lay off, will you? You've been at me all afternoon about that and I'm too tired to think about it after all that drilling and screwing and dragging those logs around. Anyway, you haven't been doing so well yourself lately!

I've provisionally given up, Elle says. I've got Soph, you, Lilith, my study, my band, my other women friends. My family when they're talking to me. Isn't that enough?

I don't know, Marie says. Is it?

Elle stares out the window to Grey Street. Well, no, it isn't really, she says. I do want something more, but it's not a man. I've been thinking of going back to Sicily.

You what?

I want to go back to Sicily.

When did this happen? I mean, shit, Elley, we've been working together the whole afternoon and you've never even mentioned it.

I didn't really know myself until just then. I mean, I've sort of been considering it but I haven't really said anything about it to anyone. It's just ... like, sometimes I think there's nothing in this country to fill you up inside. It's all so easy, so shallow, you know? Like all you have to do to be a good citizen is consume, consume,

consume other people's products, other people's ideas. But there has to be something better than that, hasn't there? I mean, there's no heart in anything here, it's like there's just a desert where the heart should be. Every now and then I get a glimpse of something more, something I could put some passion into like Lilith talks about — but then it disappears. So what I want, I guess, is to be somewhere where people believe in something. Something real that's worth living for.

⊹ ⊹

GIUSEPPINA STREPPONI goes to Paris, the opera capital of the world, to teach the daughters of the emerging bourgeoisie how to sing. Well, what else could I do? she says. They're the only ones with any money these days, and I've got to make a living somehow.

She has been working with Verdi, managing his correspondence, advising him, enjoying his companionship. Maybe she has even been sleeping with him. He writes to her before she leaves Italia. He tells her he loves her, that he wants to see her in Paris. She reads his words a thousand times, kisses them, reseals them, and returns them to their hiding place. They shall rest this letter on my heart when they bury me, she writes in her diary. The year is 1846, the year Marie Duplessis marries her Edouard in that English registry office.

A waiter deposits two lattes on the varnished particleboard table. Thanks, Elle says mechanically as she wraps her hands around a hot glass. Marie lifts hers and sips while she absorbs the significance of Elle's words. I think I need a sugar hit after what you've just told me about going back to Sicily, she says.

There's no sugar on their table so she looks around the cafe for the closest spare bowl, or someone who can bring her one. Everyone is busy: the waiter is rearranging hot-house tulips in a giant hand-blown glass vase, the chef is beating brown sugar and butter into a dozen egg yolks on the other side of the counter, and the kitchen hand is stacking still-warm flan cases onto multi-storey cooling racks. A few tables up, three women are talking house renovations across their pastries and latte glasses, but no sugar bowl. Marie scrapes her chair against the concrete floor and strides towards the counter where a row of half-empty sugar bowls is waiting to be filled. She takes the closest bowl and returns to her seat.

Damn, a six! That means another random event! says Anonymous John, and tosses again. A five. He reaches for the rule book to check the table. That means we've got to proclaim another truce, he says. This time it's for the Olympic Games! But I suppose that's better than another Helot revolt!

Or another plague, Anonymous Alexie the banker says. Look what happened to Heinrich. He lost 4500 troops and a third of the population of Athens in the last random event.

Don't you worry about Athens, Heinrich says. I've still got plenty of tricks up my sleeve. And we'll win at the Games too — plague or no plague.

And so to Elis, that part of the Peloponnese that is forever home to the proprietors of the deli where Heinrich buys his milk, and to a sacred spring in a sacred grove beneath a sacred hill, the sanctuary of Olympia.

Zeus's temple is the biggest structure within the sanctuary, all gaudy blue and red triglyphs and dripstones, monumental pediments, and metopes carved with the most recent version of Greek history. The deity himself, the heavenly father, is a chryselephantine giant sculpted upon his throne by an Athenian refugee called Phidias, from all-too-human clay decorated with a slave-mine of gold, a herd of ivory, a whole rainforest of ebony.

Hera's house, the Heraeum, is much smaller than Zeus's temple, and much older, as old perhaps as the Pelopion next door which was built for Pelopia, the mother of the Pelopids and of all the Peloponnese. But no one remembers her because she was overthrown by yet another conqueror who called himself Pelops after he stole her name. This young hero marched into the Greek imagination on the crest of yet another invasion to begin a pathology of violence which Aeschylus says could only be resolved when another young conqueror called Orestes murdered his mother, Clytemnestra of the Pelopids clan, after she stabbed his father, the warlord Agamemnon, while he was taking a shower with Cassandra, the prophetess he'd captured at Hissarlik, a town in Turkey that's also known as Troy.

Agamemnon had sailed off to sack and pillage Cassandra's town decades before with Achilles and their mates, and, en route, had sacrificed Clytemnestra's daughter Iphigenia to the goddess Artemis, for a wind to fill their patriarchal sails — which is one of the reasons Clytemnestra wanted him dead. What neither Orestes, nor his mother, nor even Agamemnon knew at the time however, was that Iphigenia was still alive. She'd been snatched from the pyre by Artemis herself just as the flames were scorching her flesh, and taken to the Taurus mountains. Iphigenia became a priestess in the goddess's temple there and in her spare time hunted sailors off the Turkish coast. She decapitated them and nailed their heads to wooden crosses in memory of her father's deeds.

All this allegedly occurred because Pelops hired a groom called Myrtilus to fix a race in Elis so he could marry Hippodamia who was descended from Pelopia, the deity herself — because that's the only way he could steal the goddess's name. He shot Myrtilus after the wedding so he wouldn't talk, but what Pelops didn't know at the time was that the groom was the son of Hermes who was the son of Zeus and the virgin Maia — which meant that Myrtilus's death came to the attention of the holy father. And so it was Zeus himself who set these events in motion as retribution for the murder of his grandson. Or that's what Aeschylus says.

Hercules, who founded the Olympic games, was also closely related to Zeus because his mother, Alcmene of Thebes, slept with the god too. Or so Pindar says. Who knows how many mortals Hercules himself slept with, or how many children he sired, because history only records the sons and there were at least eighty of them. They're collectively known as the Heraclids, the Dorian conquerors of the Peloponnese from whom the people who own the deli in Fitzroy Street claim descent. Where Heinrich buys his milk and Anonymous John his Gitanes that are shipped from that other Greek colony, Marseilles. Because everything in the universe is entwined.

THEY leave pagan George's in the twilight, Elle and Marie, to cross Grey Street together then part, Elle to shortcut to Lilith's place through St Kilda's back streets and lanes, and Marie to return to her flat. She passes old Jeannie the bag lady shuffling up the Grey Street hill to the Salvos' crisis centre for her evening meal, a couple of free sausage rolls and sweet milky tea in a polystyrene cup with the other refugees. Lunch was at the Sacred Heart, one block further up the hill. The usual meat stew and three donated veg plus jelly and custard for dessert. Or cake. Marie nods to Jeannie and turns the corner into Fitzroy Street. Past the chemist, the bank that'll soon be closing down, the all-night food store, the newsagent, Chichio's cafe with its gallery and poetry and jazz, the pawn shop, the post office that'll also soon be gone, the public phone booths where all those pale young women in very short skirts buy their pills and powders from men with tats and mobile phones. Past the cafe that got busted a few months back. Past Chronicles bookshop and Monroe's, the licensed temple to the goddess Marilyn. Past the fish-'n-chip-'n-pizza facades hiding St Kilda's nineteenth-century palaces that are now being resurrected as fashionable apartments and post-mod delis selling sun-dried tomatoes in virgin olive oil, smoked Tasmanian salmon and King Island brie. Past another pawn shop, the Guardian Family Care Chemist and bulk bill clinic that was once another bank, Angel's cutprice cigarettes, the Thai BYO, the Great Australian Ice-creamery, Angelo and Jana's USA cafe, Dan's Vietnamese hot bread shop, the 24-hour-seven-days-a-week amusement parlor, the Chinese eat-all-you-can-for-$6.90, another pawn shop, the entrance to Joey's upstairs nightclub ... past all that and into the Phoenician take-away where Feyrouz is singing Arabic along a coiled magnetic tape: peace to Beirut with all my heart and kisses, she sings. To the sea and clouds, to the rock of a city that looks like an old sailor's face. From the soul of her people, she makes wine. From their sweat, she makes bread and jasmine. So how did it come to taste of smoke and fire? this diva sings.

The exhaust fan hums. The embers glow. The spit turns above the altar ... for I am the lamb which is made ready with pure wheat to sacrifice. Come, put bread upon the table, bread, and pour wine into the cups. In the golden goblet, the blood of trees.

DEAR PIAVE,

You can imagine whether I wanted to stay in Paris, after hearing about the revolution in Milan. I left there immediately after hearing the news; but I only got to see these stupendous barricades [and not the fighting]. Honour to these heroes! Honour to all of Italy, which is now truly great.

The hour of her liberation is here; be sure of that. The people want it: and when the people want it, there is no absolute power that can resist. Those who want to impose themselves on us by sheer force can do what they want, they can conspire as much as they like, but will not succeed in cheating the people of their rights. Yes, yes, a few more years, perhaps a few months, and Italy will be free, united, and republican. What else should she be?

You talk to me now about music!! What has got into you? Do you think that I want to bother myself now with notes, with sounds? There cannot be any music welcome to Italian ears in 1848 except the music of cannon! I would not write a note for all the money in the world: I would feel an immense remorse, using music-paper, which is so good for making shells. ...

I have to go back to France because of obligations and business. You can imagine that — in addition to having to write two operas — I have a lot of money to collect there, and other money to collect in bank drafts.

I abandoned everything there; but I cannot ignore the sum of money which is, to me, quite large; and I have to be there in person to salvage at least a part of it, given the present crisis. As for everything else, no matter what happens, I will not be troubled by this. If you could see me now, you would not recognise me. I no longer have that long face that scared you! I am drunk with joy! Imagine that there are no more Germans here!! You know what kind of feelings I had for them! Addio, addio, say hello to everyone. A thousand good wishes to Venturi and Fontana. Write to me soon, for [even] if I leave, I shall not do so right away. Of course I will come back!

G. Verdi

LILLIAN is at her desk again. The book she is writing, *The death and resurrection of Hypatia*, is a mythic reinterpretation of the rise and fall of patriarchy in the West, though the fall is still wishful thinking, she keeps reminding herself. But if I believe in anything, it's this: that words still have generative power and that therefore they are female. She lifts her fingers from her loom, rests her elbows on the desk and sighs. In the beginning was the word, she whispers to herself. And the word was Om. The antique Tantric bronze deity in the corner of Lillian's study smiles at this primal sound — because it was she who first uttered it, Kali Ma or her Vedic sister Vac. I'm pregnant with sound, Vac had claimed. I dwell in the waters of the sea, spread from there through all creatures, and touch the sky with my crown.

Vac's sky is darkening now and the Babylon palms are whispering like shadows on the other side of Lillian's front fence. A single street light is illuminating her camellia grove and the buds and full-blown blossoms are brushing against one another in the evening breeze. Pale pink petals are dropping, one by one, onto Hsi Wang Mu, Lady-Queen of the West. Tonight, in this tiny inner-city Shalimar, a light dew will fall. Lillian sighs again. The dew on the petals, the lingam in the yoni, the child in the womb, the corpse in the earth — what lovely tantric words, she says. Like om-mani-padmè-hum, the jewel in the lotus ... Oh, damn you Sokrates, why are you distracting me so much tonight? Why is Alexandria so far away? And she reaches for the phone.

THE Olympic games continue in Heinrich's second bedroom. The Lesbians of Mytilene have rebelled against Athens and have sent a team of supplicants to negotiate membership of the Peloponnesian League. The formal talks are being hosted by the Boeotian delegation in the board room of Zeus's temple.

Until our current policy reversal, we'd been allies of Athens and members of the Delian League, as you know, the Lesbian envoy says. We joined that League to fight the Persians and, like you, watched with despair as Athens transformed our alliance of autonomous states into a subject empire. The strategy was to pick off the weaker powers first, exploit their resources and at the same time isolate the more powerful allies like Mytilene so we'd be easier to subjugate next. We did all we could to preserve our autonomy. We wooed the Athenian demos, we bribed their leaders, we entertained their priests, we dedicated gifts to their temples — and of course, we invested heavily in our own navy. But we always knew that as soon as the Athenians thought they could get away with it, they'd invade and annex us too — which is why we've rebelled. To preserve our freedom. And why we're seeking your support. Because in these polarised times, we know we can't survive alone. We need you, and you need us and our navy. Because Sparta and the Peloponnesian League will never defeat Athens without a very strong fleet.

⇥ ⇤

AND NOW it's Roma's turn. The Pope has fled and a quarter of a million adult males are about to vote for the first time in their lives. The three Giuseppes are all in town to celebrate: Mazzini, Garibaldi, and Verdi, who has arrived with the score of a new opera under his arm, *La battaglia di Legnano*. He's rehearsing it at the Teatro Argentina. Viva Italia! Sacro un patto utti stinge I figli suoi! his chorus sings. A sacred compact unites her people. Chi muore pa la patria alma si rea non ha. Whoever dies for Italia does not have a guilty soul.

La battaglia di Legnano surges through the city's streets like adrenalin. Viva Italia! Chi muore par la patria alma si rea non ha. At the Teatro Argentina, a thousand Arrigos and Rolandos are demanding seats for the dress rehearsals because they can't wait for opening night. From the Teatro they go straight to the polling booths. The result is a foregone conclusion. Soon the new Assembly of the People will proclaim that the temporal government of the papacy in Rome is at an end, and that Rome has become a pure democracy which will take the glorious name of The Roman

Republic and enter into such relations with the rest of Italy as common nationality demands.

On every street corner, in every cafe, another knight is enlisting in this crusade to free Italia, and in every bed another young woman waits for her hero like Lida, the heroine in Verdi's new opera. But in the real world of the Po valley, the Lombard League is being defeated by the armies of the new Barbarossa in La battaglia di Novara. Milano falls. The old king of Piedmont abdicates. The new king signs an armistice. And all Italia trembles.

We must act like men who have the enemy at their gates and at the same time like men who are working for eternity, Mazzini says.

The Pope responds from the safety of his exile: The city of Rome, the principal seat of the Church, he says in his Allocution of April 20, 1849, has now become, alas, a forest of roaring beasts, overflowing with men of every nation, apostates, or heretics, or leaders of communism and socialism. It is the moral duty of all Catholics to destroy the Republic.

No, no, no, Mazzini says. It's the moral duty of all Romans to defend it. All we want to do is ameliorate the material condition of the classes least favoured by fortune. And if that means giving ecclesiastical land to the landless poor, and teaching the masses how to read and write ...

The past versus the future in this moral war of words. They meet five leagues from Rome: an officer of the Catholic Republic of France doing his moral duty and a guard of the Roman Republic doing his. Or that's what Alexandre Dumas père says (or his translators) in his strand of this eternal web, the *Memoirs of Garibaldi*.

What do you want? the Roman says in Dumas' words.

To go to Rome, the French captain says.

That's impossible, says the Roman.

We are speaking in the name of the French Republic, the officer says.

And we speak in the name of the Roman Republic; so then, gentlemen, be good enough to retire.

And what if we don't retire?

We'll endeavour to compel you to do so, in spite of your demands.

And how, pray?

By force.

If that is the case, the French officer says as he turns to his men — then Fire.

Fire, says the Roman guard.

⊹— ⊹—

THE ROLL OF DRUMS, the toll of bells, barricades and guns. Lupa howling on the Capitoline, the she-wolf who suckled those fratricidal twins. Lupa howling, and the screams of Rhea Silvia who gave the twins their birth. Rhea Silvia's screams and the tears of Acca Larentia who pulled them from their mother's womb. Acca Larentia's tears and the wailing of the gens Romulia from whose deep this city flows. The wailing of the Romulians and the neighing of Pales, their sacred ass. Pales neighing on the Palatine and Vesta weeping at her sacred hearth. Vesta weeping with her virgins and Tanaquil, the goddess mother of the Tarquin kings; and Aurora, Roma's mater matuta, mother of the sun; and Astraea the starry one who gave to Rome her natural law. Iustucia et aequitas, this deity always said. Justice and equity. And Mensa who taught her people how to mensurate, how to calculate and count; and Carmenta, the mother of the charms, who taught them how to write the Latin script; and Uni, Etruria's mother of the Universe; and Menrva, the Etruscan mother of all wisdom; and Cybele in her cavern, the mother of the deities; and Bona Dea, Roma's holy womb; and Juno Populonia,

⊹— 115 —⊹

the mother of the people; and Fata Scribunda, the fate who writes our destiny; and Venus Libertina, omnipotens et omniparens. All powerful and parent of us all. And Sapientia, thou unbegun and everlasting Wisdom, sovereign substantial Firsthood, sovereign goddess, sovereign good. And Maria, queen of Heaven …

Our sons, our sons, these mothers cry. Why hast thou forsaken us? For you know not what you do.

But let's not talk about Rome! Giuseppe Verdi says in a letter to a friend. Because force once again rules the world! And justice? What use is that against bayonets?

A souvlaki, please, Marie says. The lamb sizzles on its spit as Muhammad sharpens his knife and cuts. Slivers of roasted flesh fall onto his waiting plate. He lays the plate on the counter. The lot? he says as he reaches for a circle of Lebanese bread. She nods. Lettuce, tomato, onion and very pink turnip pickled by his mother. Yoghurt and chili sauce. And the hot sliced flesh of the lamb. He rolls the bread around the salad and meat and stuffs it into a bag with two paper serviettes. The best souvlaki you'll get anywhere, he says as he passes it to her. She hands him four bucks and a smile in return, plus her only word of Arabic. Shookran, she says, which means thank you, or that's what she hopes it means.

Outside, Fitzroy Street is neon darkening and the moon, the evening stars are already trapped between the tram cables. A double lane of suburbans is hunting pre-dinner parking spots and Mary White and her clan are collecting coins for the bottle shop. Across the road, outside Marie's block of flats, Jeannie is waiting with her sausage rolls and Safeway bags for someone to let her in.

You're only encouraging her, Daphne Downstairs says through her window as Marie digs into her pocket for the key.

What harm does it do, her sleeping under the stairs? Marie says. She's not hurting anyone. Daphne shakes her head and threatens to ring the welfare again. It won't do any good, Marie says. She'll only come back.

But she's an eyesore, Daphne says. What will people think?

⤚ ⤙

THE BLOOD has hardly dried between the cobbles when Giuseppe Verdi and Giuseppina Strepponi arrive back in town, and another Bonaparte is about to crown himself emperor.

Fancy all those Republican dreams translating into this! Strepponi says.

Verdi reaches across the cafe table for her hand. There's a new play opening at the Vaudeville, he says. By that young Dumas, old Alexandre's son. You gave me the novel when I was visiting you here once, about Marie Duplessis. Remember? La Dame something or other. Camellias or daisies or violets ... But apparently the play's much better than the book.

Aux camélias, Giuseppina says. And yes, it'd be nice to go to the theatre again without all that small-town gossip we have to put up with in Bussetto. Maybe you'll even find a new opera in Dumas' script. Something contemporary for a change ...

She remains dry-eyed until Act IV, the ball at Olympe's house. Marguerite arrives on the baron's arm while Armand Duval arrives alone. He's been drinking again and gambling. Tonight the game is baccarat. Unlucky at love, lucky at cards, he says as he wins another two hundred louis from the baron. But now they want to fight a duel ...

Marguerite beckons to Armand. You must leave, she says in the words of young Dumas. I have suffered so deeply in the past month that I can hardly find strength to say what must be said. There is a burning pain here that takes away my breath. For the sake of our past love, for the sake of anything that you have ever held dear or

⤚ 117 ⤙

sacred in your life, return to your father and forget that you have ever known me.

I understand, he says. You are afraid for your lover. It would be a thousand pities if a pistol shot or a sword thrust were to put an end to your present good fortune.

You yourself might be killed, Armand. That is the danger.

And what difference would it make to you? Did you care whether I lived or died, when you wrote to me that you were the mistress of another? If that letter did not kill me, it was only that I might live to be revenged. You thought that you could arrange everything very simply and that I should take no further notice of you and your accomplice. But I tell you that between the baron and me there is a quarrel to the death. For I shall kill him.

The baron is not to blame for this, Marguerite says.

You love him! That is reason enough for me to hate him, Armand says.

You know that I don't love this man, that I never could love him.

And yet you left me and went to him. Why?

Don't ask me Armand, I can't tell you.

Then I will tell you, he says in Dumas' words. You gave yourself to him because you don't understand the meaning of loyalty and honour; because your love belongs to the highest bidder and your heart is a thing that can be bought or sold; because when you found yourself face to face with the sacrifice that you were going to make for me, your courage failed you, and you went back to the past; because I, who would have devoted my life to you and my honour, too, meant less to you than your horses and carriages and the jewels around your neck.

Yes, it is all true, she says. I am a worthless and ungrateful creature, who has cruelly betrayed you, and who never loved you. But the more degraded you know me to be, the less you ought to endanger your life for my sake, and trouble the peace of those you love. Armand, on my knees, I implore you, before it is too late, to leave Paris.

I will, on one condition, Armand says.

I agree to it, whatever it is.

That you come with me.

Never!

Never!

Oh my God, help me, she says.

Listen Marguerite, there is madness in me tonight, Armand says. I am capable of anything, even a crime. I thought that it was hatred that was driving me back to you, but it was love, Marguerite, angry, remorseful, torturing love, love that despised itself and was ashamed, for there is shame in my loving you after all that has happened. Say just one word, and I will forget everything. What do I care for this man? Only tell me that you love me and I will forgive you, Marguerite. We will leave Paris and the past behind us, find some solitude and be alone with our love.

I would give my life for one hour of such happiness, Marguerite says. But it is impossible. Go, forget me. You must. I have sworn it.

To whom?

To one who had a right to ask such a thing.

To the baron?

She grimaces. Yes, she says.

Because you love him! Tell me that you love him and I will go.

Then yes, I love him.

Armand grabs her and hurls her to the floor. Giuseppina Strepponi reaches for Giuseppe Verdi's hand. He takes a linen handkerchief from his breast pocket and passes it to her. Do you see this woman? Armand is shouting from the stage. Do you know what she did? She sold all that she had to live with me because she loved me so much. It was noble and generous, wasn't it? You shall hear how vilely I treated her! I accepted this sacrifice and gave her nothing in return. But it is not too late. I know now that I was wrong and I wish to settle the account between us. I call upon you all to witness that I owe this woman nothing.

And he throws a wad of notes to the floor. All the money he has won at baccarat.

UPSTAIRS, Alfredo is performing his most passionate arioso yet again. Lunge da lei per me non v'ha diletto! he is singing. Life gives me no pleasure when she's far away from me. Ah si, that languid legato of my Portuguese cellos, Guilhermina Suggia says from her portrait on Marie's wall. Io vivo quasi in cielo, io vivo quasi in ciel.

Marie hums her own orchestration as she climbs the stairs to her flat, inserts her key into the lock, enters and turns on the TV news. Yeah, just more of the same, she says and snaps the TV off. She collects a plate from the kitchen, flops into her only armchair, removes the souvlaki from its bag, and bites. Yoghurt and chili sauce dribble down her wrist. A bright pink piece of pickled turnip misses the plate and falls onto her lap. She picks it up, eats it, goes to the kitchen for a tea towel to wipe away her spills, and retreats into her bedroom. One fruit crate becomes her dining table, the other her chair. The smell of lanolin, of sheep. Pine forests. Wood dust. Shadows on the wall. And that Czech baritone ... si, si, dell' universo immemore io vivo quasi in ciel, he's singing. Ever since that day she asked me to live with her, the day she told me she'd always be true, I've forgotten about everything else in the world. I feel like I'm in heaven. Ah si, io vivo quasi in ciel, io vivo quasi in ciel.

Marie stares at the silent Murray pines that are her half-completed bed. Wood dust. Shadows on the wall. When will he be in Melbourne again? she says and nibbles her souvlaki. Yoghurt is dribbling down her wrist. She licks it and lets her lips linger. Her skin is soft and warm and spicy. She sighs. Ah, the fever, the ardour, the passion, the fire of my youthful spirit, Alfredo is singing ... De'miei bollenti spiriti ...

But what if it's not him I'm wanting, Marie says. What if it's not a man but something more?

VERDI'S in the fallen Republic of Rome again rehearsing another opera. Strepponi's waiting for him in Livorno on Italia's western coast. He's sent me into exile as if he's the tyrant of Syracuse, she says. But everyone knows we're lovers so I don't really see the point, and I'm so lonely and bored here without him. I'm living like a Trappist monk and my only regular companion is a little mouse who comes to eat the crumbs I drop on the floor when I dine in my room alone. I'm no longer afraid of rodents the way I used to be, but I wish it were my Pasticcio who's visiting me ...

She's sitting in her hotel room re-reading his latest letter. He complains about the rheumatism in his right arm and says he simply can't compose. Hardly a note of music since I arrived in Rome ... Well, what can you expect, Giuseppina Strepponi says to herself, without me tucked away in an armchair in your study, saying to you This is beautiful, Wizard. This is not. Stop. Play that again. This is original.

She picks up her pen and dips the nib in ink. One word from you and I'd be right there by your side, she writes. Because I have to confess that this separation is far more painful for me than many of the others. Without you, I'm body without a soul ...

They'd travelled by carriage to Genoa from the farm at Sant'Agata, and from Genoa they'd taken a steamer to Livorno, where they spent a few days together before Verdi caught another steamer to Civitavecchia. From there he went by carriage to Roma, where his librettist, Francesco Maria Piave of the now-fallen Re-

—✁— 121 ✂—

public of Venice, had already booked him into a hotel. A suite at the Europa with big windows and plenty of sunshine, Verdi had said. And a piano please and a reading stand because we've got to finish that piece for Venice. Amore e morte. Love and death. Or that's what the working title is. About this courtesan who …

Piave and Verdi had been working on something else for Venice, but the ideas just wouldn't flow. What we need is a completely new theme, Verdi had said one evening as he was opening another bottle of Sant'Agata wine. Something great and beautiful and daring and contemporary for a change. I'm sick of having to hide everything in the past.

What about Dumas' book? Strepponi had said.

Verdi and Piave worked like madmen after that and finished the first draft in just five days. But that was at the farm. In Rome with all those French troops occupying the streets and no Strepponi to inspire and help him work …

You can't imagine how impatiently I'm awaiting your return! she writes. I've started reading, and I read, read, read until my eyes are red; but I'm afraid that sadness and boredom will attack me violently during these days when you've condemned me to a cell. You will say Spend money and have a good time. First of all, I don't like you telling me Have a good time, when I don't know where to look for amusement! If I could see you for a quarter of an hour out of every twenty-four, I'd be in high spirits, would work, would read, would write, and the time would pass if anything too quickly. As it is … but let's drop this argument because I'm about to cry.

She sniffs, wipes her nose, sighs, and stares out the window to the bay. Five, ten, fifteen minutes pass and now her nib is dry. She dips it in the ink again: I am travelling to Florence tomorrow because, as you know, I still have business there. I might try to find a doctor who'll bleed me again and, if I'm feeling well enough, I'll go on to Pisa to hear Piccolomini sing. I'll arrange to have my mail sent on from here so please keep writing to me at this address. And remember to rub your arm with oil of camphor and stay out of cold drafts my sweet Wizard.

She lays her pen on the desk, gets up and goes out onto her private balcony to inhale the fresh sea air. A group of barefooted children is playing on the foreshore. Their voices reach her in an atonal Allegro animato she can't understand. She responds in Molto mesto. Sad, very sad. It could be my little Giuseppa playing there, she says to herself. I tried, I really tried. Those three screaming, sleepless weeks after she was born seem like a nightmare now, but what else could I do except leave her in Florence? At least I know she's being cared for there and I might even get a glimpse of her tomorrow when I go to pay her bills ...

A small pleasure boat is tied up at the jetty in front of the hotel. A man is helping a young woman ashore. She lifts her face to his as she steps from the boat and kisses him. He puts an arm around her waist and they kiss again, long and languorously, then walk arm-in-arm down the jetty towards the hotel. From her vantage point above, Giuseppina Strepponi searches for a gold ring on the young woman's finger. I hope she's doing it in the right order, she says. It's so hard when you don't, especially when it's not by choice, like for me who has to live secretly in sin with the man I love to protect his reputation, while my babies are either dead or strangers to me. And the doctors say I can't have any more ... Another tear is falling. She wipes it and sniffs. Yes, that young woman has a ring, I can see it on her finger. If I had one ... but the man I want is in Roma with the randiest poet I've ever known, instead of being with me.

She quickly returns to her desk, sniffs again and dips her nib in ink. And one more thing, she writes. Please beware of that lovely devil Piave! I worry that his erotic zeal might be contagious! We will not have children (since God perhaps is punishing me for my sins by preventing me from enjoying any legitimate joy before I die)! Well, not having children by me, I hope you do not hurt me by having any by another woman.

Love me as I love you,

Peppina.

Upstairs, the faint soprano voice of Annina the maid. Something about Violetta selling all she owns to support her lover, but Marie is performing in her own soap opera, she and her souvlaki — until Guilhermina's cellos warn her that once more that time has come. D'Alfredo il padre in vedete! a male voice is singing. Alfredo's father.

Oh god no! Marie says. Now I have to listen to all that crap about how his angelic daughter won't be able to marry the boy she loves unless Violetta sacrifices herself ... Deh, non mutate in triboli le rose dell'amor, the father sings. Don't turn the rose of my daughter's love into thorns.

But what I wanna know is, how come Verdi and Piave can do this to Violetta, and yet work so hard to liberate Italia? she says. Why can't they see their inconsistencies?

Per voi non avran balsamo I più soavi affetti, Alfredo's father is singing. The future can bring you no balm, since this relationship is not blessed by heaven.

E vero! Violetta sings. It's true. God has never blessed our love. Così alla misera ch'è un dì caduta di più risorgere speranza è muta! All hope of forgiveness is gone for this wretched woman who one day sinned.

Marie puts her souvlaki aside and wipes her mouth and hands on the old tea towel. Why can't that silly bitch see what's going on? she says. Why can't she just tell Alfredo's father to fuck off and leave her and his son alone to sort things out themselves? I mean, she's even singing a duet with the bastard! And the worst part is, Verdi has written them such a beautiful melody!

Violetta is staring out the window. She's weeping. Piangi, o misera, piangi, Alfredo's father is singing.

Soon the cellos are weeping too, and Guilhermina Suggia from her portrait on the wall, and Marie astride her fruit crate, she and her half-eaten souvlaki. Warm forest smell, wood dust, shadows on the wall and her own cello leaning there. She lifts the dust cover, carries the instrument, the bow to the fruit box, spreads her legs, places the cello between her thighs, bends over it and rests her head against its neck the way she always does. She plucks a string and listens. Ah, dunque sperdasi tal sogno seduttore, Alfredo's father is singing. Ah then, reject this seductive dream. Be instead the consoling angel of my family. E Dio che ispira, o giovine, tai detti a un genitor. It's God who inspires these words from a parent's lips ...

Marie lifts the bow and scrapes it across the strings. Vibrate, damn you, she says. Screech, squawk, howl, scream, sob, anything that isn't complicity with what's going on upstairs. She slashes the strings, lashes and whips them with her bow. Move, damn you, she says, shift yourself from this inertia.

The air begins to pulse. Dammi tu forza, o cielo, she says. O cielo, give me strength ...

Music is flooding her bedroom like moon-blood now, like a storm in a wine-dark sea. Sempre libera, her cello is singing. Set yourself free, and that man's daughter. For he would keep us in chains.

BUT HER REAL NAME is Helen Porter Mitchell, who was born in Melbourne in 1861 to a Scottish mother who was christened Isabella for a Spanish queen, and to Dave, the son of tenant farmers from far-off Forfarshire.

Colonial Melbourne was drunk on gold when Dave and Isabella stepped ashore. Helen was the third child born but the first of ten to survive. Her mother died from too many pregnancies while Helen was still growing into womanhood. After his wife's death, Dave moved to Mackay, a deep-north sugar town, and took young Helen with him, which is how she met Kangaroo Charlie, the jackeroo son of an Anglo-Irish baronet. A remittance man. She became Mrs Armstrong because that's what women did, but then she left, she and George, her baby son, to escape a loveless, lonely Queensland marriage, she said. And poverty. Sempre libera, Ursula sings upstairs. The music spills into Marie's flat below.

Helen returned to Melbourne with her baby George, and from there sailed to London where she auditioned for Sullivan of the Savoy. Ah, fors'e lui. Is he the one I dream about? No dear, no vacancies this season, but perhaps a small part in *The Mikado* next year, the Maestro said.

So then to Paris where she sang a top E, pure and pianissimo for Mathilde Marchesi. Helen clenched her fists in the folds of her dress, bit her lip and held her breath while she waited for the Parisienne to speak, because she knew her top E was good. Ah, this is the one I've been waiting for, Marchesi said. At last I have a star.

More lessons and a debut in Brussels as Gilda in *Rigoletto*. Soon sapphires, diamonds, rubies, pearls for this single mother from Melbourne with the most perfectly conformed throat. But by now, her real name is Nellie as in Melba and she's about to meet her Alfredo: Louis Philippe, Duc d'Orléans, who's also known as Tip, the exiled great-grandson of the last king of France and Pretender to the throne. Tip is twenty years old and Nellie is twenty-nine. Ah, fors'e lui che l'anima solinga ne'tumulti godea sovente pingere de' suoi colori occulti? she sings. He's the one my soul, lonely in the tumult, secretly imagined ...

OK boys, the truce is passed, Anonymous Alexie the banker says. Time to pay up for the last round before we go on to the next. He looks at Heinrich of Athens. By my reckoning, you've got a hundred ships ravaging the Peloponnesian coast, another hundred guarding Attica, Euboea and Salamis, and around fifty blockading Potidaea and Lesbos. According to the rules of this game, that's 2000 talents you owe treasury for your ships and then there's your sea costs at 400 talents per operation. Plus your land forces. Two drachmae per day per hoplite for besieging Potidaea, for instance: now that'd have to be at least another 3000 talents. And Mytilene, what have you got there? A thousand heavy infantry? That's another hundred talents, plus the cost of getting your men to Lesbos. And all those skirmishes in Thrace and the Peloponnese. And what about your lines of communication to the Black Sea? The rules say if they're broken you owe the treasury another 1500 talents per game turn because you can't get your wheat and timber and slaves out through the Euxine, but the lines seem clear so far.

He looks at Anonymous John. How come you haven't pulled off a few more insurrections along the coasts of Thrace and Ionia or the Hellespont, mate, to slow this bastard down? Is Lesbos all you've got?

I'm not going to be provoked into revealing my strategy, Anonymous John says and lights another Gitane.

Good for you, Anonymous Alexie says as he deducts 6500 talents from the Athenian treasury. That takes you right down to your emergency fund, he says to Heinrich. You're just about broke, mate.

Looks like I'll have to impose a new tax then, Heinrich says. A property tax, say, or a tax on goods and services so all those war-boomers get to pay their fair share. They're the only ones with any money these days! And an extra levy on my allies too, really hassle the ones who're slow to pay. Like with Wehrmacht and jackboots!

Ah, the isles of Greece, the isles of Greece! Where burning Sappho loved and sang, says Anonymous Carlos of Persia.

A knock on the back door. It's open. Can I come in? Denis says. Marie's in her bedroom sorting out her past. Yeah, sure, she says amid the clothes and junk that are spread across her floor: one grandfather's tie from before he died, a 1960s crotcheted granny shawl that her mother once wore, a length of golden sari silk, an old shirt she borrowed from her father and never returned, a fake fur stole that never felt quite right, a pile of knickers that've seen much better days, a straw hat from a more nostalgic phase, three pairs of laddered black opaques, her favourite little mini kilt — I wonder if that still fits me, she says to herself as she holds it to her waist …

I've never seen you in a skirt before, Denis says from the doorway.

Marie spins around and blushes. This one's from when I was trying to look sexy, she says, but I don't think it ever worked!

You always look sexy, he says. And this bed! It's a-mazing. When I saw all that old timber on your floor I thought you were mad! And it stank of sheep shit!

Yeah, well perhaps I was mad, Marie says. I still haven't finished the damn room yet because there's all this stuff I've got to find space for. Like where did it all come from? All these old clothes! And look at those books I've still got to get on the shelves …

I never have that problem, Denis says. I move around too much. But it looks like I won't be moving around much more.

What do you mean?

These lumps.

How long since you've seen your doctor?

About a month. She said I was OK then. Like my T-count was down a bit but …

Marie puts an arm around him. What a shit, she says.

Yeah, Denis says.

You wanna cup of coffee?

Yeah, he says.

She goes into the kitchen.

Hey, what's this? Denis says from the bedroom. Is it real?

Marie turns around. Denis has draped himself in her old fur stole. No, fake, she says. Don't know where it came from. I must have picked it up in an op shop in one of my weaker moments.

I just love it, Denis says. And these boots! And this hat!

Marie laughs. You look — unspeakable, she says.

Is that bad or good?

I think you look fucking beautiful. But darling, where's your make-up!

Oh, shit, Denis says. Have you got any lippy? Pink, I think. Or bright red? I'll worry about the lumps tomorrow.

Marie kisses him on the cheek. Denis, you are one of the most amazing people I've ever known, she says. The lippy's in the bathroom drawer. And the hat and fur are yours. If you want them, that is! But I'm keeping the boots!

IT'S late. Ursula's on her third cream sherry. There's a sticky circle beside the keyboard of her baby grand. Act II, Scene II. Her fingers glide across the ivory, the ebony in Allegro moderato. Urns of weeping ferns and flowers. White camellias, magnolias, azaleas. Marble statues of Venus and Aphrodite. Mirrors with big lush golden frames. And Verdi's floor show, the obligatory ballet. Romany fortune tellers dancing in bright twirling skirts decorated with tinkling bells. Gypsies, Slavs, Jehovah's Witnesses, Gays and Jews, Ursula says to no one in particular. We're all Romanies from far away. Noi siamo zingarelle venute da lontano.

D'ognuno sulla mano leggiamo l'avvenir. Se consultiam le stelle null'avvi a noi d'oscuro e i casi del futuro possiamo altrui predir. Vediamo! Voi, signora.

We can read people's fortunes from the palms of their hands.

When we consult the stars, nothing is hidden from us because we have the power to predict the future.

A whole chorus fills her tiny flat, a whole dance troupe of Romany women swirling and whirling and beating their tambourines. A veil hides what's happened in the past, they're singing. What's been has been, think only of what's to come … Già quel ch'è stato è stato, badate (badiamo) all'avvenir.

And now the men. A troop of Spanish matadors. Five bulls in a single day. Cinque tori. Con tai prove i mattadori san le belle conquistar! With such feats, we conquer beautiful women! they're singing. Matador, Minotaur, Tauromachia, Taormina, that little village on Sicilia's cliffs … Ma qui son più miti i cori; a noi basta folleggiar. But here it's enough for us to frolic. Si, Si, let's frolic then, Ursula and her guests are singing. Si, allegri. With carefree gaiety. But before we do, we'll test Fortuna's humour …

Two marble statues emerge from the wall and between them, a gaming room opens. The baron leads Ursula towards the tables. But there's Alfredo … Cielo! Il vedo, Ursula says, in Violetta's words. I see him. The baron squeezes her arm. You will not say a single word to him, or even look at him, he sings to her. Not one word! Not one glance.

HEINRICH had thought Lesbos would be a pushover. He'd planned his invasion for the day the people of Mytilene were to honour Apollo at the Malea temple outside the city walls — but Mytilene's spies in Athens had sent a warning, so the festival was postponed. Heinrich ordered the troops in anyway, one thousand heavily armed Athenian hoplites with full military support. After a few inconclusive skirmishes and some minor coastal ravaging, the hoplites set about methodically deforesting the island to build a fortified wall while the Athenian navy interdicted all vessels approaching Mytilene's ports. Heinrich's plan was to starve this former ally into submission, as he had done with Potidaea.

The roaring winds from across the mass of Asia that hovers off this island's eastern coast blew even harder as the siege tightened. The people of Mytilene grew hungrier every day. Soon there was counter-revolutionary gossip in the streets about the ruling oligarchs and their secret food caches. People began building barricades and arming themselves with guns. But there were other voices in this crisis, quiet whispers at the public wells where the women went for water, at the hearths where they spun and wove, in the temples and schools where they practised charis or grace, their arts of music, drawing, dancing, poetry, philosophy, and womanly love in all its most tender, compassionate, and sensual manifestations. For in Lesbos, women have always sought their own satisfaction, their own freedom.

When I gaze at you my sisters, I can no longer speak, Sappho sings. My voice is silent, my flesh burns, I cannot see, my ears are ringing; sweat pours from my brow, and I tremble all over ...

She glances through her window at the armed men in uniform marching down her street. The notes of her lyre choke silent from her fingers and a new trembling seizes her. So why bother defending our city if all we'll be doing is repeating the past? she says.

ALFREDO strides towards the gaming table as Ursula turns the page. Her notes are tense. Fast. Un quattro! Alfredo says. A four! He glares at the baron. The baron glares back. Frenatevi, o vi lascio, Ursula sings to him. Restrain yourself, or I'll leave you. She turns away. What will happen? Pietà, gran Dio, di me! she sings in just a whisper. Take pity, dear God, take pity on me!

A hundred louis on the right, the baron is singing.

On the left, a hundred.

Ace, jack, Alfredo wins.

Double?

Good, double.

The cards are dealt. A four. A seven.

Ancora! He wins again!

Ursula pours another sherry. In the mirror, a servant is announcing dinner. A table of polished mahogany. Silver cutlery, crystal, the finest porcelain glistening in the candle-light. Trails of ivy and camellias, big bowls of fruit. Bottles of sparkling wine in ornate silver buckets. Yarra Valley methode champenoise. But Alfredo's in danger. She beckons to him.

Mi chiamaste? You called me? he sings. What do you want?

Leave this place. Questi luoghi abbandonate.

I shall leave, but first promise that you'll follow me wherever I go.

Ah, no, never. Giammai. Go! Forget a name which is tainted, Ursula sings. Go — flee this instant. I swore a sacred oath to leave you. Un giuramento sacro.

To whom? A chi potea?

Someone who had the right.

Was it the baron?

Si.

Dunque l'ami? You love him then?

Ebben ... l'amo. I love him.

Alfredo explodes through the mirror. Or tutti a me, he sings. Everyone — come here!

Ne appellaste? Che volete?

He points accusingly. You don't know what she's done ... Che facesse non sapete ...

Ah, taci! Ursula sings. Be silent. Her old fingers are dancing more slowly now, her every knuckle is aching and the gold ring on her finger has never felt so tight.

Ogni suo aver tal femmina per amor mio sperdea, Alfredo is

singing. This woman was about to lose everything she owns because of her love for me and I, thoughtless, cowardly, destitute, could accept it all. But there's still time! Ma è tempo ancora! I want to wipe out this stain. I've called you here to witness that I've settled my account with her …

Wooden chairs scraping across the floor in Ursula's tiny apartment, crystal glasses spilling methode champenoise … Oh, infamia orribile tu commettesti! her guests are singing. Un cor sensibile così uccidesti! What a dreadful infamy you've committed! To kill this sensitive heart! Go away, you vile man, you fill us with horror. Di qua allontanati, ne desti orror!

Alfredo collapses against the piano. Ah sì — che feci! What have I done? Ne sento orrore. I fill myself with horror …

Raging jealousy and disillusioned love tear at my soul — I've lost my sanity. She can never forgive me now. I tried to escape her but it wasn't possible! I came here on impulse and now that I've vented my anger, I'm sick with remorse — oh, wretch that I am.

Gelosa smania deluso amore mi strazian l'alma — più non ragiono. Da lei perdono più non avrò. Volea fuggirla — non ho potuto! Dall'ira spinto son qui venuto! Or che lo sdegno ho disfogato, me sciagurato! — remorso n'ho.

⊷⊶

CHORDS LIKE TIDES waiting for the moon, Giuseppina Strepponi says as she sight-reads her lover Giuseppi Verdi's new opera on her piano at Sant'Agata. Allargando e diminuendo e allargando e … Ah, here's where he'll put the cellos in …

Her nose is dribbling again. She sniffs and lifts one hand from the keyboard to find a handkerchief. Once I could have sung this as well as anyone, she says, when I had my voice. But these years with Verdi mean more to me than all the praise my voice could bring.

Another melody is emerging from her fingers: Ah fors'è lui che l'anima solinga ne' tumulti, she sings, solinga ne' tumulti, godea sovente pingere de'suoi colori occulti! Ah, he is the one my soul, lonely in the tumult, secretly imagined in such soft, romantic colours! A quell' amore quell' amor ch'è palpito dell' universo, dell' universo intero, misterioso, misterioso, altero, croce, croce e delizia, croce e delizia, delizia al cor. Love, the very pulse of the universe, mysterious and noble, both crucifix and joy of the heart. Croce e delizia, delizia al cor.

This music is the only colour to Sant'Agata's lonely monotone. Snow is falling on the trees outside her studio window, the sycamore they planted for *Rigoletto*, the oak for *Il Trovatore*, the weeping willow for *La Traviata*. And those vines and fruit trees we pruned last month, how can those bare skeletons ever bloom again? she says. If he were home ... But he's in Venice trying to stop those marketing executives from turning Violetta into a period piece. Louis XIV, would you believe!

Ah, my poor Pasticcio, do they think that seeing a diva dressed as a contemporary courtesan would corrupt their morals? Because every woman knows the truth, that at every performance of every opera in every opera house in the world, every woman in the audience is a Violetta. We've all been there before. She sniffs, coughs; but I feel so stifled here, she says. I've got to get outside.

She goes to the kitchen, puts on her farm boots, which she keeps at the kitchen door, borrows her lover's woollen work coat, collects some apples from the cook, and braces herself for the cold. Her ponies, Solfarin and Menafiss, whinny from the stables. She gives them each an apple and feels their soft velvet lips on the palms of her hands, their hot steamy breaths, the wetness of saliva mixed with apple juice. She strokes them both and lets them nuzzle her again. Yes, you miss him too, don't you, my darlings, she says. Then goes back into the house to write.

⊯ ⊯

Sant'Agata
23 February 1853

My poor Wizard, how painful it was for me to see you these recent days, working like a Negro and having the additional [burden] of seeing me ill — you cannot imagine! But it will be well again and I will try with my good humour to make you forget the troubles of the past. You are so good to your Long-Term Tenant, and I am desolate that I cannot repay you for everything you do for me! ... Write when you can; hurry up with the rehearsals; and come back to your hut.

SHOPPING day and Marie, Elle and Sophie are wheeling a Safeway trolley around the most fundamental questions about the future of the world. Is bleached toilet paper made from office waste better than unbleached from plantation pulp? Is brown paper packaging better than plastic? Does shampoo have phosphates in it, and what does it do to the bay? They stop at the household detergents. This is where I feel like giving up, Marie says. I'm trained as an architect for Christ's sake, not as a biochemist. I haven't a clue how to assess the ecological impact of all these things.

But what about the dolphins? Sophie says.

That's tinned fish you've got to worry about dolphins with, Elle says.

Yeah, but they're washing up on the beaches of the Mediterranean so contaminated they have to be disposed of as toxic waste, Marie says.

Look, this is fucking Saturday morning and I've just got up! Elle says. We're doing the groceries right, and sure, I'm feeling really

⊯ 135 ⊯

guilty that we're not doing it at South Melbourne markets, or Friends of the Earth, or even the local food co-op, so just now I don't want to know about toxic dolphins!

Me neither, Marie says, and moves to the cheese and yoghurt. Is Gippsland organic mild better than Jalna skim milk natural with no added chemicals or preservatives? Can you recycle the plastic container and anyway, what do they do with all the cow shit at the dairy? Do they use it for biogas and fertiliser, or do they just pollute the nearest creek? She chooses Jalna because it's cheaper and less fattening and dismisses all the other fundamental questions as too hard.

Elle and Sophie are still at the biscuit shelves arguing about chocolate-coated teddy bears. Marie leaves them there and joins the checkout queue to browse through the women's mags on the rack and catch up on the latest gossip about Princess Di. She lets a man with a tin of Whiskas pass her while she skims through *Woman's Day*. It'll give me something to talk about with Daphne, she says in response to Elle's raised eyebrow.

SOPHIE won the argument about the chocolate-coated teddy bears and opens the pack as soon as she reaches Acland Street. Lilith must be doing one of her Saturday mornings with her refugees at Scheherazade's, Elle says, because there's Abelard waiting outside. Sophie rushes towards him. Abelard wags his tail, his whole body when he sees her. Sophie offers him a chocolate-coated teddy bear. Lillian watches from inside the cafe, frowns a less-than-serious protest and beckons Elle, Sophie and Marie to join her. Sophie elects to stay outside to share her teddy bears with Abelard.

... but the one I liked best was Sous les pavés la plage, one of Lillian's now-greying companions is saying as Marie and Elle enter the cafe. Beneath the pavement, the beach.

It's nostalgia time again, Lillian says as the young women make themselves comfortable. We're reminiscing about our favourite graffiti. Mine was Prenes vos désires pour des réalities! Take your desires for reality. I nearly wept when I saw that scrawled across a wall for the first time.

Or what about La liberté est le crime qui contient tous les autres. Elle est notre arme absolue, someone else says. Remember? Freedom is the crime that contains all others. It's our major weapon.

Or L'imagination au pouvoir! says Lillian.

One of the refugees winks conspiratorially to Marie. All this because boys weren't allowed into the girls' dormitories in the university colleges! he says.

Lillian rises to the bait. What rot! she says. Don't you remember how the universities and schools were in France before sixty-eight? Hardly changed since Napoleon's time! And the Left was just as out of touch! Which is why, by May, there were a million people in the streets demanding change.

Yes, but they were halcyon days, the conspirator responds. A bursting economy, very low unemployment, and the Vietnam War to give people a bit more than themselves to think about. You'd never get a million people in the streets now, Lil. Young people these days … He glances apologetically at Marie and Elle.

As far as I can see, the main difference is that young people today are smart enough to know that barricades and good graffiti are not enough! Lillian says in her most didactic lecturer's tone. And they have a sense of the planet as a whole that your generation never had.

Well, that ends nostalgia for today! the conspirator says as he nervously taps his fingers on Scheherazade's table.

Marie ignores the tension. But were you at the barricades, Lilith? she says.

Lillian relaxes again and grins. La Place Denfert-Rochereau with my students! The cops waited till two in the morning to fire the first round of tear gas but the wind was on our side and blew it all away! You should have heard the cheers! In the end, it was the same old story though: the blood-rimmed tide of innocence is loosed and everywhere the ceremony of innocence is drowned, as Yeats once said.

At least we had something to believe in then, says another refugee. At least we had ideals.

~ — ~

Rows of young wheat in the paddocks, bunches of blossoms on the trees, buds and creeping tendrils on the once bare vines. They're walking Sant'Agata's furrows now, and in the distance they can hear the cannon fire. Is it one of ours, do you think? Giuseppina Strepponi says.

Who knows from here? says Giuseppe Verdi. Sounds like it's near Cremona. That's where they say the next big one'll be. Tens of thousands of soldiers trampling across wheat crops like this one of ours ...

They hear the cannon again, see smoke across the river.

Someone's farm has been hit, or another village, Giuseppina says. How can people slaughter one another on a glorious day like this? Do you think the Austrians will really dynamite Piacenza?

Only if they're losing, Giuseppe says. They've already destroyed anything that'd be of any strategic value to us around here. He lifts his telescope and unconsciously hums a line from his *Vepres Siciliennes*. There they are, across the Arda, he says. From here they look like toy soldiers.

He passes the telescope to Giuseppina. When I was a baby, it was the armies of the Holy Alliance fighting Napoleon's troops across these plains, and my mother and me hiding in the village church, he says. The Austrians claimed Italia was only a geographical expression then and nothing to be taken seriously! If you were writing an opera … He kicks a clod of earth towards the river.

My son Camillo would be old enough to fight by now, Giuseppina says from her own furrow. I keep hoping he'll find me, but I know it's better that he doesn't. And your son, if he'd survived …

Verdi kicks another clod. Everyone's son, he says. We sow our seed and then …

Another clod across another furrow.

A whole family was executed the other day, he says. The Austrians thought one of them was reporting troop movements to our side.

They tread their tracks in silence until Giuseppina speaks. Do you think Italia's worth dying for? she says.

Isn't death all there is in life? says Giuseppe.

HEINRICH had thought Lesbos would be a pushover. It wasn't, but in the end it didn't matter because he had the biggest guns. After the capitulation, the Lesbians requested leave to plead for mercy before the Athenian Assembly. I'm a demokrat after all, Heinrich had said, so I'll abide by whatever demokratia decrees.

And so the delegation sails the Aegean to address the imperial marketplace. Their words are heard in silence and are followed by boos and jeers. A leather manufacturer, war-boom rich, jumps onto the podium. His name is Citizen Cleon. Mytilene was our ally, he says. We treated you well but still you rebelled, so don't look to us for mercy. What we have to do now is teach you a lesson that no so-called ally will ever forget. Kill all the men, and sell all the women and children into slavery! he says. And let these envoys be the first to die.

His fellow demokrats cheer. Cleon grins, clicks his heels, thrusts an arm into the air. Kill them, kill them, kill them, the demokrats chant as the Lesbians are led away. Almost immediately, a galley is launched for Lesbos with demokratia's decree.

A hush over this tyrant city as those who remained silent reflect upon their crime. Why have we let this happen? they say. Many good citizens are unable to sleep that night. Many good women refuse to let them. In the morning an emergency meeting is called in the marketplace. Again Cleon speaks. You are all wimps, he says. All that binds our empire together is our strength. Any pity you show our allies now will be interpreted as weakness and will only encourage others to rebel. Mytilene's revolt was deliberate and wanton, an attempt to ruin us by siding with our bitterest enemy. It was completely unjustified. I say the decision we made yesterday should stand. Punish the Lesbians as they deserve, and show the world that the penalty for rebellion is death.

A hum in the marketplace as Citizen Diodotus, one of those who could not sleep last night, climbs onto the podium. Citizen Cleon is too hasty, too narrow-minded, too short-sighted in considering the matter of Mytilene, he says. The question before us is not their guilt but our best interests. The people of Mytilene may deserve to be punished, but will that stop other cities from rebelling? I doubt it. Many states have enacted the death penalty but people still offend, and subject peoples still rebel. So let's not be foolish enough to make it impossible for those who rebel to change their minds — while they can still pay us an indemnity and be useful to us. Cleon's policy would compel every rebellious city to hold out to the uttermost and leave us nothing but ruins. And what use are ruins to Athens? Diodotus says.

The citizens vote. The leaders of the revolt will be tried by firing squad and everyone else can live — but as a subject people. And so another galley sails across the Aegean with another Athenian decree. The sailors row till their hearts are ready to burst to save their Lesbian cousins. They sleep in shifts, eat a few barley cakes kneaded in olive oil and wine, and then row some more. They dock at Mytilene just as Heinrich is reading the first decree. Hey wait! the galley captain screams. Hey, wait a minute ...

THE phone rings in Marie's bedroom. Wow, I was just thinking about you, she says into the receiver. Yeah, it'd be lovely to see you too. Dinner? OK, when? Friday at Monroe's? Fine, I'll meet you there ...

A tremor as she returns the phone to its cradle. Why does he make me feel like this? she says as she unconsciously slides her hand under her jumper. It's like we're already familiars, like we don't even have to speak. But I wouldn't want to live with him, I mean I wouldn't want to be a couple with all those proprietorial rights. Separate apartments maybe, but close enough so you could ask for love and sex and companionship whenever you needed it. Or a massage, she says as she slides her hand across her breast to the back of her neck. Because that's what I need more than anything else right now, a long and lingering full-body massage. With lavender oil. My neck, my back, my legs, the soles of my feet, between my toes. His fingers all oiled and soft and fragrant sliding back up my legs, my thighs, my ... but why's he so far away? Hurry up Friday night!

THEY go to Vienna, Nellie and her Tip, and take a box at the opera to watch one of her rivals sing Elsa in that Wagner piece, *Lohengrin*. Next day, the headlines: prima donna and her toy boy; Duc d'Orléans and his mistress. They sell newspapers like Diana and her James, Camilla and her Charles, Fergie and her Texan. Kangaroo Charlie wants to shoot a duel with the young duke but says he'll accept a settlement instead — because by law Nellie is still his property and his property has been stolen. For Nellie there's no defence, nor for her young Tip. His family sends him on a long and lonely safari to Africa followed by a long dynastic marriage to the Archduchess Maria Dorothea of Hungary, daughter of the Pretender to the Austro-Hungarian throne. No heirs are ever born of this union; perhaps Tip and Maria Dorothea never fucked. And Nellie? She keeps singing. Sempre libera ...

Elle is late — she always is. Marie's waiting for her at Leo's cafe. Three blokes are talking at the gelati bar about the shade of green the skinny one is painting his house with. Brunswick green. A doctrinaire heritage colour like the terribly authentic baby-poo brown the Council has painted the pavilion with at the end of St Kilda pier. The house painter's hands corroborate his story: Brunswick green is under his fingernails, around his quicks and etched into every line of his palms. Heritage colours, heritage minds, Marie says as she stares out the window into Fitzroy Street. She wants them to be talking the colours of the future, not these shades from the past. But they never do.

The younger one's a poet. He pulls a notebook from his jacket and claims the next pause. Unicorns sipping celestial pearls ... he reads. A daughter conceived in nylon nights ... All but these brave lines are drowned in the space between the tables. Marie collects them with the froth from her coffee. She doesn't see Elle slide into the spare seat, only feels a touch on her arm.

You're miles away, Elle says. Don't tell me! It's that bloody guy from Sydney you had dinner with last night.

Actually I was thinking of something else just then, Marie says in monotone. But yeah, that guy from Sydney. He raped me.

What? Elle says.

Well, it wasn't like he did it in the street, or beat me up, or held me down. I mean, it wasn't anything like you'd read about in the *Herald-Sun*, or call the cops for. But we went back to my place after dinner, we were just talking, touching one another, you know, then he pulled my knickers down and stuck it in like he couldn't wait. Without a condom. I mean, he just assumed — you know …

Fuck! Elle says as she signals Dominic for her first cappuccino of the day and a second for Marie. But what man hasn't done that at some time in his life, and what woman hasn't let him! That's how I got Sophie … But of course I wouldn't turn history back now, even if I could.

ANOTHER toss of the die in Heinrich's second bedroom, another rebellion against the United States of Athens. This time an attempted coup led by five colonels and their oligarch mates on the island of Corcyra off Greece's Adriatic coast, near the border with Albania.

Oh good, Corfu! Anonymous John says as he reaches for a rebellion-marker. I've always wanted to go there.

Almost immediately, boatloads of refugees flood into the Mediterranean. President Pethias, the leader of the Corcyra People's Party, is arrested, charged, and subjected to a show-trial for a ritual crime against the state, that of enslaving Corcyra to the tyrant yoke of Athens. He's acquitted and rallies his People's Party to accuse his accusers of a crime against the deities: that of cutting young Aleppo pines from the sanctuaries of Zeus and Alcinous, for vine stakes! Or so Thucydides says.

The colonels are arrested, tried, found guilty by President Pethias's court and fined one stater per Aleppo pine — which they claim they can't afford and could they pay in instalments please? President Pethias insists on the full letter of the law. The colonels are rich landowners and this is politics after all, he says. And now to the business of the day, that alliance with Athens. All those in favour …

A hush descends on the gallery of the Senate. Because the colonels are voting too. With guns and bayonets. President Pethias is the first to fall. Which is why Anonymous John is sailing to the

Adriatic in a Corinthian destroyer, and why Heinrich is already waiting off the coast on one of his aircraft carriers.

On the island itself, the supporters of the People's Party have taken refuge in the acropolis and around one of the city's two harbours. Their leaders promise anything to anyone who'll fight. Even Liberty, Fraternity and Equality. Even Peace, Land and Bread. And even to rural slaves and women. The oligarchs on the other hand, offer hard currency. In return they get well-equipped mercenaries from the mainland and booty from miscellaneous other war-profiteers — plus Anonymous John's military aid from the Peloponnesian League. But it isn't enough, not against populist rhetoric. By dusk the city is ablaze and the colonels and their oligarchs are seeking sanctuary in Hera's temple.

Next morning a delegation from the People's Committee of Public Safety visits the temple and promises a fair trial to any oligarch who'll voluntarily leave. Fifty accept the invitation, are found guilty and guillotined. Those remaining in Hera's protection hang themselves in the sacred enclosure with strips of their own tunics. By evening an oligarch is dangling from every sacred tree.

Outside the temple grounds, the all-too-human Terror. You have to step over decapitated bodies of children, the man from Reuters says. Eight-year-olds, six-year-olds, two-year-olds. You trip over their heads in the grass, chopped clean through with machetes while they were running away, and dogs and cats eating their flesh. Little girls' heads with their hair still tied back with brightly coloured ribbons, and their parents slashed to pieces in the streets or thrown alive into pits of burning tyres and covered up so us journalists couldn't see. People herded into sports stadiums, machine-gunned, bulldozed into mass graves, or allowed to die slowly. Pregnant women with their bellies slashed open, men tied up and their genitals cut off and stuffed into their mouths, or their feet amputated with axes so they bleed to death as they drag themselves away.

The Kagera River is clogged with bloated bodies, the CNN reporter says. I've counted three hundred floating by in the last hour towards Lake Victoria 250 kilometres downstream. Hundreds of bodies are already washed up on the shore. Neighbours are killing neighbours, she says. Husbands killing wives. Brothers killing brothers. Fathers killing their sons and daughters. Half a million people, maybe more, butchered in the past month. Why? And what has happened to us that we've let this occur?

Death raged in every shape, Thucydides says in his account of the war. The most dreadful examples of the most dreadful crimes: of reprisals exacted by the governed who had never experienced equitable treatment or indeed aught but insolence from their rulers; of the iniquitous resolves of those who desired to get rid of their accustomed poverty, of the savage and pitiless excesses into which men who had begun the struggle, not in a class but in a party spirit, were hurried by their ungovernable passions. There was no length to which violence did not go, he says. Words had to change their ordinary meaning. Reckless daring came to mean the courage of a loyal ally; prudent hesitation the excuse of the coward; moderation was held to be a cloak for unmanliness; ability to see all sides of a question [as a sign of] inability to act on any. Frantic violence became the attribute of manliness and the lover of violence was always trusted — while anyone who opposed him was always suspect. Until even blood became a weaker tie than party, and revenge held of more account than self-preservation, Thucydides says. Until the whole world was engulfed in madness.

IT was on the couch, Marie says. We were just talking. Well, more than that. He sat down next to me, close like, and started stroking the nape of my neck. I was mesmerised, I guess. I knew what was happening but it was like a movie and I wanted to know what would happen next. It was like I was completely detached, like a zoologist observing the mating behaviour of a new species. But his fingers were so soft, so sensual, Elley. I felt him undoing my buttons and still I said nothing. Then he stroked my nipple. Well, how can you stop your nipples reacting! He told me I had beautiful breasts. He kissed them. Sucked them. But I hardly knew the man, Elle, nothing about him, except that I'd met him in Sydney. We'd chatted, talked about his work. My work. About his latest book. He took it for granted I'd read his stuff. I hadn't, of course. Never heard of him. Then he rang to say he'd be in Melbourne and could we do coffee, and the next time he was in town it was dinner.

Look, I remember what you were like when you got back from that conference, Elle says. You had the hots for the guy, admit it! You really liked him. He would've picked up all that non-verbal stuff like you were shouting it at him.

Just because I found him cute and he thought my tits were nice, I mean, it's hardly justification for pulling my knickers off and sticking it in!

But it's not like he forced you, or you jumped up and screamed at the first stroke of your neck. Or even said no.

Elle, you're not being very helpful. There's a big gap between that and fucking me. It may be academic to you — and to him, even to a jury, but … oh shit. Look, he didn't do it with my consent. I felt like a whore. Like he'd paid for me along with dinner — which I said I'd pay half of anyway, but he said no, he earned more than me. And I didn't want to make a scene. Anyway, I didn't think this still happened. I thought he was enlightened. A reconstructed new age male — if such a creature really exists! And I just wasn't ready …

But did he come? Elle says.

Well, actually no! I rolled him off and his dick shrivelled up to about five centimetres long!

The two women look at one another and spontaneously burst into laughter. Hey, Dom, pull us a couple more cappuccini, Elle says towards the espresso bar.

All this stuff is so confusing! Marie says. I mean, I really liked him, but I didn't want it to be that way. What am I going to do?

THAT was the year Plato was born. The year the plague visited Athens again, the year the Peloponnese was shaken by earthquakes, the year a tsunami swamped the islands and the mainland coast, and the year of the 88th Olympiad in Heinrich's second bedroom.

Plato. Mother Perictione, father Ariston. Rich, well-connected. Two elder brothers, Adeimantus and Glaucon, and one sister, Potone. Ariston died while Plato was still sucking his wet nurse's breasts and Perictione remarried. Soon a half-brother called Antiphone who, Plato said, spent most of his time playing polo.

Perictione's new husband was her uncle Pyrilampes, a demokrat and close friend of Pericles, the wealthy general who made a reputation as an orator in Athens' market place. He was particularly famous for the funeral speeches Aspasia of Miletos wrote for him. He and Aspasia were lovers until he died of a random event during the last Athenian plague.

Perictione's other uncle, Charmides, as well as her cousin Critias both disapproved of her second marriage. They were oligarchs and friends of Socrates but their story is yet to come.

The men who get to tell the history of this time will call it the fifth century. Some will add the suffix BC, others, the more enlightened, will write BCE for Before the Current Era. They'll wax lyrical, these apologists, about how great the fifth century was, but it was no time for a kid to be born, especially not a philosopher kid like Plato. And the demokratia he was born into was very selective, even in its best years — though there weren't too many of those. It was OK if you were a citizen because then you could make speeches in the marketplace and raise your hand to vote. You could even get elected to public office, draft foreign policy or become a general if enough people voted for you. But most people, those who were too poor, or slaves, or serfs, or resident aliens, or barbarians, couldn't, and nor could us women because these sons of Theseus had done a deal with Poseiden. Or was it Zeus? Or Apollo? They got him to legislate from Mount Olympus that women couldn't vote. Or own property. Or pass on their mothers' names. Or learn to read and write. Or participate in or, some say, even attend athletic games or theatre performances. Or have a career. Or drive a car. Or open their own bank accounts. Or choose their sexual partners. Or enjoy any freedom at all really — except the freedom to obey.

From that moment, women too became a subject race. Soon Plato's student Aristotle would write in his *Poetics* that women may be said to be inferior beings, mere vessels indeed for male seed. For millennia, many people believed him. Even many women.

⇥ ⇤

The Ritz Hotel
Piccadilly
Tuesday 25th March, 1919
Evening

My dear Nellie, what can I tell you of the tender emotion that I have felt again after so many years? It seemed to me that it was yesterday that I said au revoir to you and that I found myself near to you the same, in spite of the age I then had nearly thirty years ago.

I was so happy to find you inspite of your sufferings moral and physical, the same Nellie who has never changed and who remains in my life, sometimes so sad, the only constant and faithful friend towards whom — even in the delirium of death that I so closely escaped — my soul and heart reached across space. For you know me and understand me! In spite of all the world has done to separate the one from the other. I am satisfied because the confidence you gave me is my recompense. Thank you for the few moments in which you have really made me happy in evoking the past years of my youth that I have relived through you and with you. I count the minutes that separate me from the moment when I will see you tomorrow evening, I hope for longer than this evening? I have so many things to say to you that I cannot write. But that tomorrow evening will come of themselves from my lips when I am near to you. I hope you will give me time to tell you all that I have in my heart. Meanwhile, my dear Nellie, I kiss most affectionately your pretty hands and am always your old

Tipon

I kiss most affectionately your pretty hands, my only constant and faithful friend. Through you, I relive the past, the years of my youth. My Violetta, my soul, my heart reaches out to you ... The notes seep through the floorboards like years into Marie's flat below. And then he dies. Of pneumonia in Sicily. The year is 1926.

BUT she dies too, this divina, in February 1931 at St Vincent's Private Hospital, Sydney, Australia, from a facelift that was botched up in Europe. Only the hospital staff and her embalmer see the pus leaking from the scars. Lie about my disfigured face, Dame Nellie says. Make me young and beautiful again.

She takes her final bows on the Melbourne Express. A special viewing window is fitted to the carriage and her coffin is covered in red roses. Thousands of people line the tracks, the streets to the kirk her father built, and the whole of Melbourne stops to say goodbye. They bury her in flowers at a place called Lilydale and on her tomb are engraved the words she sang as Mimi in *La Bohème*, that Puccini piece. Addio se za rancore. I leave with no regrets.

But legends never leave because upstairs Ursula is singing her back into life and Marie's grandmother saw her once in Ballarat. We followed her back to the hotel after the concert, she said, we stood under her balcony and shouted that we wanted to see her, to hear her once more. We want Melba, we want Melba. The French windows opened and there she was in an old dressing gown and a turban that looked like a towel wrapped around her head. All we needed was one small aria but instead this Melba, she abused us. I wish all you buggers'd go home and let me get some bloody sleep, she shouted. The shame we felt, Marie. We cursed her then. My father called her Louis-Philippe's whore, the Duke of Orleans' tart. She was a married woman after all, my dear, and the duke a Catholic. And so public about it too, grandmother said. Though someone told me once that it wasn't Dame Nellie who shouted at us, but a journalist who did it for a laugh. I was only a child at the time. All I remember is what my father said. But yes, she could sing. And she must have made a lovely Violetta.

I⊤'S morning and now she needs to talk to him about what happened on that night. A woman answers. Sorry, he's taking the kids to school, she says. Marie mumbles a message about asking him to return her call, puts the phone down and stares blindly out the window. The number sixteen tram is peak-hour passing with a number ninety-six close behind. Old Jim's at his street bench, he and his Josephine and his racing guide, and someone's ghetto-blasting the footpath with country-and-western music. Mary White and her clan.

Marie grabs her purse, her keys, the morning paper, and leaves. Jeannie is housekeeping her Safeway bags under the staircase. Marie ignores her and old Jim in the street. And the traffic lights. Watch out, sister, a voice calls from the koori camp in the park. A screech of brakes like she's blind and deaf and numb …

The bay is sparkling clichés again, all bobbing boats and gulls. The bay, the beach, the palm trees and Jesus on his steeple reaching out to clutch St Kilda's weak and wounded to his sacred heart. She reaches the end of the pier. The chef in the cafe there is playing Frankie Ifield, a coffee and croissant duet. Three hearts in the fountain, Frankie and the cook are singing, each heart longing for its home. From Marie, three tears. She wipes them with the back of her hand, orders a latte and stares out across the clichés of the bay …

… when somebody loves you, it's no good unless he loves you all the way, Frankie is singing. An old couple passes the pavilion, he carrying fishing rods and fold-up chairs, she pushing a shopping trolley filled with bait, a thermos flask and lunch box like they've been doing this for fifty years. The breeze rises. A young hetero couple passes. Her blonde hair is blowing clichés too. Like Frankie's. Like the sunshine blue of the bay. Like the seagulls. Like his wife and kids in Sydney. And yeah — he didn't tell me, she says. And no, I didn't ask.

THERE was a time before all this, a Time Before People, when ancient forests covered the soils, when the air, the water ran wild and free. The earth remembers.

What's left now is something rather like the skeleton of a body wasted by disease; the rich, soft soil has all run away leaving the land nothing but skin and bone, Plato says in the piece he named for Critias, his mother's most reactionary relative.

As recently as my father's day, or my grandfathers', the rocky plains were covered in rich soil, the mountains in thick forests. The trees provided roof beams for huge buildings, many of which are still standing. People cultivated trees then, unlimited numbers of them in great plantations to produce fodder for their stock, but the only things that grow on those slopes now are spindly herbs for honey bees. The rain runs off the bare earth and erodes it even more, but in those days it was absorbed to filter down from the highest places into the valleys and bubble forth again as springs and rivers, he says. The shrines you see at these now dry springs are proof that what I say is true …

And even the springs that seep from the sacred groves of Delphi, the Womb of Creation beneath the snowy peak of Mount Parnassus, are threatened. Here, drink in remembrance …

They did, the first peoples, they drank and bathed and gave meaning to the earth. Who are we, where have we come from, where are we going to? they asked. Their priestess answered them, she who chewed the sacred laurel leaves to soar high over Mount Parnassus, to float deep within. She said a rainbow serpent whispered in her ear, he who slept at night in the mother's cave and shared her deepest secrets. But then Apollo Shootafar, the sungod son of Zeus, the celestial archer, the blond-maned lion king, claimed Delphi. New peoples, new deities, new words invaded Creation's womb with new questions, new answers, new meanings like an arrow through the serpent's heart. Torn with cruel pain the monster lies shuddering, Hesiod says. He plunges into the forest and twists on the ground, now here, now there, until the moment when, with poisonous breath, he exhales his life in a torrent of blood.

And so Apollo is crowned lord of Delphi. It is he who whispers now the secrets, and his priests who now give prophecy to his words. The earth remembers this conquest. And we women too.

SHE'S walking along the beach alone because she can't yet face her traitor phone at home. Because what is there to say to him if he returns my call? Him with his wife and kids …

A stick lands in the bay. Abelard lumbers past, grabs the stick, bounces up the beach to Marie, deposits the trophy at her feet and shakes himself. The bay spins off his fur like a storm.

Abelard! Come here, damn you! Lillian says as she pulls a large white handkerchief from her trouser pocket to wipe the bay from Marie's face. I've been watching you dragging yourself along the shore, she says. You look as though you've got the weight of the whole world on your shoulders today!

Yeah, Marie says. She picks Abelard's stick up and throws it into the waves. He races after it, then veers to chase a seagull across the sand bar at the mouth of what was once the creek that drained the wetlands that are now Albert Park Lake. The two women walk on in silence to the wooden footbridge. The hollow echo of their feet upon the timber boards.

It reassures me, this little estuary, Lillian says. Just a storm-water channel really, but look at that. Together the two women lean over the railing. Marie sees only a dark soup of plastic bags, dead Coca-Cola bottles and scum.

No, look! Lillian says and points to a school of tiny wiggling shadows struggling against the current to feed on stray food particles that have washed from St Kilda's streets and footpaths. Don't you think that's heroic? she says.

It's a wonder they're still alive, given the crap that must wash down that drain, Marie says.

But they are alive, and even apparently healthy. Although I don't know what they're accumulating in their fatty tissue, or what'd happen to us if we ate too many of them!

The way I'm feeling today I don't really care, Marie says. The whole world can sink into its own toxic waste as far as I'm concerned. It's like we're all of us living in a storm-water drain that was once a pristine creek … Or in Sarejevo, say. This Croatian film critic says Sarejevo is proof that civilisation has failed, that you can't talk about humanity any more with any sense of hope. He says they used to sip coffee and talk all afternoon in the cafes then drive to Vienna for dinner, and now all they've got is irregular food aid, intermittent water from a single public tap, and snipers shooting at them whenever they try to fill their buckets. And this Bosnian journalist, like he's about my age, he reckons his life is over, that the war has made him old. He says he used to want to change the world but now all he wants to do is survive. Well, that's how I feel today, Lilith. Like I just don't care any more.

Lillian puts an arm around Marie's shoulders as they walk, and listens silently as the younger woman unloads her pain. And did you read about Zaire in the paper this morning? Marie says. This President Mobutu, he's one of the richest men in the world and his government can't even pay the army, so the soldiers survive by shooting and looting and raping and pillaging civilians. This relief agency guy calls it the battered-wife syndrome. He says everyone's a victim in Zaire. But how can this happen to a whole country, Lilith? Why hasn't someone shot the bastard? Why hasn't the international community intervened?

See, you do care, Lillian says.

I don't know. All this stuff's so hard, this fucking human condition we're part of. And then there's all that other stuff that's not our fault. Like you're an Indian, right, just going about your business and someone sneezes on you — so next thing, you've got bubonic plague, the medieval Black Death at the end of the twentieth century. Or take that earthquake the other day. Some tectonic plate moves deep inside the earth and whole villages disappear. Thirty thousand people dead, thousands more injured and hundreds of thousands left homeless. Like, they were celebrating some festival of a Hindu deity, Ganesh I think it was, who's meant to bring them good luck! And hi-tech doesn't save you either. Look at Kobe. A sophisticated city in one of the wealthiest nations on earth and in thirty seconds it becomes a heap of wood chips and broken girders. An act of God, they call it. Well, what sort of deity is this, Lilith?

I'd rather think of it as an act of nature, Lillian says. And nature's indifferent to human suffering. Nature just is and we're part of her.

Is HIV nature too? Is Denis maybe dying with AIDS, is that nature? Marie says.

The retrovirus is, but there's an issue there about the consequences of human behaviour — not necessarily Denis's but the behaviour of all of us, Lillian says. It seems HIV is just one of many pathogens that have jumped from one species to another because of the way we're colonising the ecosystems in which they've evolved. I'm afraid it's just one of the laws of the universe that all human actions carry many unexpected consequences, global and local as well as personal ...

You're sounding very judgemental, Lilith. You can be such an obsessive old thing, sometimes, and I mean, I could have AIDS too, just because I had sex with someone I trusted and shouldn't have — though Denis thinks he got his from sharing needles. But he didn't know the consequences then.

Is that why you're so depressed? Because you think you might have AIDS?

A long silence.

Nah, it's not that, Marie says.

Another long silence.

I just found out that a man I really like is married. With kids. And I didn't know.

DELPHI. Warriors are gathering here from all over the Balkans to hunt Heinrich and his men who are hiding at Naupactus on the Corinthian Gulf after being defeated by the mountain people, those barbarian pre-Hellenics who've inhabited these highlands since before even Greek history began. It'll be a picnic, Heinrich had said. Just primitive tribals living in unwalled villages. They don't even wear armour or fight in proper battle formation, just hurl their spears and fire a few arrows, then run away. Or so I've heard. They worship little statues of women with big tits and bums. And someone said they're cannibals, that they eat the flesh of anyone they kill in battle. They'll probably welcome us when they know how good civilisation is.

For some reason the mountain people rejected civilisation. Every time Heinrich and his men entered a village, they found only deserted huts. But the mountain people were watching from their peaks, watching, planning and waiting for the right moment — which came at Aegitium, the next unwalled village.

There's something funny going on here, Heinrich says as he watches the huts of Aegitium burn. Something's not quite right but I can't ... A war scream interrupts and a flash of javelins. An avalanche of half-naked warriors is rushing down the side of the mountain, darts and arrows are tearing through the air.

It wasn't fair, Heinrich says. Every time we got ourselves back into battle formation, they'd attack us from a different angle. My blokes were falling all around me. They'd never experienced anything like it and just panicked and ran into the forest to hide. I never saw most of them again because these fucking natives set fire to the undergrowth to burn my boys out. And for all I know, they ate them. I mean, these motherfuckers were so primitive they didn't even speak Greek ...

And now all these primitives want is for the Athenians and their civilisation to leave their mountains forever. Which is why they've sought an alliance with Anonymous John and his Peloponnesians. Which is why the Peloponnesian army is assembling at Delphi. Which is why John is purifying himself in the sacred spring — though don't ask me why you've got to ladle freezing cold water all over yourself, he says. A meaningless ritual if you ask me. But if it keeps the deities happy ... So he bathes himself in cold water as tradition prescribes, pours the prescribed libations, kneels the prescribed genuflections, sacrifices the prescribed animals, dedicates the prescribed gifts, offers the prescribed bribes, recites the prescribed prayers — then petitions the Pythia for an oracle. Apollo himself whispers the secrets in her ear and his priests interpret her words. Then, confident that Apollo is on Sparta's side, Anonymous John marches his toy soldiers through the sacred mountain passes to Naupactus on the Corinthian Gulf — where he bombs the shit out of Heinrich and his men. Not because he wants to save the mountain tribes but because he too wants Greece's wild, unknown heartland in his hands. Coast to coast control: Phocis, Locris, Aetolia, Acarnania, Epirus, Doris, Thessaly, east into Macedonia and Thrace, and west towards Italia, then across that narrow strait — to Sicily. The Promised Land of pristine forests, deep, rich soils and unfished seas.

He fires a Delphic oracle across the war table in Heinrich's second bedroom. Heinrich ducks and hurls back a grenade.

OK, if you're going to be like that, says Anonymous John, let's toss a coin for her then. We'll let destiny decide.

WHAT am I going to do? Marie says.

Lillian puts an arm around her shoulders. There's nothing I can tell you that you don't already know yourself, my darling Amazon. And I'm sure you don't want me to repeat all those old platitudes about how time heals a wounded heart!

I wouldn't believe you if you did! Marie says. But I feel so unhappy, Lilith, like all my values have been shot to pieces. I seem to have felt every emotion possible since it's all happened, and now I just feel numb.

They cross the wooden footbridge in silence and wander through the reintroduced native grasses on the western bank, the flowering saltbush, the billabong reeds. Oh look! Lillian says, the little succulents we planted are beginning to flower. Now even you would have to admit that revegetating beaches and degraded estuaries is not something people do when they've lost all hope in the future.

You're just trying to distract me! Marie says as she steps between two blushing strands of succulent that are slowly creeping across the once-barren dune. But yeah, it is beautiful, she says. And I guess you're right, Lilith. I do care. And I do want more than to just survive. But right now ...

She bends towards the tiny pink flowers that are bursting from between the fleshy leaves, feels their feather softness, strokes them with her fingertips then stands and stares out to sea. This must've happened to so many of us, she says. This betrayal. And worse. Because on the grand scale of things, it's nothing really, what I'm feeling. Well, not like Zaire or Rwanda or Bosnia or East Timor or Southern Sudan or any of those places. Or Greenhouse. Or AIDS. But why do people do these things, Lilith? And why does it hurt so much?

YES, WHY? And how do these things happen? Like the rise and fall of Rome, the little village on the Tiber that once claimed the Mediterranean as her own. Mare nostrum, her writers always said. Our sea. From the Oceanus Atlanticus to Helle's Pont and her Euxinus, which once great Athens also lusted for. Even Persia's Gulf became a mare nostrum, and that Red Sea between the legs of Aegyptus and Arabia Petaea. But then all Roman seas were red, like those dark pink slashes across Britain's once great maps, or those New World shirts in Uruguay, los camicia rossa. Rossa so the stains from the slaughter house won't show on Montevideo above the Rio de la Plata where Giuseppe Garibaldi is hiding out. Another refugee dreaming of a republic of free and equal men who speak the same language, tread the same earth, are strengthened by the same sun and inspired by the same memories, like his hero Mazzini says. Young Garibaldi wants to fulfil this dream but on his first attempt, he failed. He was captured and escaped by jumping out the prison window to be condemned to death in absentia. He read about it in a cafe in Marseilles — which is why he sailed the Atlanticus to Montevideo in Uruguay.

This is the age of wars of the oppressed against the oppressors, the poet Shelley says. And every one of those ringleaders of the privileged gangs of murderers and swindlers, called sovereigns, look to each other for aid against the common enemy and suspend their mutual jealousies in the presence of a mightier fear. Of this holy alliance all the despots of the earth are virtual members. But a new race has arisen throughout Europe, nursed in the abhorrence of opinions which are its chains, and she will continue to produce fresh generations to accomplish that destiny which tyrants foresee and dread, Shelley says.

In South America, the empires of Spain and Portugal's royal despots are imploding, and from the debris new tyrants are carving out their own — and so Garibaldi becomes a mercenary. In Montevideo in Uruguay a bale of cheap red linen shirts is lying in a warehouse for the workers at the local abattoir. Buy them, Garibaldi says. They'll do as uniforms for my men.

OUTSIDE, a flash at lightning speed and a delayed response of thunder at the speed of sound. Inside, the slow and laboured fall of wood dust as she sands, the incense smell of Murray pines, the lanolin scent of sheep — and Verdi's music still dripping through her ceiling. Piangi, piangi, o misera.

I can't stand this any longer, Marie says. And anyway, it's eleven o'clock at night. What the fuck does Ursula think this is?

Weep, weep poor girl, I see now that I am demanding a very great sacrifice, Alfredo's father is singing. Be brave, and your noble heart will vanquish all. Coraggio — e il nobil tuo cor vincerà!

Be brave and your noble heart will vanquish! What would he know, that bourgeois prick! She lifts her eyes to the ceiling. I don't need all this victim stuff, she says. And why is Ursula so obsessed with this drivel anyway, she and all those other divas who ever did La Trav?

Ah, but my Portuguese cellos, Guilhermina Suggia says from her portrait on the wall, those sweet and bitter harmonies.

Ah! dite alla giovine, Violetta is singing. Tell your daughter, so beautiful and pure, that a woman who has suffered greatly will sacrifice the only ray of light that shines in her life — e che morra. And then will die.

Piangi, o misera, piangi, Alfredo's father is singing.

Ah! dite alla giovine, sings Violetta.

The melodies diverge, converge, diverge again in this most familiar of dialectics, the oppressor and the oppressed.

So tell me what I must do, Violetta sings in her most defeated voice.

Tell him you don't love him.

He won't believe me.

Then go away.

He will follow.

Marie reaches for her cello and begins to play. Breathe with the bow, her teacher always said, intonate with your whole being, your deepest emotions. She's pouring them into Verdi's music now as she plays along with Ursula, piangi, piangi, o misera … Your whole being, your most intimate emotions, all that you've been in the past, all that you hope to become, her teacher is saying. Because music is about relationships through time, single notes, whole chords one after the other in the eternal process of becoming … an opera, a symphony, a song. If you stop playing then all you have is silence, but silence is important too, her teacher says, because silence is where you feel your pain ...

Piangi, piangi, o misera, Alfredo's father is singing. But I just want to hold him, to lie with him again, Marie says. Come and rest beside me on the couch, he said. He held my hand, stroked it, raised it to his lips, so soft, so sweet, so gentle, like Aeneas did on Dido's couch before he founded Rome, or Zeus on Wisdom's, or Ares on Aphrodite's, and even she, a goddess, fell in love. Come, my dear, he said in ancient Greek, let's sit together. He caressed her, kissed her, sucked her breasts, the most perfect breasts I've ever seen, he said, so how could she resist?

Qual figlia m'abbracciate forte cosi sarò, Violetta sings. Embrace me as your daughter so I will be strong.

A change of key, the Portuguese strings, the woodwinds soar. Ah generosa! Alfredo's father sings. O generosa. Marie puts down her cello and writes: Dear Sydney ...

ALCIBIADES, the toy soldier who — on Heinrich's back landing at the beginning of this war, was wearing the ostentatious purple cloak of office instead of the more traditional red — is down at the Piraeus wrestling school again, the all-male gym where Plato goes to meet his hero Socrates. As leader of the pro-war party, Al is a big man in Athenian politics now, and is living way beyond his means. He's sketching a map of the future in the wrestling-ring sand: Libya, Carthage, Sicily, the Italian peninsula, that's what it'll look like, he says. Our western empire. And maybe the Iberian peninsula too, because you can never fix an exact point where the future ends. We've reached a position now where we shouldn't be content to simply retain what we already have, but must scheme to extend it — for if we cease to rule others, we're in danger of being ruled ourselves.

Socrates nods his approval. Yes, my boy, he says, you're really beginning to talk like a statesman now!

Alcibiades smiles and brushes a long strand of hair from his face. But Sicily's the key, he says. Deep, rich volcanic soils, coast to coast forests, and great fishing. They say the tuna just leap into your boat. And the best brood mares in all the Mediterranean. So the sooner we leave the better, as far as I'm concerned.

MORRO! Violetta sings. For I shall die.

No, generosa, vivere, Alfredo's father sings. You must live and be happy. Mercé di queste lagrime dal cielo un giono avrete. One day Heaven will reward these tears ...

But let him know the sacrifice I made, she sings. That the last beat of my heart will be for him. Che sarà suo fin l'ultimo sospiro del mio cor.

Your heart's sacrifice will be rewarded, his father sings. D'un'opra così nobile sarete fiera allor. You'll be proud of the noble thing you've done. Si, si, si ...

No, no, no, Marie says. Dammi tu forza, o cielo! O cielo, give me strength!

WE'LL have the biggest fleet you've ever seen for this expedition! Big Alcibiades is saying as he stuffs his clothes into his gym locker. Athens will be invincible and we'll all get very rich!

His fellow wrestlers are already lounging in the spa. He winks at them, wraps a fluffy white towel around his hips, opens the door and pulls in the nearest flute girl. Oh thou holy goddess! he says to her, Oh thou virgin whore! He rips her chiton off, lets his towel drop onto the floor and tells her to bend over and spread her legs. One thrust, two and ah — I've conquered Sicily! he says.

The spa explodes with splashes and ribald laughter. Al withdraws his cock and wipes it on the girl's dress. He doesn't even wait for his breathing, his pulse to slow. OK then, an orgy at my place to celebrate our impending victory! he says. I'll supply the wine and virgins and you blokes bring the rest.

Big Al's parties are famous in Attica, especially amongst the young aristocrats who spend their time in the polo clubs and gyms. On this occasion they interpret Al's invitation to bring the rest with considerable licence. Equipped with hammers and chisels and a large bag, they attack the city's hermae, those little erections on the corners of every street that are named for Hermes, the Conductor of Souls, the Psychopomp, the Logos spermatikos, whose name, for some reason, is Ancient Greek for protect.

ELM trees clawing at her window, blood-red neon dripping down her pane. Violetta died again an hour ago and Ursula Upstairs has drunk herself to sleep. The wet rise and fall of prowling cars, the abrasive rasp of sanding up and down the grain. And all I want to do is be with him, she says, but I'm alone — while he's at home. In bed with someone else.

Wood dust falling in her grotto as she sands, the incense smell of Murray pine, the lanolin scent of sheep. His hands were soft and gentle, and his lips, he sucked my breasts, the loveliest breasts I've ever seen, he said. The neon splash of rain, the lash of thunder at the window pane, a shout, a scream, the shattering of glass. You fucking whore, a male voice says. She looks outside. A woman is standing in the middle of the road with one bare foot and one stiletto. She's weeping and pulling her skirt down. Piangi piangi o misera …

THE wealthy men of Athens compete for the honour of financing the biggest, the sleekest, the most powerful ships for their invasion of Sicily, and the best trained and strongest crews. A preliminary armada of 134 triremes and hundreds of smaller craft is waiting in the harbour for the offshore breeze. On board are 5000 heavily armed citizen hoplites, 25,000 other combatants, and enough grain, wine, olives, almonds, dried figs and salted fish to conquer the whole island with.

Almost the entire human population of Attica is at the harbour for the farewell — Plato too, although he's still only eleven years old, and his hero Socrates, who's already middle-aged. The elected generals, Nicias son of Niceratus, Lamachus son of Xenophanes, and Big Alcibiades son of Clinias, wait on board their triremes while the usual libations, hymns and prayers are offered to the deities and the usual speeches are made. But all that unfinished business Big Al is leaving behind, like the mutilated hermae ...

It's a plot against democracy, one of his enemies says. A wrestler from the Piraeus gym is arrested. He confesses under torture and names names. More wrestlers are arrested, tried, found guilty and sentenced to death.

But wait, there's more! Thessalus son of Cimon of the deme Laciadae says. I saw Alcibiades dressed up like a hierophant mimicking the sacred Mysteries by pretending a common slave girl was the goddess, and he was doing unspeakable things to her.

DEMETER herself is becoming more reflective as Lillian's story unfolds. Having that child is the best thing I've ever done, she says as she watches Persephone carrying a water jug down the track to the village well with her young cousins. The girls giggle and jostle one another as they wind the bucket into the depths, pull it up, pour the cold water into their jugs, balance the jugs on their heads and with infinite grace, walk back up the track to the house. It happens every day, this ritual. But on this one particular day they stop to pick flowers where the white poppies grow. Persephone puts her jug on the ground, bends to pick a poppy, then moves on. Red spots appear on the poppies where she stood. She moves again, and another poppy turns to red. She picks it, touches the petals. They're wet and sticky. She lifts the flower to her lips. It smells, tastes like blood. She raises her skirt and touches herself. Her finger reddens like the poppies and a red trickle runs down her thigh. She drops her bunch of flowers, clutches herself between her legs and runs back up the hill. Mum, Mummy, I'm bleeding, she screams, I'm hurt. I must be dying.

Demeter hugs her daughter, clings to her and weeps. She calls to her own mother, her grandmother, her sisters, nieces, cousins, aunts. Kill a young goat, she says, bake honey cakes, unplug last year's wine. My little girl has blossomed. She's a woman now. She can have children of her own.

WINE from my vineyard, honey from my hive, fresh water from my spring, here drink of me. My sweet mother milk your earliest, your most sacred memory, but now the feeling's gone and a whole orphan night is scratching at my window trying to get inside, a whole street of shadow-people searching for their paradise.

The moon through the clouds through the elm trees through the window onto this island bed where Marie is trying to sleep. Elm trees, Elohim, Elysium, shadows on the wall. The Doppler swish of cars is just a trickle now, the nightclub beat of bass guitars and flashing neon lights. Are you man enough to ride shotgun with me? a video voice is yelling from the amusement parlour across the street. Are you tough enough to take on Mad Dog II? Or do you wanna save the universe from an evil warlord, or duel video graphics with the terrorists Sturm und Drang? Maybe Denis is there, she says, and Heinrich, or maybe they're at the Prince of Wales with their mates, but that noise, it's like someone's playing Daytona with the volume turned up loud, the video revs, the roars, two-fifty, two-sixty, two-seventy US miles an hour but shit, that's not Daytona, that's overhead. The helicopter gunship. The police say it's to keep St Kilda safe but it's the police you gotta watch because they shoot people. Like Colleen.

Big Al is impeached for the heresy of mimicking the mysteries of Demeter and Persephone and revealing them to his mates at the gym ... and for wearing a dress like that which a hierophant wears. Or so Thucydides says. Instead of returning to Athens to defend himself against these highly politicised charges he defects to Sparta and arrives in town the same week the Sicilian delegations are appealing for military assistance against the Athenian invasion. Al takes the Sicilians' side and urges the Spartans to intervene on the island on their behalf: We Athenians sailed to Sicily first to conquer the Sicilians, and after them, the Italians also, and finally to assail the empire and city of Carthage, he tells the assembled Spartan generals. In the event of all or most of these schemes succeeding, we were then to blockade the Peloponnese from the sea and assail it with our armies by land until Sparta and all her allies submitted to our rule.

I can tell you that the Sicilians are very inexperienced in battle and must succumb to Athenian might if you do not help them immediately. The Syracusans have already been beaten in one battle and their city is blockaded from the sea. They will be unable to withstand the Athenian armament that is already there without your help — and I needn't tell you that if Syracuse falls, then all Sicily falls also, and Italy immediately afterwards. And from that time the future of the Peloponnese is also threatened unless you send troops that can row their own ships, and serve as heavy infantry the moment they land. But what I consider even more important than the troops is a Spartan as commanding officer to unite and discipline the forces already on foot and to compel recusants to serve. The friends you have already will thus become more confident, and the waverers will be encouraged to join you.

Meanwhile you must carry on the war more openly on the mainland, so that the Sicilians, seeing you don't forget them, will put heart into their resistance, and so the Athenians will find it more difficult to reinforce their armament. As a matter of urgency you must fortify Decelea in Attica — which would be the one blow that the Athenians are most afraid of. And I needn't tell you that the surest way of harming an enemy is to find what he fears most and to choose this means of attacking him, since everyone naturally knows better than anyone else what his own weak points are.

Finally, I hope that none of you will think any the worse of me if, after having passed as a lover of my country until now, I actively join its worst enemies in attacking it, or that you'll suspect what I say is the fruit of an outlaw's enthusiasm. I am an outlaw from the iniquity of those who drive me forth, not, if you will be guided by me, from your service. My worst enemies are not you who only harm your foes, but they who forced their friends to become enemies. I cannot love my country when I feel I'm being wronged, but only when I feel secure in my rights as a citizen. Indeed, I do not consider that I am now attacking a country that is still mine; but rather I'm trying to recover one that is mine no longer. The true lover of his country is not he who consents to lose it unjustly rather than attack it, but he who longs for it so much that he will go to any length to recover it.

For yourselves, I entreat you to believe that your most capital interests are now under deliberation; and I urge you to send the expeditions to Sicily and Attica without delay. By sending even a small force you will save important cities on the island, and you will destroy the power of Athens both present and prospective. After this you will dwell in security and enjoy a supremacy over all Hellas based not on force but upon consent and affection.

Such were the words of Alcibiades. Or so Thucydides says. Or his translators.

SOMEONE else was watching Persephone picking poppies in Lillian's story: her Uncle Hades, Demeter's brother.

Your daughter's grown into a woman, Hades says next time he sees the girl's father Zeus. I'd like to pick her now she's ripe and plough her virgin field!

Sure, mate, Zeus says. Pick her any day you like.

So the next time Persephone is wandering down the track to the village well, the earth quakes and a chasm opens at the place where the poppies grow. Her uncle whips his stallions through the hole, leans over the side of his chariot, grabs Persephone, throws her onto the back seat and spins his horses around to re-enter the gorge. He pulls them up hard in front of a blond brick mansion with white columns on the banks of the river Styx. He drags the girl from his chariot and carries her screaming through the front door, up the stairs, and into his bedroom. Persephone lifts her head with goddess pride. I belong with my mother, she says. I'll never stay here with you. He laughs at her, locks the door and slowly unbuttons his pants …

Demeter blows her nose, wipes her eyes, and stares numbly through her study window to the poppy field. The flowers have all turned red. Only one deity could be responsible for this atrocity, she says as she lifts her fingers to her loom. They skim across the keyboard: no rain will fall, no crops will grow, no trees will fruit, no flowers will bloom, no birds will sing, no creatures will be born, her message reads. The days will shorten, the air will freeze, and famine will visit all living things until I see my daughter again. This is not an idle threat.

She faxes the global warning to her brother Zeus, books a flight to Mount Olympus and phones a cab to the airport. Zeus refuses to see her when she arrives at his office, so she leans on his lintel and waits. Helios her cousin is passing by, the one who rises each day from the wetlands in the delta of the Nile. It wasn't Zeus, he says. It was Hades. But he married her. Zeus even gave her away. He's the girl's father, after all, and as head of the family …

Demeter passes her hand across her throbbing forehead, rubs her bloodshot eyes and leans even deeper into Zeus's closed door. Can you help me get her back then, cousin? she says.

Don't really see what I can do, Helios says, but I suppose I could have a word with her father.

You do that, Demeter says. And remind him of my fax. That if the human population starves to death or freezes, there'll be no prayers, no praise, no sacrifice and without these, there'll be no gods. We female deities, on the other hand … well, just tell him that. I'll wait for his response.

ELM trees, Elohim, Elysium, shadows on the wall. Marie is dozing now, the nightclub beat of bass guitars, the flashing neon lights, are you man enough, are you tough enough, the helicopter gunship, but no, you wanna save the universe with the terrorists Sturm und Drang. Her brain waves are slowing. But tonight the Reichstag burns, he says and from the ashes shall rise a brave new world. Are you man enough, are you tough enough? The sound of video revs and roars … Her sleep is deeper now, her breathing is irregular. The muscles of her face are contracting into a grimace and her eyes are moving rapidly under their lids. For I am he who is ordained by God and our philosophers and I alone can make our nation great.

Elm trees, Elohim, Elysium, shadows on the wall. Her muscles are twitching. Her heart is beating irregularly as is normal in Rapid Eye Movement sleep. Is this real or is this a nightmare that she's dreaming, this storm, this stress? For God builds today upon us Germans, that is the knowledge, the certain truth that has filled my soul for years. Elm trees, Elohim, and even Jesus was a German and they lie who say he was a Jew. The nightclub beat of bass guitars, neon shadows on the wall and whenever German blood's been weakened, we've been robbed of our right to rule. So all you Jews, Slavs, Gypsies, Pooftas and other deviants must be eliminated because our God-given task is to transform the human race. The neon splash of rain, the lash of thunder at the window pane. A shout, a scream, the shattering of glass, you fucking whore, and the means towards this end is German women whose only role is to bear a brand new race of blond, blue-eyed Aryans in the image of the Lord. Elm trees, Elohim, Elysium, shadows on the wall. A violently active, intrepid, brutal breed with not a hint of tenderness who'll sacrifice themselves willingly for their Fatherland. Are you man enough, are you tough enough to accept with blind obedience, what I, their Führer says? Because the Nation and the Fatherland are all there is in this new law and order, Elm trees, Elohim, shadows on the wall, and it's the duty of every citizen to fight for the state's security, for the existence and increase of our race, our nation, for the nourishment of its children, for the purity of its blood that our nation may ripen for the fulfilment of the mission appointed for us by the Creator of the Universe. Are you tough enough, are you strong enough because that is what the future is: the thousand-year-long Reich.

I'M a bride, Persephone says. I've never been a bride before. I'm dressed in white with orange blossoms in my hair, and my face and shoulders are covered with fine lace. My dress is silk, soft and very short, with a full skirt and petticoats. The bodice is tight like Marie Antoinette's and it pushes my breasts up like Hollywood. I feel chaste, pure and I just stand there without even daring to lift my eyes.

He's in a scarlet uniform with golden buttons and braids. He moves towards me, slowly lifts my veil and tells me I look exquisite, like a flower ready to be plucked. Your only desire is to give me pleasure, he says. He kisses me lightly on the lips, caresses my cheek, holds my neck tight for a moment and then moves his hand down my shoulder to trace the softness of my breast. He slips his finger beneath the silk, touches my nipple and smiles. My nipple doesn't lie. You've never wanted anyone as much as you want me, he says. I lean towards him and gaze into his eyes. I'm starving for him. He brushes his lips against mine, nibbles my ear lobe. I can feel his hand under my petticoats tracing the top of my stocking, moving across my thigh. The lace of my knickers, his fingers, his hand, he clutches my pubic mound, slips a fingertip ah, but you know where. I'm wet. I've never been so wet before, my breathing is in sighs. I lean my head on his shoulder and my little dress falls into a pool of silk at his feet. He lifts me in his arms, carries me to his bed and lays me there — like a sacrifice on an altar. He unbuttons his jacket, his pants. Dark, dark hairs on his chest and further down. I want him desperately. He pulls my panties off, throws them behind him. Only my stockings protect me now and they are no protection. My legs open spontaneously. My nipples, my breathing, please pick me, I whisper, take me. My body arches towards him. You'll never be riper than this, he says as he tests the wetness between my legs with his finger. And then he's on me, in me - but as he comes, I disappear — because I'm no longer the object of his desire. I fade into the satin sheets, evaporate like spilled perfume.

ELM trees, Elohim, Elysium, shadows on the wall. The Doppler swish of cars, the nightclub beat of bass guitars, neon flashing lights, and Hiroshima which, for a single beat, shines brighter than the sun. $E=mc^2$ or energy and mass are one — if you multiply the mass by the square of the speed of light, and from the sum, a chain reaction proven in a test called Trinity and documented in a sonnet by a seventeenth-century priest. Batter my heart, three-personed God; for You as yet but knock, breathe, shine, and seek to mend;

that I may rise and stand, o'erthrow me, and bend Your force, to break, blow, burn, and make me new.

Break, blow, burn and make me new like a poem falling from the sky, from the belly of a bomber called Enola Gay after the pilot's mother. Here drink of me, my sweet mother milk your earliest, your most sacred memory, here, come rest beside me on the couch, he says in Ancient Greek, like Aeneus did, or Zeus, or Ares, or Apollo, let me caress you, kiss you, suck your breasts, the most perfect breasts I've ever seen, him with his wife and kids. And lo, they called him Little Boy because that's how he was shaped. A gram of uranium 235 times the square of the speed of light equals fifty, sixty, seventy thousand incinerations at millions of degrees Centigrade plus a less instant equation for many thousands more.

Elm trees, Elohim, Elysium, the neon flash and then the shadow … Here it comes, the sergeant says from thirty thousand feet. The mushroom shape, it's coming this way, a mass of bubbling molasses, it's spreading, maybe a mile or two wide, half a mile high, it's growing up and up, nearly level with us and climbing. It's very black, but there's a purplish tint and the base of the mushroom is shot through with flames. The city, the city must be below that.

THE last great battle of this invasion was fought in the harbour of Syracuse and in the surrounding mountains, marshes and streams, by independent allies, mercenaries, subject peoples and slaves from all the known world, boat to boat, deck to deck, hand to hand, cheek to cheek.

The Syracusans and their Peloponnesian allies drove the Athenian navy into the shore in their first attack then drifted a lighted merchantman down the wind to burn their remaining ships. The Athenians towed the incendiary away before it did any damage — so the Syracusans blocked the harbour exit. The harbour turned to blood. The Syracusans and their allies erected a trophy and went home to celebrate.

If the Athenians had been wise, they would have escaped over-land before the Syracusans had time to recover from their hang-overs, but they were tricked into delaying their action and spent the spare day fishing the bodies of their dead comrades out of the harbour. But it was the living dead, the sick and wounded who were to be left behind that really defeated them ... the whole Athenian army was filled with tears, with remorse, Thucydides says. And distracted after this fashion [they] found it not easy to go even from an enemy's land, where they had already suffered evils too great for tears and in the unknown future before them feared to suffer more. Dejection and self-condemnation were also rife among them, he says. Indeed they could only be compared to a starved-out town, and that no small one, escaping; the whole multitude upon the march being not less than forty thousand men ...

The Syracusans were waiting for them at the gorge of the Anapus River. The Athenians who survived the crossing, were attacked on the next hill, which turned red and muddy with the slaughter. The remaining Athenians fortified themselves in an olive grove as best they could and waited for the protection of night. But night is little protection against javelins and darts, and again the earth turned red. Six thousand Athenians surrendered and were led into slavery. The survivors pushed on to the Assinarus River in the all-too-frail hope that they could still escape the terror.

With every step, more men fell. Those who reached the Assi-narus panicked and rushed into the gorge like stampeding sheep. The Syracusans were waiting for them along the cliffs. Those who tried to escape the massacre were hunted down by the cavalry. The injured were killed or left to die. The survivors were forced to march to the stone quarries of Syracuse, a prison that is an open pit — the heat of the sun and the stifling closeness of the air tormented them during the day, Thucydides says, and then the nights, which came on autumnal and chilly, made them ill by the violence of the change; besides, as they had to do everything in the same place for want of room, and the bodies of those who died of their wounds or from the variation in the temperature, or from similar causes, were left heaped together one upon another, intolerable stenches arose; while hunger and thirst never ceased to afflict them, each man during eight months having only half a pint of water and a pint of [grain] given him daily.

For some seventy days they thus lived all together, after which all, except the Athenians and Siceliots or Italiots who had joined the expedition, were sold. The total number of prisoners taken would be difficult to state exactly, but it could not have been less than seven thousand.

This was the greatest Hellenic achievement of any in this war, Thucydides says, or, in my opinion, in Hellenic history ... The Athenians were destroyed, as the saying is, with a total destruction, their fleet, their army, everything was destroyed, and few out of many returned home.

ELM trees, Elohim, Elysium, shadows on the wall, the video revs, the roars, two-fifty, two-sixty, two-seventy US miles an hour but shit, that's not Daytona, that's overhead and something's falling, slowly floating down by parachute, and then this flash like Amaterasu dropping from her sky but much, much brighter than the mother sun. And this heat, it's searing my skin, I'm turning black, blisters, and this wind, a cyclone, I cling to something I don't know what, and then a thunder clap like it's right between my ears, the loudest sound I've ever heard. Then silence. Darkness. A black cloud and the sun's like an ancient copper plate. I try to scream but no sound comes. I cover my mouth with my hand but my mouth is gone. My face is melting, peeling away, my hands, my arms, my legs, strips of shredded skin and open wounds, and my clothes, my shoes have disappeared. Everything I know is gone and I'm all that's left — but there's a scream, a voice somewhere near me, please help me, please help me, he's saying. It sounds like Denis, a dark shape, a body twisted under something, a beam, I can't move it, I peer at him, his face looks like cooked octopus and blood is leaking from his ears. I can't tell for sure if it's really him but he's thirsty, he's calling for water, he's whimpering and then the whimpers stop and I know I should be praying for him, I know I should be gathering flowers but I'm too numb to pray and there are no flowers, not even trees or grass, and all I want is my parents, my friends, where are you, please don't leave me here to die alone. I start to crawl, to walk, to run to I don't know where, and all these dazed dark shapes trailing strips of skin and blood, and maybe they're Elle and Sophie and Lilith, or my neighbours, but I can't tell, and Fitzroy Street isn't there and the sky is turning red, a wall of flames, a man is screaming, running towards the flames like he's being chased by demons and I start running too, stumbling, tripping over bodies, people, cats, dogs, pigs, and there's a woman, her belly's slashed open and a baby's hanging out, a pool of blood, a man with his entrails spilling from where a piece of flying glass, a window, has sliced him through and there's no air and I'm gasping and I'm numb and I just keep moving on and there's my great-great-grandmother's grave, I can see her name cut into the stone and a bodhisattva's sitting on the marble slab. I try to weep but no tears come. I try to pray but life passes this buddha says, like a flash of lightning, like a mountain stream and all around me dark shadows are throwing themselves into the water, it's red and thick and bodies are floating by like swollen balloons, and all I want is to throw myself into the torrent to be reborn, but then the rain, black oily smudges burning down my body and someone's washing me, bandaging my head and torso, a soft familiar voice that sounds like Lilith's and she's singing. Piangi,

piangi o misera, she sings but I can't see her, only feel her. I touch her face, her head, her hair has fallen out. It's a new disease, she says, and our lives will never be the same.

A chill wind is blowing around Mount Olympus and the fields lie fallow and bare. Our grain's all gone, our kids are starving and now our sheep and goats are dead, the peasants say. What have we done to deserve this fate?

… the figures for last quarter are looking bad, Zeus's accountant reports. Formal prayers and sacrifice are down and again we've had to print our own praise.

Zeus frowns from behind his desk. It's that fucking Demeter, he says. How much longer can we hold out? The accountant shakes his head. Then you'd better show her in.

Demeter marches into her brother's office. My words at last have meaning for you then, she says. Zeus adjusts his tie and offers her a drink. Nectar perhaps? No thank you, she says as she crosses her legs into a chrome and leather chair. Let's just bypass the formalities and not waste any more time.

So, you want to see our daughter, he says.

And you want your profits up.

He buzzes for his nymph. Put me through to the underworld, he says. Tell Hades it's me.

They wait in silence for the call.

Hades? Yeah, oh I'm going fine, mate. No, Heaven's great. Just wondering how my daughter is. Oh good, good. Could you put her through?

He's just calling her now, he says to Demeter. She nods.

Hello sweetie, how are you? Zeus says. Oh good, good. Look, your mother's here, she wants a quick word.

He passes the phone across.

Demeter walks the phone to the other side of the office and

stares out the plate glass to the city streets seventy floors below. She's fighting tears. Persephone darling, can you talk? she says.

Mum, I miss you. I want to go home.

Demeter closes her eyes and leans against a marble pillar. I know, darling, I'm working on it. I love you.

The phone goes dead. She breathes deeply then turns to Zeus. If you don't get her out of there within twenty-four hours, she says, your next quarter's figures'll drop down your screen like they've been pushed from this window. And what's more, there won't be a single mortal left on this planet for you to exploit. And you know what that means for corporations like yours …

He stares at her and buzzes his nymph. Get me Hades again, he says. A pause. Look, mate, this business with Persephone. How about letting her go back to her mother for a while? Yes, I know I said that, but things have changed.

N O, no, don't wake her, Guilhermina says from her portrait on the wall. She stirs anyway, the young woman in the big wooden bed.

Annina?

Comandate?

Dormivi, poveretta? Were you asleep, poor child?

Si, perdonate. Forgive me.

Osserva, è pieno il giorno? Violetta says. Is it daylight outside?

It's seven o'clock. Sett'ore.

A knock at the front door. Annina answers it. Il signor di Grenvil! she says. The doctor.

Oh, il vero amico! Violetta says. He's a true friend. But please help me up.

She rises but collapses back onto the pillows. Annina rushes to help her to the sofa.

How do you feel? the doctor says.

Soffre il mio corpo. My body suffers but my soul is tranquil. A priest came to console me. Religion is a great relief to the suffering.

He nods. And how was the night?

I slept peacefully.

Corraggio adunque. Courage then. Your convalescence isn't far away.

She smiles. La bugia pietosa ai medici è concessa, she says. The little white lie is allowed to a doctor ...

THE bay has turned to porcelain after last night's storm, purple and soft rose. The sun is rising from behind the 'Nongs and Jesus on his steeple on the hill is first to see. But it was the sparrows that raised her from her nightmares, the sparrows in the elm trees, and the number sixteen tram. She couldn't get back to sleep after that — which is why she's stepping now between bales of seaweed on the beach, clumps of mussel shells, lost shipping buoys, scraps of polystyrene foam, dead Coca-Cola bottles ... and yet her feet imprint upon the wet sand as if no one's trod this path before. For the first time in days, she feels calm like the bay, but what a night! she says. All I can remember is that goddam tree scraping across my window pane, the neon flashing lights and video games across the street and the usual Friday night gunship overhead. And that woman screaming. But something else must've been happening because my bedclothes looked like I'd been fighting World War II. Yet I woke up ready to start the day like I haven't woken up for months. Not since before ... but that's all over now. Something's cleared inside my head like the storm has cleared the bay. There's hardly a ripple on the surface and the water is like crystal — and except for this detritus on the beach, you'd never know what was going on last night.

A penguin surfaces, stares at Marie and dives again. A school of sand whiting. A flight of gulls. A lone cormorant. She almost steps on a small pink plastic doll's leg. Wonder how come that's washed up here? she says. Ahead of her, a whole colony of mussels lies across her path, a great brown beard of molluscs that must have been torn fresh from their rock or pylon in the middle of the night. She stops and squats on the sand for a closer look. They say the water in the bay's still OK because all the crap gets diluted to relatively safe levels here, it's not quite like overseas yet, so I don't suppose fresh mussels'll kill me, she says as she tears one of the larger molluscs from its protective weeds. The shell is closed tight with only a few strands of hair protruding from its lips. She takes her jacket off, spreads it on the sand, and begins her harvest. Mussels for breakfast, she says as she selects the biggest and healthiest looking shells.

She completes her harvest, ties up her load by the sleeves, sits on the wet sand and gazes across the bay. The salt smell of the mussels in the early morning chill, the air moving gently across her face. She inhales, exhales deeply and closes her eyes. I am the gatherer and the gathered, she says. The fisher and the fished. The self and the other. Her breathing, her pulse rate slows. The bay, the beach, the womb, she says. My planet, my culture, me.

She opens her eyes. There are ripples on the water. A dorsal fin, a second, a third. A dolphin surfaces. And another. She can hear the air passing through their blowholes. She savours the moment, immerses herself in it. One dolphin is much smaller than the others, a calf with its mother and aunt perhaps. They ignore her. From their perspective she's just another piece of flotsam washed up by last night's storm. The dolphins dive, circle and speed away. Marie watches then gets up to continue her walk along the line of froth and bubbles that separates liquid from solid, the bay from the shore. She almost treads on a small pink one-legged doll. It's a blond male sans genitals, Barbie's boyfriend Ken. She picks him up, brushes the sand and seaweed away, puts him in her makeshift haversack with her harvest of fresh mussels, then turns to find his lost leg, the one she nearly stepped on back along the beach.

WHEN news was brought to Athens, for a long while they disbelieved even the most respectable of the soldiers who had themselves escaped from the scene of action and clearly reported the matter, a destruction so complete not being thought credible, Thucydides says. When the conviction was forced upon them they were angry with the orators who'd joined in promoting the expedition, just as if they'd not themselves voted for it, and were enraged also with the reciters of oracles and soothsayers, and all other omen-mongers of the time who'd encouraged them to hope that they should conquer Sicily. Already distressed at all points and in all quarters, after what had now happened, they were seized by a fear and consternation quite without example. It was grievous enough for the state and for every man in his proper person to lose so many heavy infantry, cavalry and able-bodied troops, and to see none left to replace them; but when they saw, also, that they didn't have sufficient ships in their docks, or money in the treasury, or crews for the ships, they began to despair of salvation. They thought that their enemies, inflamed by so single a victory in Sicily, would immediately sail with their fleet to the Piraeus; while their adversaries at home, redoubling all their preparations, would vigorously attack them by sea and land at once, aided by their own revolted confederates. Nevertheless, with such means as they had, it was determined to resist to the last, and to provide timber and money, and to equip a fleet as they best could, to take steps to secure their confederates and above all Euboea (on which they depended for food, especially since the Spartans had occupied Decelea); to reform things in the city upon a more economical footing, and to elect a board of elders to advise upon the state of affairs as occasion should arise. In short, as is the way of a democracy, in the panic of the moment they were ready to be as prudent as possible.

Or so Thucydides says.

ALL Paris is going mad — è carnevale, says Annina as she opens the shutters.

In all this merrymaking Heaven knows how many unfortunates are suffering! Violetta says. How much is left?

Annina opens the dresser drawer and counts the remaining coins. Twenty louis.

Take ten and give them to the poor.

You'll only have a few left then.

For me it will be enough. Hurry please. Sollecita, se puoi.

Annina leaves. Violetta withdraws a crumpled letter from next to her heart and reads: Teneste la promessa — la disfida ebbe luogo! You kept your promise. The duel has taken place! The baron received a wound, however he is getting better. Alfredo has gone abroad; I told him about your sacrifice myself and he will return to ask your forgiveness; I'll come too. Take care of yourself. You deserve a better future. Signed Giorgio Germont.

She kisses the letter and slips it once more beneath the lace.

E tardi! It is late. I wait, I wait — they never come to me! She looks in the mirror and brushes a strand of hair from her face. Oh, come son mutata! she says. How I've changed. The doctor told me there was still hope, but with this disease all hope is gone. Adieu to the bright dreams of the past, the roses of my cheeks are already fading. I miss Alfredo's love which once comforted and sustained my weary soul. Ah, della traviata sorridi al desio. Smile upon this fallen woman, she says. Forgive her, O Dio! Receive her into your arms! Ah! Tutto, tutto fini. All is finished. Or tutto fini.

B<small>UT</small> what is? And if it is fini, then when, where, how did it begin? With Giuseppe Verdi and his music? With Francesco Maria Piave and his words? Was it then, with them, or with Alexandre Dumas and his book? Or Marie Duplessis whose real name is Alphonsine? Was it her? Was it there? Was it then? Or here in Fitzroy Street, St Kilda, with Ursula's sherry dreams seeping through the floor into Marie's flat? Or with Lillian as her fingers dance across her loom? Or with Plato and his ancient Greeks? Or was it before even their story began?

S<small>IGNORA</small>! Signora!

Che t'accadde? What's happened?

You're feeling better today, aren't you?

Si, perché? Why?

Promise to stay calm?

Si. What do you want to tell me?

Una gioia improvvisa! A wonderful, unexpected visit!

Alfredo! Ah, tu il vedesti? You saw him? He's coming! L'affretta! Hurry then. Colpevol sono — so tutto, o cara!

The door opens. Amato Alfredo! Amato Alfredo! My love. Oh gioia!

Mia Violetta. Oh gioia! Oh joy!

G changes to E major. They're kissing, embracing, falling into one another's arms.

Darling, I know everything, he sings. Colpevol sono. I know I'm the guilty one.

Io so che alfine reso mi sei! All I know is that at last you've returned to me!

Da questio palpito s'io t'amo impara. Let my passion teach you how I love you. I can't live without you.

If you've found me still alive, I believe no amount of sorrow can kill me.

Forget your anxiety, donna adorata, forget it and forgive my father and me.

What is there to forgive? It is me who's guilty; but I did it for love alone.

She collapses onto the couch, her head falls back, her eyes close.

Gran Dio! Alfredo says and kneels beside her to clutch her limp body to his chest. Violetta opens her eyes. It's my illness, she says. A momentary weakness! Now I'm strong. Vedi? See? I'm smiling. Help me dress, Annina.

Wait, Alfredo says. Attendi. Tears are streaming down his cheeks.

No. I want to go out.

She undoes the buttons of her nightdress and lets it slip over her thin shoulders. Annina lays a pale lace gown across the sofa. Violetta reaches for it but collapses against the cushions. Gran Dio, she says. Non posso! I can't do it. She closes her eyes.

Cielo! Alfredo says in F sharp minor. Che vedo! He's panicking now. Annina, get the doctor! he says. Va' pel dottore. Quickly.

Violetta is still conscious. She opens her eyes. Tell the doctor that Alfredo has returned to his lover, she says. Tell him I want to live again.

Ma se tornando non m'hai salvato a niuno in terra salvarmi è dato. Ah! Gran Dio! Morir sì giovine, io che penato ho tanto! Morir sì presso a tergere il mio sì lungo pianto! Ah, dunque fu delirio la credula speranza! Invano di constanza armato avrò, avrò il mio cor!

If your return can't revive me, then nothing on earth can save me and my death is inevitable. Almighty God! To die at such a tender age and after such suffering. To perish when I'm so close to wiping my slate clean. Ah! but my hopes of future happiness were nothing more than the fantasies of a credulous woman. All my attempts to protect my heart with dreams of constancy have been in vain.

MARIE is sitting at Elle's kitchen table scraping vegemite across a slice of buttered toast. Elle is waiting for the kettle to boil, two early-morning cups of tea. The mussels are in the sink, still tied up in Marie's jacket.

So, you sick or something then? Elle says. I mean it's not like you to be up and about at this hour. Me neither for that matter!

Nah, just couldn't get back to sleep, Marie says.

That Sydney bloke?

Nah. Well, yeah, I guess that's what started me off last night but now that I think about it, I suspect it's more to do with what you said at the George. Remember? That day we'd been working on the bed? About trying to find some meaning in your life, something you could really believe in? But like, that's really scary too because it's so much easier to go along with the crowd. And like, last night, all I could hear above the storm and the noise of the street was that line from La Trav. You know, Piangi, piangi, o misera, and all that paterfamilias shit where she finally capitulates. And then this woman just below my window, right, she must've been working Grey Street and this bloke, he'd picked her up and he was probably too pissed to do anything so he dumped her half-naked in the middle of the tram tracks and began swearing and throwing bottles at her. And all that stuff with that bloke from Sydney ... I know I'm not making any sense but it all seems to be connected somehow. I must have had a bad dream about it because my bedclothes were all over the place when I woke this morning and I keep getting these flashes ...

She passes the slice of toast and vegemite to Sophie. All this crap and yet the bay is so beautiful this morning, Elley. And there was a penguin swimming near the beach and these three dolphins, it was like they were my totem or something, and for a moment I had this feeling of absolute clarity. Like — I'd been walking along the beach right, and there was all this rubbish washed up, polystyrene and Coca-Cola bottles and stuff, and I know it's going to sound really obvious and corny, but like, I realised that sure we're the disease, but we can also be the cure.

Elle raises her Sicilian eyebrows and reaches for the tea. You're talking to someone of Italian descent, remember, she says. And every prophet, every priest, every philosopher since even before Pythagorus or Plato's time has said he's gunna cure our ills. And every politician. Did you watch that Bertolucci film on SBS the other night? *1900*?

A few hours of it, Marie says. I couldn't get past the scene where that bloke smashes the kid's head against the bedroom wall. It made me so sick I had to turn the TV off. But what's that got to do with anything?

Fascism, Elle says. That's what. My relatives lived through Bertolucci's film in real life so if you're talking about some grand new narrative about making the world a better place ...

She pauses for a bite of toast and vegemite. I was working on my thesis again last night, she says. Doing some more reading. And remember that Futurist poet Filippo Marinetti, the one who got so pissed off with all the fin-de-siècle pessimism and conservatism last time round that he published that Manifesto about how war was the world's only hygiene and how there couldn't be any beauty without conflict, or any masterpieces without aggression? He was into militarism and patriotism and what he called glorious death-giving ideas. And contempt for women. Some of those architects of yours were into all that too, remember! So then we got Mussolini and his brown shirts. Like — ideas about the future can be really dangerous, Marie. Because sometimes they become real!

Yeah, but all that stuff you're talking about, it's boys' stuff, Marie says. The world doesn't have to be that way, Elle. Does it? And don't we need some sort of vision to fill us up inside, to give us something worth living for that's more than the latest TV commercial? Or a job. Or a man and kids! I mean, they're our lives we gotta live, Elley, and we gotta do something with them that matters. Or else what's the point of getting up in the morning? I mean, if we keep giving in to the past, we're just being Violettas too. And we can't let Marinetti and his acolytes write the libretti forever. Can we? Or am I just being naive?

PLATO, who has grown into adulthood by now, is reconsidering his options too, as his letters to his Sicilian student Dion reveal. In my youth I went through the same experience as many other men, he says in the words of one of his many translators — a J. Harward from Warwick in Queensland, who was Director of Education in Ceylon under the British Raj, and presented his translations of Plato's epistles to the Melbourne Classical Society in 1920.

I fancied that if I were to become my own master early in life, I should embark on a political career, says Plato in the words of his Australian translator. And I found myself confronted with the following occurrences in the public affairs of my own city. The existing constitution being generally condemned, a revolution took place, and fifty-one men came to the front as rulers of the revolutionary government — namely, eleven in the city and ten in the Piraeus to take charge of the market and municipal matters, while thirty were appointed rulers with full powers over public affairs as a whole. Some of these were relatives and acquaintances of mine, and they immediately invited me to share in their activities, as something to which I had a right. The effect on me, as a young man, was not surprising. I believed that they would manage the state in such a way as to bring men out of a bad way of life into a good one — so I watched them very closely to see what they would do.

In quite a short time, however, they made the former government seem precious as gold — for among other things they tried to send a friend of mine, the aged Socrates (whom I have no scruples in describing as the most upright man of the day), with others to arrest a fellow citizen who was to be executed. They wanted him to share their guilt, but Socrates would not obey them and was prepared to risk any consequences rather than become a partner in their iniquitous deeds. Seeing all these things and many others, I disapproved of what they were doing, and withdrew from any connection with the abuses of the time.

Not long after that a revolution terminated the power of the thirty and the form of government that they had instituted. And once more, though with more hesitation, I was moved by the desire to take part in public affairs and politics. Well, even in the new government, unsettled as it was, events occurred which one would naturally view with disapproval, and once more it happened that some of the ruling elite brought my friend Socrates to trial before a court of law, laying a most iniquitous and inappropriate charge against him: for it was on a charge of impiety that he was prosecuted, condemned and executed.

The more closely I observed these incidents and the men engaged in public affairs and the more carefully I examined the laws and the customs of my society, the more I realised how difficult it was to handle public affairs aright. For it was not possible to be active in politics without friends and trustworthy supporters; and finding these was not an easy matter, since public affairs in Athens were not carried on in accordance with the manners and practices of our forefathers; nor was there any ready method by which I could make new friends. The laws too, written and unwritten, were being altered for the worse, and the evil was growing with startling rapidity. The result was that, though at first I had been full of a strong impulse towards political life, as I looked at the course of affairs and saw them being swept in all directions by contending currents, my head began to swim. Finally it became clear to me that all existing States were one and all misgoverned. For their laws had created problems that were almost incurable, except by some extraordinary reform supported by good luck. It became clear to me that it was only through true philosophy that men could see what justice in public and private life really meant. Therefore, I said, there will be no cessation of evils for the sons of men, till either those who are pursuing a right and true philosophy receive sovereign power in the States, or those in power in the States, by some dispensation of providence, become true philosophers.

With these thoughts in mind I came to Italy and Sicily ...

LILLIAN is sipping her first cup of tea for the day, jasmine tea from China because it's meant to be good for my health, she tells herself. She has just let Abelard out for his early morning sniff around the garden and is standing barefoot on her front verandah in her old chenille dressing gown investigating the damage from last night's storm. Hsi Wang Mu, Lady-Queen of the West, appears to have taken a direct hit. She's gazing at the world through a thick veil of fallen palm fronds and is leaning dangerously to the right. The lawn of the park is littered with fronds and some of the glazed green tiles have fallen off the ziggurat to the local boys who died fighting Boers. The stelae to some of the 100 million victims of the next two wars seem to be undamaged, and the white marble bas-relief of the man with the gun is washed clean and sparkling. But the Babylon palms, those trees of life, of knowledge ... I will go up to the palm tree, I will take hold of the boughs thereof, Lillian says to herself. Now also thy breasts shall be as clusters of the vine, and the smell of thy nose like apples; and the roof of thy mouth like the best wine for my beloved, that goeth down sweetly, causing the lips of those that are asleep to speak.

Oh dear, I'm thinking about sex again! she says. The Old Testament's Song of Solomon no less. I would cause thee to drink of spiced wine of the juice of my pomegranate.

Is there anything that doesn't have hidden erotic meaning? she says. But of course not, how could there be when genital intimacy is the very source of life and love, and in Babylon, palm trees were the dwelling place of Astarte, or was it Ishtar, the biblical whore, whose Hebrew name was Tamar, which means Palm Tree; and her lover was called Phoenix, the rising god of Phoenicia, the Land of the Palm. His head is filled with dew and his locks with the drops of night, she recites. His mouth is most sweet: yea, he is altogether lovely. This is my beloved, and this is my friend, O daughters of Jerusalem.

The early Christians called their Great Mother the Holy Palm too, or so I'm told, so this little park beyond my picket fence is a far more sacred site than St Kilda's founding fathers ever knew. She sips her green tea again. Abelard is scratching around in the camellia grove and is attempting to lift his neutered leg over the Lady-Queen of the West. Lillian smiles. Isn't that the truth! she says. Males will piss on anything! But I've never visited Babylon, only seen its wall in that museum in Germany. I could stop over in Iraq on my next trip to Alexandria, or Sokrates could even meet me there. We could follow Alexander's path, or my own mob's for that matter, to and from slavery in Egypt, and to and from in Babylon. She sighs. Ah, those Great Escapes — and here I am just a few millennia down the track having already lost both my goddesses and my gods. And it's such a damnably difficult job picking up their shards and recycling them into something new to believe in! But Babylon in Sumer, aye? Or Babylon here in St Kilda, the ziggurats, stelae and bas-reliefs in the little park beyond my fence — because some things never change no matter where they are.

Like the Vulture Stele incised by Eannatum of Lagesh's scribes in the third millennium to let the war god Ningirsu know his king was intending to conquer Sumer — as were all the other rising despots in all the other mud-hut villages along the Euphrates and the Tigris. Like the boy-child Sargon of Akkad just north of Babylon who was found by Akki, the divine water-drawer, floating down the river in a cradle made of bulrushes and was raised by the goddess Ishtar — or was it Inanna? — in the wilderness. His scribes said he married her, that it was she who gave him his power. The marriage covenant must have included all the land from the Persian Gulf to the Mediterranean and from the highlands of Iran to the foothills of the Caucasus because never had the world seen such an empire. Or such a man — until his grandson Naram-Sin, who was named for another Mesopotamian deity, Sin the Father-Moon. The Shebans claimed this god lived in Sinai with Inanna and that it was on her sacred mountain that he received the Tablets of Law from Tiamat, the primal Mother of Creation, just as — years later — Moses received his from Yahweh on that mountain, or Hammurabi from Marduk, or Zoroaster from Ahura Mazda.

All those deities handing down their laws, Lillian says, and all the other patterns I'm part of, like all those unfathered baby boys floating down the rivers of the world in cradles made of bulrushes: the goddess Cunti's child, the sun, who was found in a woven basket in the Ganges, Sargon of the Euphrates, and Moses of the Nile, he who gathered together those twelve tribes of alien workers after they'd been expelled from Egypt, and led them to the Promised Land — where one of my pagan deities, David, founded a mud-hut empire of his own by stealing the throne of Balkis, the Queen of Sheba, Mother of the Moon. Or so the Koran says. And then Queen Bath-Zabbai's son Solomon, the sun god of On ... Thou hast ravished my heart, my mother, my sister, my spouse, King Solomon sang. How much better is thy love than wine and the smell of thine ointments than all spices! Thy lips, O my spouse, drop as the honeycomb: honey and milk are under thy tongue; and the smell of thy garments is like Lebanon. A garden enclosed is my sister, my spouse; a spring shut up, a fountain sealed. Thy plants are an orchard of pomegranates, with pleasant fruits; camphor, spikenard, and saffron, calamus and cinnamon, frankincense, myrrh and aloes.

My beloved is mine and I am his, his Shekina sang to him. His head is filled with dew and his locks with the drops of night. His mouth is most sweet: yea, he drinks of me, the spiced wine of the juice of my pomegranate. This is my beloved, this is my friend, O daughters of Jerusalem.

BUT anyway, what are we going to do with these mussels? Marie says. I thought you'd be really pleased to have a jacket full of fresh seafood land on your doorstep for breakfast!

Sorry, Elle says. I'm never my most positive first thing in the morning!

Have you got any wine then? And a few onions or shallots and some herbs and things? And some lemon juice?

There's a bit of dry white in the bottom of that cask on top of the fridge, and Lilith sent some lemons back with Soph yesterday, Elle says.

Well, that settles it, Marie says. It's Moules à la Marinière for breakfast, like it or not! Come on Soph, let's get some of these molluscs scrubbed and into the pan.

We saw a dolphin yesterday too, Sophie says as she scrapes a mussel shell with a vegemite coated bread and butter knife.

Where? Marie says.

Near the jetty. Lilith says they belong to Aphrodite.

Well, why hasn't Aphrodite stopped us pouring all our crap into their habitats then? Marie says.

I don't do that, Sophie says. I go to the toilet.

But where's it go after that?

I don't know.

To the bay, that's where. It gets treated a bit but then most of it gets pumped into the bay along with all the muck that gets flushed into the drains. Because it's people like me who design it that way! Architects and planners and engineers. And it's not just the sewers, it's all the run-off from the streets as well, and the stuff that people chuck into the gutters. The cans and plastic bottles and cigarette butts. But fortunately our bay's so big the crap gets diluted and there aren't that many people living around it yet, but in other bays in other places like the Mediterranean.

What's with all this mea culpa all of a sudden! Elle says as she peels an onion. Those dolphins must've given you a really hard time this morning for you to be giving us such a lecture! You sound like old Lilith! And should we really be discussing this while we're preparing shellfish for breakfast!

Sorry, Marie says. She puts an arm around Sophie and kisses the crown of her head. I didn't mean to snap at you, sweetheart, she says. But there was an awful lot of rubbish on the beach this morning, and I guess I'm also kind of reassessing my life. She resumes her shell-cleaning. Here I am farting around the edges of my profession feeling very self-righteous about a bit of green design, but when you look around at the real world — I mean most of the new public buildings are still air-conditioned as if we don't know how to design structures that maintain their own micro-climates, and none of them harvest the sun, wind or rain in any way that's going to make a difference to the world, and they all have these huge basements designed exclusively for cars, and if not basements, then above ground car parks, and architects are still justifying themselves by saying they're just following their briefs or providing what the market demands — which I reckon is like an army massacring a whole village and then the soldiers telling you they're just following orders! I mean where's the morality, Elley?

She gets up from the kitchen table to carry the scrubbed mussels to the sink. Elle is already frying onions in a large skillet. For God's sake lighten up, Marie, she says. We haven't even had breakfast yet! And pass me the wine so I can drown these onions before you chuck the mussels in. Soph, can you pick some herbs from the window sill please?

I don't know what to do, Marie says as she reaches for the wine cask from the top of the fridge. I can't make up my mind whether I should compromise and try to join the mainstream in the hope that one day I'll get to make a difference from inside. Or whether I should stay on the fringe like you, and subsidise my own work in whatever way I can, because like, you can really touch people with your music, Elley — even if not many people get to hear it yet.

THOSE poor bedraggled Trees of Knowledge, Lillian says as she returns to her kitchen to make herself another cup of tea. I expect the Council workers'll clean them up sometime during the day though and I'll attend to my own storm damage when I've got dressed. But what a night in Babylon — as if the deities themselves were warring. Marduk versus Tiamat, Creator of the Universe, who, from her menstrual deep created Apsu and lay with him, and then all the other deities. But it was matricide, what Marduk and his brothers did, only worse — they had their victory documented as the Epic of Creation.

They marched to war, they drew near to give battle.

The Lord spread out his net and caught her in it.

The evil wind which followed him, he loosed it in her face.

She opened her mouth, Tiamat, to swallow him.

He drove in the evil wind so that she could not close her lips.
The terrible wind filled her belly. Her heart was seized,
She held her mouth wide open.
He let fly an arrow, it pierced her belly.
Her inner parts he clove, he split her heart,
He rendered her powerless and destroyed her life.
He felled her body and stood upright on it.

HE clove his mother's body in two as if he were filleting a fish, and from one half created the vault of heaven, home of the gods, and from the other made the solid land and everything upon it, including us. And to make sure we mortals never forgot his power, he sent the king of Babylon those seven tablets of clay and commanded him to read them aloud every year for all the world to hear. But even Marduk's magic was not enough against Assyria's sky-god Ashur and his earthly servant, King Ashurnasirpal II, she says to herself. I flayed all the chief men who revolted, and I covered the pillar with their skins, Ashurnasirpal claimed in the inscriptions on the walls of the grand entry of his new imperial palace in Nimrud. Some I walled up within the pillar, some I impaled upon the pillar on stakes, and others I bound to stakes round about the pillar; many within the border of my own land I flayed, and I spread their skins upon the walls; and I cut off the limbs of the officers who had rebelled.

Not one of the 60,000 guests who were invited from throughout Ashurnasirpal's terrified empire to celebrate the completion of his new palace doubted the truth of these inscriptions. Soon the Assyrian king's phalanxes would penetrate even the valley of the Nile.

Ah, how the empires have waxed and waned in these fertile mother-crescents, Lillian says to herself as she sips her tea. Akkad, Babylon, Nimrud and Sargon II's new capital at Nineveh, but from here the view's so hazy, just mirages in the desert of men seeking immortality, stealing it from the lives of others like those boys whose names are listed on the stelae in the park, and all the other victims of all the other wars whose names were never recorded. As Assyria declines, Babylonia rises again and so another divinely inspired army besieges Jerusalem, she says. Destroy the city and send all the survivors to the gulags, King Nebuchadnezzar told his field commanders. Oh my country, so lovely and lost! Nabucco's captives sing in Verdi's opera. Oh, remembrance so dear and so fraught with despair, sings Giuseppina Strepponi.

But at that time, over two and a half thousand years ago, Babylon was considered the most culturally and linguistically diverse mud-brick city in all the universe, with artificially irrigated roof-top gardens filled with plants from all the known world, ornately decorated temples to its thousands of deities and many brightly glazed ziggurats, those Mountains of Heaven which reached from the flat alluvium of the delta higher than any mortal plains-dweller could have imagined. Nebuchadnezzar's ziggurat, the Tower of Babel, was seven storeys high, one storey for each of the heavenly spheres, and seven deep, a storey for each of the nether spheres of the underworld. On each level was a hanging garden, a fecund glade of ferns and running water, of camellias, lotuses and lilies, pome-granates, date palms and figs; and at the very top, the Holy of Holies to which Marduk himself would descend each year to lie with Mother Earth.

But ziggurats made of blood and sweat and river mud crumble and blow away as do men's vain empires. And so it was that, while Babylon waned, other empires were on the rise. The fundamental-ists amongst us rejoiced when we saw the chariots and cavalry at Babylon's gates, Lillian says. Babylon the great is fallen, they told us. The mother of harlots and all the abominations of the earth. For all nations have drunk of the wine of their fornication with her, and the merchants of the earth have grown rich through the abundance of her delicacies. Come out of her, ye captives of Judah, that ye be not partakers of her sins, and receive not of her plagues, the tripped-out authors of the Book of Revelations said.

And, at that very moment, as if from nowhere, a hand appeared in the King of Babylon's palace and wrote these words in candle soot on a plaster wall: mene mene tekel apharsin. Only one man could translate them, a soothsayer and astrologer named for Dan-El, the Phoenician deity of divination who received his power from the goddess Dana and her sacred serpents. Thou art weighed in the balances and found wanting, Daniel told the king. God hath numbered thy kingdom and finished it. He hath divided it and given it to the Medes and to the Persians.

PLATO'S first visit to Sicily was not the success he had hoped it would be. He went there to turn the tyrant of Syracuse, Dionysius, into a philosopher statesman as a first step in his personal crusade to make the world a better place. But the tyrant, a former colonel who'd been given emergency powers during the last war against Carthage and had maintained them by force, didn't want to be either a philosopher or a statesman, and what's more, he found Plato really irritating. After tolerating him for a few months, Dionysius sold his would-be teacher to an African slave trader in the hope that both the philosopher and his philosophy would disappear forever. But unfortunately an anonymous benefactor bribed the slave trader to release his captive. When Plato offered to repay the cost of the bribe, his benefactor lectured him about how he should use the money to teach the next generation of rulers how to be philosopher statesmen — seeing he wasn't having much luck with the current generation. There's a vacant plot in the gardens of Academus just outside the walls of Athens, the benefactor said. You could build a school there. Call it the Academy or something, and run courses in rational thinking.

Yeah, but what did the doctor tell you? Marie says.

That my T-cell count was down and that I should think more positively about myself! To let my mind do the healing!

They're sitting on the back stairs, Denis and Marie. He's just finished washing Heinrich's dirty dishes. She's been watering the plants.

The doctor wasn't much help so I snuck into the Sacred Heart to pray, he says. To Saint Sebastian. He's the one who's got all the arrows sticking out of him because he tied himself to a tree, an oak tree I think, so he wouldn't fall down in front of his enemies. I felt a bit silly in the church because I've never really prayed before but the door was open and no one else was there — except the organ player and she was playing too loud to hear. So I went in and told Sebastian how I felt. And Mary too. I figured she'd understand — because my own mother doesn't seem to. I think she's scared. But what if what they say is true, Marie? All that stuff about going to hell …

When Dionysius I of Sicily died, his son, who was also called Dionysius, inherited most of the island. Plato had met the boy on his last trip there but it was Dionysius II's maternal uncle, a young man called Dion whom Plato was closest to. They were probably lovers, and it was to Dion that some scholars believe the epistles J. Harward of Warwick, Queensland, translated were addressed. Dion became chief minister in his nephew's court, and one of his first initiatives was to invite Plato to return to teach the new tyrant — but Dionysius II was no more receptive to Plato's ideas than his father had been, and dismissed them as utopian. The politics of the situation became so fraught that Dionysius banished his uncle

Dion who, rather than just disappear from history as he should have done, decided to enrol in Plato's new Academy in Athens to learn how to become a philosopher statesman himself.

But to be a philosopher statesman, first you first need a state — which is why Dion and two of his fellow academicians, Callipus and Timonides, returned to Sicily with an army of one thousand mercenaries. We know this is true because Timonides kept a log of the invasion and sent it to one of Plato's nephews, who hid it in his bottom drawer. Or so the story goes.

When they arrived back in Syracuse, Dion, Callipus and Timonides told the Sicilians that they'd come to liberate them from tyranny. The lessons they learned in the Academy didn't translate very well into the real world, it seems, because soon Dion was assassinated by his friend Callipus who in turn, was driven out of Syracuse by Dion's nephew Hipparinus. The former tyrant, Dionysius II, engineered a brief return to power, and Carthage also intervened, but it was a young and hitherto unknown Corinthian military officer called Timoleon who eventually cleaned up the mess Plato's students had created, after he landed with his own small army of mercenaries near the tourist town of Taormina. We know this is true because a local man called Andromachus witnessed the invasion, and his son Timaeus wrote a book.

Of course Plato never imagined for a moment that what he had taught his students at the Academy would lead to this. It was the world that was the problem, not his theories. But by any objective evaluation — if such a thing were possible — Plato's ideas were a disaster for the island. And for his students too.

ALFREDO is singing in Ursula's upstairs flat. Parigi, o cara, noi lasceremo, la vita uniti transcorreremo. Darling, we'll leave Paris to live our lives together. We'll make up for all our heartache, your health will bloom again, you'll be the light of my life and the future will smile upon us. Ursula can feel his lips against hers. Si o caro, we'll go away to live our lives together, she sings. My health will bloom again and you will be the light of my life …

Si, si, si, Alfredo sings. We'll make up for all our heartache and the future will smile on us.

Ursula gets up from the piano, sways and stumbles. Ah, no more now, she says. Non piu, a un tempio. Alfredo grabs her, holds her in his arms. Let's go to church to give thanks for your return, she sings to him.

You are my breath, my heartbeat, the delight of my life! Alfredo is singing. My tears will flow with yours. But believe me, we have need of constancy more than ever now. Don't close your heart to hope. Tutto alla speranza non chiudere il tuo cor. Don't close your heart …

Ursula is trying desperately not to close her heart — but that sherry, and all the sadness of her life. What a cruel end! she sings.

The door opens and the doctor enters her small flat accompanied by Alfredo's father, Giorgio Germont.

La promessa adempio, o generosa, Alfredo's father sings. I'm fulfilling my promise. I've come to embrace you as a daughter.

You've arrived too late! Ursula sings. But I'm thankful you've come. Doctor Grenvil, see! I'm dying in the arms of the only loved ones I have in the world.

Dying? What are you saying! Germont sings. Oh cielo — è ver! It's true.

La vedi, padre mio? Alfredo sings. Do you see her, Father! Tears are streaming down his cheeks.

Don't torment me any more, Germont sings. My soul is already consumed by remorse. Her every word strikes me like a bolt of lightning. Oh thoughtless old man! Only now do I see the harm I have done.

BUT HER REAL NAME is Anna Maria Ribeira da Silva de Jesus, who's also known as Aninha or Anita. She was born in a peasant hut built on wooden piles beside a stream in a village in Brazil, to Marie Antonia and her husband, Bento Ribeiro da Silva de Jesus. No record exists of Aninha's birth or her baptism, but it's said to have occurred around the time King John gave Brazil to his young son, Dom Pedro, and returned to Portugal to reclaim the throne Napoleon had stolen from him.

Aninha's father, Bento Ribeiro de Jesus, dies a few years after King John's departure, so Maria Antonia bundles her babies into a cart and takes them to the slums of the nearest big town, Laguna, where Aninha grows into a wild, illiterate adolescent with dark slanted eyes, long black hair, brown skin scarred by small pox, freckles and firm young breasts. One morning she's walking home along a narrow, lonely track. A rich boy gallops past, stops around the bend, dismounts and waits for her. She tries to ignore him but he grabs her as she passes him, pushes her against the tree, presses his body against hers, and attempts to kiss her. She turns her face away. He undoes his fly and pulls her skirt up. She bites him so hard he loosens his grip. She breaks free, snatches his whip from his hand and flogs him, then jumps onto his horse and gallops to the nearest police station.

But such a scandal in Laguna's slums! Who does this girl think she is? Her mother decides to marry her off to a cobbler named Manuel Duarte di Aguiar before she causes any more trouble. He's twenty-five years old and she's fourteen, sixteen years at the most. They exchange vows before the baroque altar of the church of Santo Antonio dos Anjos in August 1835, but the union is not a happy one. And Brazil is at war with itself again. Manuel enlists on Emperor Pedro's side and abandons Aninha — or that's what some books say. Others that he's wounded in the battle for Laguno and is left behind when the Imperial army retreats. In this version of history, Aninha nurses him at home. One night, a rebel leader in a red shirt knocks on her door and demands bed and board for his men. You'll have to ask my husband but he's too ill to be disturbed, she says. The stranger offers to take Manuel to the rebel hospital for treatment. Aninha accepts on condition that she goes too — because you never know what these rebels might do, she says.

Aninha stays at the hospital to nurse her husband, or so the story goes, and when he dies, she nurses the other wounded men. Giuseppe Garibaldi doesn't mention this. In his version of events, the first time he ever saw Aninha was from the deck of his ship one day when he was daydreaming about finding a woman to comfort him. I felt totally alone in the world, he says. I needed the love of a women, someone who would stay close to me forever. I felt that unless I found such a person immediately, my life would become intolerable.

And lo, through his telescope he sees a young woman with long dark hair carrying a bucket of water up the hill towards the slums of Laguna. He launches a dinghy and rows ashore to find her. By the time he reaches the hill she has disappeared, but a local man recognises him and invites him home for coffee. In the man's kitchen a young woman with long dark hair is roasting coffee beans. It is her, the one he has rowed ashore to find. We gazed on each other like two people who'd met before and were searching in each other's eyes for something which would help us recall the forgotten past, Garibaldi says. The moment seemed like hours and then at last, I greeted her in Italian. You must be mine, I said. My insolence was magnetic. I had formed a sacred bond, pronounced an edict, which only death could annul. I had come upon an illicit treasure, but yet a treasure at great price!

So — who was the man who invited Giuseppe Garibaldi home for coffee? Was he Aninha's brother? Was he her lover? Was he her boss? Or was he her husband Manuel? Was Garibaldi lying when he said Manuel had died? It doesn't matter now which story you believe, because Giuseppe and Aninha sail off together to fight for freedom. There's a battle against the tyrant's men, they're outnumbered, a whole army is pursuing them, carbines, bullets, Aninha's horse is shot from beneath her, she runs into the forest, trips, the tyrant's men encircle her, she's trapped, they grab her, tie her up. But in the dead of night she loosens the ropes around her wrists, steals the captain's horse, mounts him bareback and gallops into the moonlight. The captain and his soldiers wake and reach for their guns, she reins the horse into the river with fifty men firing from the bank. She slips off the horse's back, and shields herself with his body. The air, the water boil with bullets as she swims. She scrambles up the opposite bank, jumps onto the horse's back again and for four hungry, sleepless days and nights, rides through virgin forest to find her man. And by some Hollywood miracle, she does. He's starved and exhausted too, but just when you think they can ride no more, they reach an escarpment. The camera pans across the valley. A clearing in the forest. A plume of smoke. Rows and rows of young coffee trees. An encampment. And cauldrons of rice being cooked for the plantation slaves. Garibaldi reaches for his sword, his gun …

HE'S losing the battle, Heinrich says. I've just taken him to Fairfield. They reckon it's PCP.

What? Marie says.

Pneumocystis carinii pneumonia.

They're passing on the staircase, Heinrich and Marie. He going up, she going down to another Tuesday morning tutorial. She's in a rush because she's late but Heinrich wants to talk.

He was only positive, for Christ's sake, and people can go on for decades being positive. He said he'd told you …

Yeah, but can't he still go on for years? she says. I mean, he said he was getting fevers but …

He's on a drip, he can't breathe without oxygen, and he's got practically no immune system left to fight with any more, Heinrich says. He turns his face away so Marie can't see the tear that's threatening to unman him. His lip is quivering. I don't want him to die, he says.

Heinrich has never talked to Marie like this before. He's never talked to anyone like this. He's embarrassed. She is too. Anyway I'd better go and have a shower and shave, he says. I'm already late for work.

Why don't you take the morning off, or the whole day, she says. I'll ring for you and tell them you're sick if you'd like me to.

He turns his head away again. Another tear is about to fall. I'll be fine, he says. And rushes into his flat.

⊢⊱   ⊰⊣

SHE'S STANDING on the steps of the basilica named for a fisherman, the one who bequeathed Roma to the popes. But by now her real name is Anita Garibaldi, the intransigent, obstinate twenty-eight-year-old who insists on fighting by her lover's side — even when he's losing. She's pregnant again, her fourth, and in her last trimester. A long red shirt hangs over her swollen belly, and below her shirt she's wearing a black pair of men's trousers. Her head is covered by a soft dark hat with a single ostrich feather, a sabre and pistol are hanging from her belt, and across her shoulders she has draped the green, white and red of Italia. She is listening to her lover speak. Where we go, there Rome shall be, he says to the thousands who are now assembled in St Peter's Square on this northern summer day in 1849. His red shirt is stained even redder, and his sword is so bent it will no longer fit into its sheath.

Soldiers! he says. You who have shared with me the labour and the dangers of fighting for our patria, you who have won a rich share of glory and honour, all you can expect if you follow me into exile is heat and thirst by day, cold and hunger by night. No other salary awaits you except hard work and danger. You will live in the open, without rest, without food, and there will be long night watches, forced marches and fighting at every step. Let him who loves his country follow me.

They leave the Eternal City as the sun is setting on Saint Peter's dome, to march across the Campagna, a retreating, defeated rebel army of three, four, five, ten thousand freedom fighters, depending on which story you believe. Cavalry, infantry, baggage train, one lone cannon drawn by a team of horses, and Anita with her unborn child.

By early morning they've reached Tivoli in the foothills of the Apennines where they stop to rest and collect the cash they need for bread and meat and wine; bread carried on a string around each warrior's neck, meat bought on the hoof to be killed en route (a stab to the heart like on Montevideo in Uruguay), and wine bought by the local hog.

From Tivoli they cut west to the valley of the Tiber. It's Garibaldi's birthday and he's forty-two. Anita dismounts and rests in the shadow of a rock near an old stone bridge. He sits beside her, picks up a pebble and throws it into the stream. They'll rise up, the rural people, he says. We'll mobilise them along the way. You'll see. Then we'll turn around and march again on Rome.

Anita kisses him. You're forgetting the priests, she says. They've got a weapon far mightier than your sword or your dreams of freedom! All they have to do is threaten the peasants with excommunication and tell them they'll go straight to hell, and no peasant wants that, my darling. They already know what hell's like.

I think you hate priests even more than I do, Giuseppe says.

I'll be happy if I'm wrong, she says.

The butcher's assistant lays a bullock haunch on a nearby rock. Garibaldi rises to gather bark, twigs and some rotting logs. He arranges them as he did on the pampas and strikes a light. Soon his single flame becomes a barbecue, and his private moment, public. To my wife, he says as he lifts his mug towards Anita. She's a very valiant lady, he says to his comrades across the fire. Did I ever tell you about that day her horse was shot from under her in Uruguay?

The Garibaldini have heard this story a thousand times, but they're happy to indulge their general once more. She was fighting on the left wing and she was captured, taken prisoner, he says. I thought I'd never see her again. But in the dead of night she stole the captain's horse ... I'm sure I've told you this story before....

A small wooden suspension bridge across the creek. Marie stops, gets off her bike and leans over the railing. Platypuses have recolonised this tributary of the Yarra since the plastic bags and blackberries have been replaced by native plants. But platypuses don't perform for passing cyclists, and anyway, Denis'll be waiting ...

The hospital is isolated from the rest of the world by bush and parkland. Not for aesthetic reasons nor for the benefit of the patients, but because it was built in a bygone age for people with contagious diseases like tuberculosis, cholera, bubonic plague and now, HIV/AIDS. As a consequence, almost every room overlooks sweeping English lawns, rose gardens and at this time of year, flowering wattle trees and gums, even Denis's room in Acute. He's waiting for her by the fish tank, he and his bactrim drip. In loving memory of Mark Henstridge May 1991, the plaque on the fish tank says. Please don't overfeed the fish.

Well, what's wrong with you? Marie says as she reaches past the drip to embrace him. You're looking great.

You should have seen me when I arrived! he says. And you should see my room! I've got a balcony and the wattle's out. You get better much quicker when you've got something nice to look out to.

Marie follows him down the lino corridor into number seven. She lays her back-pack on the bed and removes a long narrow box wrapped in recycled pink tissue paper. I've got something for you, she says.

Denis sits on the edge of the bed. You shouldn't have … he says.

Yeah, but I have and it's kinda special.

He unwraps the paper and opens the lid. A small blond doll with arrows sticking out.

Sebastian! Where did you find him? Denis says.

I made him for you. In his past life he was Barbie's boyfriend Ken, but I had to operate on him to tie his arms to the branches of his oak tree and poke the arrows through. I thought he could keep you company when there's no one else around.

Denis strokes the doll's matted hair, the tiny hand-made arrows, the carefully pruned elm tree twig that's meant to be an oak. Darling, I don't know what to say. He's beautiful. He'll give me strength to do what I have to do.

VIOLETTA is trying to open a drawer in her bedside table to find a medallion she knows is there. Listen, beloved Alfredo, she sings, take this portrait painted in times past. It will remind you of she who loved you so much.

No, don't say that, you're not going to die, Alfredo sings. He's sobbing now. Darling, you must live. A strazio si terribil qui non mi trasse Iddio. God wouldn't return me to you to cause me so much anguish.

His father is clenching his fists. His face is pale. Forgive me for the suffering I've caused your noble heart, he sings. Cara, sublime, sublime vittima d'un disperato amore. Dearest, most sublime victim of this hopeless love.

Violetta ignores the older man. If some chaste young girl in the flower of life should give her heart to you, marry her, she sings to Alfredo. It's what I would wish. Then give her this portrait. Tell her it's a gift from one who is in heaven among the angels, and prays for her and for you.

No, death can't take you from me, he sings, and buries himself in her arms. She strokes his hair. He raises his head from her breast and gazes at her. She rises too.

E strano, she sings. How strange.

Che?

The spasms of pain have gone, she sings. An unexpected energy is bringing me back to life! Ma io ritorno a viver! Oh joy.

━━ ━━

ONLY BRIDLEPATHS between the villages now, and the hills and valleys are ruled by priests. Those Garibaldini are wicked men, the priests are saying. If you stop to talk with them, even for a minute, you'll go straight to hell.

Looks like what I said is true, Anita says as she rides through the deserted villages.

At one village a Garibaldino is caught stealing a chicken and is summarily executed. Are we here to defend the people or to oppress them? Garibaldi says. Many of his warriors no longer know and no longer care. At Orvieto they find the gates of the city closed. Garibaldi orders his men to wheel the cannon into place. Food or else we'll shoot, he tells the municipal fathers. At the next town, Cetona, the gates remain open. The Chief Magistrate even offers Anita a bed — but my dear, you can't come to dinner dressed like that. She sits down to her meal in a hastily made-to-measure green brocade gown and borrowed jewels.

They pass through ancient Clusium early the next morning, Lars Porsenna's town, that Etruscan warlord who sacked Roma in the goddess Uni's name. How times have changed, says Anita. Near Clusium they cross the border from the Papal States into Austrian territory. Oh Uni, give us strength, Anita says.

That night she can hear young men weeping, and by dawn some of them have disappeared into the Tuscan hills. Those who are caught are shot. That's how I treat deserters, Garibaldi says. At least he's trying to maintain law and order, says the abbot of the monastery at Montepulciano. I've seen retreating armies before and know too well what they can do in an isolated place like this. He orders a banquet to welcome the remaining warriors — just to be safe. Veal and venison, roast pork and goat. Fresh bread and yes, we'd better offer them wine. They'll take it by force if we don't.

And on through the great forests, ridges and ravines of eastern Tuscany to the closed gates of Arezzo. The cannon is rolled into place again and a small forest is logged for ladders to scale the walls. But what would we do with the wounded? Garibaldi says. We can't take them with us and if we leave them here, they'll be shot. And we can't stay ourselves because the Austrians would surround us in next to no time. He negotiates. You know we could blow your gates to pieces, he says. And we know the people of Arezzo would rise up in our support. But if you, their municipal leaders, are generous with food, wine and cash …

The Austrians intercept the retreating freedom fighters on the Metaurus plain. Five Garibaldini are captured and executed, and many more are massacred in Sant'Angelo. The survivors retreat to an orchard near Macerata. Keep faith, my heroes, Garibaldi says. Tomorrow we'll be in neutral territory in the Republic of San Marino, and from there we'll head to Venezia where we'll be free at last. Anita looks at him as if to speak, then faints. She's sweating and feverish. He picks her up. Oh Mary, mother of God, he says, don't let her die. I need her more than ever now.

THE strings quiver, the brass, the woodwinds soar. The sound of clapping from the auditorium, hearty cheers and sobs. Maria Callas rises from the couch and curtsies. Alfredo Kraus takes a bow, and the rest of the cast follows him. The conductor gestures towards the members of the orchestra. Someone presents Callas with a bouquet, white camellias and young ferns. Another curtain call. And another. And another. Until slowly the clapping dies …

✦ ✦

ANITA GARIBALDI wakes and says she's fine. Only exhaustion made me faint, she says, because this baby's so heavy in my belly now.

Garibaldi leaves her to negotiate their entrance into the Republic of San Marino and orders her pages to help her mount. They cross one ravine after another in single file, horses, mules, men and one lone woman with an unborn child. All of them are hungry, exhausted and dripping with sweat. They stop in a gully beside a spring and collapse onto the rocks to rest. Garibaldi is watching from Monte Titano on which the tiny Republic is perched. On the next mountain he sees a line of descending white uniforms. His wife and his exhausted rebel army seem unaware of this approaching threat. He mounts his horse and spurs it down the track. The Austrians are already firing their guns. A woman is yelling abuse. He recognises her voice. Fight damn you, get off your arses and fight! she screams as she cracks her whip. And load that cannon! What do you think we've dragged it across all these bloody mountains for?

THEY'VE settled into the balcony, Denis and Marie. The wattle is smooching up against the railing like a contented yellow cat.

You have to face a few facts when you get in here, Denis is saying. Everyone's nice and bright and breezy and telling me I'm doing fine but I know I'm not. And somehow the knowledge that I'm dying is making me stronger than I've ever felt before. I think it was seeing Heinrich so upset because now I know he really loves me. It's the first time in my life I've ever felt loved like that. Funny what you discover when it's almost too late …

Marie reaches out and takes his hand. The one with the bactrim drip.

The next ward is for the terminals, he says. When you go in there, you know you won't be coming out alive — unless you're there for respite care. There's this guy — I mean we're not meant to see but you get to know — and it's like he's made of plastic dry-cleaning bags and coat-hangers he's so thin. And another guy, he's in a room by himself. Apparently he was really bright, an academic like, and now he's totally blind. No one comes to see him much, so I guess his lover's already gone. And another one who refuses to see anyone because he doesn't want his mum and dad to know he's gay. And a guy who's in for respite care because he's throwing up and shitting all the time and his partner needs a break. But the worst thing, darling, is when you get demented. I'd never want Heinrich to see me like that. Or like a coat-hanger covered in plastic bags. Or blind. Or shitting and pissing myself all day. I want him to remember me as young and beautiful. Because soon memories'll be all he'll have. And you know how vain I've always been!

What are you trying to tell me? Marie says. She's still holding his hand.

That for the first time in my life I'm going to do something I can be really proud of, he says. I'm not going to let Heinrich suffer by seeing me turn into a dribbling, shitting, pissing, demented, skin and bones mess. Because that's what'll happen if I don't do something soon.

Marie squeezes his hand and remains silent.

If I hang on too long, I might dement and not be able to do it, he says. So I've got to pick the right time. I know how to and where to get the stuff and, like I've seen plenty of people do it before. And I've thought about it often, I mean who hasn't, but for some reason I've lasted long enough to find Heinrich and to know he loves me. So I want to do something for him now that'll really make me proud.

Marie is staring past the wattle to the sweeping lawns. Have you talked to Heinrich about it yet? she says.

No, Denis says. I want to choose the right time.

SOKRATES has arrived in town. He rang twenty minutes ago from Tullamarine airport. The train from Alexandria, Egypt Air from Cairo, a night in Bangkok and here I am, he said. I've booked in to the Novotel, which I'm told is somewhere near your place, so if you're free, I'll meet you in the cocktail lounge for a drink in an hour or so, and we'll see where we go from there.

Lillian was shocked by the phone call although not unpleasantly, as she admitted later. She put the kettle on and made herself a cup of tea — because coffee is too strong for my constitution these days, she says — and now she's sitting at the kitchen table trying to collect her thoughts. Abelard pads over to her and puts his head on her lap. She scratches him behind the ears. Well, my old mate, it looks like you won't be the only male in my life for a while, she says, but I don't think it'll be terminal! Abelard wags his tail. I don't really know how I'll cope, though, she says. And whatever will I wear? She shakes her head at her own confusion. I'm carrying on like a teenager and at my age! Maybe I'll just have a quick shower to freshen up, put on a clean shirt and wear these same old trousers I've been wearing all day ... But why on earth didn't he give me any warning? And why has he come here anyway?

The Novotel Hotel where she is to meet her lover is one of the ugliest and most controversial pre-stressed slab constructions in all

St Kilda. It could be any cheaply constructed tourist hotel anywhere in the world except for the two fake cupolas attached, à la Venturi, as vernacular references to the other domes that grace St Kilda's landmarks. Lillian is forced, by the hotel's very proximity, to look at it every day, but she has never been inside. It has no authenticity at all! she says. I'm sure Sokrates would never have wanted to stay there if he'd known — unless he's changed a lot since our last time together. How long ago was it? A year? That's right, in Rome. I was in Paris and he in Athens, so we decided to meet halfway. But Egypt to Australia is a little more of an effort than a quick flight from Greece to Italy. He must be getting lonely in his old age.

She takes her cup into the bathroom, undresses, showers, dries herself, pulls on her old chenille dressing gown and goes into her bedroom. Yes, but what am I going to wear? she says again. This is ridiculous! I think I must still be in shock! And do I want a man in my life again anyway?

MARIE leaves the hospital, unlocks her bike, mounts it and cycles through the ornate gardens to the bike path that runs along a small tributary to the Yarra. He's gunna die, she says over and over again as the wheels of her bicycle turn, as the creek beside her flows. He's gunna die. It's always been so abstract before but now it's real, and it makes no sense, no rhyme nor reason, just the falling of the dice, and my life too because what'll it matter in a thousand years, or a hundred, or even fifty, and yet I want it to, I want to find some meaning, make some sense like Denis has. But not in death. Not in St Sebastian.

The wheels of her bicycle turn, the creek beside her flows. I tied him to an elm-tree twig and pretended it was an oak, she says. Because that was his destiny, to be tied to a European tree and pierced with pagan arrows so his blood'd flow upon the earth. He was washed up naked on St Kilda's shore so I took him home and tied him to his twig and pierced his skin with matches, but not so Denis would die. Tears streak her cheeks as she pedals. In front of her, a storm-water drain is leaking dirty runoff into the creek and willow trees, blackberries and kikuyu have colonised the slopes. She wipes her eyes with the back of a hand. I wanted Sebastian to give him strength to live, not strength to end it all, and now it's me who needs the strength, and a tree that's part of me, not these exotics that are killing this little creek. A gum tree, one with roots deep into this earth like it's been here for hundreds of years, not these shallow-rooted weeds that my forebears planted because this place wasn't like home to them. And now even the songs of the birds are from somewhere else and what's that roar, that crescendo like a rising storm? She looks up. Two giant freeway bridges are scrawled across the sky. She sighs. And how dare they think that's still an OK thing to do! she says.

She's pushing her bicycle up a hill now, her lungs are burning, she's hot, she's sad about Denis, she's confused about her own life, and now above her, sixteen lanes of automobiles are speeding to and from foreign countries like Balwyn, Doncaster and Donvale, places that are filled with brick-veneered fortresses and no one in the streets at night, only more cars and gangs of bored suburban youths. How dare anyone think that's an OK way to live!

She stops to rest between two of the giant freeway pylons. At this level, they function as public galleries but the current exhibition is hardly inspiring. Fuck the Police, the first artwork says. Fuck the Nazis. Fuck Asians. Stop Police Violence Rally 2nd November. She looks across the creek. Nazi Alan MacSmith lives at 36 Vere Street Collingwood, KILL HIM, a pylon screams. Beside it the familiar black circle with a capital A inside. And next to that a metre-high signature piece in decorative pastels which is as content-free and illegible as any other contemporary tag on any other pylon in any other city in the Western world. Marie sighs again and looks around. So this is where we've got to at the end of the twentieth century, she says. But why should I care?

⤝⥤ ⥢⤜

FROM THIS HOUR, I release my companions-in-arms from all obligations whatsoever, leaving them free to return to private life, Garibaldi says. He's standing in the piazza of the Republic of San Marino. But I remind them that they must not remain in a state of disgrace and that it is better to die than to live as slaves of the foreigner.

Archduke Ernst of Austria is camped nearby with two and a half thousand men. He says he's acting on the Pope's behalf, and what the Pope wants is unconditional surrender: Giuseppe Garibaldi and his wife to leave Italia forever.

Holy Mother of God! Garibaldi says. I can't accept that! We may have failed this time, but I'll never surrender. To those who follow me I offer fresh suffering, great danger, perhaps even death itself. But treaty with the foreigner, never!

Then we'll have to escape, Anita says. And tonight!

But the doctor says you're too weak.

Nonsense! she says.

He helps her dress and lifts her into the saddle. By morning they've reached the village of Cesenatico on the Adriatic coast, where they hijack a small fleet of fishing boats and sail north towards the Republic of Venezia. Anita is sweating and drifting in and out of consciousness. Garibaldi wipes her brow. Don't die, he says. Don't leave me now — because I don't know how I'll carry on without you.

He beaches the boat near a coastal lagoon and carries Anita to a peasant's cottage. You can't stay here, the man says, because the Austrians will find you. Garibaldi lifts his lover in his arms again and wades through the coastal swamps to a shepherd's hut and lays her on a bed of straw. He prepares a bowl of thin gruel and sits beside her. Just one swallow, he says, please Anita.

In the morning, he lifts her in his arms once more. A punt across the marsh, a horse, a cart, a farmhouse ...

> Now to your hearth and home, my weary band
> of young companions in arms, return!
> Yet do not tell your wife you tried, and left
> Our Italy in foreign thrall, but say
> To her that you were bid farewell, and swore
> To save your country from servitude
> So soon as you to service were called back!
> And meanwhile see me following, who am
> Cast out, rejected from this land I deeply love,
> And with me see my wife, inseparable
> Companion of the Outcast, fearless ... Ah,
> So sick unfortunate! She never more
> Will see her darling babies! On the sands,
> The shifting, empty sands of Adria
> Her miseries will end. No stone, no cross
> Will signal to the passer-by the bones
> Of one who dies for Italy, who oft
> Urged on her warriors to free our land.
> Oh woman of my heart! How hard it was
> To give this sacrifice to Italy!

BEYOND the freeway bridge, the creek Marie has been following meets its river at a place called Dights Falls. Once-upon-a-time, perhaps as little as 150 years ago, the only falls here were natural rapids where the then-wild waters of the Yarra rushed across a basalt reef and around a cliff of sedimentary rock. The land Marie is standing on had probably already been cultured for thousands of years by the time the last lava-flows cooled into these boulders, but the cliff on the other side of the river dates from a much more distant past, a time long before human consciousness began. The grains of sand that now constitute this cliff eroded from a primeval landmass that, in retrospect, is called Pangaea, and settled in horizontal layers on the floor of a primeval sea around 400 million years ago. Marie knows this because she has read it on an information plaque near the falls. But those once-horizontal layers of Silurian sand are now thrusting upwards at forty-five degrees as the solid rock foundation of a very different island continent. She shakes her head. How can I comprehend these forces? she says to the cliff face. And what's 400 million years mean anyway? It's hard enough imagining a millennium, or even 400 years for that matter. And in the context of a single human lifetime ...

She leaps from one basalt boulder to the next to reach the wedge of land that separates the creek from its river. This is Kulin territory, or at least it's the Koori Revegetation Project in what is now Yarra Bend Park. On this sacred triangle, all the exotics have been replaced with pre-European species. Instead of willow trees, blackberries and kikuyu, there are now young acacias, casuarinas, manna gums, river reds and native grasses. Marie sits on this re-sanctified ground and crosses her legs. Above her, tiny native birds chatter in the branches of a eucalypt. A light wind rustles the leaves. She closes her eyes and from across the river hears soft guttural chattering and laughter from another time. A platypus surfaces then dives quickly into its hollow. A roo with a joey in her pouch hops lazily from under an ancient river red gum. A sacred kingfisher flashes across the sky. And from out of the shadows emerges a clan of stately women and pubescent girls. As they reach the water's edge, three of the girls throw their possum-skin cloaks to their elders and leap across the exposed rocks to a carefully constructed series of stone channels. They laugh, signal back to their mothers, grandmothers and aunts then reach into the shallow water. A splash, a giggle, a shout of encouragement from the shore, and with a movement too quick to be seen, a large glisteningly silver fish is launched from the bottom of the stone trap towards the river bank. An older woman picks it up as it lands, snaps its head and drops it into the finely woven basket she's carrying over her shoulder. Another fish follows, and another.

Marie opens her eyes. The Kulin disappear and their stone fish trap becomes a concrete wall across the full width of the Yarra. To the left, a canal diverts some of the flow through a partly restored bluestone mill. She stands, stretches and walks along the path to where she left her bicycle. Almost two centuries of European progress stretch before her: in the foreground, the old mill which, a century ago, supplied colonial Melbourne with flour; and above it the nineteenth- and early twentieth-century factories that turned this river into a sewer. The Yarra ran putrid then and the ancient trees that lined the banks became fuel for the factory boilers. Those same factories have now been retrofitted as inner-city apartments for young upwardly mobiles, or as offices for software designers. You can see the newcomers leaning over their bolt-on balconies sipping Yarra Valley wines across a view that looks like an English picture postcard. Willows lapping at the water, green lawn carpeting the banks. But all I want is an old gum tree, Marie says. One that's been here for hundreds of years.

She leaves the path to take a shortcut back to her bicycle and passes through a knee-high forest of plastic tree-guards. At last she allows herself a smile. Because inside each of these topless, bottomless triangles is a tiny eucalypt, wattle, paperbark, or tree violet. Looks like the Koori Revegetation Project is being repeated on this side too, she says, but not for me. I'll be long gone by the time these trees are as old as what I want them to be. But shit, I'm sick of thinking about the fucking future!

Lillian arrives for her meeting with Sokrates in a black Chinese silk jacket over matching pants she picked up cheap in Hong Kong. She is early and has brought the latest *New Scientist* to distract her while she waits. She asks for retsina for sentimental reasons but the woman behind the bar doesn't know this Greek favourite, so she orders a gin and tonic instead and chooses a table by the window.

Although the Novotel is postmodern ugly on the outside and international nondescript on the inside, the view of the bay from her table is St Kilda's best. Even the terracotta troughs of pink and red geraniums on the terrace, the urns of lemon trees and lavender and the al fresco furniture in its grove of canvas umbrellas are as pretty as a postcard. They remind her of somewhere else which is exactly what they're meant to do. Two men at the next table are speaking Russian. They signal the bar attendant and with great difficulty order two strawberry daiquiris. Lillian sips her own drink. Her stomach feels very tight and her emotions are in a knot. How can I still get in such a tizzy over a man? she says as she flicks through her *New Scientist*. One article in particular attracts her attention: a physicist is suggesting that rational arguments and economic tools have failed to change human behaviour. We need a complete change of values, he says. Lillian is so delighted to find such subversively sensible notions being expressed by a scientist, that she fails to notice Sokrates until he's almost at her table. But when she does, all the old clichés occur simultaneously.

The bicycle path Marie has been riding along has become two flights of steep stairs and a footbridge that leads into European parkland on the opposite bank of the river. She dismounts, carries her bicycle up the stairs, wheels it to the middle of the footbridge and stops. Beneath her, the Yarra flows for one last sluggish brown meander before it's subjected to the tides of Port Phillip bay and the ballast and swill of the port itself. To the right, the roofs of the nineteenth-century inner suburbs stretch towards the horizon, a dense conglomeration of factories, warehouses, corner stores, cafes, verandah'd shops, two- and three-storey pubs, small single-storey timber cottages with picket fences, two-storey brick terraces with iron lace balconies, three-storey blocks of walk-up flats, bluestone churches with steeples, and wedding-cake municipal buildings surrounded by green splashes of trees or lawn, and all set within a traditional nineteenth-century grid of narrow roads, tram lines and cobbled back lanes. But what attracts her attention most is the cluster of grim, cheap, concrete towers that are the Collingwood Housing Estate. She grimaces. How did Corbusier and Gropius and their modernist mates I spent all those bloody years at university being so respectful of get away with it? And why did they do it? Like Corbu, I mean there he was riding around the back streets of Paris when he was still that painter Charlie Jeanneret, dressed up like an absolute dork in his tight black suit, Homburg hat and really spooky black-rimmed glasses, and like, he'd tie his bike up to a lamp post, climb the stairs to his studio and sit down at his drawing board to sketch the future. And what was it? Rows and rows of these blank-faced concrete towers separated by empty expanses of lawn, and with all the diversity that makes a metropolis a rich and exciting place to inhabit carefully segregated into separate boring zones. I mean how could he deny his own subjectivity like that, the fuck-wit, his own everyday lived experience?

And old Gropius too, he knew what the great German cities were like when they were at their best, and yet he told his students to start from Year Zero as if he were Robespierre or Pol Pot! How come these guys got so trapped?

She's leaning on the railing and staring into the brown water below. But I guess they lived through two world wars, so that's a good enough reason to wanna start from scratch, she says. And yet World War II was their lucky break. All that death and destruction followed by all those baby-boomers. Perfect conditions if you're a modernist architect with a drawer full of designs for mass-produced machines-for-living for the mythical common man, but never of course for the common woman because we didn't exist in modernism. Right ideology, right timing, right economics, right technologies, right demographics, and who cared whether the so-called common man actually wanted to live in depersonalised concrete towers or not, because he was intellectually undeveloped and had to be re-educated to know what was good for him. Or so Gropius said. Because architects are the engineers of people's souls. Or was it Stalin who said that?

A Coca-Cola bottle is bobbing ever on towards the assemblage of glass and steel and concrete towers on the skyline, which from this distance looks suspiciously like one of Corbu's sketches for a city of three million. But those old modernists, even though they got it all so dreadfully wrong, at least they had a vision of the future they believed in, she says, and faith that they could change the world. And fuck 'em, they did! They changed the way people think about cities and in the process, invented a completely new aesthetic. And there's the proof, the Collingwood Housing Estate and those office towers on the skyline and all that carefully differentiated homogeneity beyond the nineteenth-century grid.

She stares at the river stretching before her again. A fine line of bubbles is moving around the bend. Something's growing in the mud, something new, she says. Bubbles, like the ones Gautier could see last century before Corbu and Gropius got to do their thing … Mankind, Gautier said — though I can hardly bring myself to repeat the term — will produce a completely new kind of architecture that's inspired by railway stations, suspension bridges and conservatories! Which is exactly what we got! But maybe these bubbles are a radically different aesthetic rising up from the muddy depths. Like — what if you could evaluate a building's beauty, a city's even, by the way it performs? As the inverse of its impacts upon natural systems, say, and by how good it makes you feel? She clutches the bridge railing, inhales deeply and stares straight ahead. The bubbles continue to rise. Oh shit! she says. That means beauty's a moral imperative now! How did I get from a stream of bubbles to … Wow! What am I gunna do now?

THEY didn't sleep together that first night, Lillian and Sokrates. After talking over drinks for several hours they had dinner together at Jean Jacques by the Sea, an arm-in-arm stroll along St Kilda beach and a nightcap back where they started. They embraced in the hotel lobby, kissed one another again, discussed where and when they'd meet for breakfast, then went to their separate beds on opposite sides of the park. They both fell asleep very quickly and dreamed strange archaic dreams. Lillian's was in Ancient Greek. She's on the beach. It looks like St Kilda but there are paperbarks, eucalypts and wattles in full bloom instead of Babylon palms and buildings, and the foreshore is covered with native grasses and wildflowers instead of lawn and asphalt. Her body is young again and she's wearing a finely woven linen chiton. Her nipples are bursting through the cloth into the early morning chill and she's carrying a bunch of white lilies, tuberoses like in Alexandria. She can smell their sweetness even in her sleep.

A man approaches. He's also wearing a white chiton but his chest is exposed and she can see the dark hairs that cover the curves of his muscles. She embraces him and feels his cock grow hard against her belly. She withdraws, hands him a lily and wanders with him, arm in arm, along the dune. Who is this spirit called love? the man asks. Who is the mother, who is the father? After all, everything has a mother and father, a beginning and an end.

Lillian looks at him as though he were a child, sits him down on a dune and holds his hands. Aphrodite, as you call her now, had no beginning, she says quietly. Aphrodite is older than time but you men seem to have forgotten that. You've done some deal with your deities and I fear the worst for the next few thousand years.

She pauses and caresses his hand. Their knees are touching. She can feel his melancholy. But let me tell you a story about love in a way you might understand, she says. One day your deities threw a party for Aphrodite, a kind of big symposium although I must say the gods behaved just like those academicians you hang out with now and then. They lay around all day getting pissed on nectar, making sexist jokes and molesting the goddesses and nymphs! Poros was there, the god of Plenty. He got drunker than most and fell asleep under an apple tree in Zeus's garden. Penia was there too — she's Poverty — and even though she was already immortal, she wanted a child. Her womb was ready and waiting and all she needed was one good healthy ejaculation. But because she didn't want her child to ever be hungry or cold or alone like she often felt herself, she planned her parenthood carefully. So which god should she choose to fertilise her egg?

She nearly tripped over Plenty as he lay sprawled in the grass under the apple tree. He seemed fit and strong enough with no obviously transmittable diseases. He wasn't much of a role model, she admitted, but a child with his genes should never starve, and there'd be no danger of emotional attachment to him on her part. So she slipped her hand beneath his chiton and quietly, gently — like this, Sokrates — massaged his organ into a sceptre Hermes himself would be proud of. She straddled him, did what she had to do — and conceived a son. She named the child after the one thing Plenty's wealth could never buy, something many of the gods didn't even acknowledge. That's right, Sokrates: Love. Unconditional, tender, compassionate, sensual, committed mother-love.

And despite what your romantic friends might tell you, this child was neither gentle nor fair, but rough and squalid. He had no shoes and slept in the streets or in the doorways of rich people's houses. But like his father, he was also bold, enterprising, strong and a mighty hunter so, as his mother had predicted, he never starved. He was a philosopher too, an enchanter, a sophist and a sorcerer who was neither mortal nor immortal but lived between these states. When he was in plenty he was alive and flourishing; when he was in poverty, he was a vanquished hero. He was never in want and never in wealth. He was neither ignorant nor wise. But like you, he was forever seeking wisdom.

You know all this, Sokrates. You know it, you feel it, the nature of Love, its contradictions — and its contractions! Look at the way you squeeze the muscles of your arse when I touch you there, Lillian says as she moves her hand beneath his chiton. The way you unconsciously thrust your pelvis, arch your back; the way you squint your eyes and spontaneously smile. Ah Sokrates, you feel the ecstasy and the agony of this thing called Love. Why do you want to analyse it?

I just want to understand it, Sokrates says. I want to master it.

Lillian removes her hand from under his chiton and lets his sceptre fall. Do you think that's wise? she says. To master Love?

Do I think that's wise? Look my darling teacher, I'm just a character in someone else's book. I wouldn't exist except that young Plato had a crush on me and wanted to make me immortal. As for wisdom, if I possessed it, I wouldn't be seeking it, as you yourself have said. I wouldn't be lying here on this distant dune with you.

BUT HER REAL NAME is Rachel Chiesley, a Scot, who married a judge in Edinburgh and became the Lady Grange, sister-in-law to the Earl of Mar, who was also known as Bobbing John the Jacobite, one of those who wanted a Stuart prince back on Britain's throne. James Edward Stuart was the rightful heir, the Jacobites said, the

Catholic son of Mary of Modena and England's second James, who fled to France when Wilhelm of Orange sailed up the Thames — but that's another story. And if we can't have James, then his son Charlie the Bonnie Prince will do.

The Stuart princes lost and so, therefore, did the Jacobites. And Rachel? Well, she didn't count, her husband says, because she's a woman and she's mad and she knows too much. So one night in 1732 he goes down to his Club and shouts his mates a round, the MacLeods, Frasers, and MacDonalds, and a deal is struck. They threw me down upon the floor in a Barbarous manner, Rachel says. I cried murther murther than they stopped my mouth ... their hard hands bled and abassed my face all below my eyes they dung out some of my teeth and toere the cloth of my head and toere out some of my hair ... Oh alas much have I suffer'd ofen my skin made black and blew, they took me to St Kilda. John MacLeod is called Stewart of the Island, she says, he left me in a few days no body lives in but the poor nataive it is a viled, nasty and stinking poor isle.

The St Kildans looked after her as best they could but she was never grateful, even for the food they brought: rough bread made from the island grain, cheese from milk from the island cows, birds' eggs collected from the island cliffs, oatmeal porridge boiled with dried puffins or fulmars, boiled or roasted gannets garnished with wild greens, and gibben which is the oily fat of gannet chicks and stinks beyond belief.

To the islanders, the sea birds that arrived each year to nest on their cliffs were their very soul, their sustenance. The guillemots and razorbills came in early spring, followed by the puffins and gannets, and then the solan geese. The skies darkened when the geese arrived, and their shit stained the sea. But the fulmar petrels were the islanders' favourites, or more specifically, the petrel chicks.

The arrival of the birds heralded spring and meant that another all-too-brief summer was near. A few weeks of eternal northern light and then the northern winter. Twenty-four hours of darkness and only smouldering peat and body heat to keep you warm. The manure stench of cows inside your hut, the reek of fulmar oil burning in the lamps, the soft purr of the spinning wheels ... I have heard the gannet upon the sea, the women sang as they spun in the pools of light leaking from their bird-oil lamps. Thanks to the Being the gannets are come, yes, and the big birds along with them. Dark dusky maid, a cow in the fold! A brown cow, a brown cow, a brown cow beloved. A brown cow, my dear one, that would milk the milk for thee.

Ho ro ru ra ree, playful maid, dark dusky maid, cow in the fold! the men respond as they weave the island tweed. The birds are a-coming, I hear their tune!

But Rachel heard and saw none of this. She hid all day inside her hut and wandered the island at night. Sometimes, when the moon was full, you could see her dancing around a stone circle, or laying wreathes of wild irises beside the island springs. On the windiest nights she'd tempt fate by standing at the very edge of the highest cliffs, but the fairies always saved her, the St Kildans said. The fairies or the Celtic Sluagh, the mysterious spirit host that soars through the northern nights like a flight of solan geese. And sometimes you'd see her throwing letters into the sea or hiding them in skeins of wool or bolts of tweed bound for the outside world. Once a message even reached someone who was literate: When this come to you if you hear I'm alive do me justes and relieve me, I beg you make all hast but if you hear I'm dead do what you think right befor God. The note was dated January 1740 but by the time it was acted upon, her husband and his Jacobite mates had been forewarned. The MacLeods, Frasers, and MacDonalds ...

And so it came to pass that one hundred years after Rachel's note was read, a yacht called The Lady of St Kilda sailed to the other side of the world to be moored for months near this beach, this knoll, this village that required an old-world name. St Kilda.

Yeah, so he's waiting at Quarto, Elle says. Staying in Augusto Vecchi's house, some villa behind the Spinola Palace overlooking the sea. Like this, I guess ... She gestures through the plate-glass window to the bay. They've just completed another game of pool, Elle and Marie, and now they're sipping cider in the front lounge of the Espy with their feet up on the window sill. They're trying not to think about Denis, and Marie still hasn't mentioned her ride along the Yarra, nor her epiphany on the footbridge.

Quarto was rural in 1860, Elle says, all vineyards and woodlands, but it's probably covered in suburbia or tourist resorts by now. And all over Italia, people are raising funds for his expedition — well, his invasion really, an invasion sponsored by public subscription. Because no state can be seen to support Garibaldi, not even Piedmont and its king, and especially not that Cavour, the king's prime minister. So everything's being done on chook raffles and through local Committees for the Succour of Sicily! Councils are even voting their rates to the Million Rifles Fund, or sending money to Garibaldi direct. Everyone's involved. Like officers are deserting the royal regiments to be part of this crazy dream of national unity, this Risorgimento, or Resurgence, or Resurrection, or whatever you like to call it. But no one gives a fuck about the Sicilians.

She sips her cider. What's meant to happen, she says, is that a couple of blokes'd capture these two steamers in the harbour and sail 'em along the Italian Riviera to rendezvous with Garibaldi and his conquerors, who're meant to be waiting out at sea in little dinghies with all the guns and provisions and stuff that has to be loaded onto the steamers so they can all sail off into the sunrise to conquer Sicily.

The first blokes captured the two steamers OK. Swung on board in the middle of the night and pointed their pistols at the crews — though once the sailors knew what the ships were for, the pistols were hardly necessary. They did everything right. Stoked up the fireboxes, wrapped the chains in rags so no one could hear the anchors being hauled, all that — but then they tried to start the engines, and sure enough, one was completely stuffed! After wasting hours trying to make it work, they decided to take the boat in tow, so of course they were terribly late for their rendezvous with the dinghies.

The boys in the dinghies weren't going too well either! Back at the palace gardens Garibaldi was busy playing the romantic hero in his grey sailors trousers, red shirt, South American poncho, black felt hat and battered old sword — he was always one for theatricals — and his warriors were into being heroes too. But what they were meant to be doing was hopping into the waiting dinghies and rowing off to meet the steamers — but the trouble was there weren't enough dinghies to go around! So they had to do it in shifts! And when the first shift arrived at the rendezvous and found there were no steamers there ... Well, you can imagine! It was almost dawn before the steamers appeared! And still no sight of the ammunition, because these other blokes who were meant to be collecting it were lost somewhere in the Ligurian sea without their mobile phones! So not enough dinghies, no ammo, and apparently not enough coal for the boilers, or oil or grease for the engines either, nor even enough food and water for the men! Though most of them couldn't've eaten anyway because they were too busy throwing up over the rails.

Marie shakes her head and laughs. You telling me this is how nation states get built?

Apparently! Elle says.

Maybe if ... nah. Forget it, Marie says.

What? Elle says.

Doesn't matter, Marie says. But did they ever get their coal and oil and stuff?

Eventually. Hassled the officer in charge of the government store at Porto San Stefano until he gave them the key to the state coal shed. And they got their ammo too. They dropped anchor in Tuscany, at this little village called Talamone, and one of the Garibaldini, this Magyar bloke, he asks the commandant of the fort to open up the arsenal and hand over all the weapons and ammunition because this mad revolutionary in a red shirt and poncho wants to invade an island that's part of the neighbouring Kingdom of Naples! I mean, you can understand if the commandant's a bit nervous! So this Magyar says what if the orders come direct from King Vittorio Emanuele? Because Piedmont's just helped liberate Tuscany from Austria, see, and there's been this plebiscite, part of the whole unification thing. So he starts writing this letter to his mate in the public service in Turin asking him to ask the king, et cetera, but the letter'd take days to get there and then days for a reply and by then Naples'd be alerted and the Neapolitan king and every other monarch in Europe'd be ordering their navies to intervene, and the commandant was probably on Garibaldi's side anyway, probably even bought tickets in the chook raffles!

So guess he just says fuck it and turns his back while they load up their wagons! Marie says.

Don't suppose he had much choice, really! Elle says. Not with two battalions of volunteer conquerors marching up and down the beach! And all of them boys, of course, except for one woman who's married to this Sicilian called Crispi. Most of them were from the northern cities, plus a few dissidents from the Kingdom of Naples and the Austrian empire, and four or five Hungarians. And a Frenchman — that's Garibaldi — plus a South American, one of his and Anita's kids. All ready to sail off into an Odyssian sunset to make Romantic poetry real!

⇥= =⇤

THEY LAND on Sicily's western shore at Lilybaeum, a city founded by Phoenician conquerors and renamed Marsala by the Moors. By the time Garibaldi and his freedom fighters step ashore, Lilybaeum's an English colony in the territory of the Bourbon King of Naples. The Poms grow grapes there and make mercantile wine. And now the Neapolitan navy is about to attack. The first shells fall short. The Bourbon sailors fire again — and overshoot. Instead of Garibaldi's steamers, they hit an English winery. Casualties for this first round in the liberation of Sicily: one man wounded in the shoulder, one dog wounded in the hind leg, and one hole in a cellar wall. Or so George Macaulay Trevelyan says, that Cambridge don who wrote the book that pisses Elle off so much, *Garibaldi and the Thousand.*

At dawn, the first march. Marsala to Salemi through a landscape still dreaming its past. To the north, Mount Eryx the goddess's breast, the Sican and the Elymian's natural mother and the mother of the peoples they dispossessed. Sicily was a forest then: these conquerors pass through desert. The Arab conquerors called it Sciara, but Allah was still in Al-Lat's womb when these scars were made.

Desert becomes prairie as they march — open treeless slopes once tilled by the slaves who grew the grain that kept the Roman empire fed. Plantation agriculture. Row upon conquered row of captives harvested from battle, raided from coastal villages or bred to live in chains, because no empire can survive without slaves. But the Romans also knew another truth: that every slave we own is an enemy we harbour within. And on these Sicilian slopes, there were tens of thousands of enemies. More than once they broke their

⇥= 229 =⇤

chains, and more than once they nearly won and were hanged from the last wild trees.

Slaves become serfs, and tonight Garibaldi's conquerors camp by a mediaeval tower called Rampagallo. It's cold and there are no fires to keep them warm because all the trees have gone. In the darkness they see the ghosts of mediaeval peasant women collecting the last twigs to bake their last loaves of bread.

Then Salemi, which took its name from Salaam, the Arabic word for Go in peace. Another castle, another village and the sounds of bells tumbling down the hill from another campanile. Viva Italia, Viva Vittorio Emanuele! Viva Garibaldi! the villagers are shouting. Behind them, their ex-feudal Don sits astride his Andalusian mare. Across his saddle is a hunting gun inlaid with mother-of-pearl, and behind him a brigand band of Sicans armed with pikes and scythes and ready to fight for Italia. But they stink, the freedom-fighters say. They're unwashed, uncouth, uncivilised and we can't understand a word they speak. Do we have to fight with them?

Si, Garibaldi says. They're Italians too.

MARIE has almost finished her bed, even the sculpted steps, and now she's waxing the timber, that sensual honey feel of hymenopterous, the veil-winged bee named for Hymen, the deity of the honeymoon whose other name is Aphrodite, the deity of love. Long even strokes of molten wax along the timber grain, the lanolin smell of sheep, the incense scent of Murray pine, and see those bands, her grandpa said, they tell the story of this tree. Another year, another ring, another page and who knows how many pages before someone cuts it down. Blood on this Murray pine, she says. How many died fighting? My great-great-grandmother helped sew the flag, it was silk, she worked all night by candle-light hemming the stars, tucking the edges, the points, then a double row of fine running stitch. A flag as big as a double sheet, she said as she watched it unfurl. But your place is at home sewing, washing, cooking, cleaning, having babies, she was told. No, she said, you're wrong, because I too dream dreams. And I stitched the stars on the Southern Cross …

But it's only white male sovereignty they're fighting for, so what's Eureka matter? Marie says. Like whether or not Archimedes, that physicist from Syracuse in Sicily, ever took a bath. He yelled Eureka too when his tub overflowed but it wasn't him who made the water rise. It rises every time a physicist takes a bath — yet we still call it Archimedes' Principle. A body floating in fluid displaces a weight of fluid equal to its own weight, what was called Specific Gravity once and then someone changed it to Relative Density. Names are funny that way, like Archimedes' Screw, and his Lever and his Fulcrum. Give me a lever and I'll move the world, he said. Or someone did. But his lever didn't save him because a Roman soldier killed him in Syracuse in one of those wars against Carthage. But what's that got to do with waxing a bed on an island at the end of what some people still call the twentieth century?

＊━　━＊

ANOTHER DAWN, another day, another march, another village, another church, another villa, another fort, another valley, another hill, Pianto dei Romani, the wailing of the Romans, the scene, some say, of a Roman defeat. Others call it Chianto di Rumani, the place where the Rumano family once grew their grapes. Pianto or Chianto, it doesn't matter which — because one day someone will erect a monument to a battle that's about to be fought. The wailing of the Neapolitans. Here we make Italia or die, Garibaldi says as he unsheathes his sword and steps into the line of fire. For us, there's no retreat.

LILLIAN and Sokrates are doing dinner at Scheherazade's, that Jewish BYO in Acland Street named for a nightclub in Paris named for Rimsky-Korsakov's symphonic suite named for a Muslim woman, who, by the grace of Allah the All-Merciful, did good stories for some sultan in Baghdad a thousand and one nights ago.

The older I get, the more things stay the same, Sokrates says like he's never heard the phrase before.

I know what you mean, Lillian says as she mentally notes the fuzzy orange roses that have been dropping their petals from this cafe's wallpaper since the 1970s. They're on their second glass of red and have already ordered their first course, two bowls of barley soup, but that was twenty minutes ago. I don't know why I keep coming here, Lillian says. It can't be for the service, and gefillte fish and sauerkraut have never been part of my culture. My Jewish forebears arrived here last century from their dark Satanic mills in northern England. I remember this place when it was O'Shea's milk bar!

Sokrates laughs. From the way you talk about your Saturday morning coffees here I thought this place had been Scheherazade's since time immemorial, he says, that this cafe was one of the few grand constants in life! But that's not what I was talking about when I said the older I get …

I know, Lillian says. You listen to the news every day, read the papers, and the patterns just keep repeating themselves …

She's interrupted by the barley soup. Sokrates tops up their wine glasses as the bowls are laid on the fake timber table.

The whole universe of barleyhood in a single grain, Lillian says.

What's that?

Just a phrase. I was showing little Sophie how to make a Garden of Adonis before you arrived and I found it abandoned among the journals on the kitchen table this morning. I promised her we'd throw it into the bay when the barley sprouts were dead so Adonis could be born again. Remember how we used to do that in Alex? Sappho explained the tradition to me. She had a lift that actually worked with a delicate glass door — very, very slow, but as you went up you could almost imagine you were in Alexander's crystal sarcophagus ascending to the Vault of Heaven. Is she still in that apartment in Midan Saad Zaghloul?

She's still there, Sokrates says. And she still throws her kernos into the Mediterranean at Easter time. Her apartment overlooks the Caesareum that Cleopatra commissioned for her Antony, or where the Caesareum used to be, but of course they suicided before it was completed. You know the story!

Lillian smiles. She's familiar with it, of course, but she lets him talk because she knows how passionate he is about Alexandria's complex past. Your great Jewish philosopher, Philo, says it was covered in gold and silver and all its libraries, halls and groves were filled with works of art, he says. Can't you just see it, Lil! And between the Corniche and where the trams run now, those two great granite obelisks, each mounted on four giant crabs, and at the very top, statues of Hermes and Victory. When I see them in New York and London now, I almost weep, and to think they're called Cleopatra's Needles ... That stone was cut for the Temple of the Sun in Heliopolis and they were already fifteen hundred years old when Cleopatra was a girl! But at least they've been preserved which is more than I can say for the Caesareum. Athanasius turned it into a Coptic church but it was completely destroyed in that theological war against the Arians. So then the Copts built their cathedral on the site and that's where they tore your Hypatia to pieces, or at least in the street in front of the cathedral. And where, a few centuries later, they betrayed the city to the Arabs.

And who knows what other atrocities have been committed on that piece of ground! Lillian says. Cleopatra's Caesareum was probably built on the ruins of another temple to another deity, who was probably female.

But that's why I love Alex so much, Lilly, because of the depth of history there. I don't have that feeling here, even though I know people have occupied this continent for forty, sixty, a hundred thousand years or more. It's just not part of me like the Mediterranean is — but I know that's not how you feel. He pauses and reaches for her hand. I told you that UNESCO had asked me to do some work on the rebuilding of the Library, didn't I? God knows North Africa needs a modern library, and the dream of resurrecting one of the world's great intellectual institutions ... Why don't you join me, Lilly? That old bed in Alex is getting far too big for me without you — and my mind is getting far too small.

—+►◄ ►◄+—

THEY'RE ON THE LAST TERRACE before the summit of the Pianto, just three hundred more yards to go. A priest lunges up the slope, musket in one hand, crucifix in the other. You can hear the Neapolitan officers ordering their troops to shoot lower so they don't let that damn padre through.

Another adrenalin rush. Four students from Pavia University capture a Neapolitan cannon. A cheer from the three-hundred-yard line — but by now, there are only a few hundred freedom fighters left. Italiani, qui bisogna morir, Garibaldi says. Italiani, here we must die. Even the atheists are praying. Even Garibaldi. He's leaning forward like he's on bended knees. A stone hits him on the back. He looks up. The Neapolitans are throwing rocks, clods, anything they can reach. Avanti, avanti, he says. Look, they're out of ammunition! Our Maria has heard our prayers. He storms up the hill. His sword turns red. His conquerors follow. No one remembers what happens next but soon the Neapolitans, or those of them who are still alive, are disappearing into the next ravine. In terror.

THE whole universe of barleyhood in a single seed, Lillian says to herself. Sokrates has gone to find the toilet and she is left alone at

Scheherazade's fake timber table with her glass of red. She sips it and lets the sounds of the cafe lap around her. An argument in Yiddish from the kitchen. A Jewish grandmother trying to coax her grand-daughters to taste the food of her own youth but all the kids want is McDonald's from down the road. A very loud family reunion between two overweight brothers, one of whom is speaking Ameri-can, their very middle-class wives, and their matched pairs of home boys complete with baseball caps turned the wrong way around. Lillian pushes her empty soup bowl aside and rests her elbows on the table. A whole universe of peoplehood in a single cafe, she thinks. Like the refugees who own this place, the mother printing leaflets about the coming revolution with a young man called Josef, and a few years later, risking her life to save the lives of others on the battleship Potemkin. And yet when the revolution came, she was branded a heretic and sent to Siberia, the father too. To Vilna in Lithuania next to begin a new life, but then young Josef did his deal with Adolf, the KGB took the father, and the Nazis did the rest.

The stories go on and on until its seems the only things that change are the means by which they're writ. But why am I being so morbid? Sokrates has just asked me to go back to Alexandria to help rebuild the Library where my Hypatia worked. The old Serapeum. Why aren't I rushing home to pack my bags? There's still so much I could do there and not just on my Hypatia either but Jewish scholars too, like Philo, and the more recent Muslim phi-losophers ... She sips her wine and smiles. That's what I'll do, she says. I'll go via Babylon. The Tigris and then the Nile. We could meet in the Emirates, him from Alexandria and me from here, and sail together up Persia's Gulf ...

THE NEOPOLITANS retreat to Calatafimi then Alcamo then Partinico — where the Sicilians resist. When the Garibaldini pass through the village, the houses are still smouldering. The bodies of the villagers are rotting in the street, and the village dogs and crows are tearing them to pieces. On the crest of every hill, on every mountain, a beacon fire is burning. A signal, Garibaldi says, that the island is just biding her time.

Yes, please, Lillian says as Sokrates gestures towards the bottle of red that's still sitting on Scheherazade's laminex table. I was getting rather melancholy on the last glass!

That's not like you Lil, he says. Must've been the barley soup!

Lillian laughs. I think it's just that I'm growing old. And the patterns seem much clearer now …

The young waiter arrives with the main course and Lillian moves the glasses to make room for the plates, one of goulash and the other of schnitzel with over-boiled carrots and potato. She winks at Sokrates. He grins and shakes his head. Well, traditional Greek cuisine's not that much better! he says.

How true! Lillian says. But I can't imagine Melbourne without souvlaki or baklava! She moves a piece of veal around her plate. Look, about going back to Alexandria … she says. It's surprising, really, how we've just fallen back into our old ways since you've been here. We even hold one another in bed the same way we did thirty years ago. I like that, the familiarity and body-to-body intimacy, she says. But I also like it when we're not physically together, when you're in Alex and I'm here and we have to make a special effort to see one another. I had a feeling you were suggesting something a little more than that …

Sokrates finishes cutting a mouthful-sized slice of schnitzel, pushes it onto his fork and looks at her. I'm not sure what I was suggesting Lilly, he says. I admit that I had considered asking you to marry me again, but I've since decided you'd only laugh at me.

Lillian reaches across the table and takes his hand. I wouldn't have laughed, she says. But I wouldn't have accepted either. Not because I don't love you or want you in my life. It's just that I like the freedom we both have now to get up and leave at any time.

But we're not getting any younger, Lilly.

I know. But I'm rooted here. I have my de facto family, a community I'm part of, my work, and besides that, I simply love this place. Not just St Kilda, but this whole continent. It's part of me. You say it doesn't have any depth of history and what you mean, I think, is that it doesn't have much history that Europeans can identify with, which is true, but that's one of the reasons I want to stay. Because what's happening is that people from every other continent, every cultural tradition on the planet are bringing their own pasts with them and, whether they like it or not, are being forced to change — and together we're dreaming something new, a new kind of society that's never existed before. It's not happening rationally or by design, but in some complex, chaotic way this continent — the climate, biodiversity, geomorphology — is changing everyone who comes here. And the indigenous peoples are changing us newcomers too. She pauses and strokes his hand. Her goulash is already cold. So with the few years I have left, my love, I want to be part of this country's growing. But there's plenty of research I could do in Alex for my current book — if you'd like me to go back for a while. And I'd love to spend more time with you.

You could have your old study back, Sokrates says and squeezes her hand. And your old desk overlooking the sea.

Lillian smiles. What about meeting me in Babylon then? she says. I know you'll think it pretty wild, but every time I look at those palm trees across my front fence ... And I've never been to Babylon.

My nights have been many to see the brown waters of the Tigris under black-veiled stars, Sokrates says.

What are you talking about?

The Thousand Nights and One Night, Sokrates says. The Mardrus translation. One of Shahrazad's stories, the Sultana of Baghdad, which is just a few millennia north of Babylon. It's a tricky time to visit Baghdad though …

Lillian smiles. We could fly to the Emirates and catch a coastal steamer, she says. You could be Sinbad sailing up the Persian Gulf into the mother of all estuaries like in Rimsky-Korsakov's suite. The one this place is named for.

I think I'd rather play Shahrazad's Sultan so you could tell me a new story every night before we made love, Sokrates says. And after the first thousand nights, I'd bathe you in rosewater and finally admit to you that you are my salvation, my repentance — like her Shahriyar does at the end of volume four. Because as Allah the All-Merciful knows, we men need salvation and repentance more than anything else these days!

Especially you and your Plato, Lillian says and laughs.

Oh, leave poor Plato out of this, will you. But are you really serious about sailing up the Tigris?

Yes.

Why?

Because I think my Jewish patriarchs abandoned our goddesses in Babylon and I want to rediscover them. After I've done that, I'll sail through the Red Sea with you back to Alex, like Lilith did. Because there's still so much for me to learn and love in your Old World.

Sokrates takes her hands and kisses them. And so much for me to learn and love here in your new one, he says.

They're gazing into one another's eyes again, smiling and holding hands. Golden petals are falling from the roses on Scheherazade's walls and the cafe din of cutlery on crockery has become a symphonic suite. But what about your own past, Lil? Sokrates says. Do you ever celebrate Passover, that first sip of wine to the northern spring? The bitter herbs, the salt water and sweet charoset?

You're making it sound so pagan, Lillian says. But no, I haven't done Pesarch for decades. I think I must be too assimilated to do it here, or too much of a heretic! But sometimes the old melodies … She hums a few bars and lets the words of an ancient hymn flood back. Boruch atah Adonai, she sings. Eloheynu melech ha-olam …

Sokrates lifts his glass. To freedom, he says.

To Babylon, says Lillian. And to old lovers.

THE waxing's done and the bed is built and polished. Now all that's left is the cleaning up, Marie says. Those clothes and books and memories still to be hung and stacked and shelved, and my drawing board, because there's something special about staring at a sheet of paper with a pencil in your hand that's different from staring at a computer screen, though don't ask me what it is. And those piles of books waiting on the floor, the ones I've read because I've had to, the ones I didn't have to read but did, and all the other ones I bought because I thought I should and have never even opened. Like that one there, Plato's *Republic* — I mean, it might as well be in Ancient Greek to me. She picks it up and skims. Jeez, she says, did anyone ever believe this stuff? Just as well he's dead and buried now — or maybe that's the point, that he's not really dead and buried at all …

The book falls open at part eleven, The Immortality of the Soul: After seven days spent in the meadow the souls had to set out again on the eighth and came in four days to a place from which they could see a shaft of light stretching from above straight through earth and heaven like a pillar, closely resembling a rainbow, only brighter and clearer; this they reached after a further day's journey and saw there in the middle of the light stretching from the heaven the ends of the bonds of it; for this light is the bond of heaven and holds its whole circumference together, like the swifter of a trireme. And from these ends hangs the spindle of Necessity, which causes all the orbits to revolve … and the whole spindle turns in the lap of Necessity. And on the top of each circle stands a siren which is carried round with it and utters a note of constant pitch and the eight notes together make up a single scale. And round about at equal distances sit three other figures, each on a throne, the three fates, daughters of Necessity: Lachesis, Clotho and Atropos; their robes are white and their heads garlanded, and they sing to the sirens' music, Lachesis of things past, Clotho of things present, Atropos of things to come …

Hey, but that's not Plato's story, Marie says. That's much older than him. So what's it doing in his book?

⊱ ⊰

THE CLOUD CLEARS, a pause in the rain, a nightingale. Below them, two thousand feet, their destination, the city of Palermo where twenty thousand Neapolitan troops are waiting with an imperial navy in the bay.

Garibaldi's conquerors are in rags by now, and many are marching with bare and bleeding feet. They camp in a natural fortress called Cozzo di Crasto, but the king's spies are watching — so Garibaldi orders a tactical retreat. To the people of Palermo, the line of men, carts and cannon returning inland looks like San Giuseppe is abandoning them, and somewhere along the road to Corleone he and his conquerors disappear. They spend the night under Arcturus, the red giant of Ursa Major, the Great She Bear. My favourite star, Garibaldi says. And he's very bright tonight, a sign that Sicily will soon be free. From a forest floor on an island in the middle of an almost land-locked sea on a small blue planet at the edge of the Milky Way, a thousand dreams reach out to the fourth-brightest star in the northern sky, thirty-six light years away. And in the morning …

DENIS is home again after another visit to Fairfield. He's resting on the back staircase talking with Marie, who's sweeping up the possum poo from last night's raid — because, yes, the possum family has returned.

So I told him, Denis says.

What does he think then? Marie says.

He said what if they find a cure? But I don't think they will. Or not for me. I'm not going to last that long, and I can't afford the drugs. It's just the luck of the toss I guess.

You saying life's just a casino game? Marie says.

I didn't meant it like that, Denis says. It's too hard to talk about this stuff any other way, and if I'd wanted to leave everything to luck or fate or God or whatever you want to call it, I wouldn't be making the plans I'm making now. Heinrich says he'd do the same if he had to — in his own way. Except I hope he never has to. But we've spent some really nice times together since we first talked about it, and he's changed, Marie — even though you wouldn't know to look at him. He's softer now — and I am too — and when he wants to go to sleep, he doesn't turn over with his back to me like he used to do. He usen't even to let me touch him when he wanted to sleep and I hated that because it made me feel rejected. Now we fall asleep in one another's arms as if it's absolutely natural, and when we move — like you know how you do when you're asleep — he'll often wake up and reach out to make sure I'm still there. Sometimes I lie awake in his arms thinking how lucky I am to have found this at last — because maybe I never would've otherwise. We could've gone on for years without him ever snuggling up and telling me he loved me. And now it's other things than sex that matter. I guess it's always been that way, but we'd been too scared or dishonest to admit it. Or too desperate. And there'd always been that gay thing about fucking around meaning you're liberated, and how you look and what you own being the most important things. But what I've discovered — and promise you won't laugh at me — is that men can be really loving people.

He pauses. I know this is going to sound really old-fashioned, he says, but seeing you're into men too — what I think is that you should find a good one who really loves you. It's my only piece of advice! Because that last bloke, it wasn't love he wanted to give. And from all accounts, you didn't even get as far as the bed!

Fuck, Denis, Marie says. Don't do this to me. It's too confusing. And I hadn't even thought about him much in weeks. It's you I've been worrying about. Because I don't want to lose you.

She rests her possum-broom against the railing, sits beside him on the step and wipes away a tear. Denis wraps an arm around her. Hey, she says with a nervous laugh, isn't it me who's meant to be comforting you!

We'll comfort each other, he says.

They sit in silence while Marie searches for a way through her emotions. When she speaks, her voice is very soft. So what've you got planned then?

I'll do it at the Prince of Wales, he says. Because that'll be gone soon too. It was sold for millions the other day and the new owners won't be wanting all us pooftas hanging around the place for long, or the ferals and diggers in the other bars. So I'm gunna buy the stuff with my last pension cheque, the best deal on the street, and do it at the Prince. A kinda last supper! Because everyone who drinks at that bar is either positive or knows someone who is. They don't talk about it much but there's this kinda solidarity — except that I've always been a bit too queer even for most of them!

Marie squeezes his hand. And then what? she says.

Someone'll check that they can't revive me, a doctor who said he'd help. And then they'll call the ambulance. You wanna come?

Nah, she says. I think I'll say goodbye another way. I'd feel a bit uncomfortable in that pub, I think, and I couldn't trust myself not to cry and mess things up. But all your gay friends will be there, and I'll be around for Heinrich if he needs me. And for you.

I know you will darling, he says. That's why I've told him you'll play the cello at the church.

What!

I'm going to have this service at the Sacred Heart and you and Elley are doing the music. If I'd had a wedding, I'd have asked you to play at that, so my funeral's the next best thing!

Marie buries her head in his shoulder. It's soft and warm. I don't know if I can, she says.

Of course you can.

She inhales deeply and lifts her head. What do you want us to play?

La Trav. Remember when you and Elley and me went to that film and sobbed our hearts out.

The whole thing?

Fuck no! We'd be there all day! Just that song, you know, the one Ursula's always playing. About freedom. Really belt it out. I'd like to ask Ursula to do the piano but I'm too shy. It'd sound all wrong without her though. I checked it out with Ernie and Barry, they're the priests at the Sacred Heart, and there's an old piano in the church down near the altar.

Do you want me to ask Ursula for you then?

Could you? And get Elley to sing? You know, like she did at the Espy that night we all went? Make it sorta gothic and loud — with a bit of gutsy blues.

She won't sound anything like Ursula's Callas! Marie says.

Yeah, but I'm not Violetta either, darling!

MORE HILLS, more valleys, more olive groves, more orchards, more cacti, more poplars, more streams, more red poppies. Garibaldi calls a council of war. The decision is unanimous: tomorrow Palermo. And every man wants to enter her first.

A Hungarian journalist working for the London *Times* hands over a coded letter from the Underground detailing troop movements, numbers, positions, gun batteries, and barricades. The least defended entrance is Porta Termina, the journalist says, and once you're in the heart of the city, once you've penetrated the alleys and back lanes ...

An American officer unbelts his holster and passes it to Garibaldi. A pistol for Italia, he says. But remember, we're officially neutral. If anyone asks, I'll deny this meeting ever took place.

SHE'S waiting for Elle at Leo's and her latte is already well sipped. The *Age* lies half-read in front of her. Bosnia again, and the French. Because their government wants to test more bombs in the Pacific, the Ocean of Peace. But isn't that what we all want? she says. Peace and happiness? And if Leo's is not completely peaceful and happy, then at least at this time of day it belongs to us locals. All the paid and unpaid arts and sex workers, health carers, taxi drivers, waiters, single parents, students, teachers, pensioners and this under-employed young architect who call St Kilda home. And there's Daphne from Downstairs getting onto the tram, where's she off to I wonder? And all those solo cars running late for work. Such a funny way to organise your life, your whole society, but it doesn't have to be that way ...

She's doodling on the front page of the *Age* to give image to her thoughts. The Moorish arches on the colonnades of the historic building across the road, the fine lace of the budding elms against the morning sky, but what if it's a different picture outside, she says, with no cars or asphalt? Not Sous les pavés la plage like that 1960s graffiti said but Under the pavement, the earth. This cafe spilling into the outside world like it's part of nature too, and landscape design that replicates the ecosystems that were here before. Like we'd be doing coffee right, organically grown of course like in permaculture, and there's this lizard stalking an insect for breakfast and this parrot, wild and red and green and it's chatting to you from the back of a vacant chair, while down the path there's a whole mob of them feeding on native grass seeds that have fallen on the ground. Some kids run past and the birds screech and whirl and alight again when the kids have gone, and if we planted some gum trees now, in sixty, seventy years say, there'd be hollows in them for the parrots and possums to nest in and blossoms for the local bees. And other trees. Public orchards of nuts and berries, oranges and apples, with some kind of mass transit track running through the groves, like our trams today only more efficient and not powered by brown coal, and a path for little privately owned or pooled vehicles that elderly and disabled people can use and anyone else who's got a good enough reason not to walk or use the public transit system. All zero emissions of course, because everything's zero emissions now, like maybe you'd plug your vehicle in when you parked it but the energy'd be co-generated from the sun or wind or water. Like the whole community, the whole city system'd be energy self-suffi-cient. That expanse of roof on that ugly brick thing across the street, the one where the cops shot Colleen, it'd be covered in photovoltaic tiles, or the windows'd harvest the sun like leaves do with chloro-phyll, and there'd be a garden on the roof with vegetables and flowers among the solar collectors. And we'd harvest the rain and store it and recycle all our greywater so we'd be self-sufficient in water too, not enough perhaps for European lawns but who needs them when there are indigenous species that are already adapted to this country? But we wouldn't harvest all the water that fell as rain because other systems need it too, so we'd design our cities to let rain filter back into the earth which means no more impervious pavements, no more asphalt and no more concrete canals where creeks and streams should flow. Which means, shit, there's so much work to do just ripping up the concrete and revegetating the water courses to create habitat for native fish and frogs and water beetles again. We could even do that to Albert Park Lake, make it a swamp again! And all our sewage and industries would have to be closed-system processes because we couldn't allow any contaminants into the air or soil, or into our creeks and streams and rivers and bay, or our watertables, and that means no more flushing loos because it's hard to avoid a build up of nutrients with them, so we'd have to go for self-composting numbers instead and whole new industries to support them, because nothing can ever be considered waste again, especially not human excreta. And we wouldn't have to import fertilisers then. We could probably even be self-sufficient in basic food, I mean it's possible even in a city because London and Paris were net exporters of food during the last world war which means we wouldn't need all those monocultures to feed us, nor those transport fleets and we'd keep most of our food production local because local is where we live. And even global problems start out local somewhere like the hole in the ozone layer or nuclear bombs because the factories that produce these things are all next door to someone, as Vandana Shiva says. But it all gets so big and complex then and —

Elle is tapping on the window from outside.

I wish you wouldn't do that, Marie says when she joins her.

I couldn't resist it! Elle says. What were you dreaming up this time?

Just doodling. Like I've been reshelving my piles of books and I came across some of Corbusier's stuff again and Plato's *Republic* so I figured that if they could have their own republics, then so could

I. But one you'd really want to live in because you wouldn't want to live in theirs! It's hard stuff, though. It's not the technology so much, I mean we've got all that and we know what's gotta be done, it's the people stuff. Changing the culture. Like getting from here to there.

Is that what you wanted to see me about? Elle says. Some imaginary republic?

Nah, this is just my own private doodling while I'm waiting for you! But what I wanted to tell you was … well, it's about Denis. He's organised his own funeral at the Sacred Heart and he wants us to do the music. And guess what he wants you to sing!

✢ ✢

MOONLIGHT down Gibilrossa, the red mountain pass. A dry river bed through the city's skirt. A horse pigroots. Panic. Confusion. A musket blast, two, three, four. A dog barks, howls. Then every dog in Palermo. Adrenalin. Cold sweat. A piano in the darkness. A woman's voice. Sempre libera, she sings. The conquerors breathe again. But the enemy has heard.

THE Haddad brothers are talking Arabic across the espresso bar. A carpenter interjects. You can tell he's a carpenter by the hammer hanging from his belt and his leather pouch. He's talking Aussie Rules and says his team's gunna win but the reason why is drowned in the gap between where he's at and where Elle and Marie are sitting. I mean, of course shit happens in St Kilda, Elle is saying, and it's an ecological disaster like everywhere else. But in spite of that …

Yeah, I know what you mean, Marie says. I think it's because we've all got our little niches here. Like look at this place. People from everywhere but we've all got our favourite tables that we come to all the time, and Tony or Michael or George are always there to meet you whoever you are, and you can always find someone to talk to. And take the Prince, or the Espy. Like for the price of a cider or a local beer …

Not for long! Elle says. We won't be playing pool and music at those places much longer the way the developers are queuing up!

But if people wanna live in diverse communities like St Kilda, then it's really stupid to turn everything into quarter-million-dollar apartments and homogeneously posh places that only serve fancy food and wine and imported beer, Marie says. Or worse still, to transform the whole place into a tourist attraction for those 'burbans who come here for a bit of authentic culture because there's nothing left where they come from! I mean it's us locals who give this place its authenticity, Elle, just by the way we live. But professionally speaking, I don't know how you'd design a place that'd work like St Kilda does because I suspect most of what makes it so good happened by default when the authorities weren't looking. It's like we've all come here as refugees from mainstream cultures to live the way we want to live, and everyone and everything is normal here, no matter how we dress or speak or think or look or where we've come from. Whereas in other places most St Kildans'd be considered deviants, especially single women like us who want to live alone, or in your case with a kid, and want to do non-mainstream things. Like every cafe's full of us and it doesn't matter that most of us are poor — because it's all the other stuff that counts, like having somewhere cheap to meet for coffee any time of the day or night, and places to perform or listen to our own kind of theatre or poetry or music, places for everyone to perform or listen to their own kind of stuff no matter what kind of stuff it is. And if some of us fuck-up for a bit, then we know we can get support from our friends or from the Sacred Heart or the Salvos or the Baptist Centre. Or even a free coffee from the Jesus is Lord van! Because it's like we've got a bigger vision of what it is to be human here, a bigger kind of citizenship, and I don't know how you'd enshrine that into any set of building regulations or planning codes or urban design guidelines or even a bill of rights like some people are talking about! But if you don't define it somehow, then the developers and all those other suspect characters'll get away with murder, and it's really begun to bother me, especially since I read Plato's book. Because that's what blokes like him do, they define the future in their own image as though the rest of us don't count, and then everyone else has to tag along because they don't leave you any other choice.

There must be a way, though, Elle says. Like a set of indicators for what makes a culturally rich and fulfilling place to live in, with some sort of complexity or diversity quotient or something. And some measure of the flow of new ideas into local communities so people can collectively adjust and change rather than atrophy and destroy themselves. Like Easter Island or even the island of St Kilda in the North Atlantic. Remember Lilith telling us those stories? It could be part of that new aesthetic you've been talking about.

So then you gotta analyse what makes a good society, Marie says. And when you're analysing it, you're not living it! You're just looking in from the outside.

But we've gotta do something to protect what we've got and make it even better, Elle says. For all of us — because I mean, we can only survive as villages within the bigger fabric. Those old ideas about people being individuals were never very helpful. And if St Kilda becomes just another monoculture, like even of the trendy kind … Because then people like you and me won't fit. And as for Denis, or Old Jim and his Josephine, or Jeannie the bag lady, or Mary White and her clan, or even, at the other end of the spectrum, our dear old Lilith, who's probably rich enough to support us all …

Marie smiles. So you've changed your mind about going back to Sicily then!

≫— —≪

AVANTI, CACCIATORI! A voice before dawn. Forward, into the city's heart! But a barricade is blocking the gates. They tear the stones with their bare hands. Shells from the gunship bombard them, bullets ricochet from the walls.

Avanti, avanti ...

The barricade collapses.

Arcturus the red giant in Ursa Major is smiling now, and Rosalia, Palermo's patron saint. They must be related, an old woman says, because Rosalia's father's name was Sinibaldi. Garibaldi's coming home. Viva la Talia e Garibardi amicu, the people of Palermo scream, men, women, children all rushing from the city's slums. At dawn they disperse to fight the Neapolitans in dialect: kitchen knives, daggers, sticks, iron bars, stones, cauldrons of boiling oil ... And then the imperial retribution. Whole city blocks are sacked, looted, burned by the king's soldiers. Whole families are slaughtered. We'll raze the entire city, His Excellency says, if that's what submission takes.

DAPHNE Downstairs has invited herself to the rehearsal even though she claims she's not very musical. She has brought a box of tissues and promises to turn the pages of the now very revised and photocopied scores of *La Traviata*, the fallen woman, if the musicians tell her when. Verdi will be rolling over in his grave with what you're doing to his music, she says.

Nonsense, Elle says. He'd be delighted that we're liberating it from all those stuffy old opera buffs.

Well, I don't know what my husband would have thought, Ursula says from her baby grand.

He might have liked it too, Marie says. But can we go through it once more? This waiting is killing me.

Another siren. Another flashing light. It's the police. The four women rush to Ursula's upstairs window. The siren goes straight past. They relax. A bottle of open champagne and four half-full glasses are waiting on the baby grand.

Tonight, on the other side of the street at the Prince of Wales, Denis is doing his Last Supper with Heinrich and some of their gay friends.

Marie settles on her stool again and rests her cello between her legs. Elle opens her accordion and prepares herself to sing. Ursula raises her hands to the keyboard and nods. Let the music begin.

How strange! His words are carved into my heart! Would a true love be bad for me? What decision are you making, my troubled soul? No man has ever affected me like this. Joy that I've never known, to love and be loved! Can I reject what he offers for the emptiness of my present life?

E strano! E strano! In core scolpiti ho quegli accenti! Saria per me sventura un serio amore? Che risolvi, o turbata anima mia? Null'uomo ancora t'accendeva. O gioia ch'io non conobbi, esser amata amando! E sdegnarla poss'io per l'aride follie del viver mio?

—⋅—

THEY FIGHT despite the odds, the conquerors, the people of Palermo. Their city becomes their fortress, with barricades every hundred yards. His Excellency is panicking. He begs the Admiral of the British Fleet to give him safe passage to the port. The Admiral refuses. He says he'll speak with Garibaldi, that he'll ask the Italian for permission to let His Excellency leave.

But Garibaldi's a terrorist, His Excellency says. I'll bombard this place to hell before I'll allow anyone to negotiate with him on my behalf.

Meanwhile, the terrorist is sitting quietly by a fountain in a small piazza. The Neapolitans are aiming their artillery at him but are hitting women and children instead. The shells are being directed by semaphore. When this happened in forty-eight we draped curtains across streets so they couldn't see, an old man says. They couldn't signal our positions to their gunners then.

The women of Palermo sew all night and in the morning their curtains are draped. At last, the fighting can take place in private — one window, one doorway, one wall, one house, one street, one piazza to the next. Sniper to sniper, blade to blade, person to person, blood to blood.

The cathedral is the first public building to be liberated, and then the archbishop's house. The freedom fighters attack the royal palace across the road next, but His Excellency's men rally and push them back. Another bugle call, another rush, one that Garibaldi can't afford. He lifts his telescope. Two battalions of fresh German recruits are waiting on a ship in the bay. He watches them disembark then counts his remaining cartridges …

ANOTHER siren. Daphne looks out the window then sits down again. A collective sigh from around the baby grand. The music continues.

He is the one my soul, so lonely in the tumult, secretly imagined in such romantic hues. It was he who kept vigil so humbly while I was ill and inflamed within me this new fever: love, the very pulse of the universe, mysterious and noble, both crucifix and joy of the heart.

Ah, fors'è lui che l'anima solinga ne' tumulti godea sovente pingere de'suoi colori occulti! Lui che modesto e vigile all'egre sogile ascese, e nuova febbre accese, destandomi all'amor. A quell'amore ch'è palpito dell'universo intero, misterioso, altero, croce e delizia al cor.

— —

His excellency, the king of Naples' man, is thinking the unthinkable. Eighteen thousand of his Neapolitan troops are trapped, with food and water running out. Eight hundred of them are wounded and all medical supplies are gone. And every one of them is blaming His Excellency, the king of Naples' man.

Whore mother of god, he says as he reaches for his quill to write to Garibaldi: Your Excellency, he scrawls to this now-former terrorist. If we could meet and talk about this, a conference perhaps on the British flagship …

By the time he reaches the flagship, the king of Naples' man is very tense. We have correct procedures to follow, in disputes such as these, he says at the negotiating table. What's required is a humble petition to His Majesty the King, to advise him what His people truly wish. Only then can He decide what's best for them, because that's His divine right.

Garibaldi stands and thumps the table. The British Admiral's cabin shakes. What are you here for, then? he says. A glass of marsala? The time for a humble petition is gone. If you want an armistice, let's have an armistice, but if you don't, then stop wasting my time. The people of Palermo and I have a war to win.

He picks up his hat and sword and leaves. He wanted you to address a humble petition to the king, he tells the people of Palermo. A humble petition to let him know what you really want. But, I said, is he blind, is he deaf? The people of Palermo have already spoken and what they've said is that they don't want you here! You or your king!

A risorgimento from the piazza, a crowd with a single cheer.

— 253 —

Garibaldi lifts his hand. And one more thing, he says. We have our ceasefire. Let's use this peace to win.

ANOTHER siren. Another flashing light. Daphne is at the window. Her face is expressionless. Marie, Elle and Ursula keep playing but their music has slowed to a dirge. Marie's clutching the cello tight between her knees like her teacher told her not to. She keeps playing but silent tears are flowing down her cheeks. Her nose is running — but she dares not rest her bow to find a handkerchief. Elle's voice has gone all husky and plaintive. She's sniffling each time she inhales.

> I must always be free to enjoy myself, to never refuse a good time. I dedicate my life to pleasure and I'll live it to the full, always seeking new delights and ever more exciting thrills.
> Sempre libera degg'io. Folleggiare di gioia in gioia, vo' che scorra il viver mio pei sentieri del piacer. Nasca il giorno, o il giorno muoia, Ah! Sempre lieta ne' ritrovi. A diletti sempre nuovi dee volare il mio pensier.

One more stanza until the finale. You can hear Marie sobbing now. Elle too. The piano has become a machine beneath Ursula's fingers. Daphne is staring at the street. Two police cars have pulled up as well as an ambulance van. A body is being wheeled through the door of the Prince. The music continues.

> Love is the very pulse of the universe, mysterious and noble, both crucifix and joy, crucifix and joy of the heart.
> Amore, amore e palpito Dell' universo intero Misterioso, misterioso, altero, croce, croce e delizia croce e delizia, delizia al cor.

MARIE and Lillian are walking along the beach. They've been talking about Denis, his outrages, his naivety, his generosity, his despair, the way he lightened their lives — and those dreadful cut-off jeans that exposed the cheeks of his arse. But what else is there to say except that there's a gap in their lives where he once was.

The sun is setting on another day. Lillian gestures towards the horizon. I salute you, oh Goddess, bless us and fulfil all our desires, she says. The sun was feminine, you know, before those old patriarchs rewrote our stories ... She steps into the foam, this crone, stares across the bay to the setting sun and trawls her memory for the ancient Greek she knows is hidden somewhere in the depths. Slowly she drags the words to the surface, and gives them voice:

> Drawn in his swift chariot,
> he sheds light on gods and men alike;
> the formidable flash of his eyes pierces his golden helmet;
> sparkling rays glint from his breast;
> his brilliant helmet gives forth a dazzling splendour;
> his body is draped in shining gauze whipped by the wind.

Aphrodite's husband, the smith Hephaestus, built the chariot, she says, and the Horae harnessed the horses each day, nine of them, all dazzling white with flames spurting from their nostrils.

Marie laughs for the first time in days. The sun's irradiating her, making her glow. You'd think there'd be traffic jams on Beaconsfield Parade every evening and people rushing down to the beach to watch! she says. I can really understand why the ancients worshipped it. If I'd been born before science, I'd have worshipped it too.

Bugger science! Lillian says. To science, it's just a ball of gaseous flotsam from the Big primeval Bang. A nuclear furnace, a rather small and dying star. She sighs. And science is the only reason it looks so good this evening, she says. All those twentieth-century pollutants in the lower atmosphere ...

At least we can still gaze in awe at something! Marie says.

Lillian ignores her comment and throws the stick again for Abelard. When it's low on the horizon like this, she says, you can sometimes see magnetic storms on its surface. Sunspots. If you squint.

They stop and stare with squinted eyes like mad women. Photons hit their retinas at 3.0×10^8 metres per second to react with the living tissue of their eyes, and lo, by some cosmic miracle, they see: hundreds of thousands of tonnes of solar hydrogen exploding every second into helium at millions of degrees Centigrade — and about to sink into the bay with hardly a sizzle.

Can you pick them? Lillian says. The spots? There was this German Jesuit once who spent hours staring at them through a tube fitted with ground glass. He was one of the first to notice them but he got into terrible trouble with the Church when he wanted to publish his findings, so he used another name. Galileo got into trouble too when he said the sun was pock-marked.

Marie's still pulling faces at the horizon. Her eyes are just slits. I'm not sure what I'm looking for, she says.

They're a little darker than the rest of it, Lillian says. Plasmic vortexes. Knots and twists in the magnetic fields. Because the sun's like a magnetic ball of plasma and the middle's spinning at a different speed from the poles, which means the magnetic fields get so twisted that they burst through the surface and we see them as these spots. When the knots are really tight, you get great cathartic flares that spew plasma hundreds of thousands of kilometres into space and send shock waves across the whole solar system to interrupt our radio reception and … I remember once, she says, 1972 I think it was. I'd just returned from Paris and couldn't sleep, so I came outside, and the sky over the bay, it was shimmering, Marie, luminescing green and white with flashes of pastel pink, like … like the folds of Aurora's veil, if that doesn't sound too romantic. According to science, it was just another flare bombarding our planet with elementary particles and exciting the molecules of the upper atmosphere into throwing this silken light — but it was so beautiful. So mysterious and magical. We explain the phenomenon in our own ways now, but what stories must past generations have told?

She's in lyric time now, this elder, waxing, weaving dreams. Marie's walking in silence beside her. Abelard's frothing in the St Kilda foam.

Sometimes I just sit here, Lillian says, just sit and listen to the waves on the sand and feel the breeze on my skin and try to imagine the world like a pre-modern might have — because I want to feel part of all this, not alienated from it like we Westerners have been taught these past few thousand years — that we're separate from nature, and all those other dualisms. For years I've been wandering the planet like a beggar to visit other cultures like they're op-shops, in the hope that I'd find a set of clothes that fit: Africa, India, south-west Asia, south-east Asia, South America, northern Australia. I've even visited the past to try to find some meaning. But I always leave as just another visitor, forced to accept that all I have is what I am and the stories of my own place, my own time.

And so I return to the bay to stare at the sun, or the moon, or the stars like they're grains of sand, and sit and sift through my own culture's stories to find something that's the truth, that's certain. Even a decent theory of causality'd do! But all I have is a statistical probability that something might or might not have happened. A trace. A quantum of nothingness. An Uncertainty Principle. Even poor old Einstein was shocked. Remember? God doesn't play dice with the universe, he said. He was no quantum mechanic, that old Einstein!

Nor was that deity of his! Marie says. More like a modernist architect really! But (and here there's a long pause) is there a design, do you think, even if there's no designer?

Well, you know what I think about that! Lillian says. Do you have an answer?

No. Not definitively. Guess that's uncertainty for you!

They're both walking barefoot now. Wavelets are lingering between their toes, blue and pink with the evening cold.

Well, it's not enough, this uncertainty, Lillian says. I don't want a maybe/maybe-not universe. I want more. And sometimes when I'm listening to the waves, feeling the breeze on my face, I even find it, a kind of transcendental connectedness that I'm sure you've felt too. For a few magic moments I know that I'm part of all this, that the fundamental particles of my being are recycled from the very moment of creation and will continue to be recycled into ever more creation long after whatever I am is gone. That's the only certainty left to us now, Marie, and it makes us all at last — immortal!

She laughs. The great bonus is of course, that once more Creation's done without those dreadful male deities! she says. Much easier to believe in now that Chaos and Gaia have been resurrected as solid working metaphors ... In the beginning, there was Chaos, nothing, she says in mock Hesiodic tones. And from Chaos came Gaia the deep breasted, the universal mother. Who begat Uranus the night sky then lay with him.

Her Big Bang! Marie says — then giggles. I'm sorry, I shouldn't have said that. I've spoilt the moment.

No, I deserved it for being such a didactic old bag again! Lillian says, laughs at herself, and throws an arm around Marie's shoulders. Look, there's Jean Jacques', she says. Come and do fish and chips with me. We'll order a bottle of rosé and drink to old Gaia getting it off with her bloke. Abelard, where are you? Don't you wish you had balls, you silly, darling dog!

THE maître d' recognises Lillian as old St Kilda money so ignores the battered Birkenstock sandles she's still carrying, and refuses to notice her bare and sandy feet. He offers her an inconspicuous table for two at the far end of the restaurant away from the early stockings and high heels, the suits and silk ties. Abelard is wagging his tail from the other side of the plate glass.

The rosé arrives. To the big primeval bang, Lillian says as she lifts her chalice.

To Gaia and her bloke, Marie says. And I hope they do good fish and chips at this place!

I know what you're thinking, Lillian says. That it's bourgeois and expensive — and very pretentious. But it's also warm and close by and, as I discovered recently with Sokrates, it's just right to watch the evening pass into night. And what's more, I'm paying.

It must be heaven then! Marie says.

The fish and chips is scallops followed by octopus grilled over charcoal with rosemary, and a whole flounder criss-crossed too with chargrill scars, with side dishes of slim French fries and a bowl of fashionable red and green foliage dressed in virgin olive oil and basalmic vinegar. A meal much the same as any other that's been cooked on this foreshore over the last ten or so millennia — except for the oil and vinegar. And the French fries. Before that, chargrilled marsupials, freshwater fish, reptiles and flat Pleistocene bread made from the stone-ground seeds of native grasses. Because this bay was dry land before the last big climate change.

But much more recently, like a day or so ago, the scallops were happily filtering plankton on the other side of the beach. Or so the waiter says. Dreaming of spring when rising temperatures would set their gonads fluttering. Scallops are hermaphrodites, so when they spawn they ejaculate both eggs and sperm. The probability of scallop eggs and scallop sperm actually meeting is very low, but obviously some do. Some even grow into adulthood to be dredged, ripped open, torn apart, thrown into a pan, and sautéed in butter and garlic as an entrée for a young woman in jeans and with blazing red hair.

According to the waiter, the octopus and flounder were also swimming in the bay, perhaps even as recently as last night. The octopus was stalking bivalves and crabs, grabbing them with her (or his) eight legs then salivating neurotoxins into their flesh. As for the flounder, she (or he) was just lying around on the bottom in that flat flounder sort of way until she (or he) lurched at something that looked like food and became entangled in the net of a third-generation fisherman of Italian descent called Mario, who took her (or him) to the fish markets at Footscray. From there to the hot coals of Jean Jacques' grill, and from the grill to Lillian's plate. And so the story continues.

THE autopsy's over, the paper work is done, and the coffin is covered with flowers. Geraniums and pelargoniums picked from between the pickets on the way to the Sacred Heart. Daffodils and jonquils from Safeway in Acland Street. Azaleas and magnolias stolen from the flats in Robe Street. Bluebells, pansies and primulas from St Kilda's parks, and slightly wilted lilies from the local cemetery. Bunches of wattle, the koori flower of death. And in the centre, long wild branches of Sasanqua camellias from Lillian's garden with a simple note: Denis, we love you. Thank you for what you gave in life and for what you're giving us now in death. Near the coffin, a candle burns to represent the resurrection, the priest says, and incense fills the church like rising prayers.

Heinrich is in the front pew. Anonymous John of Sparta is sitting beside him, because Denis rang him secretly a few weeks ago to tell him Heinrich might need some support. John of Sparta's wife Julie is also there. Anonymous Carlos of the Persian empire is sitting next to Anonymous Pete of Macedonia and his partner, George. Marie, Ursula, Daphne and Elle are waiting by the piano. Lillian and Sophie are in the second row. Sophie is nursing the kernos of withered barley sprouts she retrieved from Lillian's kitchen table and will throw into the bay, after the service. The bar attendant from the Prince of Wales, Terri-Anne, is in row three with some of her trannie friends, including Renate and Priscilla, and behind in row four, are Ralph the Rat and Monica from the Mission where Denis went for lunch, Danny from the Salvos who knew Denis when he was into smack, and Harold and Jacko who're looking for somewhere warm. Old Jim and his collie Josephine are also there, though the priest said Josephine should wait outside. Martha who feeds the cats at the back of the Fitzroy Street motel is sitting in row four, on the far side, near some of the women who work Grey Street late at night. (One of them has brought her two-year-old daughter who's sound asleep in her arms.) Across the aisle are Mary White and some of her koori cousins, and in the shadows, Jeannie with her Safeway bags.

The priest is speaking the words of a psalm. My flesh pines for you, he says. My soul thirsts for you like a parched and lifeless land. He sprinkles the coffin with holy water to wash away Denis's sins. Our days are like those of grass, like a flower of the field we bloom, he's saying. The wind sweeps over us and we are gone and this place knows us no more.

He sits down and nods towards the piano. Elle stands, adjusts her accordion straps and inhales. Marie lifts her bow. Daphne nervously prepares to turn the pages of Verdi's re-orchestrated score. Ursula nods. The music begins. E strano! E strano! Elle is singing in a wild-woman tempo. In core scolpiti ho quegli accenti! His words are carved into my heart!

Soon the air in the church is pulsing, every molecule, every atom. The stenciled acanthus leaves on the ceiling, pillars and walls are rustling, and from the windows the saints are glowing like they're made from coloured glass. Josephine the border collie barks. Old

Jim tells her to sit down. Renate from the Prince where Denis used to drink clicks her fingers in time with the music, sways her head, her shoulders, her whole torso until she can restrain herself no longer. She stands and excuses herself past everyone else on the pew and claims the empty spaces in front of the altar for a strong and sensuous tango in emerald green tights. Heinrich hardly knows whether to be angry or to laugh. Renate blows him a kiss. He blushes and wipes away a tear. Her friend Priscilla squeezes past the others in her row and leaps onto the dance floor too. Renate's solo tango becomes a sexy pavane à deux.

Che risolvi, o turbata anima mia? Elle is singing. What decision are you taking, oh my troubled soul? O gioia ch'io non conobbi, esser amata amando! Joy that I've never known, to love and be loved too! Amore, amore e palpito dell'universo intero. The very pulse of the universe. Both crucifix and joy of the heart.

Marie's fingers are gliding along the strings as if she and the music are one. The arthritic aches and pains in Ursula's fingers have gone. Amore, amore e palpito dell'universo intero … Elle is singing. Love is the very breath … You can feel it on your cheeks, against your lips and in your hair, like a warm breeze from the sepulchre. And another voice. Amore, amore e palpito dell'universo intero … It's Mary, she's singing too. She's stepping down from her pedestal, she's turning, beckoning like she's summoning up a chorus, a massed choir. You can see them in the distance. Hundreds, thousands of them, dark polished-basalt women, ochre women, limestone-pale women like beaches of quartz sand. Naked women, women in long diaphanous dresses, women with shields and spears. Amore, amore, they're singing. The very pulse of the universe. Both crucifix and joy of the heart.

Mary's greeting them like they're her sisters. Nana the queen of the Tigris and Euphrates rivers who taught her people how to read and write and irrigate. Nut the Vault of Heaven and her daughter

Aset of the Nile. Uni the mother of the Universe. Amaterasu the sun and Gaia the mother earth. Asherat, Astarte and Artemis. Isis. Hera, Rhea, Demeter, Persephone. Metis and her daughter Athena. Aphrodite and Venus Libertina. Vesta and her virgins. Tanaquil the mother of kings. Mensa who taught her daughters how to count. Aurora the mother of the dawn. And Sapientia and her sister Sophia, though unbegun and everlasting Wisdom, the sovereign-substantial Firsthood, sovereign Goddess, sovereign Good. Ishtar and Kali Ma, the beginnings and the ends. From every culture these sisters come. From every forgotten time and place. And mortal women too. Hippodamia of Pelopia's clan. Clytemnestra and her daughter Iphigenia. Cassandra and Helen of Troy. Sappho and her Lesbian sisters. Plato's mother Perictione and her daughter Potone. Socrates' teacher Diotima, the priestess of Mantinea who's quoted in Plato's *Symposium*, Pericles' speechwriter Aspasia of Miletos, and Lillian's Hypatia of Alexandria. The medieval philosopher Heloise and her child. And Anne du Mesnil d'Argentell and her daughter Marie Deshay of Normandy and her daughters, Delphine Plessy and Alphonsine, who's also known as Marie Duplessis, our lady of the camellias, and her son, who until now, she thought was dead. The seamstress Catherine Labay of Paris with her son too, young Alexandre Dumas. And Helen Porter Mitchell of Melbourne who calls herself Nellie to sing these songs, and is re-united now with Tip, the man she loved. And her son George, and her Scottish mother, Isabella, named for the Spanish Queen. And Rosa Cornalba of Italia and her daughter Giuseppina Strepponi. And all Giuseppina's lost children. And Maria Antonia of Brazil, with her daughter Anna Maria Ribeira da Silva de Jesus — who's also known as Anita Garibaldi. And her children. And Maria Callas of Greece and New York who sings for Ursula Upstairs. And Rachel Chiesley, the lady of St Kilda. And Colleen who was shot by the cops on the corner of Fitzroy Street and Park Lane. And Colleen's mother and her mother and her mother and no, don't shoot me you fucken gubbas because this is my country and I'm not gunna take no shit from no one, see. And Marie's great-great-grandmother too, who sewed the stars on the Southern Cross, and great-great-grandmother's children, and their children, and their children and look, Mum, this is me playing the sound of cinnabar velvet, like I always wanted to. Like Guilhermina Suggia. And there's that beautiful blond boy with kohl around his eyes. Sempre libera, he's singing. I must always be free to live life to the full ...

GARIBALDI got what he wanted, of course, Elle says. Complete capitulation. His Excellency and his soldiers to leave forever.

But did anything really change? Marie says. On the island?

Nah, not really. Only the names and faces. But it didn't have to be that way.

ACKNOWLEDGMENTS

Republic of Women is not an historical work although real people from the past walk through its pages, including Plato, Socrates, Sappho, Thucydides, Alcibiades, the French courtesan Marie Duplessis, Alexandre Dumas *fils* and his father Dumas *père*, Giuseppe and Anita Garibaldi, Giuseppe Verdi, Giuseppina Strepponi, Dame Nellie Melba, and Rachel Chiesley, the Lady of St Kilda.

Republic is not an autobiographical work either, although I live in St Kilda where its contemporary stories are set, and anyone who is familiar with this inner-Melbourne bayside suburb will recognise some of the local identities, including Jim, the guardian of Fitzroy Street, Colleen Richman who was shot by police in 1994 outside the Hanover Welfare Centre, and the Haddad brothers who own Leo's Spaghetti Bar, one of Melbourne's most significant cultural institutions, where two of my fictional characters, Marie and Elle, regularly meet for coffee.

Leo's Spaghetti Bar deserves special acknowledgment because much of *Republic* was researched and written there at my regular corner table overlooking Fitzroy Street. Indeed Tony, Michael and George Haddad and their staff subsidised my work by allowing me to linger for hours over single caffe lattes and plug my laptop into their power supply. They also supplied me with many complimentary glasses of their house wines — to help me write better, as Tony once told me! And sometimes I really needed a glass of Leo's red!

Republic of Women has been woven from diverse threads, many of which were spun by other people many years ago. The war games played by my fictional character, Heinrich, are based on *The Peloponnesian War* by Thucydides, for example, a work that is as fresh and relevant today as it must have been when it was written two thousand five hundred years ago. The words 'Or so Thucydides says' are repeated like a mantra throughout my *Republic*. The translation I used was by Richard Crawley completed in 1876 and revised by R.C. Feetham in 1903. My battered Everyman's Library edition was published by J.M. Dent and Sons, London, in 1963. I also drew on famous translations of Thucydides' work by Jowett and Bury, and referred to more contemporary texts including Donald Kagan's *The Fall of the Athenian Empire* (Cornell University Press, Ithaca, New York, 1987), J. Bury's *A History of Greece* (St Martins Press, New York, 1967), and the many books on Ancient Greece by writers such as M.I. Finley, H.D. Kitto and R.W. Hutchinson.

Both Plato and Aristotle are there too. I found Plato's Epistle VII, as translated by J. Harwick of Warwick, Queensland, in an old volume at Melbourne University's Baillieu Library (*Platonic Epistles*, Cambridge University Press, Cambridge, 1932). Some of Plato's reflections about environmental degradation are based on Sir Desmond Lee's translation of his *Critias* (*Timaeus and Critias*, Penguin Classic, Middlesex, 1977) and Plato's reflections on the Spindle of Necessity come from Lee's translation of *The Republic*, Part Eleven, The Immortality of the Soul (Penguin, Middlesex, 1987). The extract I have used is reprinted by permission of Penguin Books, London. Lillian's dream in ancient Greek is inspired by the lesson Diotima, the priestess of Mantinea, gave her student Socrates in Benjamin Jowett's translation of Plato's *Symposium* (William Kimber & Co., London, 1963). Aristotle's infamous comment about women being mere vessels for male seed can be found in his *Poetics*.

Some of the sources I've drawn on are even older than the works of Plato and Thucydides. Many were first inscribed in cuneiform on clay tablets, or as hieroglyphs on stone stelae up to five thousand years ago. My *Larousse Encyclopedia of Mythology* (Hamlyn, 1990), the *Penguin Chronicle of the World* (Chronicle Australasia, 1991), *The Woman's Encyclopedia of Myths and Secrets* by Barbara Walker (Harper and Rowe, San Francisco, 1983), and *The Women's History of the World* by Rosalind Miles (Salem House, Massachusetts, 1989) were especially useful to me in discovering these ancient threads. For example I found Dhorme's translation of the Babylonian Epic of Creation (Table IV, vs 93–104), and the Greek poem Lillian recites to Helios the Sun, in Larousse, and have borrowed lines from some of the hymns to female deities I found in Barbara Walker's wonderful book. Leonard Woolley's reflections about the impacts of Sumarian land-use practices in southern Mesopotamia are borrowed from *A Green History of the World* by Clive Ponting (Penguin,

Middlesex, 1992), although Ponting acknowledges that they come from Woolley's own 1936 publication, *Ur of the Chaldees*.

Many of the Sumerian, Babylonian, Assyrian and Egyptian hymns of praise and other ancient texts I have appropriated were repeated — although usually with the gender of the supreme deity reversed — in the Bible from which I borrowed verses from Song of Solomon, Psalms, the Book of Daniel, and the Book of Revelation. (King James version, Thomas Nelson, Nashville, 1977).

A number of the more recent texts I've referred to have been as central to the way Western thought has developed as the earlier texts we now call myths and fables have been. I've used Gerard Winstanley's *A New Year's Gift* written in the seventeenth century which I found in *Divine Right and Democracy: an anthology of political writing in Stuart England* edited by D. Wootton (Penguin Classics, Middlesex, 1986), Thomas Paine's 'The Rights of Man' (republished as a Penguin Classic in 1987) and Thomas Jefferson's 'Declaration of Independence' written in the eighteenth century, and snippets of the work of other visionaries such as Karl Marx and Giuseppe Mazzini. From the twentieth century, I've drawn on Adolf Hitler's autobiography, translated as *My Struggle* (Paternoster Library, 1937) — which I very uncomfortably struggled through myself to write Marie's nightmare scenes. William L. Shirer's *The Rise and Fall of the Third Reich: a history of Nazi Germany* (Secker & Warburg, London, 1960) was useful in this context too, as was *The World Atlas of Warfare: military innovations that changed the course of history* edited by Richard Holmes (Viking Studio Books, 1988). I found Sergeant George Caron's chilling description of the mushroom cloud rising over the city of Hiroshima in a chapter of this book contributed by John Pimlott from the War Studies Department of the Royal Military Academy, Sandhurst (Chapter 18, Destroyer of Worlds).

Many of the people whose personal histories have become part of my *Republic* were European nationalists from the century in which the nation state as we know it now was emerging: Verdi, Strepponi and Garibaldi, for example. Because I am so regrettably monolingual I had to rely on English sources in my explorations of their lives, and the life of Anita, the young South American who fought with Garibaldi and had children with him. Garibaldi himself documents his love for Anita and his despair at her death in his Canto X, a translation of which I found in *From Rome to San Marino: a walk in the steps of Garibaldi*, by Oliver Knox (Collins, London, 1982). An extract from the Canto and various quotations from Garibaldi are reproduced with permission of HarperCollins, London. Jasper Ridley's book, *Garibaldi* (Constable, London, 1974) was helpful to me in researching Anita's background. The translation of Garibaldi's speech to his defeated freedom fighters in St Peter's Square, 2 July 1849, and miscellaneous other comments he allegedly made during his retreat from Rome, as well as the Declaration of the Constituent Assembly of Rome, February 9, 1849, are from Denis Mack Smith's *The Making of Italy* (Macmillan Press, 1988). Mack Smith acknowledges their original nineteenth-century sources, including *Storia della rivolizione di Roma*, by G. Spada, published in Florence in 1870. The translation of Mazzini's vision of a 'republic of free and equal men' that inspired so many nineteenth-century males is borrowed from Stephen H. Roberts' *History of Modern Europe* (Angus and Robertson, Sydney, 1956).

Two books by English historian George Macauley Trevelyan were also useful to me in exploring both Mazzini and Garibaldi's contribution to the re-unification of Italy. They were *Garibaldi and the Thousand: May 1860*, a 1931 edition republished by Cassell Publishers by arrangement with Longman Group (London, 1989), and *The Defence of the Roman Republic* published by Thomas Nelson in 1928. Trevelyan's books gave me Pio Nono's Allocution of April 20, 1849, and a number of comments Garibaldi and Mazzini allegedly made.

One of my most exciting discoveries while I was researching Italian nationalism was R.S. Garnett's translation of *The Memoirs of Garibaldi* (Ernest Benn, 1931), as told to (or edited by) Alexandre Dumas *père*, the author of *The Three Musketeers* and *The Count of Monte Christo*. The account I've used of the first shots being fired between the defenders of the newly proclaimed Roman Republic and French soldiers loyal to the Pope are from Garnett's translation of Garibaldi's memories of the event — as dramatised by Dumas.

This Dumas was, of course, the father of the young Alexandre who wrote *La Dame aux Camélias*, which is integral to *Republic of Women*. The son claimed he had an affair with Marie Duplessis in 1844 when they were both twenty years old and he based what was his first novel on this experience.

If only half of what is said about Marie Duplessis is true, she must have been a remarkable young woman. She was born in Normandy in 1824 and by the time she died of tuberculosis at the age of twenty-three she had become one of the most famous women in France. In *La Dame aux Camélias* she is fictionalised as Marguerite Gautier, the lover of Armand. I have appropriated the first few paragraphs of Dumas *fils'* novel, as translated by David Coward (Oxford University Press, Oxford, 1986), and they are reprinted by permission of the publisher. Likewise the final letter from the fictional Marguerite to Armand, and several lines of direct speech.

While Dumas *fils'* novel is written from the male lover's point of view, my re-telling of Marguerite's story is written from the female's perspective. Fortunately Duplessis' life is well documented so it wasn't too difficult, even with my limited resources, to feed my imagination with historical facts. David Coward's introductory essay to his translation of *La Dame aux Camélias* and books such as Nickie Roberts' *Whores in History: Prostitution in Western Society* (Grafton, 1993), and Joanna Richardson's *The Courtesans: the Demi-monde in Nineteenth-Century France* (Weidenfeld and Nicolson, 1967) were particularly helpful to me in this context.

Marie Duplessis was killed by tuberculosis, a disease which is now understood and treatable, as is the plague which killed a third of all Athenians in Heinrich's fictional war game and in the real-life Athens of Thucydides' time. My fictional character, Denis, suffers a more contemporary disease, HIV-AIDS, but he chooses to suicide rather than wait for his immune system to collapse completely. I have to say I wept over Denis and I didn't want him to die! As part of my research for him, I made several visits to Melbourne's Fairfield Hospital — and those who knew this famous institution before it was 'restructured' will recognise the description of the wards and the fish tank memorial to Mark Henstridge. My thanks to the Fairfield staff for answering my naive questions and for showing me around. Books such as Derek Humphry's *Final Exit: The practicalities of self-deliverance and assisted suicide for the dying* (Penguin,

Ringwood, 1991), John Dwyer's *The Body at War: The story of our immune system* (Allen and Unwin, Sydney, 1993), and *AIDS Care at Home: The complete source of medical, psychological, and nutrition information and practical advice for day-to-day living,* by Judith Greif and Beth Ann Golden (John Wiley & Sons, USA, 1994) were also very useful to me, as was George M. Carter's pamphlet *ACT UP: the AIDS War and Activism* (Pamphlet 15, Open Magazine Pamphlet Series, Open Media, New Jersey, 1992).

While I was thinking about Denis's funeral — and worrying about how I was going to tie all the diverse threads of my fiction together in some kind of emotionally satisfying 'climax' — I knocked on the door of the Sacred Heart Mission in Grey Street, St Kilda. Barry Whelan, the parish priest who was on duty at the time, listened to my queries, reassured me that the Mission would support someone like Denis who wanted to script his own funeral, and leant me his copy of *Through Death to Life* by Joseph Champlin (Ave Maria Press, Notre Dame, Indiana, 1979). Denis's funeral scene owes much to Barry's generosity to this non-believer. Thank you.

The historic model for my fictional Denis, Marie Duplessis, died in 1848, a year of bloody revolution in Europe. *La Dame aux Camélias* was written and published in that same year. Four years later Dumas *fils'* stage adaptation of his novel received its first performance in Paris and soon after was translated into English — to become known as *Camille*. I have borrowed part of Act Four of this play, which I found in *Camille and Other Plays,* published in 1930 by Hill and Wang with permission of Ernest Ben, London, and translated by Edith Reynolds and Nigel Playfair. Giuseppe Verdi was apparently in the audience of the 1852 Paris production, and soon after wrote *La Traviata* — and so Dumas' Marguerite becomes Verdi's Violetta.

My fictional character, Ursula, is obsessed with one particular live recording of *La Traviata,* that sung by Maria Callas and Alfredo Kraus in Lisbon in 1958, and digitally re-mastered by EMI in 1987. I played this CD over and over again as part of my research and followed the score from a very old and yellowed edition of *La Traviata* which was published in a time when you could buy vocal scores with pianoforte accompaniments for two shillings. It was lent to me by my friend Louise Byrne.

The libretto for this opera was written by the Venetian poet, Francesco Maria Piave, but the translation in Louise's edition was so dated and over-the-top that, after considering the alternatives, I decided to translate Piave's nineteenth-century words myself, with only my school-girl Latin and French to help me, plus a now very dog-eared Italian-English dictionary. My apologies to both Piave and Verdi for any inaccuracies or purposeful manipulations I might have made along the way.

Verdi's own story is central to *Republic of Women*, because, as a composer and public figure, he was politically engaged in the struggles of his time, and because he loved and eventually married another extraordinary woman, the singer and music teacher, Giuseppina Strepponi. Extracts from Strepponi's letters to Verdi, plus a letter from Verdi to Piave are reproduced from *Verdi: A Biography* by Mary Jane Phillips-Matz (Oxford University Press, Oxford, 1993) with permission of Oxford University Press. In re-imagining Verdi and Strepponi's life together I also referred to George Martin's *Aspects of Verdi* (Robson Books, London, 1989).

Strepponi never actually sang the role of Violetta, or at least not in public, but Australia's Dame Nellie Melba did, and so her personal history has also been appropriated. I came across the letter allegedly from her lover, the Duc d'Orleans, in *Melba: the Voice of Australia* by Therese Radic (Pan Macmillan, Melbourne, 1986). Therese Radic found it in Lady Maie Casey's short self-published essay *Melba Revisited* (Melbourne, 1975). Dame Nellie Melba's niece, Lady Pamela Vesty, has since told me that she translated the letter from its original French and gave it to the late Maie Casey as a gift, but that she had no direct evidence to support the claim that the author, who signed himself 'Tipon', was indeed the Duke with whom Melba was also associated. The letter is reproduced in *Republic of Women* with Lady Vesty's blessing, nevertheless.

Verdi's *La Traviata* is only one of many musical works I've integrated into my own fiction. I've also referred to three of Verdi's other operas, *Battaglia di Legnano*, *Les Vepres Siciliennes*, and *Nabucco*; to Puccini's *La Bohème*, and to Wagner's *Lohengrin*. Franz Liszt's Liebesträume (or Love-dreams), Nikolay Rimsky-Korsakov's *Scheherazade*, and Sir Edward Elgar's Cello Concerto (as played by the late Jacqueline du Pré with the Chicago Symphony Orchestra conducted by du Pré's husband, Daniel Barenboim) are also important musical threads.

Perhaps my need to write music into my own work reflects my deep regret that I can't play an instrument myself. A number of very gifted musicians helped me fill a few of the gaps in my knowledge while I was writing *Republic*, including pianist Louise Byrne, composer Tony Hawkins who dragged his cello up my stairs one day to show me how to hold and bow the instrument and 'feel the vibrations', and cellist, Helen Mountfort, from the Melbourne band My Friend the Chocolate Cake, who lent me her copy of William Pleeth's book on the cello (Yehudi Menuhin Music Guide, compiled and edited by Nona Pyron, MacDonald & Co., London, 1982).

I've also drawn on more traditional music. The song sung by the birders of St Kilda island off the west coast of Scotland, for example, was recorded in writing by Alexander Carmichael in 1865 from an eighty-four year old island poet, Euphemia MacCrimmon. I found it in *The Story of St Kilda: The Island on the Edge of the World* by Charles MacLean, published as a Canongate Classic in 1992 (Edinburgh). I also borrowed the extracts of letters written by Rachel Chiesley, the Lady Grange, from MacLean's book. Both the song and the letters are reprinted with permission of the publisher.

Another song I've used comes from a brief reference in an article by Robert Fisk of the London *Independent*, republished as 'Letter From Lebanon', in the Age, Melbourne, 26 September 1994. This is the song Feyrouz sings in Arabic at the Lebanese take-away in my book.

I've used an excerpt from a contemporary popular song: 'Change', as sung by Australian performer Kate Ceberano, reproduced by permission of MCA Music Ltd © 1998. My fictional character Marie hears it at her gym, the Seaspray, which is based on Fernwood, the Women's health and fitness club in Fitzroy Street, St Kilda. Words and music of this piece are by Jolley/Jolley/Harris.

Other people's visual images have also been woven into *Republic of Women*, including photographs by Wilhelm von Gloeden, Augustus

John's portrait of Guilhermina Suggia, 'Psyche Crowning Eros' by the eighteenth-century painter Jean-Baptiste Greuze, and Francois Boucher's 'Triumph of Venus' from the same period. The most significant borrowed image is the rosebud painting, 'The Initiation', which hangs on a wall in my fictional character Lillian's house. The real painting is by my friend, Bogan Gate artist Apollinario Cruz.

And finally the poets whose work I've borrowed: Hesiod, Sappho, an unknown Gnostic who wrote about the Virgin and the Whore; John Donne; William Blake; Lord Byron; Percy Bysshe Shelley; William Butler Yeats and the Futurist, Filippo Tommaso Marinetti. To these giants, thank you.

So, as you can see, many people from many different times and many different places have contributed to my *Republic*, and many people from my own time and place have supported its writing and publication in ways that I haven't mentioned here. They are part of my personal life and I'll thank them privately. Perhaps I could say, however, that some of them are men — my friends, my brothers, my lover — and none of them has felt intimidated by this book's feminist title. I hope other men will feel that my *Republic* speaks to them in the same non-threatening way. And that many women will identify with the characters and feel that this *Republic* is also their own.

St Kilda
January 1999

CENTRAL CHARACTERS

ABELARD Lillian's neutered fictional Labrador dog named for the Medieval philosopher, logician, and theologian Peter Abelard (1079–1142) who was also the lover and covert husband of the scholar, Heloise. Abelard retired to a monastery after he was castrated by thugs employed by Heloise's uncle, the canon of Paris.

AGAMENON The mythic warlord responsible for the sacking of Troy, husband of the last matriarchal Queen of Mycenae, CLYTEMNESTRA, and father of IPHIGENEIA, whom he sacrificed for a wind to fill the sails of his fleet. His heroics are immortalised in *The Iliad* attributed to Homer.

ALCIBIADES An Athenian general who was central to the conflict between the Peloponnesians and the Athenians that is the subject of the war game HEINRICH and his mates are playing. Alcibiades' extraordinary career is documented in *The Peloponnesian War* by THUCYDIDES.

ALFREDO GERMONT The lover of VIOLETTA VALERY in Verdi's opera, *La Traviata*.

ALPHONSINE PLESSIS The name MARIE DUPLESSIS was given at birth.

ANITA GARIBALDI, nee ANNA MARIA RIBEIRA DA SILVA DE JESUS The daughter of Maria Antonia and Bento Ribeiro da Silva de Jesus, born in a village in Brazil in about 1821. GIUSEPPE GARIBALDI fell in love with her while he was in exile in South America and she accompanied him on his return to Italy. Anita fought with Garibaldi in campaigns in South America and in Italy and died on their flight from San Marino.

ANONYMOUS JOHN OF SPARTA, ANONYMOUS CARLOS OF THE PERSIAN EMPIRE, ANONYMOUS PETE OF MACEDONIA AND THEBES, ANONYMOUS ALEXIE THE BANKER Henrich's mates and fellow war gamers.

APOLLINARIO CRUZ   Australian visual artist born in the Philippines. His real-life painting "The Initiation" hangs in the fictional house of the fictional character Lillian in St Kilda.

ARMAND DUVAL   The lover of MARGUERITE GAUTIER in DUMAS' fiction, *La Dame aux Camélias*.

ASPATIA OF MILETOS   A scholar, priestess, mother and resident alien of Athens who taught both SOCRATES and PLATO and wrote speeches for her lover, PERICLES.

CLEON   Citizen of fifth-century Athens, whose speech to the demos is documented in *The Peloponnesian War* by THUCYDIDES.

CLYTEMNESTRA   The last matriarchal queen of Mycenae, the mother of IPHIGENEIA and Orestes (who murdered her), and the wife of the warlord AGAMEMNON.

DAPHNE DOWNSTAIRS   Fictional seventy-three-year-old woman who lives in the flat immediately below Marie, in Fitzroy Street, St Kilda.

DE PERRIGAUX, COMTE EDOUARD   A French nobleman and Marie Duplessis' lover whom she married in a Kensington Registry office on 21 February 1846. The couple seem never to have formally lived together, and even after her marriage, Duplessis maintained her own business and her independence.

DE STACKELBERG, BARON   Marie Duplessis' elderly patron.

DE VARVILLE, BARON   The rival of ARMAND DUVAL and one of MARGUERITE GAUTIER'S lovers in DUMAS' fiction, *La Dame aux Camélias*.

DEMETER   Meter is Greek for 'mother', and De is Delta, the female genital sign of birth, death and erotic paradise. Demeter represents the trinity of life, death and rebirth. Many of the rituals her initiates practised in ancient Greece were sexually explicit and involved the eating of flesh and the drinking of blood.

DENIS Fictional St Kilda resident, Marie's friend, Heinrich's lover, and a former sex worker and intravenous drug user.

DIODOTUS Citizen of fifth-century Athens, whose speech to the demos is documented in *The Peloponnesian War* by THUCYDIDES.

DUMAS, ALEXANDRE *FILS* The author of *La Dame aux Camélias*, born in Paris in 1824 to a seamstress who raised him with minimal assistance from his father, the established writer ALEXANDRE DUMAS *PÈRE*. The young Dumas claimed he had an affair with MARIE DUPLESSIS in 1844 and based his first novel on her life. As he grew older, he became more austere, conservative, anti-feminist and messianic, and died in 1895.

DUMAS, ALEXANDRE *PÈRE* The author of *The Count of Monte Cristo, The Three Musketeers,* and *Memoirs of Garibaldi*, whose illegitimate son, also known as Alexandre, wrote *La Dame aux Camélias.*

DUPLESSIS, MARIE (Also known as ALPHONSINE PLESSY) A French woman and acclaimed beauty who was born in Normandy in 1824 and died of tuberculosis in Paris in 1847. In her twenty-three years she established herself as one of the most successful sex workers in Paris. In 1846 she married her lover, COMTE EDOUARD DE PERRIGAUX, and added the title La Comtesse to her name. She is buried in Cimetiere Montmartre. Alexandre Dumas *fils* claims he had an affair with her in 1844 and later wrote a fictionalised account that was published in 1848 as *La Dame aux Camélias.* VERDI'S opera, *La Traviata*, is based on Dumas' fiction.

ELLE A fictional twenty-something resident of St Kilda, post-graduate student, single mother and rock musician. She was born in Turin where her Sicilian parents worked at the Fiat factory but spent most of her youth in Ballarat, Victoria, where her parents have a fruit and vegetable store. She now lives with her daughter, Sophie, in a converted stable behind St Kilda's Esplanade Hotel.

FLORA A character in Verdi's opera, *La Traviata*, and friend of the heroine, VIOLETTA VALERY.

GARIBALDI, GUISEPPE   A sailor and mercenary who was born in what is now France but became a hero of Italy's Risorgimento. He was a central figure in the invasion of Sicily in 1860, and in the defence of the Roman republic in 1848.

GASTON, VICOMTE DE LETORIERES   The character in *La Traviata* who introduces Alfredo Germond to the heroine, Violetta Valery. Alfredo becomes her lover in the opera.

GIUSEPPINA STREPPONI   Italian soprano who created Abigaille in Verdi's opera, *Nabucco*, in its premier performance in Milan in 1842. She stopped singing professionally in 1849 and married Verdi ten years later, after living with him for many years. She died in Busseto in 1897.

GUILHERMINA SUGGIA   Musical prodigy who became an internationally renowned cellist. She was born in the Portuguese city of Oporto in 1888, and died there in 1950. She studied with Catalan cellist, Pablo Casals, in 1906 and later married him. Augustus Johns painted a startling portrait of her, a copy of which belonged to Marie's fictional grandmother. The print now hangs in Marie's fictional bedroom in St Kilda, Australia.

HEINRICH   Marie's fictional next door neighbour and Denis's lover who works as an accountant and plays war games in his spare time.

IPHIGENEIA   Daughter of CLYTEMNESTRA and AGAMEMNON, who, in Greek mythology, was sacrificed to ARTEMIS by her father and snatched from the flames by the goddess to become the high priestess of her temple in the Taurus mountains.

LILITH   The Great Mother of Sumero-Babylonian mythology who refused to 'lie down' for the biblical Adam when he insisted on the male-dominant 'missionary' position. In the Bible Lilith is replaced by the more docile Eve, whom the Hebrews' patriarchal deity, Yaweh, created as Adam's second wife. MARIE and ELLE's nickname for LILLIAN.

LILLIAN   A fictional, retired professor, close friend of Marie and Elle, surrogate grandmother to Elle's fictional daughter, Sophie, and an acclaimed author of scholarly feminist works. She is currently writing a ficto-criticism called *The Death and Resurrection of Hypatia*. Marie and Elle affectionately call her LILITH, in honour of the Sumero-Babylonian Great Mother. Lillian's lover, SOKRATES, calls her LILY, after the flower that represents the goddess's genitals — although we can't be sure that Sokrates is familiar with this interpretation of the name 'Lily'.

LOUIS PHILIPPE, DUC D'ORLEANS Who may have been known as TIP or TIPON. The exiled grandson of the last king of France and pretender to his throne, and NELLIE MELBA's lover until both her estranged husband and D'Orleans' father intervened to end the relationship. Louis Philippe later married Archduchess Maria Dorothea of Hungary but apparently maintained contact with Nellie Melba throughout his life.

MARGUERITE GAUTIER The central character in ALEXANDRE DUMAS' first novel, *La Dame aux Camélias*, based on the real-life sex worker, MARIE DUPLESSIS. VIOLETTA VALERY, the central character of Verdi's opera, *La Traviata*, is based on Dumas' fictional Marguerite.

MARIE A fictional twenty-something resident of Fitzroy Street, St Kilda, born and raised in Ballarat, a regional city in Victoria, Australia. She trained as an architect and is now tutoring in that discipline at a Melbourne tertiary institution while she develops her expertise as a 'green' designer. She also plays the cello.

MELBA, NELLIE Internationally acclaimed Australian soprano who sang the role of Violetta. She was born in Richmond, Melbourne, in 1861 where she was christened Helen Porter Mitchell. She died in Sydney in 1931 and was buried at Lilydale on the outskirts of Melbourne.

OLYMPE A character in DUMAS' fiction and friend of MARGUERITE GAUTIER.

PERICLES Athenian general and progressive politician for whom his lover, ASPATIA OF MILETOS, wrote some very famous speeches. He was born around 493 BCE to Agariste, the niece of Cleisthenes the lawgiver, and to Xanthippus, the victor of the battle of Mycale, and was educated by the best teachers available, including the philosopher Anaxagoras.

Pericles died in 429 BCE in a plague that killed one third of the Athenian population. His death left Athens without a strong leader.

PERSEPHONE   Demeter's daughter, and one aspect of the complex virgin, mother, crone trinity. In the version of her story recounted in *Republic of Women*, Persephone is raped and abducted by her Uncle Hades and taken to the Underworld from where her mother negotiates her release.

PIAVE, FRANCESCO MARIA   Italian nationalist and Venetian poet who wrote the libretti of ten of VERDI's operas, including *La Traviata*. He died in Milan in 1876.

PLATO   Athenian philosopher born around 428 BCE. Over twenty dialogues are attributed to Plato, including the *Republic*, and *Symposium*, most of which feature his teacher SOCRATES, the Athenian philosopher. Plato died in about 348 BCE, having witnessed the complete collapse of the Athenian empire.

RACHEL CHIESLEY   Lady Grange of Edinburgh who was kidnapped in 1732 and imprisoned on St Kilda island in the North Atlantic, by the Jacobites. She became known as the Lady of St Kilda. St Kilda, Australia, was named after a yacht bearing that name.

SCHEHERAZADE   The central story teller in the vast collection of ancient Muslim fictions known, in English, as *The Arabian Nights* or *The Thousand and One Nights*. The Russian composer, Nikolay Rimsky-Korsakov, named his Symphonic Suite, Opus 35, composed in 1888, for Queen Scheherazade. In 1948 Jewish refugees, Masha Frydman and Avram Zeleznikow, celebrated New Year's Eve in a Parisian nightclub also named for Scheherazade, and when they leased a shop in Acland Street, St Kilda, ten years later, they called their new business after that night club. St Kilda's Scheherazade has since celebrated its fortieth anniversary — which makes it one of the oldest cafes in Australia.

SOCRATES   The Athenian philosopher born in about 470 BCE who featured in the writings of his student Plato. Socrates wrote no philosophical works himself and died in about 399 BCE.

SOKRATES   A fictional classics scholar of Greek descent who lives in Alexandria, Egypt, and is the long-term lover of LILLIAN.

SOPHIE   Elle's fictional six-year-old daughter and Lillian's surrogate grand-daughter, named for Sophia, the Gnostics' Great Mother, and the spirit of Female Wisdom symbolised by the dove of Aphrodite.

SYDNEY   A fictional man from the city of Sydney with whom MARIE has a brief liaison.

THUCYDIDES   The Athenian naval commander and author of *The Peloponnesian War*, who was born in Attica about 460 BCE and died, probably in Thrace, in about 401 BCE.

URSULA UPSTAIRS   A fictional singing teacher who lives in the flat above Marie's in Fitzroy Street, St Kilda. She plays Verdi's *La Traviata* over and over again, especially when she is drinking sherry alone at night.

VALERY, VIOLETTA   The central character in Verdi's opera, *La Traviata*, which is based on the stage adaptation of *La Dame aux Camélias*, by nineteenth-century French writer, ALEXANDRE DUMAS *fils*.

VERDI, GIUSEPPE   The Italian nationalist composer born in 1813 at Le Roncole, near Busseto, in Parma. His operas include *Nabucco* (1841), *La Battaglia di Legnano* (1848), *La Traviata* (1853), and *Les Vepres siciliennes* (1854). He was GIUSEPPINA STREPONNI'S lover for many years, and married her in 1859. By the time he died in Milan in 1901 he was acclaimed as one of the world's greatest composers.

WHITE, MARY   A fictional Aboriginal resident of St Kilda's public open spaces, and Queen of Fitzroy Street.